LORI WICK

Who Brings Forth the Wind

HARVEST HOUSE PUBLISHERS
EUGENE, OREGON

All Scripture quotations are taken from the King James Version of the Bible.

Cover by Terry Dugan Design, Minneapolis, Minnesota

WHO BRINGS FORTH THE WIND

Published by Harvest House Publishers
Eugene, Oregon 97402
www.harvesthousepublishers.com

Library of Congress Cataloging-in-Publication Data
Wick, Lori.
Who brings forth the wind / Lori Wick.
p. cm. — (The Kensington chronicles)
ISBN-13: 978-0-7369-1323-2 (pbk.)
ISBN-10: 0-7369-1323-8 (pbk.)
1. Married people—England—Fiction. I. Title. II. Series: Wick, Lori. Kensington chronicles.
PS3573.1237W49 1994
813'.54—dc20

94-10718
CIP

Printed in the United States of America

07 08 09 10 11 12 13 / BC / 23 22 21 20 19 18 17 16 15 14 13

For my grandmothers
Mabel Carrie Strebig and
EOline Elizabeth Johnson Hayes.
Thank you for the heritage of hard work
and boundless love.
I dedicate this book to you from
the bottom of my heart.

About the Author

LORI WICK is one of the most versatile Christian fiction writers in the market today. Her works include pioneer fiction, a series set in Victorian England, and contemporary novels. Lori's books (more than 3.9 million copies in print) continue to delight readers and top the Christian bestselling fiction list. Lori and her husband, Bob, live in Wisconsin with "the three coolest kids in the world."

Other Books by Lori Wick

A Place Called Home Series
A Place Called Home
A Song for Silas
The Long Road Home
A Gathering of Memories

The Californians
Whatever Tomorrow Brings
As Time Goes By
Sean Donovan
Donovan's Daughter

Kensington Chronicles
The Hawk and the Jewel
Wings of the Morning
Who Brings Forth the Wind
The Knight and the Dove

Rocky Mountain Memories
Where the Wild Rose Blooms
Whispers of Moonlight
To Know Her by Name
Promise Me Tomorrow

The Yellow Rose Trilogy
Every Little Thing About You
A Texas Sky
City Girl

English Garden Series
The Proposal
The Rescue
The Visitor
The Pursuit

The Tucker Mills Trilogy
Moonlight on the Millpond
Just Above a Whisper

Other Fiction
Sophie's Heart
Beyond the Picket Fence
Pretense
The Princess
Bamboo & Lace
Every Storm

The Kensington Chronicles

DURING THE NINETEENTH CENTURY, the palace at Kensington represented the noble heritage of Britain's young queen and the simple elegance of a never-to-be-forgotten era. The Victorian Age was the pinnacle of England's dreams, a time of sweeping adventure and gentle love. It is during this time, when hope was bright with promise, that this series is set.

Prologue

LONDON
NOVEMBER 1852

"YOU'RE A BUFFOON, HENRY. I was a fool to have married you and an even greater fool to have given you sons. They're sure to grow to be just like you."

"Please, Ramona, please come back to me. Leave that man and return home. If not for my sake, then for William's and Tanner's. They need you."

"Get out of my sight, Henry, and take those brats with you."

"I'm sorry to disturb you, your Grace, but—"

"You forget yourself, Price. My brother, William, is the duke."

"I'm sorry, Lord Tanner, but your brother is dead. A fire at his London town house. Your wife was found with him. She died also."

Lord Tanner Richardson, Duke of Cambridge, woke with a start, sitting up in one violent motion. The bedclothes were drenched with sweat, and Tanner's chest heaved as he recalled the nightmares that so vividly portrayed his past.

The dreams hadn't changed in all these years. His mother's laugh was just as scornful, his wife's infidelity just as real. Bleakly content that he hadn't dreamt about either of them in ages, he threw the covers back and rose, ignoring his robe as he went to the window of his bedroom. The room was cold and the night dark, but his eyes still caught the images of bare trees blowing in the wind.

"Do you need something, my lord?" a voice spoke softly from the doorway.

"No, Price. Go back to bed." The duke's voice was cold, but the experienced servant knew better than to take this personally. The door was closed silently. It was some minutes before Tanner moved back to the bed.

Climbing back onto the mattress, he recalled the words his Uncle Edmond spoke during dinner.

"You need a wife, Tanner. You can scowl at me all you want, and even walk from the room, but it won't change the fact that you need another wife."

Tanner now gave a mirthless laugh as he settled the covers around him. If his uncle broached that forbidden subject again, he would stop him, even if he had to plant his fist on the older man's mouth to do it. He fell asleep telling himself that Edmond was wrong; he had no need of a wife, no need at all, none...

One

MIDDLESBROUGH, ENGLAND
MARCH 1853

ANASTASIA DANIELS SAT on the creek bank and stared down at the fishing line that lay undisturbed in the water. Four fish on another line lay at her side, but she'd set a goal of five and was not leaving the bank until she had them. However, her mind was beginning to wander. She pushed a stray lock from her face, wishing she had taken time to brush the honey-gold mass or at least secure it out of her eyes.

"Lady Stacy," a voice spoke from behind her, succeeding in drawing her attention from the surface of the water.

"Oh, good morning, Peters."

"Good morning, my lady. Breakfast is ready, and your grandfather is asking for you."

Stacy was on the verge of telling him she would come immediately when the pole twitched in her hands. She gave all her attention to the catch, and in just moments expertly pulled in a fat trout. She then turned to Peters with a huge smile that he found most contagious.

"Tell my grandfather I'll be right along."

Peters went on his way, and Stacy rose gracefully from the bank. The weighty line in her hand felt wonderful as she stepped lightly over the path and headed for the kitchen.

"Here you go, Mercy," Stacy nearly sang with triumph. "I think we'll enjoy these for lunch."

"I'll see to it, Lady Stacy," Mercy, the family cook, told her fondly. She shook her head with true tenderness as Stacy rushed out to clean up for breakfast.

Forty minutes later Stacy and her grandfather, Viscount Andrew Daniels, were finishing their morning meal.

"Did I tell you I caught five fish for lunch?"

"Five!" the old man exclaimed. "Why didn't you take me?"

"I went very early," she explained. "It took me forever, though. I must be losing my touch."

Andrew's only reply to this was a small grunt of disbelief.

"Peters says there's a letter here from London," Andrew commented.

"Oh, it must be Lucinda. Why don't we go into the salon, and I'll read it?"

Stacy began as soon as they were settled:

> The weather here is cold right now, but I can tell that spring is around the corner. It will be welcome as the cold gets into my bones these days as never before.
>
> I had two of Mother's pieces reset, the emerald and the ruby, and I'm hoping Stacy will be interested in them. They're quite lovely and up-to-date in style. I'll hold onto them until such a time as Stacy can view them herself.

Stacy stopped reading at that point, and after a moment her grandfather questioned her.

"Is that all she says?"

"No," Stacy admitted, the letter still in her hand. "She goes on about my age and birthday, both of which she has wrong."

"That's normal," Andrew muttered. "If she mentions your age, then she must have a bee in her bonnet about your coming to London."

Stacy said nothing to this, only sat quietly and watched her grandfather where he rested in his favorite chair. He returned her look, but she knew he saw little; his eyesight seemed to weaken daily.

"Read the rest, Stacy." The command was soft, but Stacy complied immediately.

> Stacy will be 21 at the end of October, and I can't believe she's never come to London. It's criminal of you, Andrew, not to let her come and try to make a life for herself here. I'm still angry with you that she had no coming out. It's time Stacy marry and start a family. I know you agree, but you're too stubborn to admit it.
>
> I'll forgive and forget all the past, however, if you'll allow Stacy to come next month and stay for the entire summer, from the first of May to the end of July. I won't settle for a day less. I've been begging you for years, and it's the least you can do.
>
> I await your letter. Please do not let me down, Andrew. Love to you and Stacy.
>
> Lucinda

Andrew listened as Stacy folded the letter and wished he could see her clearly enough to read her expression. He knew she would go in an instant if he asked her, but he wasn't certain she would tell him the truth as to whether or not she *wanted* to go.

From the time she was a little girl Stacy had hated confrontation or unhappiness of any type. Andrew was quite certain that she would walk on hot coals if she thought it would please him.

"Would you care to go to London, Stacy?"

"Would you like me to?"

The old man smiled. He had known very well she would answer his question with a question of her own.

"As a matter of fact, I think it might be a good idea," he said after a moment, keeping his tone carefully neutral. "I don't feel as Lucinda does, that you need to make a life for yourself there, unless of course you want to, but it might be a summer you would really enjoy."

"All right," Stacy agreed, but her voice told him something was wrong.

"You're worried about something."

"Two things, actually," she admitted. "I'm afraid Lucinda will be determined to marry me off."

Andrew nodded. Stacy was a tall girl, nearly six feet and with a statuesque figure. None of the local boys had wanted a wife, even one with the face of an angel, who towered over them.

"I'll set her straight long before you go," he assured her. "What else troubles you?"

"The train ride. London is so far away, and it frightens me a little to contemplate making the ride alone."

Andrew's heart sank. He had been hoping that she would be bothered by something plausible, such as London itself, so that he could with a clear conscience tell Lucinda she wouldn't be able to come.

He did not have the extra staff to send someone on the train with Stacy. However, just the week before his man, Peters, had told him the Binks were headed to London with their daughter Milly to shop for her coming out. He knew they would be delighted to have Stacy with them.

Careful to keep biased emotion from his voice, he told Stacy this. If Stacy believed he wanted her to go, she would pack that hour. If she sensed he was hesitant, nothing could draw her away.

In just a matter of words it was settled. Andrew dictated a letter to Stacy for his sister on the spot, informing Lucinda of his expectations for Stacy's trip. He also reminded his forgetful sister that Stacy was approaching her twenty-*second* year and that her birthday was at the *beginning* of October.

He sent Stacy to post the letter as soon as it was ready and then rang for Peters.

"How did she seem?"

"Fine, my lord."

"Not upset?"

"No."

"Her face? What was on her face?"

This line of questioning was quite common for Peters, so he answered without hesitation as he led his lordship to his bedroom.

"She looked thoughtful, sir. Not upset or overly excited, just thoughtful."

Andrew heaved a great sigh of relief. Next he would have to check with his cousin's young wife, Elena, for Stacy would be certain to visit her while in the village. If Peters had missed anything, Elena certainly would not.

Elena Daniels sat across the parlor from Stacy just an hour later and marveled, not for the first time, at her looks. She was like a Viking queen with her thick, honey-blonde hair that hung as straight as a line and her beautiful figure, neither of which Stacy seemed to be aware in the slightest. She carried herself proudly, and just looking at her, one would not guess how shy and timid she could be.

"So what do you think?" Stacy, who had told Elena all about the plans, wished to know.

"I think if you want to go, then you should." It sounded harmless to Elena, and she was able to answer Stacy calmly. She was just two years older than Stacy, but her marriage to Noel Daniels, who was 24 years her senior, along with the birth of two daughters, made her feel years older.

"I think Papa wants me to go, and I know it would make Aunt Lucinda happy," Stacy told her.

There goes that word again, Elena thought. *Stacy must see to it that everyone is happy.* When would she see that the only true happiness anyone could have was found in pleasing God?

"What about you, Stacy? Will it make you happy?"

Stacy's huge blue eyes were thoughtful. She knew she could be very honest with Elena, but wasn't certain she should be. She suspected that her grandfather would be checking with Elena as he always did with Peters.

If the truth be told, Stacy said to herself, *I would never leave Middlesbrough and the safe haven of Papa's home.*

She had never seen London with her own eyes, but the drawings and paintings she'd studied made it look very large and crowded.

"I think I've lost you," Elena commented, and Stacy was swift to apologize.

"I'm sorry, Elena. I was thinking of London and how big it must be. I'm to have three new gowns." Stacy's face took on a look of excitement. "I'm hoping Aunt Lucinda will approve of them."

"Will that be enough? Maybe you should wait and shop for a complete wardrobe there," Elena suggested.

Stacy looked doubtful. "I don't know if Papa can afford that."

"What about your dowry?"

Stacy sighed; she'd thought of that. "He would never agree. He's so certain that I'll marry someday."

"You could ask him."

Stacy's look of longing turned to one of fear. The question might anger her grandfather, and she would hate that.

"Would you like me to ask him?" Elena offered, accurately reading Stacy's mind. Quite suddenly Elena wanted Stacy's trip to London to be very special, and thought that an extra dress or two might help.

"No, Elena, but thank you for the offer."

Elena nodded. "I suppose you're wise to let it rest," she commented. "You'll need that money when you marry."

Stacy didn't reply, not wanting to contradict Elena. It wasn't that she was against marriage, but if the suitable young men Stacy had grown up with were any type of gauge, Stacy was probably right in believing that she would never be wed.

It was true that she was as sweet and lovely a girl as any man could hope to find, but her height was a definite disadvantage. Stacy had had numerous dreams of meeting a tall stranger who would not be put off by her height, but so far no such man had materialized. *Maybe in London...* Stacy let the thought hang.

Elena, who had noticed Stacy's thoughtful face but not commented on it, had her own thoughts about the men in London—men who might flirt with Stacy, making promises with their eyes that they never intended to keep.

Stacy had been raised in a sheltered world, one that made her very trusting. The thought of someone hurting Stacy was so painful for Elena that for a moment she couldn't breathe. Maybe it was best that Stacy not have those beautiful gowns.

Both women were pulled from their thoughts when Elena's daughters, Harmony and Brittany, suddenly entered the room. They were thrilled to see Stacy, who was one of their favorite relatives. After swarming into her lap, they begged their mother to let them stay with the adults for tea. All thoughts of London were put aside.

"WELL, WHAT DO YOU THINK?" Stacy asked of Hettie. Hettie Marks was the housekeeper for her grandfather, and had been long before Stacy was born. She had been like a mother to her since before her second birthday, when Stacy had come to live with her grandfather at Morgan, their centuries-old family estate.

"I think you'll do. Of course..." Hettie, who always had something negative to say, added, "I've no doubt the styles in London are quite different, and you might look like a country mouse."

"But I *am* a country mouse," Stacy reasoned quietly. Hettie could only shrug.

"You'll have to wait and see what Lady Warbrook has to say."

These words were thrown over Hettie's shoulder as she exited, leaving Stacy alone in her room. As soon as the door shut, the younger woman's eyes swung back to the full-length standing mirror.

She liked her new dress—in fact she liked all three of her new dresses—but the overwhelming feeling that they all looked the same hung heavy in Stacy's mind. When she had questioned the seamstress, a Mrs. Crumb from outside the village, the woman had assured her that the change in fabrics—

a light blue silk, a pale yellow satin, and a muted shade of red velvet—would disguise any similarities.

Stacy had taken her at her word, but now that the dresses were finished and ready to be worn, she wasn't so sure. Stacy stared at herself a moment longer and then shrugged much like Hettie had. There was little she could do about it now, and because she was going to be visiting a woman past her sixtieth year, Stacy assumed they would not be dining out each night of the week.

As she changed out of her dress, Stacy's mind wandered to her trip. She would be leaving in two days. Stacy let her thoughts drift into another world. A world where she was sought after. A world where a tall, dark man would fall in love the moment he lay eyes on her and want her to be his wife.

"But then he'll want you to live in London," Stacy, straightening suddenly, spoke aloud into the still room. "That won't do at all."

With composed movements, and working to bring her thoughts firmly back to reality, she pulled the hairbrush through her hair and then headed for the door to check on dinner preparations.

It simply won't do to stand about fantasizing when there is work to be done, Stacy told herself. Still, she was seeing a tall, faceless man bending gallantly over her hand.

Stacy's heart thudded with dread when it was time to say goodbye to her grandfather. Not an overly demonstrative man, Andrew Daniels surprised Stacy by giving her a quick hug. They were nearly of the same height, and Stacy had to force the words from her throat when he dropped a kiss onto her cheek and released her.

"Goodbye, Papa."

"Goodbye, Stacy. Write when you are settled."

"Yes, Papa." She stood quietly then and just looked at him.

Andrew stared in return. His vision was better today, and he could see the uncertainty and fear in her eyes. He kept his own expression bland.

"You're going to be fine," the old man spoke, wondering if he would be able to say the same for himself.

Stacy could only nod, wanting to believe him. It was such a childlike gesture that Andrew gave her another hug, this one quite lengthy and without words. When it was over, he stood quietly and watched her step into his ancient carriage. He stayed on the steps, not only until they disappeared from view, but until he could no longer hear the carriage wheels rolling or the sound of the horses' hooves.

Lucinda Warbrook, Countess Snow by title, surreptitiously shifted the locket-watch that lay on her bosom and studied the time. She'd done so every few minutes for nearly an hour.

"Stacy will be fine, Cinda," a calm male voice told her from across the room. Lucinda's chin rose.

"Of course she'll be fine, Roddy. She is a Daniels, and all Daniels are strong. I was merely straightening my lace."

Roddy Caruthers, Earl of Glyn and Lucinda's closest friend, eyed her with doubt. Lucinda met his gaze for only a moment before she relaxed and the two exchanged a smile.

"Would you like me to go to the train station and see what might be keeping her?" He'd offered to do this twice before, and both times Lucinda had turned him down. Now she looked as though she might be considering it.

"It's just that I have pushed this issue with my brother, and if anything should happen to Stacy before she even arrives—"

Lucinda broke off when Roddy stood. She was reaching for the bellpull so Roddy's coat and hat could be retrieved when the door opened. It was Craig, Lucinda's head servant, announcing Stacy's arrival. Craig closed the parlor door as soon as he'd had his say, and Lucinda looked at Roddy, a touch of panic around her eyes.

"What have I done?" she whispered.

"You've done exactly as you should, Cinda," Roddy assured her confidently, just as the door opened and Stacy entered.

Her face was washed with fatigue but nothing could disguise the sweetness of her smile or the lovely blue of her eyes. She stood quietly for inspection wearing the yellow satin dress, her hair pulled back in a youthful style.

Even as Lucinda approached, she thought both the dress and hairstyle too young for Stacy, but no matter; she would fix all of that. The older woman nearly rubbed her hands together in anticipation of dressing this magnificent creature.

"My dear Stacy," Lucinda spoke with genuine warmth as her arms surrounded the girl.

Stacy returned the embrace, surprised and strangely relieved to find that her aunt was just a few inches shorter than herself.

"How was the train?" Lucinda asked as she led her to the settee near the fire. The room was chilly, and Stacy welcomed the warmth.

"It went well. A bit cold at times, but Milly and I snuggled together for warmth."

"Milly?" Lucinda frowned in thought.

"Milly Binks," Stacy supplied. "I traveled here with her family."

"Of course. I remember now. She was coming to shop, I believe."

"Yes, for her coming out."

Roddy, having taken a chair, sat quietly and listened to this exchange with great pleasure. He'd known for years that Lucinda wrote her brother and niece regularly and gained steady replies in return, making this instantaneous friendship quite natural. What he hadn't been prepared for was Stacy's sweetness.

She was not some nauseating creature who feigned politeness or forced good manners; she was simply a very gentle woman who obviously found pleasure in small things, such as conversing with her elderly aunt.

"Oh, goodness," Lucinda's voice broke into his musings. "You're sitting so quietly, Roddy; I nearly forgot you.

"Stacy, this is my dear friend the Earl of Glyn, Roddy Caruthers. Roddy, this is my niece, Anastasia Daniels."

Roddy stood on this introduction, and with all the court manners of a prince, bowed low and gently kissed the hand offered him.

"It is a pleasure to make your acquaintance, Lady Stacy."

Stacy, who had begun to smile at the introduction, found her eyes growing round with surprise by the time her aunt's friend was finished.

"Have I said something wrong?" Roddy asked solicitously, his eyes sparkling with good humor.

"I don't think so," Stacy spoke softly. "I've just never heard Lady Stacy sound so grand. We're all quite familiar at home."

"Ahh." Roddy's voice was kind, a smile now in full bloom. "I think you will become comfortable with our formality very swiftly." His voice was so gentle that it put Stacy's doubts to rest. Stacy gave him a huge smile, one that Roddy returned, before Lucinda spoke.

"I've ordered tea for 3:00, Stacy, if you'd like to freshen up. You will stay, Roddy?"

"Of course, Cinda," Roddy accepted with a gracious nod of his head. He watched as his hostess took her young charge from the room.

Stacy silently followed her aunt up the wide staircase of the mansion, mentally figuring how many hours remained until bedtime. Near the top she was beginning to flag, but the idea of tea drove her on. Never had she experienced such a long day. The sights and sounds of the train stations, the train ride, and then London itself were nearly more than she could take.

Watching Milly and her family walk away at the train station after such a good journey of sharing and laughter had been harder than Stacy expected, but Lucinda's coachman was kind and just 30 minutes later Stacy had been relieved to walk into Lucinda's parlor and find it warm and homey.

Stacy was looking forward to her stay with her aunt, but she was not lulled into a false sense of security about this visit. She had seen a look in Lucinda's eyes that had told her her clothing was not acceptable. And there was more. Lucinda sported the same stubborn chin that her grandfather owned. He was a man who liked to have his own way. Stacy had no doubts that as warm and loving as Lucinda Warbrook might be, she would also possess a well-used stubborn streak.

"She's lovely, isn't she, Roddy?" Lucinda said after the tea service was cleared away and Stacy had asked if she could retire to rest awhile.

"Yes, she is," he agreed softly, gazing at the excited flush on Lucinda's cheeks and thinking how lovely she was herself.

Three years past her sixtieth birthday, Lucinda didn't look a day over 50. Her dark hair was liberally streaked with white, but it gave a softness to her face that not even her stubborn chin could hide. She had a temper and was fiercely protective of those she loved, but she was also wise, sensitive, and well liked among London's elite.

Roddy wondered briefly if Stacy had any idea just how fully her aunt intended to launch her into London society.

"She hasn't many clothes, and what she does have are all wrong for her, so I'm making an appointment with Angelica tomorrow."

"Does Stacy know that?"

"No," Lucinda spoke dismissively, "but all girls like new clothes."

Something on Roddy's face made her pause.

"Do you think she'll object?"

"I honestly don't know. She's nothing whatever like I expected. She's mature and quite accepting of her lot, I would say. I could tell she was uncomfortable in the red velvet dress she changed into for tea, but even at that I detected an underlying acceptance within her over the whole situation."

Nodding, Lucinda stayed silent, digesting what he'd said. Roddy was always so good at reading people. He never worried about putting his oar in as Lucinda did, but was content to sit back, listen, and observe. Sometimes he read the situation wrong, but Lucinda felt certain he'd hit the mark with Stacy.

No matter really, Lucinda thought. *Stacy will not have to be accepting of her situation any longer. I am here to see to that.*

It crossed Lucinda's mind that her niece might not care to have new clothes and attend every ball in London, but Lucinda quickly pushed the thought away. What girl wouldn't be thrilled with the summer Lady Warbrook was about to give her niece?

Three

STACY THANKED RAYNA, the personal maid Lucinda assigned to her, while carefully keeping a smile pinned to her face. When the door closed, leaving her alone, Stacy's hands moved to her mouth and she dropped onto one side of the bed.

She simply didn't know what to do. Her grandfather would be furious if he knew how many dresses Lucinda had ordered for her today. Stacy knew they would cost a fortune, money that her grandfather didn't have. She recalled the flash of anger in Lucinda's eyes when she mentioned this, and that had been enough to make Stacy hold her tongue.

It had done little to relieve her mind when Lucinda calmed down and explained quietly that the gowns were a gift. Stacy knew her grandfather would still not approve, and in a way she understood her grandfather's belief. Stacy often dreamed of finer things, but it seemed cruel to shower a person with beautiful articles of clothing they could never have again. Stacy was convinced that it was easier to go without your whole life than to live in opulence only to have it taken away.

Suddenly the room felt stuffy, and Stacy rose to go downstairs. A walk in the garden was sure to do some good.

An hour later Roddy stopped to see Lucinda, only to be told that she was taking a rest. He was on the verge of leaving his card and a note when Craig told him that Lady Stacy was in the garden. There was something akin to concern in the man's tone, causing Roddy to reconsider and make his way out-of-doors.

The weather was still a bit cool, but Stacy seemed immune to the conditions around her. She sat on a stone bench amid the budding flowers and stared into space toward the high stone wall that surrounded the yard. She found herself wishing for the green hills of Middlesbrough, where she could walk for hours without need of an escort.

Her mind was wandering among those fields when she heard a footfall. Glad for something to take her mind from home, Stacy turned with surprised pleasure to see Roddy.

"Good afternoon, Lady Stacy," he began. "Taking in this brisk afternoon?"

Stacy smiled shyly. "My room felt stuffy. I'm afraid I've hardly noticed the weather."

Roddy took a seat across from her and studied her. Stacy sat quietly under his scrutiny, searching her mind for some topic of conversation. She had never been very good at being witty or charming. She usually just said what was on her mind, but she didn't think her wardrobe an appropriate topic right then. Stacy was still groping for a subject when Roddy spoke.

"How was your shopping trip this morning?"

"Fine," Stacy answered a bit too brightly, and Roddy's brows rose in disbelief, causing Stacy's eyes to drop to her lap.

"Lucinda likes to shop," she spoke inanely, wishing that Roddy's gaze wasn't so penetrating.

"I take it that she bought you quite a number of dresses?"

"An entire wardrobe," Stacy admitted, looking miserable. "It was really very kind of her, but I just don't know what my grandfather will say when I arrive home with an entire trunk full of new dresses." Stacy did not know what prompted her to confide in this near stranger, but he was so kind and easy to talk with.

"Your grandfather doesn't care for your having new things?" Roddy's voice held no accusation, just deceivingly mild interest.

Stacy tipped her head to the side, searching for the right words to explain. As she did so her thick blonde hair fell like a curtain over one shoulder.

"My grandfather is a proud man, just as Aunt Lucinda is a proud woman. He wants me to have all that *he* can provide. Aunt Lucinda married well. My grandfather couldn't provide that many dresses for me if he saved for a year. And in truth, I can't think where I'll wear them. Some of the fabrics look fit for a princess."

"Did you explain that to Lucinda?"

"I tried, but she didn't look too happy about it."

Such a polite way, Roddy translated to himself, *of saying that Cinda became angry and Stacy immediately closed her mouth and backed down.*

"Has Lucinda told you all she has planned for the summer?" Roddy suddenly asked.

Stacy shook her head no.

Roddy nodded. "I think you may find that you will have ample opportunity to wear the dresses. As for your grandfather's reaction, let Lucinda handle it. You certainly won't be blamed for something over which you had no control."

Stacy sighed deeply. She felt caught between the hammer and anvil where her aunt and grandfather were concerned. To please one would displease the other, and that thought alone gave Stacy a headache. But her normal good sense took over then, and she told herself that Roddy was right.

"Thank you, my lord. You've been a tremendous help."

"You're most welcome, and I really wish you would call me Roddy. It's not as if I'm a duke," he added with a cheeky grin.

Stacy smiled in return but then looked worried. "I won't have to meet any dukes or duchesses, will I?"

"You might," Roddy told her. "Is that a problem?"

Stacy shrugged uncomfortably. "I just don't know what I would say."

"Don't say anything if you don't have to. And if you do find you need to reply, just be yourself. The London elite can be ruthless, but the only thing they could find to say about you is that you're the sweetest thing to arrive in decades."

Stacy chuckled softly at the compliment. "I think Aunt Lucinda is quite lucky to have Roddy Caruthers."

"I think so too," he agreed with her, another grin in place. With that he stood and offered his arm.

"May I escort you in to tea?"

Stacy accepted graciously, not even self-conscious that he was two inches shorter than her statuesque frame.

"Did you give my letters to Craig?" Lucinda wanted to know. Over two weeks had passed since Stacy had spoken with Roddy in the garden, and during that time Stacy had been much easier about the wardrobe.

Now she was breakfasting with her aunt, and Lucinda was giving her the day's plans.

"I did give them to Craig. He assured me he would see to them," Stacy answered.

"Very good. Now, I wish to leave as soon as we've eaten. We've been invited to Andrea's, and I don't wish to be late."

Stacy nodded and continued with her meal. Her day-dresses had begun arriving just two days ago, and Lucinda had had the two of them out for tea both morning and afternoon since. Stacy had met more people in the last three days than she had in all her life.

They had all been kind, but Stacy could not shake the feeling that she was here on inspection. It put something of a damper on her outings, but most of the time she was determined to enjoy herself and go home rich with memories and experiences.

Every memory of home gave her a slight pang. She was truly pleased to be in London, but she missed her grandfather, Elena, Elena's girls, and Hettie terribly. When her feelings of homesickness threatened to overwhelm her, she thought of her dresses. They were the most beautiful she'd ever seen.

Stacy found herself feeling very pleased that Lucinda had not listened to her about her grandfather's wishes. Had she done so, she would not have been stepping out in London with clothes that made her feel as if she belonged. So often her words to Hettie about being a country mouse came to mind. Most of the time she still felt that way inside, but on the outside she knew she was at the height of fashion.

The dress she wore this day was a dark blue water silk of elegant simplicity. The neckline was high with a white lace inset. The same lace trimmed Stacy's three-quarter-length sleeves. The skirt was of a medium fullness, and the bodice accentuated the line of her waist and full bosom. As they climbed down from the carriage before Featherstone, Lady Andrea Brent's mansion, Lucinda felt a surge of pride in Stacy.

Featherstone sat on the Thames and was one of London's most talked-about residences. Stacy and Lucinda were inside, standing in the vast foyer, before Stacy learned that Andrea was a duchess.

"He said, 'The duchess will be with you in a moment,' Aunt Lucinda. Did he mean Lady Andrea?"

"Well, of course," Lucinda frowned at her. "What did you think?"

"I don't know. None of the other ladies I met this week were—" Stacy cut off her sentence when the servant reappeared and directed them forward.

He opened a door at the rear of the foyer and led them into a huge parlor. Andrea was inside and rose immediately to greet them.

"Come in, Lucinda." She greeted her with a kiss. "And you must be Stacy. Lucinda has told me so much about you." Stacy returned the spontaneous embrace, thinking that she liked Lady Andrea very much.

"Please sit down." Andrea indicated the chairs and continued to speak as they moved. "Your dress is lovely, Stacy. Something tells me the two of you have been shopping."

Lucinda looked so pleased that Stacy had to stifle a laugh. "We have been shopping," Lucinda announced proudly and went on to tell Andrea all they'd been about.

Stacy found herself quelling laughter again, this time at herself, when she remembered the quiet existence she believed Aunt Lucinda led. Why, the older woman had more friends than Stacy could keep track of! Stacy glanced up at Andrea to find her hostess's eyes on her. They shared a small, almost secret, smile, and Stacy had the impression that Lady Andrea could read her thoughts.

With an effort, the younger woman then concentrated on what her aunt was saying. She learned that they would be having tea with someone else the next day and then attending the Parkinsons' ball on Saturday night. The following Saturday it would be the Madisons' ball.

Stacy's eyes, having just been so amused, must have now shown her shock over this news. Both women smiled at her.

"You'll have a wonderful time, Stacy," Andrea assured her. "If your dress is half as lovely as it is today, you'll be the talk of the room." Andrea could see in an instant that she'd said the wrong thing. A moment later Stacy's words confirmed this.

"I don't want to be the talk of the room," she said softly, and Lucinda's voice was tight when she spoke.

"Honestly, Stacy, you would think you don't even like all the new things I've bought you or want to show them off."

"Oh, no, Aunt Lucinda," Stacy was instantly contrite. "I love my new dresses." Her answer was an honest one, but Stacy was far too timid to tell Lucinda she didn't care to be on display.

Lucinda, choosing to ignore Stacy's discomfort, nodded her stubborn chin as though she'd won the battle. Lady Brent was thankful that tea was announced. Neither of her guests noticed her scrutiny of Stacy's quiet face or her worried frown over Lucinda's control of the girl. Thankfully, tea-time passed smoothly.

Two hours later Andrea was seeing her guests to the door. The older women conversed as they walked, and Stacy was content to listen. All three of them were surprised when the front door suddenly opened and in swept the most beautiful woman Stacy had ever seen.

"Sunny!" Andrea cried and rushed forward to embrace the lovely chestnut-haired girl.

"Hello, Mum. Am I interrupting?"

"Of course not. Come and meet Stacy. You know Lucinda Warbrook."

"Of course. It's lovely to see you, Lady Warbrook."

"And this is her niece, Stacy Daniels. Stacy, this is my daughter-in-law, Sunny."

"Hello, Stacy." Sunny greeted her with genuine kindness. "I hope you're not leaving."

"Actually, we are," Stacy told her with real regret.

"My timing is awful." Sunny pulled a face that did nothing to detract from her lovely appearance. "At least I can walk you out."

This said, Sunny tucked her arm in Stacy's and began to chatter as they walked out the front door toward the waiting carriage.

"I think I know your cousin. Is her name Elena?"

"Yes," Stacy answered with surprised pleasure. "How do you know her?"

"We met a few years ago, just after she married your grandfather's cousin. She was in London for a visit, and I think she was expecting her first child."

"That would be Harmony. She's had another little girl since then; they named her Brittany."

"Those are lovely names. Do you miss Elena and the girls?"

"I can't tell you how much," Stacy told her fervently and then pulled a face of her own. "I also miss our home in the country. London is so huge and noisy."

"You forgot smelly," Sunny added.

Stacy laughed. "How could anyone forget that?"

"I prefer the country myself," Sunny told her as they walked. "Maybe you'll have a chance to visit Bracken while you're here. We would love to have you."

Stacy looked delighted and then uncertain. "I'm not exactly sure what Aunt Lucinda has in mind," she admitted softly.

The two older women were following slowly, so Sunny only had time to nod in comprehension and say just as quietly, "I think I understand. Lucinda must feel she's been given a live doll to play with."

Stacy laughed softly at the accurate description of her relationship with Lucinda and found Sunny grinning at her.

"I like you, Stacy Daniels," Sunny told her.

"And I like you, Sunny," Stacy barely had time to reply before being joined by Lucinda and Andrea.

Stacy thanked her hostess and climbed into the carriage without ceremony. As it pulled away, Lucinda commented on having just spotted the duke as he joined his wife and mother. Stacy wanted to question her on the spot, but Lucinda continued to speak.

"It had been on the tip of my tongue to ask Sunny if she was here with Brandon."

"Brandon?"

"Yes," Lucinda answered absently. "Sunny's husband, Brandon Hawkesbury, the Duke of Briscoe."

Stacy's eyes widened a bit, but Lucinda didn't seem to notice. Stacy was very quiet on the ride home.

"WELL, WHAT DID YOU THINK of her?" Andrea asked of Sunny when they were finally alone.

"I think she's the sweetest thing I've ever met. And," Sunny paused for emphasis, "I know her cousin, Elena, who happens to be a believer. We met a few years ago, and she told me at the time that she was praying for Stacy's salvation. I find it very exciting that the Lord put us together, however briefly."

"Put who together?" Brandon asked as he joined the ladies and they went in to lunch.

Sunny explained her encounter with Stacy, and when Brandon prayed before they ate, he asked God to bless Stacy and give her further contact with Sunny.

They were halfway through the meal before Brandon commented cryptically on his mother's lack of enthusiasm.

"Over what?" Andrea wanted to know, thinking she'd been quite pleased over Stacy's visit.

"I was so excited about Stacy," Sunny admitted softly to her spouse, "that I forgot to tell her."

Andrea looked from her son to her daughter-in-law, and a slow smile pulled her mouth into a huge grin.

"I thought there was something going on, Sunny." She rose and kissed her cheek. "You have that special glow about you."

Brandon and Sunny exchanged a glance, one of love and sharing. The meal continued with a discussion about how old their first child, Sterling, would be when his younger brother or sister was born.

Stacy moved into the parlor at Lucinda's and collapsed into a chair. Her feet were throbbing, but she was as light-hearted as a child. She had survived her first London ball, and it had been the most exciting night of her life.

The ballroom and dining room at the Parkinsons' had been absolutely beautiful. Stacy needed only to close her eyes to see the lovely candelabras and hear the music play. She had danced for hours.

"I think she's asleep," Roddy commented as he came into the room and made himself comfortable.

Stacy's eyes opened, and she smiled. Lucinda had invited him in to rest by the fire.

"Sleepy, but not sleeping. I was thinking of the dance."

"I was thinking of it myself," Lucinda put in as she made herself comfortable across from Stacy, eyeing her maternally. "I think Lord Culbertson was quite taken with you."

"He's so nice," Stacy commented sweetly, "and he loves to fish," she added with enthusiasm, her blue eyes sparkling.

Roddy chuckled over Lucinda's good-natured groan.

"Is that all you spoke of?" the older woman wanted to know.

"Well," Stacy sat up straight and tried to think, wanting to please her aunt, "he told me about his horses, and I told him about Noel's stables."

"My dear Stacy," Lucinda's look was pained, "Lord Culbertson raises some of the finest horses in England."

Stacy's fine mood was deserting her. She tried to think of something else they spoke of that would pacify her aunt.

"He said my dress was pretty and my hair. And he didn't seem to mind that we were of the same height."

"But you spent most of the time discussing fishing?" Roddy asked gently.

Stacy nodded, looking miserable now. "I'm sorry, Aunt Lucinda. I hope I didn't embarrass you."

Stacy's look, that of a child who had disappointed her mother, was too much for the older woman. Lucinda's own look became a mask of shame.

"You could never embarrass me, Stacy. I couldn't have been prouder of you tonight if you had been my very own daughter. I'm sure Lord Culbertson was captivated."

Stacy looked uncertain, but she did feel a little better. "At least he wasn't a duke," Stacy added as an afterthought. "They still intimidate me."

"Why is that?" Roddy wished to know.

"I guess because the only one I've ever been acquainted with is rather mean. His wife is even worse. Each time I see them, they make me feel like some sort of country vermin. It makes me feel as though I've no right to be moving in their circles.

"Sunny and Andrea are certainly nice people, but it may take some time for me to get beyond their titles. I know it must sound silly to you, but I've no lofty aspirations. My grandfather is a viscount. I've always assumed I'd marry a viscount or a baron who led a simple life, and that's always been fine."

Lucinda did not look overly pleased with this news, but Roddy was able to catch her eye and with a slight move of his head, keep her hushed. Stacy, growing sleepier by the moment, didn't notice their silent exchange.

"Goodnight, Aunt Lucinda. Goodnight, Roddy; I'll be ready in the morning," she bid them softy as she stood. They returned her wishes for a good night and watched her exit the room.

"It's silly of her to be afraid," Lucinda said immediately, her tone impatient.

"Be that as it may, she is. I see no reason to try to calm her, since it's very unlikely that she will encounter many dukes."

Lucinda didn't seem very satisfied with his logic. She named the few eligible dukes out loud, all 80 if they were a day, until Roddy stopped her with a soft rebuke.

"Cinda! You don't actually have your sights set on a duke, do you?"

"No," she admitted. "In fact, I think Lord Culbertson might do very well for Stacy, and he's a marquess."

"He's also old enough to be her father." Roddy's voice was dry.

"Well, we might not be able to be so picky," Lucinda nearly snapped.

"Why must she marry at all?" Roddy questioned, not at all put off by her bad humor. His question only gained him a quelling look, one that amused him more than anything else. A moment's silence passed before Roddy suggested the only young, single duke he knew.

"There is always Lord Richardson." Roddy worked to keep his face bland while Lucinda's flushed with anger.

"Don't be ridiculous! He's the biggest cynic in all of England and all wrong for Stacy." Lucinda's foot beat a rapid tatoo on the floor. Roddy watched her for a moment and then stood with a lazy stretch.

"This conversation has worn me out. Remind Stacy that I'll be here at 10:00 sharp for our ride."

With that he leaned over and pressed a soft kiss to Lucinda's brow. Her anger melted at his tenderness, and even though no more words were said, their eyes held for just a moment before Roddy crossed the room to the door.

"Oh, Stacy, that color is beautiful on you," Lucinda complimented her the next morning when Stacy entered her bedroom wearing a pale yellow riding habit with a white blouse and short jacket.

"Thank you. I think this one must be my favorite."

"Roddy's head will swell when he's seen in the park with you."

Stacy smiled shyly without answering. Lucinda patted the side of the bed, and she took a seat.

"Are you having a good time with me, dear?" Lucinda's eyes were eager.

"Oh, yes, Aunt Lucinda. It's been wonderful." Stacy hesitated before going on. "Are you pleased with me?"

Lucinda's answer was to tenderly cup Stacy's soft, rosy cheeks in her perfectly manicured hands and place a gentle kiss upon her forehead. Stacy was very touched by the gesture and was surprised to see tears in Lucinda's eyes. The older woman busied herself with her bedclothes to cover the fact, but Stacy had seen them nonetheless.

"Aunt Lucinda?"

"Yes, dear." Lucinda's voice held a catch.

"May I ask you a question?"

"Of course." She cleared her throat and finally looked up.

"Why have you never married Roddy?"

Lucinda's eyes, which had first held expectancy, became very thoughtful, but she wasn't long in answering.

"He's never asked me."

Stacy tipped her head to one side. "But you love him?"

"Yes" was the serene reply. "I have for years."

Stacy nodded, feeling closer to her aunt than ever before. Silence passed for a moment, a gentle silence with no hint of strain or awkwardness, before Craig knocked and announced that Roddy had arrived for Stacy.

"I'm probably the most envied man in the park today," Roddy commented from the back of his horse. Stacy smiled.

"Aunt Lucinda said your head would swell when you were seen with me today," Stacy admitted and then looked swiftly at Roddy to see if she'd offended him with Lucinda's words. On the contrary, his shoulders were shaking with laughter.

They rode on in silence for a time. Roddy took them down one of his favorite paths. They were halfway to the other side when they passed another group of riders. Stacy recognized a few from the Parkinsons' ball and smiled, but in her mind the entire event passed without exception. Not so for Roddy. Stacy glanced over to ask him a question and found his handsome face in a fierce frown.

"Are you feeling ill, Roddy?"

"No. I'm just always amazed at the ton's propensity for gossip."

Stacy stared at him uncomprehendingly.

"I take it you didn't hear that remark concerning you and me?"

Stacy shook her head no.

"Well, then, we'll let the matter drop."

Stacy nodded in agreement but was troubled by his words. It was a pity really that her friendship with Roddy had to be put in a sordid light, because it simply wasn't so. He was only a few years younger than Lucinda and like a father figure to her. Even if her heart had moved to romance where he was concerned, in her mind he belonged to Lucinda. Stacy sighed softly and did her best to do as Roddy suggested.

"I don't believe you've heard a word I've said," Lord Edmond Black complained to his nephew as their horses stood off the path in a small copse of trees. "But I'm going to say it again. I think those horses are a good investment, and I think you should look into it."

Tanner glanced at the older man for an instant, but his eyes swung swiftly back to the woman riding through the park with Roddy Caruthers. Something tightened in his chest as he watched her smile at her companion, something he hadn't felt for years.

Edmond was talking again, so Tanner turned and tried to pay attention, but almost immediately, as though they couldn't help themselves, his eyes sought out the girl once again. This time he watched her until she disappeared from view, wondering absently how long her hair might be, and about her relationship to Caruthers.

"Tanner!"

Tanner's handsome head swung slowly back to his uncle. The look he gave the older man was one of pure boredom. "I'm listening, Edmond."

Edmond grunted with irritation. "You were doing nothing of the kind. You were watching Lucinda's niece."

"Lucinda Warbrook?"

"Certainly." Edmond's voice was still testy. "Daniels is the girl's name. Her grandfather is Andrew Daniels, Viscount Claremont. She never had a coming out, but she's here for the summer and Lucinda is dressing her like a princess and introducing her all over town."

Tanner listened intently, something he was not prone to do with Edmond. Edmond loved to gossip, and Tanner simply didn't care to hear about everyone in London. However, this tall-looking girl in the yellow riding habit captivated him.

"Now as I was saying..." Edmond began again, as their ride resumed, but Tanner's mind was still elsewhere.

The younger man had just remembered the invitation he had received to the Madisons' ball. He usually hated those affairs, but the thought of possibly seeing Lucinda Warbrook's niece was enough to make him reconsider.

THE NIGHT OF THE MADISONS' BALL, Stacy was dressed long before Lucinda. She sat before the dressing table mirror and thought how lovely the emerald necklace looked with her green dress. Lucinda had done a wonderful job choosing the new settings for the family stones. In fact Stacy had already worn the ruby last week.

When Rayna finished stacking her hair high atop her head, Stacy walked downstairs to wait in the parlor with Roddy. She wondered in some amazement at how many hours he had stood in this parlor waiting for Lucinda to appear over the course of the years.

"Oh, my, Roddy," she commented as she came in. "You look very dashing tonight." Stacy moved to where he stood near the mantel and kissed his cheek. They had grown closer almost daily, and small touches were now customary and warm.

"Thank you, my dear." He accepted the compliment with a sparkle in his eye.

Stacy's grandfather had never been a demonstrative man, and now to have Roddy here to pat her hand or cheek and to accept her embraces and kisses was more special to Stacy than she could have put into words. It didn't cause her to miss Andrew Daniels any less, but it added a warm dimension to her life that she'd never before experienced.

Stacy and Roddy talked for the better part of an hour, both beginning to think that Lucinda was never going to make an appearance. Roddy's coach was waiting when she did come, however, so they were swiftly on their way.

"The Madisons are an old family," Lucinda explained on the way. "They have several daughters and one son. I would advise you to get to know him, but I think he's a bit of a libertine and a little young for you."

Stacy smiled in the darkness of the coach interior. Her aunt was forever out to see her married. Her grandfather had told Lucinda in no uncertain terms not to push this point, but Lucinda did as she wished.

"Now don't hesitate to dance with Lord Culbertson. You did well at the Parkinsons' ball; however, you must always watch who you're seen with. I want you to enjoy yourself, but spending even a few moments with the wrong person could ruin your chances." Lucinda's voice was now severe.

This time Stacy didn't feel like laughing. She wished with all of her heart that it was easier for a young woman to stay single, so that every union could be one of love. But this simply wasn't the case. Her honest desire was to marry, but at this moment Stacy wondered if she would ever meet the man of her dreams. She was comforted by the fact that she knew her grandfather would never force her. The thought made her sigh unconsciously, and Lucinda's voice came sharply from the other side of the coach.

"Did you hear me, Stacy?"

"Yes, Aunt Lucinda," she answered obediently, and the rest of the ride was made in silence.

The ballroom was crowded when they arrived, but Lucinda and Roddy were old professionals when it came to this type of entertainment. Stacy was more than willing to follow their lead, and within moments of coming to the edge of the dance floor, Stacy was swept out into a waltz.

She didn't catch the name of the man dancing with her, but she answered all of his questions and detected a gleam of disappointment in his eyes when he learned that she would not someday be the heiress to a fortune. Not until she arrived back at Roddy's side did Stacy begin to wonder if some of the young man's questions might have been out of order.

The next hour passed in much the same fashion, Stacy going from one partner to the next, some young, most old. She tried to ignore the fact that even if her hair hadn't been piled high atop her head, she would still be taller than most of them. The room grew very stuffy, and Stacy felt delivered when Roddy pressed a glass of punch into her hand.

The glass was on the way to her mouth when she spotted him across the ballroom—the tallest, most handsome man Stacy had ever seen. He was dressed all in black, and she stared at him because she seemed incapable of doing anything else. His own eyes were on her, and for the space of several seconds Stacy simply couldn't look away.

"Drop your eyes!"

The low, furious words came to Stacy's ears, but thinking they couldn't be for her, she didn't heed them. A fierce yank on her arm, one that nearly spilled her punch, finally brought her to her senses. She looked down to see Lucinda glaring furiously at her.

"I said, drop your eyes!"

"Oh." Stacy was startled and instantly contrite. "I didn't realize it was you, Aunt Lucinda. I'm sorry."

Stacy seemed to be at a sudden loss, her hands all aflutter as she changed her glass from one hand to the other. Lucinda wondered if she might not have overreacted and felt compelled to make amends.

"Here, give me your glass." Lucinda's voice was brisk now, but not angry. "Go to the retiring room and fix your hair. There's a good girl."

Stacy complied, but she honestly couldn't feel her slippers as they moved on the carpets. It was a comfort to find the retiring room empty. Head in the clouds, Stacy stood before the mirror and took in her flushed cheeks and dazed eyes. No wonder Lucinda had sent her from the room. Her own image faded as once again her mind's eye saw the man in black.

Can a person really be so drawn to someone after just one look? Stacy asked herself, and then her heart lifted. It didn't matter if no one else had ever felt as she did. He was the most wonderful man she'd ever seen.

"I wonder who he is." This was spoken out loud as Stacy's brow lowered in concentration.

Two young ladies chose that moment to enter the room, and Stacy swiftly turned and entered one of the booths. She wanted some time to herself. She came to her senses some five minutes later and knew she would have to return to the ballroom or Lucinda would miss her.

And who knows, Stacy told her heart as she moved toward the dance floor. *Maybe you'll spot him again.*

An hour and a half later Stacy knew that if she didn't get some fresh air she was going to be ill. It was dreadfully warm, and the young man who had promised her a glass of punch had left and never returned. She hadn't spotted the man in black again, but from across the way she could see Lucinda and Roddy talking with Lord Culbertson. Stacy was simply too warm to push her way through the crowd in order to join them.

With movements that were as subtle as she could make them, she moved toward the balcony doors. They were closed but thankfully unlocked, and Stacy drew in a huge breath of cool night air the moment she was outside. The breath nearly stuck in her throat, however, when a deep male voice addressed her from out of the darkness.

"I wondered how long it would take you to join me."

Stacy gasped as she spun and saw a man leaning lackadaisically against the stone railing, close to the house. Stacy was so startled by his presence that for a moment she said nothing.

Tanner, who had been watching her through the glass doors for over an hour as she danced and talked with half the people in the room, smiled at the surprise he knew must be feigned. It was an old game, often played in social circles. Not that he cared. He intended to know this woman very well before she left in the fall.

"I didn't know anyone was out here," Stacy finally spoke when her breathing returned to normal.

Again Tanner smiled. Most of the debutantes he knew believed that coyness was the way to attract a man. If Stacy preferred that method of sweet innocence, it was fine with him.

"Would you rather be alone?" Stacy asked kindly, not seeing Tanner's smile in the dark.

"Don't go in on my account," he told her. "I realize it's warm inside."

Stacy sighed with relief and moved away from the doors. She stepped to the railing a good ten feet from Tanner, thinking what a nice voice he had but wondering what he looked like. Stacy glanced out over the gardens, but the moon was very dim and beyond a shape or two, she could make out little.

"The Madisons have a lovely home," Stacy commented absently.

"It's nice," Tanner observed, his voice bored. "A little small perhaps."

Stacy stared at his silhouette and then up at the grand expanse of mansion before her. Clearly this man was accustomed to a home far larger than her grandfather's.

"You haven't told me your name," Stacy's companion suddenly said to her.

"Oh, I'm Stacy Daniels. Lucinda Warbrook's niece."

"Stacy would be short for—?"

"Anastasia."

"Hmm, Anastasia. That's a lovely name. I think it fits you." Tanner was well aware that he was doing some pretending of his own. Since he'd seen her in the park he had set about learning everything about her he wished to know. Unmarried, 21 years old, not spoken for, and of course what his eyes had told him the first time he'd seen her—tall and beautiful.

"I'm Tanner Richardson."

"Tanner," Stacy said with surprise. "I've always liked that name." Relieved that he had shared his name, Stacy chatted on about a young man from home with the same name.

Stacy would not have been quite so friendly had she been able to see the calculative look in Tanner's eyes as he studied her from the shadows. From where he was, the lights from the ballroom gave a perfect view of Stacy in her lovely green frock with its rounded neckline and short, puffed sleeves.

Stacy laughed suddenly. "I'm chattering on here, and you must be bored to death." Suddenly, her whole frame stiffened with embarrassment, but when she spoke her voice was as sweet and sincere as the woman herself.

"I'm sorry, Tanner. You must be waiting for someone, and now I've joined you and ruined it. I'll go inside and leave you alone."

"Come now, Stacy." Tanner kept his voice calm, but he wanted the game over. "We both knew you would come out here to join me."

A moment of silence met this remark. "I don't know what you mean," Stacy told him in genuine confusion.

"Of course you do." Tanner's voice lost some of its patience. He didn't care to keep up this pretense much longer. "Your eyes told me from across the room what I wanted to know."

Stacy tensed abruptly. It was *him!* Even though Tanner had not moved from the shadows, Stacy could now visualize this gorgeous man—very tall with dark brown hair and dark, compelling eyes. Lucinda's sudden hissing in her ear now made complete sense.

"I have to go in now." Stacy's voice was thick with shame and near desperation. Lucinda had warned her time and again to be careful with her eyes, but she'd never understood. Now by looking at a man and thinking him handsome, she had unwittingly given him a signal that she was interested. Lucinda would be livid.

Stacy moved back to the glass doors of the ballroom to the sound of Tanner's voice, but she didn't take in the words.

"I think Roddy is ready to leave now," Lucinda told Stacy. Stacy had come back to the dance an hour ago, and Lucinda had not seemed at all put out by her absence.

"You wait here by the cloakroom. We'll say our thanks and collect you in a moment."

Lucinda swept away before Stacy could frame a reply, which was just as well, since she was too tired to speak. She waved at a group of girls who were leaving and then slipped farther down the wall to lean against it and rest her feet. She knew it wasn't the least bit ladylike, but right now she didn't care.

"You left the balcony so abruptly that I didn't have a chance to tell you something."

Where he had come from Stacy didn't know, but suddenly there stood Tanner Richardson. He nonchalantly leaned one hand on the wall above her, and Stacy had to actually look up to see his face.

With a smile that was almost tender, Tanner turned on the full force of his charm. Stacy's heart pounded in her chest. She'd never reacted to anyone as she was doing now.

"I was going to tell you," Tanner went on quietly, his deep voice confidential, "that I *was* waiting for someone to join me. I was waiting for you."

Stacy could only stare up in stunned surprise. She couldn't

move or think, not even when his free hand reached for her and he gently touched the end of her adorable nose.

"I'll look forward to seeing you again, Anastasia," he whispered before straightening. A moment later he was gone.

Stacy didn't move or even breathe in the seconds that followed. Her heart felt as if it might pound through her chest.

"Why, Stacy." Lucinda's voice snapped her out of her trance. "Your face is rather flushed. Are you not feeling well?"

"Cinda," Roddy spoke with a laugh, "she's just danced for hours; what would you expect her to look like?"

Lucinda laughed with him, and Roddy helped her into her cloak. Stacy was thankful that no more was said on the subject as they loaded into the carriage and headed for home.

The next morning Roddy and Stacy enjoyed another ride in the park. When they returned, Stacy went directly to her room, but Roddy found Lucinda in a fury. Now he was in the parlor with his hostess and friend, making an attempt to calm her.

"Cinda," his voice was gentle, "wait to send for her. If she comes in now you'll terrify her."

"I don't care," Lucinda told him, although she did. "I've already sent Craig for her. I intend to have some answers *now!*"

Roddy sat down. When Lucinda was in high dudgeon there was simply no reasoning with her. If only she would settle down before Stacy arrived. But it was not to be. The moment she stepped into the room, Lucinda attacked.

"Where did you meet him?"

"Meet who?" Stacy asked. Her expression had gone from open friendliness to guarded fear upon seeing her aunt's ire.

"The Duke of Cambridge."

"I—" Stacy began to say that she hadn't met him, but Lucinda cut her off and began to pace.

"I warned you last night when I found you staring at him, but I can see my wishes mean little to you." She continued to rant and rave, but Stacy couldn't get beyond the fact that she didn't remember meeting a single duke the night before.

"I'm waiting for an answer, Stacy Daniels," Lucinda suddenly stopped and demanded. "When did you meet Lord Richardson?"

"Lord Richardson? You mean Tanner Richardson? He's the Duke of Cambridge?"

"Do not play games with me." Lucinda moved toward her, having completely lost her head.

"Lucinda!" Roddy's voice, sounding unlike Lucinda had ever heard it, checked her stride. She turned to find angry fire in his eyes, his face flushed. She was so startled by the change in him that she calmed slightly before turning back to Stacy. What she saw washed her in shame. All color had drained from Stacy's face, and she was staring at her aunt in stark fear.

"Sit down, Cinda." Roddy's voice had returned to normal, and Lucinda did as he commanded. She watched as Roddy approached Stacy and led her gently to a chair. Stacy kept her eyes on Roddy once he had seated himself, her eyes begging him to tell her what she had done. He did not disappoint her.

"The flowers on the table are for you," Roddy told her gently. He waited until Stacy noticed the huge bouquet of red roses before going on. "They are from Lord Richardson and came with a note telling you how much he enjoyed meeting you last night."

"Which is just ridiculous," Lucinda cut in angrily. "All you did was see him across the room. Isn't that right, Stacy? He's got more cheek than any ten men I know."

A short silence ensued before Roddy asked, "Did you see more of him, Stacy?"

Stacy nodded in misery, her eyes on her aunt, who suddenly looked crestfallen.

"I'm sorry, Aunt Lucinda. It was so warm in the ballroom, and I needed some air. I didn't know he was on the balcony. I didn't know he was the man from inside, and he never said he was a duke. I'm so sorry, Aunt Lucinda."

Stacy's face was so full of anguish that the last vestiges of anger drained completely out of Lucinda. The room *had* been like a furnace last night, and it was all so innocent on Stacy's part.

On the other hand, Lucinda was convinced that Tanner Richardson didn't have an innocent or honorable bone in his body. She was going to have to keep her head about this or lose control of the entire situation.

"Don't be upset anymore, my dear," Lucinda finally told her. "It wasn't your fault, and it's going to be fine. Did Tanner touch you in any way?"

"No," Stacy told her, and then her eyes grew huge. "I almost forgot. He did touch my nose with his finger."

Lucinda's eyes slid shut momentarily. When she regained control she asked, "Did he say anything improper?"

"No."

"You're certain?"

"Yes, ma'am."

Lucinda nodded. "Stacy, Tanner is not for you. He's young and titled, but he's also very cynical, and that is *not* the type of man for you." Lucinda looked at Roddy and gained his approving nod.

By unspoken agreement, however, neither Roddy nor Stacy's aunt went on to tell her that Lord Richardson's interest in her would not lead to marriage. Stacy was upset enough as it was, and they now knew how closely she would need chaperoning. Her trusting and innocent nature made her a possible prey to any and all disreputable men of title.

The three of them talked for a while longer before Lucinda suggested that Stacy check on preparations for lunch. Roddy and Lucinda continued to talk after she'd left.

"You can control Stacy's actions, Cinda, but you have little to say over Lord Richardson's."

"True," Lucinda said regretfully. "But if he tries anything with Stacy, he'll have to go through me."

"Well, you're certainly his match, Cinda, but have you considered the possibility of Stacy falling for him?"

The eyes Lucinda turned to him were dim with pain. Roddy moved close enough to slip an arm around her. Lucinda let her head fall against his shoulder, her heart silently contemplating how many years she'd begged Andrew to allow Stacy to come to London. Lucinda wondered that she could have been so unsuspecting of all that would entail.

Six

TANNER SWEPT INTO THE BALLROOM, completely unconscious of the picture he presented. The black pants and coat hung on his muscular frame without wrinkle or gap, and the white cravat at his throat only heightened the deep tan of his face.

He nodded to several greetings of "Good evening, your Grace," but beyond that he was left alone. His eyes scanned the crowded dance floor for a sign of Stacy. This was the third dance he'd attended this week in order to speak with her, and she hadn't been present at the first two. Tanner told himself if she wasn't here tonight, he would go directly to Lucinda Warbrook's and demand to see her.

The incongruity of the situation began to dawn on Tanner. He hadn't been involved with a woman since Leslie died. So why now? Tanner had no answer. He had met Leslie the same way, spotted her at a ball and then sought her out. Of course at the time he didn't know how self-seeking she was or how desirable the title of duke was to her, the title that his brother had held at the time.

Suddenly Stacy came into view. Just the sight of her caused Tanner's doubts to fly. He didn't know much about her, didn't know if his being a duke would matter to her or not, but he knew this—he found her unforgettable. For the moment Tanner believed this to be enough.

In order to be more discreet, Tanner moved from the edge of the dance floor and began to patiently watch her and wait for his chance to approach.

"He's danced with you twice, Stacy," the younger girl said with wide eyes. "I hope you're ready for a proposal."

"Oh, Liz," Stacy shook her head at a friend she'd come to know through her weeks in London. "I think he's only being kind."

Liz exchanged a glance with the two other girls of the group, Barbara and Annemarie, and all three giggled. Stacy laughed at their teasing and shook her head again. They all wanted to be married so badly, and now a man at the ball, one who seemed to be two feet shorter than Stacy, had danced with her twice and given them all reason to think they would be bridesmaids.

"I need to go to the retiring room," Barbara said in a sudden whisper, and Stacy, with a swift glance at Lucinda who was standing nearby, moved off with the other three.

Lucinda held her place and watched them go, finally feeling at ease over letting Stacy out of her sight. The flowers had arrived over a week ago, and Lucinda had been ready for a battle that never materialized. She mentally shook her head over her own reaction. She should have known young Richardson would never follow through. He was the type of man who wouldn't commit himself to anything.

Lucinda frowned at her own uncharitable thoughts. Why was she so adamant against the man? She knew him to be a skeptic. She also knew he'd had a terrible childhood and first marriage, but that didn't make him a brute. It was just that his looks so reminded her of her husband, dead many years now. He had not been an easy man. Never faithful for more than a month, he had been two-faced about his infidelity to boot.

As unkind as it seemed, Aubrey Warbrook's death had come as a relief to Lucinda. He had killed the love she had for him while she was still a bride. Lucinda wanted so much more for Stacy.

"I know I'll end up right back in here," Liz was saying as the four young ladies exited the retiring room, "but I must have something to drink."

"Good evening, Stacy." Tanner's low-pitched voice brought all four of them about, but his eyes were for Stacy alone.

"Hello," Stacy returned softly, forgetting for the moment who he was and thinking he was even more good-looking than she remembered. She glanced at her companions and found them staring at her with eyes like saucers. Their looks reminded her of Lucinda's reaction to her speaking with this man.

Stacy curtsied suddenly and turned to go back to the dance. The other girls had already done the same, so when Tanner moved to fall in step beside her, they ended up a little behind the rest. Not that the girls missed anything; they turned constantly to look at their companion and the duke.

As they neared the dance floor, Stacy began to panic. If Lucinda saw her with Lord Richardson, she would be very upset. With a move born of desperation, Stacy stopped, thinking she could bid this man goodbye and go back with the others. To her horror they did not stop, and she found herself alone with Tanner.

She glanced at the floor in misery, not wanting to offend him but knowing Lucinda would be outraged. When she looked up it was to find herself under Tanner's close scrutiny, a small smile playing around his firm mouth.

"You look lovely this evening, Stacy."

"Thank you, Lord Richardson," she answered, finally allowing herself to meet his eyes.

"So it's Lord Richardson now. On the balcony it was Tanner."

Stacy's hand came to her mouth in humiliation. "I'm so sorry, your Grace. I had no idea. It won't happen again."

His low chuckle sent a chill down Stacy's spine.

"On the contrary, Anastasia, I hope I hear it often." There it was again—the soft, warm sound of her name. Stacy felt lost and breathless. She stood looking at him as though she'd taken leave of her senses. Not until he repeated the action of touching her nose, ever so tenderly did she realize where she was and to whom she was speaking.

"My aunt," Stacy nearly stuttered and took a step back. "She will wonder where I've gone."

Tanner nodded wisely, knowing that now was not the time to try to talk with her.

"Go ahead, Stacy. I'll see you later."

Stacy didn't stay to question him about his words, but turned and nearly ran. Her heart, pounding from her encounter with the duke, slowed with relief when she spotted Roddy as soon as she returned to the floor. She stepped to his side, and he turned to her with a smile which died when he saw her flushed face.

"Is he here?" he asked after just a moment.

Stacy nodded.

"And you spoke to him?"

"Yes. I'm sorry, Roddy. He just appeared, and I didn't know what to do."

Roddy took her hand in his and led her onto the dance floor. As they danced he spoke softly—words to calm her, words to let her know she hadn't erred.

"I don't know how to tell Aunt Lucinda," Stacy admitted.

"Let me handle it, dear." His voice was paternal. "You just enjoy the remainder of the evening, and I'll be close by."

Stacy nodded gratefully and went from Roddy's arms to those of an older gentleman whom she'd met earlier. He and his wife had been friends of her aunt's for years, and Stacy looked forward to a relaxed dance and visit. Tanner, however, had other ideas.

The music had barely begun when he stepped forward and cut in. Stacy looked at her partner, but he didn't seem the least put out. He smiled in a grandfatherly fashion and turned her over without a backward glance.

Stacy held herself stiffly in Tanner's arms and for a long time never looked higher than his cravat.

"I'd like to see more of you, Stacy," Tanner said when they had danced for a time.

"You would?" Stacy asked, finally looking up at him.

"Yes. In fact, I'd like you to meet me tonight."

Stacy wasn't even aware of her feet as she stared into his eyes and listened to him. "Meet you where?"

"In your aunt's garden. I'll be there at 1:00."

"I'll have to ask Aunt Lucinda."

Tanner smiled, willing to go along with her innocent act just to be with her. "Oh, but I want it to be a secret, just between the two of us."

His voice and eyes made it seem special and wonderful, but as dreamy as Stacy felt she still answered immediately. "I couldn't do that. I couldn't leave the house at night without telling Aunt Lucinda."

The smile left Tanner's face abruptly. She was taking this too far.

Stacy had no idea what caused the change in him, but she saw it in his face and felt it in the arm that held her.

"I really hoped you would agree." Tanner's voice was clipped now. "Maybe one of the other women here would be interested in a moonlight stroll with me, since you are obviously not."

"I'm sorry I can't go with you," Stacy told him. Her bubble had abruptly burst, and hurt etched every word. "I hope you have a nice time with...with whoever accompanies you." Stacy's voice had grown softer with every syllable until the last word was little more than a whisper.

Tanner stared at her in amazement. He couldn't believe she was actually turning him down. They finished the dance in silence. Tanner was coldly angry, and Stacy had no idea what she'd done wrong. When the dance ended, it was a relief to be led off the floor.

"I can't believe you didn't go out there," Lucinda said to Roddy before Stacy returned to their side.

Roddy sighed. "I never dreamed he would go that far. The damage was done the moment he took her in his arms. It would have brought nothing but humiliation to stalk out there and demand her return."

Lucinda nodded unhappily and watched anxiously as Tanner returned Stacy to their side. She glared at Tanner upon seeing Stacy's pale features, but the young duke seemed totally unaware of anyone's presence.

Without a word, Stacy's confused face caused Roddy to suggest an early evening. Stacy looked so relieved at the suggestion that the three of them left immediately.

Stacy worked very hard over the next two days to put Tanner from her mind. She and Lucinda had talked, calmly this time, and Lucinda had told Stacy that considering all the circumstances, she had done well. Lucinda surprised her speechless by apologizing for underestimating Tanner's boldness and for taking her out and not staying with her.

"I've decided that we need to slow down a bit. It's always been more my desire than yours to attend a different ball every week, and now I think that for your sake, Stacy, we'll stay in for a time."

"I'm sorry, Aunt Lucinda."

"No, child, it is I who am sorry. You've gone along to please me and been hurt because of it...and after I told Andrew I would take such good care of you."

Lucinda did nothing this time to disguise the tears in her eyes. Stacy rose and went to put her arms around her aunt.

"I've had a wonderful time, Aunt Lucinda. Please don't think I'm disappointed or unhappy. It's too bad that I'm not more experienced in social settings or with men, but—"

"No, dear," Lucinda cut her off. "Never be sorry for your innocence. Your trusting nature is a precious gift. Someday someone very special will come along and treasure you and that gift for all of his life."

Tanner's face immediately popped into Stacy's mind, but she did her best to push it away, smile at her aunt, and give her one final hug.

❦ ❦ ❦

Three weeks later Roddy, Lucinda, and Stacy went shopping. Stacy thought Lucinda amazing as she careered her way through the day, never seeming to tire or grow too warm. At the last shop, Stacy had to beg off.

"If I'm going to have any energy left for the Royal Gardens, I'm going to have to rest."

"I quite agree. Cinda, you're on your own for this one."

Lucinda regarded her companions with a raised brow and condescending look before sweeping out of the open carriage and into the shop. Roddy chuckled at her departure and then looked up to see Stacy studying him.

"That's certainly a serious face," he said with a smile.

Stacy didn't smile. In fact she looked so hesitant that Roddy sobered.

"What is it, Stacy?"

"It's something that's none of my business."

"Concerning me?"

"Yes," Stacy answered and studied him some more. His look was so open that she felt emboldened. "Why have you and Lucinda never married?"

Roddy nodded and regarded her seriously. When he spoke, Stacy could tell he'd given the matter great thought.

"I value Lucinda's friendship above all else in the world. Were I to introduce romance between us when she did not share my feelings, I would ruin everything we have. I simply can't take that chance."

"But you must know she loves you," Stacy reasoned.

"Yes, she does love me, but she isn't *in* love with me. There is a difference, you know. I'm her best friend, just as she is mine. I can go on living with the knowledge that she will continue to be."

"She is in love with you, Roddy," Stacy told him softly.

Roddy didn't go so far as to shake his head, but his look was more than a little dubious.

"She's loved you for years. She told me herself."

Roddy stared at Stacy. The intensity in his eyes frightened her a little. She had started something here, and as much as she might regret it, she decided to see it through.

"When I first came to London, we talked of it. I asked her why she wasn't married to you, and she said it was because you'd never asked."

Stacy watched Roddy's eyes slide shut and felt as if her insides were being torn in two. She was not easily given to tears, but this was almost enough to make her sob.

Roddy's gaze turned beyond the carriage then, and Stacy left him to his thoughts. She knew Lucinda would be returning soon and wondered if she should apologize. As it was, Roddy quietly thanked her just before Lucinda emerged from the shop.

The Royal Botanic Gardens were riotous with color during midsummer. The day was a bit warm for a long stroll, but they walked leisurely along until Roddy proclaimed that he would die if they didn't stop for tea.

Stacy, feeling very much that Roddy and Lucinda needed a few moments alone, slowed her pace and let them move ahead. A lovely bloom caught her attention as the path wound its way back to the carriage, and Stacy stopped to take in its fragrance. When she looked up, Tanner stood some ten feet away.

His look was rather stern, but Stacy couldn't mask the softening of her eyes at just seeing him again. He scared her a little, and she knew he was not the man for her, but her heart turned over every time she thought of him.

"Stacy," Roddy's voice suddenly called to her from beyond the shrubs.

"I'm coming, Roddy," Stacy answered immediately before looking back at Tanner and a woman beyond him. Even at a distance and standing in profile, the woman looked lovely.

Stacy met Tanner's eyes as she spoke. "I'm glad you found someone to go on that stroll with you, Lord Richardson." Stacy dropped her eyes then and moved away. Tanner did not try to follow.

Seven

"I WILL NOT ALLOW YOU to see her." Lucinda's tone was calm, but her insides were trembling. "She doesn't want to see you."

"I would like to hear that from Stacy," Tanner challenged, much as he had been doing for the last half hour.

"There is no need," Lucinda insisted. "As I've said before, she cannot see you."

"Why?" Growing perilously close to the end of his patience, Tanner fired the single word at her.

"I'll tell you why, because I know you're not here to ask for her hand in marriage, and I will not allow you to play games with my niece's life.

"If in fact I have misread your intent, please correct me, but unless your intentions toward Stacy are honorable, you will not socialize with her."

Tanner stood silent, his anger at a boiling point just beneath the surface. After a moment, Lucinda's brows raised and her shoulders lifted in a shrug. Her voice was void of accusation when she spoke.

"Your silence has answered my question, your Grace."

Tanner continued to stand quiet. He grudgingly admired Lady Warbrook for the way she stood up to him, but he did not care to be thwarted. He wanted Anastasia Daniels, and Lucinda had made it very clear that the only way he could have her was in marriage. He'd been married once, and he was not going to fall into that trap again.

If he and Stacy were to form a relationship that was mutually beneficial to both of them, fine. They didn't need the confines of marriage to do it. Lucinda had said his intentions were not honorable, but to him they were. Tanner had never had a mistress before, but he knew when he finally made Stacy his own, he would treat her like a queen. He would be faithful to her, and she would know no humiliation at his hands. He was one of the wealthiest men in England and well able to care for her in any style she desired.

And when it was time to end their relationship, not that he believed there would be a need for many years, there would be no messy scenes. He would tell her goodbye and give her enough money to do anything she pleased for the rest of her life. There was simply no need to marry.

Lucinda watched as Tanner leaned down and picked up the riding gloves he'd dropped on the table. He turned toward the door without a word, and Lucinda did not try to speak to him. His pride had obviously been wounded, and she had no desire to rub salt in the wound. It was relief enough to see him go. He must realize now that she meant business concerning Stacy. Stacy, she reminded herself, must not know that he'd even been to call.

Across the foyer in the library Stacy chose the book she desired and moved back toward the door. She hadn't even bothered to close it, since she'd known just what she was looking for. Halfway across the carpet, however, she was so startled that she dropped the book and simply stared.

Tanner stood in the doorway, his eyes hooded and almost angry. Unlike the day before in the park, Stacy's gaze didn't soften; this time his look was too foreboding, and she was too surprised to find him in Aunt Lucinda's home.

Stacy watched as his eyes traveled over her dress. It was the red velvet she'd brought from home. Without moving from the doorway, he spoke.

"That color is dreadful on you."

Stacy shrugged apologetically and glanced down at the skirt. "Aunt Lucinda doesn't care for it either."

At the sound of her voice Tanner had to draw nearer; it was as though he had no choice. He stopped a foot away from her and, feeling mesmerized, just stared into her wide, blue eyes.

Every woman who's ever meant anything to me has been full of lies and deceit, he thought. *Can this sweetness in her be real, or does it only last as long as she gets her way?*

"I'm not the marrying kind, Stacy," Tanner told her without preamble.

He spoke the words as though they'd been discussing the matter, but as abrupt as they seemed, Stacy wasn't surprised to hear them. She nodded, her eyes regretful but understanding.

It was almost more than Tanner could take. He wanted her to show her true self, to yell at him or lash out, but instead she continued to offer him only sweet sensitivity.

Suddenly his hands grasped her upper arms in a grip that was firm but not bruising. It was as if he needed to be touching her to make his point.

"I'm *not* the marrying kind, Stacy, and your aunt is completely unreasonable."

His grasp had brought her so close that Stacy could feel his breath. She should have felt frightened, but instead her heart turned over with love for him. Her voice told him as much.

"I'm not sure what you want of me, but I must do as Lucinda asks. It's what my grandfather would wish." Stacy paused before going on, almost talking to herself. "July is already here. Just a few weeks now, and it will be time for me to go home. It will be easier then."

Defeat washed over Tanner. He hadn't really expected her to leave with him on the spot, but he had halfway hoped she would at least be open to some discussion. It never once occurred to him that she didn't even realize he wanted her for a mistress.

Tanner didn't speak again. He felt he had said it all. As his hands slowly released her, his eyes moved slowly over her face, as if to memorize every detail of her lovely features. When his inspection was complete, he brushed a soft kiss across her lips, moved to the door without looking back, and walked away.

Stacy found a chair and sat down hard. Her eyes focused unseeingly on the book she'd dropped on the floor. She sat for the next hour and stared at it, wondering how she was ever going to get over Lord Tanner Richardson.

Just four days before Stacy was to leave for Middlesbrough, she and Roddy took a long ride in the park. As they rode, Stacy would fall into moments of quiet contemplation. Roddy knew she was thinking of Tanner. He alone knew that she'd seen him in Lucinda's library. What Stacy didn't know was that Tanner had not given up that day. He'd been to see Lucinda twice more in an attempt to reason with her, explaining what a wonderful life he could offer Stacy.

Amazingly, Lucinda had not been offended. She had confided in Roddy that she'd seen a certain vulnerability in Tanner, one that touched her heart and caused her to put aside her reservations. It was as though she understood him, when in fact, she should have been insulted that the man wanted Stacy for a mistress and not a wife. Roddy knew that she struggled with how closely he resembled Aubrey, but she had also admitted that although Aubrey was a rake, Tanner had shown no such signs.

Roddy knew her heart was softening, and he was rather fascinated by her handling of the whole affair. However, he also knew Lucinda would never settle for less than a proposal of marriage.

Roddy's musings were cut off suddenly when a stray dog rushed from the bushes and snapped at the heels of Stacy's mount. Roddy called for her to watch herself, but Stacy was obviously too preoccupied.

Taken unawares, her horse pranced suddenly. Stacy lost the reins. She was groping frantically for control when the dog dashed forward again and the horse reared.

Roddy watched in horror as Stacy was thrown. She landed hard on the grassy turf and lay still even as Roddy jumped from the back of his mount and rushed to her side. He heard the pounding of hooves, the rush of feet, and the sound of someone coming to subdue the dog and catch Stacy's horse, but Roddy's eyes never left her white face.

"Stacy," he called urgently and placed a hand on her pale cheek. Roddy's heart pounded in fear when she did not respond. The same heart leaped in relief when someone's hands joined his own. He watched as they probed gently about her head and neck.

"We'll take her to Lady Brent's."

Upon hearing that stern voice, Roddy's eyes snapped up. He shouldn't have been surprised. The Duke of Cambridge managed to appear wherever Stacy went. There was no thought of arguing with the younger man; all thoughts were for Stacy's welfare. And if Tanner's concerned face was any indication—it looked carved from stone—she would receive the best of care.

The next minutes passed in a flurry of activity as Tanner ordered a gawking youth to Featherstone to warn Andrea of their arrival. Roddy remounted and captured the reins of Stacy's horse while Tanner lifted Stacy in his arms and swung abroad his own horse. Featherstone was just moments away, but it felt like forever to Roddy.

Stacy was unconscious through the transport and the summoning of the doctor and Aunt Lucinda. In fact nearly 30 minutes passed before she opened painful eyes to find Tanner bending over her, Roddy hovering in the background.

Lady Andrea was also in attendance, but Stacy did not notice her.

"What's happened?" she whispered, her eyes on Tanner's face.

"You were thrown from your horse. How do you feel?"

She felt horrible but didn't answer. Her head was pounding and it hurt to blink, but Tanner was there and for the moment the pain didn't matter. He looked tired to her. Without thought of place or circumstances Stacy reached and tenderly brushed the dark hair from his brow.

Tanner caught her hand and held it as though he were drowning. Roddy's gentle clearing of his throat reminded him they were not alone. After returning Stacy's hand to the coverlet, he stood and moved from her side. All of this was accomplished just before Lucinda swept into the room.

Tanner had little choice in the next minutes but to stand back and watch as Lucinda talked with Roddy, Andrea, and then the doctor when he arrived. Stacy lay silent during the proceedings, and when the doctor said she could be moved, Tanner held his place as Roddy saw her to Lucinda's waiting coach. Lucinda was on her way out when she stopped and turned back to the room. Andrea was by the sofa Stacy had just vacated, and Tanner was by the mantel, his look guarded.

"Thank you for seeing to Stacy," she began to Tanner, but had to stop and clear her throat. "She means more to me than I can say, and I am grateful for your assistance.

"I am concerned, however, that she was seen on your horse. The gossip concerning your visits to the house has been swiftly escalating. As relieved as I am that she is going to be fine, I fear this latest incident will destroy what is left of Stacy's reputation.

"Given a choice I would want you to repeat your actions in order to ensure her safety, but I find myself rather thankful that she is scheduled to leave for home in four days' time. She will be free from the gossiping tongues of London and hopefully put this painful time behind her."

The room was utterly silent when Lucinda left. Andrea was uncertain what she should do or say, and Tanner's face, although impassive, had drained of color during Lucinda's speech.

Andrea knew all the signs—Tanner and Stacy were in love. Tanner, however, had worked at his reputation as a confirmed bachelor, and Stacy was as guileless a girl as Andrea had ever met. It wasn't very hard to see why Lucinda was worried about the relationship.

Andrea searched for some words to take the pain from the young duke's eyes. When none came, she prayed. She was still praying when he thanked her kindly for her assistance and made his way for the door.

Tanner pushed his mount until the horse was blown and lathered. He'd sought out one of London's largest parks in an effort to ride and think. It would have been an ideal time to return to his estate in the country, but putting that many miles between him and Stacy was more than he could take right now.

If he couldn't take the miles between London and Winslow, what he would do in four days' time when Stacy went home for good? Tanner's torturous thoughts plagued him. When had Stacy Daniels gotten so deeply under his skin? And why? What was it about the girl that was causing him to consider marriage, something he vowed would never happen again?

His faithless wife came to mind then, as did his brother, William, along with all the pain he had experienced in the first months after their deaths. The betrayal and anger and then the cold bitterness that ate at him for more than a year before he determined not to give them another moment of thought. Now, sitting alone on horseback in a remote section of London, he let down the wall for a brief look back and was stunned that the anguish of their affair could still cut so deeply.

But in the midst of this agony he was amazed to see someone else's pain. He saw Stacy as she thudded to the ground from atop her horse, and then her eyes when they opened as she lay so pale on the couch at Featherstone. He'd known that her head hurt. Yet she made no word of complaint, only looked at him in tenderness before brushing the hair from his brow.

Tanner's chest rose with a deep sigh. He was ready to return home, slowly now, but with a solid purpose in his heart. He wasn't certain he could live with his decision concerning Stacy, but the thought of her leaving London was simply not to be entertained.

Eight

LUCINDA REGARDED TANNER with serious eyes as he stood across the library from her the morning after the accident. He had quietly and with surprising humbleness asked for Stacy's hand in marriage. It was what Lucinda had been hoping for. With this commitment, she now believed he would make Stacy a fine husband, but it suddenly occurred to her that she didn't know Stacy's heart.

Roddy had assured her that Stacy loved Tanner, but Lucinda had never heard this from Stacy's lips or really seen anything to confirm it. Lucinda's guilt over all her niece had been through weighed heavily upon her. The last thing she would do was force Stacy into a union she did not desire.

"I find your offer quite satisfactory, but I will not accept until I've spoken with Stacy."

"Are you worried that she won't agree?" One of Tanner's brows rose in what Lucinda could only label a sinister fashion.

"Exactly," Lucinda told him. "I realize it's not the custom to consult the woman, but Stacy is not some bubble-headed girl who cannot be trusted to know her own mind. I will speak to her and let you know."

Tanner's look was full of amusement now. "You'll be wasting your breath, Lucinda." He called her by name for the first time. "I assure you, Stacy will accept."

"Nevertheless," the older woman stated firmly, "I will find out for myself."

"On three conditions," Tanner told her. Lucinda knew she was now seeing the man, the duke, who always had his own way. "You must find out within the hour how she feels, and you must do so without telling her of my offer."

"And the third condition?"

"You will allow me to ask her for her hand in marriage."

Lucinda looked perplexed. It was happening a little too swiftly for her comfort, but she didn't know how to slow the process.

"Yesterday I watched Stacy fall from a horse and lie unconscious in the park," Tanner said when Lucinda remained silent. "I want the right as her intended to visit her and see for myself that she is well. I want this settled *today*."

Lucinda felt she had no choice. She had managed to hold him off for many weeks now and knew it was not wise to push her advantage. She would never have given into Tanner's request for a mistress, but now that he'd made a legitimate offer of marriage, Lucinda felt she needed to go along with his desires as much as she was able.

"As you wish. I will send word to you as soon as I know. And," Lucinda paused, "you may plan on joining us for dinner. Come early, and I will see to it that you have a few minutes alone with Stacy. And I do mean a *few* minutes."

Tanner nodded and replaced his hat. "Until 7:30?"

"Seven-thirty," Lucinda confirmed and stood quietly as he left.

"Another pillow, Lady Stacy?"

"No, Rayna, I'm fine. You don't need to stay. I'm going to sit here very quietly. I promise to ring if I need something."

The maid looked uncertain, but Stacy put her head back against the settee and shut her eyes until she knew she was alone. She smiled and opened her eyes when the door closed. They were all like a bunch of mother hens.

Most of Lucinda's staff were beyond their fortieth year, and they had all adopted Stacy when she moved in. She was surprised she had put on only a few pounds since coming—they were forever sneaking things into her room. They showed Stacy repeatedly how much they cared.

Up to now all the pampering had been fun, but after Stacy had been brought home yesterday, they'd all been frantic. She did have a concussion, but she was not dying as Rayna and Craig both seemed to think. It would be wonderful to walk in the garden, but knowing it would stop the hearts of half the staff, Stacy resigned herself to staying in her room.

When Lucinda knocked on the door, Stacy nearly lay back and pretended to be sleeping. But she had never been good at deception and simply waited for the entrance of the next anxious servant. To her surprise it was Lucinda.

"How are you, dear?" Lucinda asked after placing a kiss on her cheek.

"I'm fine. A little tired perhaps, but I'm doing well."

Lucinda smiled, seeing that it was true. Stacy's color was good, and she had already learned from Rayna that she'd had a good night's sleep. They talked on for a time, and Lucinda asked to see Stacy's needlework. It was in a basket by the settee, and in a moment Stacy had retrieved it to proudly display her art.

"It's beautiful, dear. I especially love the use of the blues."

Stacy smiled her thanks and gazed on as Lucinda continued to study the intricate needlepoint. When Lucinda spoke, her voice was so casual that Stacy was taken unaware.

"It was very kind of Lord Richardson to take you to Lady Brent's yesterday."

Lucinda watched surreptitiously as the color crept into Stacy's cheeks and her eyes slid shut with remembrance. Lucinda's own eyes closed for a moment as well, and when she looked at Stacy again, the younger woman's gaze was distant and soft. Lucinda would have felt stunned had she known that Stacy's mind was reliving Tanner's gentle kiss in the library.

"You're looking a bit flushed, my dear," Lucinda said softly when she could. "Maybe you should sleep for a time."

"Maybe I will." Stacy grasped at the chance to be alone with her thoughts. "Thank you for coming up to see me, Aunt Lucinda."

Lucinda's hand gently patted Stacy's cheek. Once out in the hall, Lucinda found that her hands were shaking. She scolded herself and tried to calm down before she was forced to dictate her note to Tanner.

Ten minutes later, back in her room, she was able to write it herself. It said simply that they would discuss the terms of the betrothal immediately following dinner.

Had Tanner not insisted, Lucinda would have kept Stacy in her room for yet another night. It helped to remind herself that Stacy had looked very well that afternoon.

"You look lovely," Lucinda told Stacy as she met her outside her bedroom door.

"Thank you," Stacy said simply and stared down at the cream-colored gown that hung with lace. Rayna had brushed her hair out long and straight, and beyond a simple comb at the crown of her head which pulled the hair from her face, she was unadorned.

"I really wanted you to stay one more night in your room," Lucinda said as she hooked her arm through Stacy's. "But you have a visitor."

Stacy glanced with surprise at her aunt, but didn't question; she simply walked along as Lucinda led her to the upstairs salon. Lucinda stopped outside the door and turned to face Stacy.

"Tanner Richardson is waiting for you. I'll give you a few

minutes alone before Roddy and I come to collect you both for dinner."

Stacy's eyes had grown large on this announcement, but she had no time to reply. Lucinda turned on her heel and marched back down the hall. Stacy looked at the back of her aunt and then at the doorknob for only a moment before turning it and stepping quietly inside.

Nearly the entire expanse of carpet separated them as Stacy closed the door and stood just inside. Tanner was by the window, looking incredibly handsome and larger than ever in formal black evening clothes, with a white shirt and black tie. He stared at Stacy before stepping to the fireplace and speaking.

"Come over here, Stacy."

Stacy obeyed without question, moving with natural grace to stand some two feet away. The distance was too far for Tanner's taste, and with a gentle touch he reached for her hand and drew her closer.

Tanner looked into her wide, trusting eyes and knew frustration. Without a doubt Lucinda would hold to her word of coming back in a few minutes, and there was so much he wanted to say to this woman.

"I have asked Lucinda for your hand, and she has agreed to my proposal," Tanner began, hearing the tick of the clock so near his ear on the mantel. "Now I wish to ask you, Anastasia. Will you be my wife?"

Stacy's breath left her in a rush. Her face flushed and her mouth dropped open. "You wish to marry me?"

For some reason her reaction amused Tanner, and a huge smile broke across his face. "Yes, I do, and if you don't answer me quickly I won't even have time to kiss you before we gain an audience."

Suddenly Stacy's smile matched his own. "You kissed me in the library. Do you remember? I thought I would have to be content with that for the rest of my life."

"Oh, sweetheart," Tanner said softly before pulling her into his arms. She was a perfect fit.

Stacy didn't think she would ever breathe again. Tanner's hold felt like a walk through paradise. She wanted his kiss to go on and on.

Fortunately Tanner's head was more level. He broke the kiss and stepped away from her just before the door opened to admit Roddy and Lucinda.

Stacy spent the rest of the evening floating on a cloud. She couldn't have told anyone what was served for dinner or who talked at the table. She was so happy that she didn't even mind being sent upstairs early so the others could talk business.

Her cocoon of joy lasted until right before she fell asleep; right up to the moment when she realized she wouldn't be seeing her grandfather in a few days as planned, and she would probably never live in his home in Middlesbrough again.

Nine

THE NEXT MORNING, before the wedding agreement could be drawn up and signed or the banns posted for the coming wedding, Stacy went in to see Aunt Lucinda. Lucinda was at her writing desk in her bedroom, already making a list for Madame Angelica concerning Stacy's wedding trousseau. She had been half-expecting her niece, so as soon as Stacy appeared, Lucinda put her task aside.

"Aunt Lucinda, may I speak with you?"

"Of course, my dear."

Both women made themselves comfortable in chairs by the window.

"I'm trying to write to Papa, but I just can't find the words," Stacy began. "I love Tanner, but I feel as though I've betrayed the man who has loved and taken care of me since I was a child."

Lucinda rose and went back to her writing desk. She opened the top drawer and withdrew a letter. Returning to Stacy, she opened it and began to share.

"This arrived just a week after you did, my dear, but there has never been a reason, until now, for you to see it. I shall read it to you.

Dear Lucinda,

I know that Stacy must be well ensconced in your care by now, and I wish you both a wonderful summer. As you may or may not realize, Stacy is the type of girl who would gladly lay down her life for someone she loves. There have been times over the years when this has not been an asset; now is just such a time.

I told Stacy that no one would push her into a marriage and I meant it, but I also fear that Stacy might deny her heart if she fears hurting me or missing Morgan. I want Stacy to follow her heart. I trust you to judge the type of man who might show interest, and if you find him worthy of my precious girl, then act in wisdom.

Stacy works hard to see that those around her are happy. Above all else, Lucy, see to Stacy's happiness, for there are times when she does not look after it herself. Give her my love and to you also.

Andrew

Stacy was not a woman given to tears, and in fact none filled her eyes, but her heart was so full she could not speak.

"I will ask you what your grandfather would at this moment." Lucinda gazed at her tenderly.

"Are you happy, my dear?"

Stacy could only nod.

"Then I will write Andrew and tell him all that has transpired. I will also say that you will be writing soon to give him the wedding date and details."

Stacy's answer to this was to throw her arms around her aunt. Lucinda laughed as she embraced her, thinking she would topple a smaller woman.

"You run along now, dear; I've got things to do."

Stacy was more than ready to comply now that her mind was set to rest. Returning to her room she sat down at the table by the window, now knowing that she could write that letter. It wasn't as easy as she believed, however. Before she'd written two words, her mind began to wander. The quill was set aside and soon forgotten. Stacy never even noticed the cool breeze coming in the window and moving her hair. Her mind was wholly taken up with Tanner and what he might be doing at the moment.

Stacy might have been pleased to know that Tanner was thinking of her, except that his thoughts were turning rather pensive. His breakfast sat growing cold as he let his mind dwell on the night before.

Dinner had been a delight, and Lucinda, with a few suggestions from Roddy, had been more than reasonable concerning the marriage contract. Not that Stacy's dowry mattered to Tanner in the least. She could come to him with nothing more than the clothes on her back, and he would still marry her.

The now-familiar tightening in his chest that happened every time he thought of her was coming on again. She was so precious. Tanner's eyes closed when he remembered the way she felt in his arms and the way she had shyly returned his kiss.

Without warning, the face of his first wife, Leslie, swam before his mind's eye, her expression very soft and open as it had been when they'd first met. She too had been sweet and seemingly innocent, promising to love and honor him for all of her days.

With an abrupt gesture Tanner rose from the table, his breakfast completely forgotten. *It isn't too late to back out,* he told himself. *The papers have not been signed or the newspapers notified.*

"I fear this latest incident will destroy what is left of Stacy's reputation."

Lucinda's words suddenly sounded in Tanner's ears, and he stopped dead on his way into his study. The way Stacy's eyes had looked last night, so full of trust, caused Tanner to shake his head as if to clear it. Still, the black cloud of his past still lingered. With a decisive turn he moved for the stairs.

"Price," Tanner bellowed. The servant appeared at the top of the stairs as if by magic.

"Yes, your Grace."

"Riding clothes. And order my horse saddled." His reply was curt, but he simply had no time to be civil. He had to see Stacy, and now. There was no other help for it.

"I wish you could have seen her face when I read that letter. She was so relieved, but I worry a little that Tanner likes to have his own way and will run right over the top of her if she stands in his way."

"I don't know," Roddy spoke contemplatively. "If you could have seen his face when he bent over her on the grass..." He let the thought hang.

They sat silently for a moment in Lucinda's small parlor until Roddy suddenly leaned forward and kissed Lucinda lingeringly on the lips. Her eyes were quite round when he pulled away.

Roddy had always been affectionate with her and a kiss from him was not all that unusual, but in the past few weeks he'd kissed her nearly every chance he had. The kisses were a good deal more personal than they'd ever been before. And when he wasn't kissing her, he was holding her hand or placing his arm about her waist.

"You're doing quite a lot of that lately." Lucinda couldn't resist commenting about the kiss. To her surprise, Roddy looked pleased that she'd noticed. His smile was almost smug.

"Any objections?" Roddy's voice was far warmer than she was used to hearing it.

"No," Lucinda said, and suddenly felt herself blushing like a girl.

"Did I cause that flush?" Roddy's grin nearly left his face.

Lucinda could only stare at him. "What has come over you, Roddy?"

She was more confused than ever when he only kissed her again and sat back in contentment. She watched him reach for the newspaper he'd been enjoying and settle down to read. He obviously wasn't going to answer her.

Lucinda might have run from the room if he had. Roddy Caruthers, who had been in love with Lucinda Warbrook for years, was now amid his plan of attack to win the lovely lady's hand.

It wasn't that he doubted Stacy's words about Lucinda's loving him; it was just that he wanted to take no chances of losing her. He was no longer afraid of rejection, but of not being taken seriously. They had been friends for so long that if he suddenly declared himself, she might not believe him sincere. Such an action would also cause her to question the change in him after so many years. He knew he would be honest with her, and in so doing might lead her to believe that Stacy had somehow betrayed her trust.

So with his usual level head, Roddy decided to bide his time. He'd waited many years; a few more months wouldn't matter. He'd be alongside Lucinda as she saw Stacy safely married; then it would be his turn.

He could still feel Lucinda's eyes on him at the moment, and indeed, was about to take pity on her and explain, but Craig entered quietly to tell Lucinda that Lord Richardson had arrived.

Lucinda's brows rose. She thought they would not see him until the next day when the papers announced the engagement, but perhaps he had come about something other than his engagement. Lucinda nearly laughed at her own thoughts when she saw Tanner's face. There was no doubt that he was here to see Stacy.

"Hello, Tanner," Lucinda greeted him as Roddy stood and the two shook hands. "Please, sit down."

"Thank you, Lucinda," Tanner responded but remained standing, "but I'd really like to see Stacy." Tanner had to bite back the word "alone."

He stood erect and waited for Lucinda's response. At the moment he was tense enough to force his way into Stacy's room, and Lucinda was obviously aware of this fact. Her voice was very gentle when she answered him.

"She's in the garden, Tanner. When you're done, maybe you'd both like to come in and join us in the large salon for tea?"

Tanner accepted with a nod of his head and moved toward the door. Lucinda and Roddy exchanged a glance after he left, but neither of them spoke.

Stacy pushed herself from the grassy turf and stood looking down at her progress. Aunt Lucinda had a gardener, but his skills among the English daisies were lacking. They were a small flower and took careful weeding. Stacy could understand why he didn't care to bother, but she loved the work.

She dusted her dirty hands together and had just wiped the moisture from her upper lip when she looked up to see Tanner approaching. With a quick glance at her filthy hands, she put them behind her back.

"Hello." Tanner's bass voice ran over Stacy's nerves as he stopped some five feet away and greeted her, his eyes serious.

"Hello." Stacy's own voice was breathless. She was thrilled to see him but knew she must look a mess.

Tanner's eyes moved over her, taking in the dirt smears on the front of her dress, her hair falling from its chignon, the hands held carefully behind her back, and finally the smear of mud above her upper lip.

"What are you hiding behind you?" he asked as he moved to a nearby bench and made himself comfortable. Stacy watched his legs, clad in knee-high black boots and gray riding trousers, stretch out seemingly for miles before she looked back to his face. His brows were raised in expectation, and Stacy remembered that he'd asked her a question.

"Just my hands," she answered honestly.

Tanner looked skeptical. "You're sure?"

"Yes," Stacy said, beginning to feel rather silly. With her hands still out of sight, she moved to the opposite bench, carefully tucking her hands under the folds of her skirt as she sat down.

As surreptitiously as she made the move, Tanner didn't miss a thing. He'd told himself if he could only see her, he would feel better, and in fact he was growing more relaxed with every passing second. She was the most restful woman he had ever known.

"How are you, Tanner?" Stacy's sweet voice broke into his musings.

"I'm doing fine."

"Are you really?" Stacy's voice seemed to lift with pleasure.

"Yes. Why do you ask?"

Color leapt into her cheeks as she admitted softly, "I thought you might have come to tell me you changed your mind."

Tanner found it very disconcerting to be read so easily. It caused him to realize just how little he really knew this woman. She was soft-spoken, graceful, and very trusting, but beyond those qualities, Tanner was at a loss.

It became suddenly clear to him that he was going to marry this woman. He knew that more doubts would surface as the days went on, but he *was* going to marry Stacy Daniels.

"I haven't changed my mind," Tanner told her seriously, and Stacy had to look away from the intensity in his eyes. She cast about for something to say and only looked at him when she was ready to speak.

"Did you see Lucinda and Roddy? They're inside." Stacy knew she sounded inane, but he was still watching her so intently that she began to feel very unsettled.

"Yes." Tanner's scrutiny eased some. "They're expecting us later for tea."

Stacy could only nod, glad she was alone with him but not certain what to say.

"When is your birthday, Stacy?" Tanner asked suddenly.

"Not until October."

"And you'll be—?"

"Twenty-two," Stacy supplied nervously. "That's rather old, isn't it?"

"Not in the least," Tanner told her emphatically, feeling quite glad that she wasn't a starry-eyed teen.

"When is your birthday?"

"Next May. I'll be 29." Tanner hesitated before a warm sparkle lit his eyes. "Rather old, isn't it?"

Stacy laughed, and Tanner found he liked the sound. Spotting a newspaper by her side then, he noticed at the same time that she was still hiding her hands.

"What have you been reading?" Tanner asked, gesturing toward the paper.

"*The London Times.* I just finished an article about Nanking."

"Nanking?" Tanner questioned her. He had read the same paper and not seen the feature.

"Well, yes," Stacy said hesitantly, wondering if he'd be bored if she shared. But he had that expectant, almost impatient look she was coming to recognize. She hurried to explain.

"Nanking, China, is a city that sits on the Yangtze River. The article says that an army of 500,000, composed entirely of *women*—" Stacy was now warming to her subject—"and led by *female* officers, was formed in Nanking during a rebellion."

Stacy stopped when she realized her hands had come out of hiding to gesture as she spoke. She quickly hid them and shrugged apologetically. "I just found it rather interesting."

Tanner did not reply but sat staring at her as if seeing her for the first time. Stacy felt like a fool. She stood awkwardly.

"If Aunt Lucinda is expecting us for tea, I'd best go freshen up."

With surprising agility for a man his size, Tanner stood, moving silently to block her path. He reached his long arms around her and gently brought forth the hands she'd hidden once again to hold them within his own.

He examined the dirt under her nails and on her palms and then looked to find her standing still with mortification. She was staring no higher than his shirtfront.

"You were weeding?"

Stacy nodded, utterly humiliated. She was engaged to a duke, and here she was digging in the dirt like a child at play. What must Tanner think?

"You did a nice job," Tanner told her as though she'd asked the question out loud. Still, she wouldn't look at him.

"Look at me, Anastasia," he commanded, and Stacy felt helpless to resist. Tanner spoke when her eyes met his.

"There is nothing to be embarrassed about, sweetheart. If you enjoy gardens, then you're going to love Winslow."

"Winslow?"

"My home in the country."

Stacy never thought of his living anywhere but London. She was still taking this in when she questioned him about the dirt.

"And you really don't mind my working in the garden?"

"Not in the least."

Stacy's sigh was of such relief that Tanner smiled.

"I even like you with dirt on your upper lip."

This time Stacy didn't sigh with relief. Her eyes widened in horror. Tanner only laughed as he gazed into those huge, blue orbs.

Ten

WHEN THE LETTER ARRIVED from Stacy's grandfather, it was nearly enough to put her in tears. He would not be at her wedding. Andrew explained very gently that he couldn't have been happier for her, but his eyesight was so unpredictable now that he feared embarrassing her by falling in the aisle or some equally foolish act.

If Stacy could have talked with him and heard this in person, she might have felt better, but reading of his decision made her feel helpless with grief. She debated going home to visit until the wedding day, but Lucinda talked her out of it, explaining that with fittings for her trousseau and dozens of other tasks, she was needed in London.

To top it off, a letter from Elena came the same day. She was expecting again, and Noel did not want her making the long trip in such warm weather. The double blow was devastating to Stacy.

She sat in the window seat of the upstairs salon, completely awash with heartache. Tanner had come to the door, not entering, but simply enjoying the way the sunlight played on her golden hair. Stacy didn't notice his presence.

When she finally heard his footsteps on the carpet, she turned. Hurting over the news from home, it was the first time she didn't feel delighted at seeing him. This was especially surprising since Tanner had just been away for a few days. He noticed the change in her immediately and tensed over what she might say. It didn't occur to him until he saw the letters in her lap that her reaction might not have anything to do with him.

With Stacy curled on the window seat there wasn't much room, but Tanner managed to sit down beside her. With a glance at the papers in her lap, he spoke.

"Bad news?"

"Yes," Stacy told him in a voice he'd never heard before—thick, almost husky. Tanner carefully studied her face, noticing not for the first time that Stacy was not prone to tears.

"My grandfather can't make the wedding."

"Not enough notice?"

"No, that's not it. His eyesight is failing so badly and—" Stacy cut off, swallowing hard. "Would you like to read the letter?"

Tanner took it from her outstretched fingers and read swiftly and silently. His look was very compassionate when he finished, but Stacy's gaze was directed out the window, her lovely profile etched in misery.

Tanner noticed the other note in her hand.

"Is there more?" he asked as he returned Andrew's letter.

"Yes. Elena can't come either. She's married to my grandfather's cousin, Noel, and although Noel is old enough to be my father, Elena is my age and we're very close."

"Yes, I remember your telling me."

Stacy looked into his wonderful dark brown eyes for just a moment before turning to the window once again. Tanner gave her the silence, his mind thoughtful.

"I'm sorry, Tanner," Stacy spoke abruptly, and Tanner watched her make almost a physical effort to cheer up. "You've come to visit me, and all I do is sit here and mope. How was your trip?" She smiled at him, but it didn't quite reach her eyes.

Tanner could have kissed her on the spot. Lucinda had mentioned to him one day that Stacy usually put the happiness of others ahead of herself, but this was the first time he'd actually witnessed it.

"Would you like to go for a walk or a ride?" Stacy asked when Tanner stayed quiet. She felt a headache coming on and wondered if the change of scene might do her good.

"I think a ride sounds delightful, but you should write your letter first."

"My letter?" Stacy asked, wondering what she had missed.

"Why to your grandfather, of course, telling him to expect us a few days after the wedding. We're going to honeymoon in the Cleveland Hills and spend some time in Middlesbrough."

"You told me you wanted to honeymoon in the south of France."

"France will still be there in a year. We'll go for our first anniversary."

Stacy's hands went to her mouth. Her eyes searched Tanner's face for signs of teasing but found only caring.

"Oh, Tanner," was all Stacy could say.

He felt her tremble as she laid her cheek against his shoulder. Never had he known someone for whom it was so satisfying to give of himself. She never took anything for granted or lightly. It had taken a gem the size of a bird's egg to gain that kind of expression from Leslie.

Tanner's heart clenched. Why did Leslie always come to mind? She and Stacy were not even remotely the same, and yet since becoming engaged, she haunted his times of peace with Stacy. He remembered the one who lied and cheated on him at times when he should have been enjoying the precious woman at his side.

"Thank you, Tanner." Stacy lifted her head so she could see his face. "I love you," she whispered, her heart so full she could hardly breathe.

"You're welcome," he spoke gently, his eyes holding her own. Stacy thought he might kiss her, but a moment later they were joined by Craig, who was there to tell Stacy that Edmond Black had come to call.

Tanner's uncle was as different from his nephew as any man could be. Tanner was very tall; Edmond very short. Tanner's hair was dark with just a touch of gray at the temples. Edmond's hair was the color of new straw, and even though he was years older than his nephew, there didn't seem to be a gray hair in sight. Tanner's frame was very muscular, from his broad shoulders to the heavy muscles in his legs. Edmond had a round look about him that could only be described as doughlike.

And this was not where the differences ended. Tanner was quiet, sometimes broodingly so. His uncle seemed to talk nonstop and loudly. He wasn't always very discreet about his subjects either, and several times Stacy noticed a look of near anger cross her intended's face as his uncle carried on raucously.

Stacy didn't really find him offensive, just boring. In fact, she had only been half-listening to him for the past hour, allowing her thoughts to wander to her honeymoon with Tanner. One sentence from Edmond's mouth, however, brought Stacy quickly back to earth.

"Been telling him for years that he needed another wife. Some say, 'The third time's a charm,' but I believe in number two myself." Edmond, who had never been married, carried on, completely oblivious to Tanner's black look or Stacy's shocked expression.

Lucinda, who had been silent through this exchange and not caring one wit about her breach of manners, rang for tea in the midst of Edmond's diatribe.

"Oh, tea," the older man stumbled. "Is it that late already? Sorry, Lucinda, must be off. Standing engagement, you know.

So nice to meet you, my dear," he offered to Stacy, never noticing how pale her face had become. "Are you coming, Tanner?"

"I'll be along." Tanner rose and watched as Edmond bid his hostess goodbye and hurried out the door to his usual Friday afternoon poker game.

Stacy still hadn't looked at him, and the paleness of her face only reminded him of Edmond's loose tongue, angering him all the more. Thinking to put the subject to rest for all time, he asked her to walk him to the door. Stacy complied.

"Edmond talks too much," Tanner's voice was tight when they stopped and were alone in the entryway.

"But you were married?"

"Yes, but we will not speak of it." Tanner's voice was livid now, and Stacy's stomach clenched. "She's dead and has nothing to do with us. Do you understand me, Anastasia?"

Stacy nodded. She realized that his anger was not directed at her, but still it terrified her. She'd rather cut off her own hand than disobey him.

"I'll come by and see you tomorrow. Maybe we'll go for the ride we missed today."

Again Stacy only nodded. Tanner had nothing more to say to her and turned toward the door without touching her. He usually ignored his uncle's indiscretion, but this time he was going to find him, and when he was through, Edmond Black was going to think twice before talking about his nephew's past again.

An hour later Tanner returned to his town house, feeling satisfied over his confrontation with Edmond.

They had not actually come to blows, but Tanner believed he'd made himself more than clear concerning Edmond's propensity to talk. He had no doubts that the older man would continue to gossip at will, but Tanner also believed that neither his, Stacy's, nor Leslie's names would be mentioned.

Back in the parlor, Lucinda waited for Stacy to return. When Stacy did not make an appearance, Lucinda sought her out in the foyer. She found her standing very still, staring at the far wall.

"Come back in for your tea," Lucinda spoke as she placed a gentle arm around the younger woman's waist.

Stacy obeyed mindlessly, sitting down and doing nothing with the cup Lucinda placed in her hands. Not until Lucinda sat beside her and touched her hand did she seem able to think.

"I had no idea."

"Of course you didn't, my dear, and I wasn't certain if I should tell you."

Stacy nodded with understanding. It really had been Tanner's place to tell her, but he didn't want the subject discussed.

Lucinda watched Stacy, her heart in pain. Aubrey had held many secrets while they'd been married, and Lucinda wanted desperately for Stacy's marriage to be different. If she didn't believe with all of her heart that Tanner really cared, she would have called the marriage off right then. There was so much Stacy didn't know, but again Lucinda was uncertain how much to share. She decided to be brief.

"Stacy," she began. "Tanner did not have a happy childhood, nor did he have a happy first marriage. In fact they were so painful that Tanner has had difficulty putting those times behind him. He's going to react harshly at times because of those memories. There will be areas that he's going to feel are better left alone. It's not very fair to you, but right now, that's the way it is. Maybe in time Tanner will feel he can share. If you have any doubts about the marriage, Stacy, you can tell me."

"No, Aunt Lucinda, no doubts," Stacy told her without hesitation. In truth, a huge weight had been lifted from Stacy's shoulders. Tanner barely knew her. In time, after they were married and had a chance to really know one another, Tanner would open his heart.

Stacy's mind went to the times, including today, that she had told Tanner she loved him. He always smiled tenderly or kissed her in response, but he never said those words to her.

Stacy knew he felt them; she knew it with all her heart. Hearing them had been important to her until now, but suddenly words didn't matter anymore. Just as Tanner would someday share his past with Stacy, he would also come to tell her about the love he carried in his heart.

Eleven

TWO DAYS BEFORE THE WEDDING, Stacy experienced a severe attack of nerves. The thought of becoming Tanner's wife, the Duchess of Cambridge, was suddenly overwhelming. Fortunately Roddy, a gentle presence in Stacy's tempestuous world, was on hand when the panic hit.

"I'm really just a country girl, Roddy. I don't know if Tanner realizes that. I've never been to court. I never even had a desire to go to court. I really am just a country girl," she repeated herself. "Have I ever told you that I love to go fishing?"

Roddy smiled at her lack of artifice. "You're going to be the loveliest bride of the year," he told her.

"But then I'll be married." Stacy stated the obvious, and Roddy had to hold his laughter at her look. "What if I'm not a good wife? What if Tanner needs me to organize a dinner party or a weekend with friends? I've never done anything on a large scale. I can't imagine what Tanner would say if he knew. I just can't imagine."

"Can't imagine what?" Tanner's voice asked from the edge of the room. Stacy turned to him, her color high, her voice sounding like that of a lost little girl.

"Middlesbrough is not London, Tanner," she told him.

"All right," Tanner answered carefully as he moved toward her.

"My grandfather is not a duke."

"I believe I knew that." Tanner's voice was extremely gentle. He'd come over because he had to see her, had to be near her calm and gentle presence. Finding her like this, eyes fever-bright with anxiety, caused him an even greater sense of satisfaction because he knew he was the one who could put her mind at rest.

"Sit down, Anastasia," he told her.

Stacy, not having heard him, shook her head in despair. "You don't understand."

"Yes, sweetheart, I do. Sit down, and I'll tell you."

Stacy sat then and stared in misery at Roddy and then at Tanner. "I don't know how to be a duchess."

"Sweetheart," he called her again and sat beside her.

"Tanner—"

"Shhhh. I am not marrying you so that you can entertain my guests or be a lovely feather in my cap, although I certainly appreciate your beauty. I'm also not marrying you to compete with some other duke or to be on the front page of the social papers." Thinking this settled it all, Tanner fell silent.

"Then why are you marrying me?" Stacy couldn't resist the question.

"Because I want you for my wife," he told her simply.

"All right," Stacy replied compliantly, wanting to please him. However, she didn't really feel much better. It would have been wonderful to hear that Tanner was marrying her because he loved her. Stacy pushed the thought away. She usually wasn't so emotional, but the largeness of what she was about to do—commit herself for life to Tanner—was beginning to weigh upon her.

Tanner, watching her so quietly, wondered what was troubling her. He only hoped Stacy would be able to calm down and enjoy the wedding and festivities. He wasn't entirely sure if she was aware of what the crowd would be like, but now was certainly not the time to tell her.

Roddy did a quick change of subject in the next moment, and Tanner was able to watch Stacy collect her wayward thoughts. By the time Lucinda joined them she seemed to be herself. In fact Stacy was calmer than Tanner by the time he took his leave. He knew that once he left, he wouldn't see her again until she walked down the aisle.

The streets of London were thronged with well-wishers for the wedding of the Duke of Cambridge. That he was marrying a virtual unknown made it all the more romantic, and the wedding coaches could barely move amid the good wishes of the gentry and common folk alike.

"How does it look?" Lucinda asked Roddy as he peeked out the window.

"Like a riot, but we'll get there." Roddy settled back and smiled at the wide-eyed Stacy, who did not return his grin.

No one spoke for a time and the young bride-to-be was relieved. How *unsheltered* her world had become in the last weeks. She would never have dreamed that a crowd of this size would gather for the wedding of a duke. She could understand if this was for the queen or a princess, but not a duke and his nearly common bride. It was inconceivable.

"Stacy, are you all right?"

"Yes," she answered her aunt immediately, but her voice was wooden.

"You don't sound all right."

The comment made Stacy sigh. "I'm just a little overwhelmed by all of this."

For once Lucinda did not lose patience with her. She smiled tenderly and spoke in a soothing voice.

"While the wedding and reception are going on, you'll be convinced that it's going to last forever, but before you know it, you and Tanner will be married and on your way."

Stacy actually managed a smile at the thought. The remainder of the ride was made in silence and not until they arrived at the church did Stacy see what her aunt's words meant.

It seemed that before she had a moment to think she was dressed in her wedding finery and standing with Tanner before the bishop. Stacy had to quell laughter over the way the poor man had to tip his head to see their faces; they literally towered over him. At one point, she risked a glance at Tanner, who had also turned his head to look down at her. Stacy watched as one lid dropped in a flirtatious wink. From that moment on the service and reception were a blur.

The coach lurched into motion and Stacy leaned back against the seat with a sigh. Her feet ached dreadfully, but she had done it—she'd married the man she loved. A glance to the side of her found Tanner leaning against his corner of the seat, just watching her. Stacy smiled with childish delight at him, and he grinned in return and reached for her hand.

She was about to speak, wanting to tell him she'd never experienced so many emotions in her life as she danced for hours and met what appeared to be half of London, but her stomach growled quite loudly. She turned away from Tanner, thankful that the dim interior of the coach hid her flaming face. In the semidarkness she heard her new husband chuckle.

"We'll eat when we get to the house," he told her.

"Winslow?" Stacy asked, curiosity overwhelming her embarrassment.

"No, Winslow is too far. Don't forget we have a train to catch tomorrow."

"I haven't forgotten," Stacy told him and looked with love into his eyes. She couldn't imagine a more caring act than Tanner's willingness to change their honeymoon plans. Just thinking of it made her want to throw her arms around him, but she didn't think the time was right for that.

Without warning, Stacy's thoughts moved to motherhood. She had never told Tanner that she desperately wanted to be a mother, but it was true. She loved Elena's girls and ached for children of her own. She wasn't good at many things, but Stacy somehow knew that she would be a fine mother.

She was contemplating the wonderful idea of presenting Tanner with a son in nine months' time when the carriage abruptly halted. The door opened immediately, and Tanner swung down and turned to give Stacy a hand. She smiled her thanks.

"I thought I'd lost you for a moment," he spoke as they moved up the steps to the front door.

"I was just thinking."

"Want to share?" Tanner asked and then chuckled. They had stepped inside the door of his London home, and he had lost her again. Most men with homes as large as Tanner's country home cared only to have a small town house in London, but Tanner was not most men. Although not as large as Winslow, his London residence was substantial. He watched Stacy's head move carefully as she saw this home for the first time. Lucinda had forbidden her from visiting while it was still a bachelor's domicile.

Tanner loved it when Stacy was awed, as she was now. He also loved it when she tried not to show it. He admired her self-control as the staff gathered. The introductions were performed by Campbell, who was head of housekeeping, and before Stacy knew it she was being shown to her room.

It was a relief to find Rayna there. Lucinda had sent her to assist Stacy for her entire honeymoon. The faithful maid had laid out one of the beautiful dresses from Stacy's trousseau and, after buttoning her into it, began to brush her hair. Tanner loved it long down her back, so after Rayna pulled it back from the sides, Stacy asked her to let it hang.

Just 20 minutes later, a very hungry Stacy entered the private dining room at the back of the house. There had been a lavish feast at the wedding, but no time to eat, what with well-wishers and every man in the room wanting to dance with the bride. Stacy frowned when she remembered that she had only danced with Tanner twice.

"That's quite a fierce look. You must be starved," Tanner commented, having arrived just ahead of her.

Stacy's face relaxed into a smile as she crossed the small room to stand before him. She loved the fact that she had to look up to see him. He was the most handsome man she had ever seen and as hungry as she was, she somehow wished they were going to be alone for the remainder of the evening.

This was an impossibility as Stacy soon learned. The thought had barely formed when the food arrived. The duke and duchess took their seats and were served a sumptuous feast of roast goose by the staff.

Tanner was well satisfied watching his wife eat. She didn't pick at her food, but ate what she was hungry for and until she had a sufficiency. Their talk over the table was equally satisfying as Stacy questioned him about the many different people she'd met at the wedding. Tanner was pleasantly surprised to learn that she knew the Duchess of Briscoe.

"Sunny Hawkesbury?"

"Yes. Aunt Lucinda and I had tea with Lady Andrea just weeks after I'd arrived. Sunny came as we were leaving. She knows Elena."

Tanner nodded. "Did you like her—Sunny, that is?"

"Very much."

"Then you'll be pleased to know she and her husband are our neighbors. They live at Bracken, less than an hour's ride from Winslow. I wouldn't be too surprised to arrive home and find an invitation to dinner or tea from them."

Stacy had never thought about their being invited as husband and wife to dine, but now that Tanner mentioned it, she found she liked the idea immensely. She decided she would have to learn who their neighbors were and have them in as well.

"Are you finished?"

Stacy came out of her musings to find Tanner watching her.

"Yes," Stacy told him, and sat still as he pushed his chair back and approached. He took her hand as she stood, and with a gentle squeeze said, "I'll see you upstairs."

Stacy smiled into his eyes before she moved away from the table and toward the door.

Twelve

RODDY TENDERLY LINKED HIS FINGERS with Lucinda's as he sat down beside her in the open carriage. It was just two days after the wedding, and Roddy had asked the woman he loved to go for a drive. He refused to say where they were headed, but Lucinda, feeling young and lighthearted with the wedding over, readily agreed.

The streets of London were rather quiet for midmorning, but Lucinda and Roddy barely noticed. They talked of the little things that only good friends share, and each time Lucinda tried to learn their destination, Roddy only smiled with mischievous delight. Twenty minutes after they had left Lucinda's, the carriage pulled onto a quiet street in a lovely part of the city and stopped before a grand mansion.

"Why, Roddy," Lucinda spoke with surprise. "This is the old Wood mansion."

"Come along, my dear" was his only reply as he stepped from the carriage and held out his hand for her. He led her to the front door. Lucinda paused in indecision when Roddy opened it without knocking and stepped inside.

"Come along," he turned back to say to her. "It's all right."

Lucinda followed him uncertainly and gaped at the interior. Not only was no one there to greet them, but Lucinda could not see a stick of furniture in any direction.

"Well, what do you think?" Roddy wished to know.

"Of what?" Lucinda asked, feeling more confused than ever.

"This home."

Lucinda looked around. "Roddy, it's beautiful, but I'm still not sure what—"

"Have I ever told you that I love you, Lucinda? I mean, really told you how I felt? I'm not sure that I have."

Lucinda was so dumbfounded by his words that she could only stare at him while he paced around and spoke.

"It's taken me forever to gain the courage to ask you about us, and I'm still nervous. It helped to buy this place, but I'm still uncertain."

"Uncertain over what?" Lucinda asked, wondering if she had heard him correctly about the purchase of the mansion.

"Uncertain if you'll take me seriously when I ask you . . . to be my wife. I'm sure you've noticed a change in me. That was to help you see where my intentions were headed. Then I found this house and thought it would be the clincher.

"Now, I still have time to back out of the deal, but if you like it, it will be ours after we're married."

Roddy stopped then. Lucinda's eyes were swimming with tears.

"I've loved you for so long, Roddy," she whispered.

"As I have you." His voice was just as soft. "Now, what's it to be, Cinda. You have two questions to answer—yes or no to my proposal, sloppy as it was, and yes or no to the house?"

Roddy paused then and took a deep breath. "Please let the first one be yes, Cinda."

"Oh, Roddy. I don't care where we live."

Roddy's chest heaved with relief for just an instant, and then he was there, standing before her, his arms reaching to hold her close. Lucinda's eyes closed when she felt his arms, and then his lips pressed against her cheek before they met her own. Lucinda's heart pounded. She was going to marry her best friend; she was going to be Roddy's wife.

Stacy's second train ride was vastly different from her first. Then she'd ridden in crowded conditions with the Binks and ate the food Hettie had sent with her. Now she was experiencing a whole new world with her husband. They ate in a private car, had a private sleeping compartment, and not once did she grow cold or have to clean up after herself. It was her first taste of life as a duchess, and although Stacy tried to take it in stride, she knew that she often looked like a child at a circus.

Tanner seemed greatly amused by her response, but also touched. He was as tender a husband as Stacy could have dreamed of, and it seemed that she loved him a little more with each passing hour. By the time they arrived at the train station in Middlesbrough, Stacy was floating on a cloud of adoration.

Price hired a coach as soon as they disembarked. Within minutes they were on their way to Morgan.

"Tanner," Stacy spoke when the coach was underway. "My grandfather is not a wealthy man."

Tanner looked at his wife's face and felt the familiar squeezing sensation around his heart. She was infinitely precious to him. He knew very well that Andrew Daniels was without substantial means and had already spoken with Price on the matter. All concerned were to see to it that Stacy was not made uncomfortable in any way.

"Tanner, did you hear me?" Stacy spoke again when he remained silent for so long.

"Yes. Does it bother you that your grandfather isn't a wealthy man?"

"It doesn't bother me; I grew up that way. I just don't want you to be, well, inconvenienced."

"Will we have a bed?"

"Of course." Stacy blinked at him in surprise.

"And food to eat?"

"Yes."

"Then I shall be quite comfortable."

Stacy nodded, tucked her arm within Tanner's, and laid her head on his shoulder with a sigh of contentment—a contentment that wavered as soon as Stacy and Tanner were alone in her bedroom. She watched him take in their modest surroundings, finishing with the small bed.

"I'm sorry, Tanner. I wish the bed were bigger."

"Oh, I don't know," Tanner said calmly. "It means I'll need to snuggle very close to my wife tonight."

"You mean you really don't mind?"

"Will you mind my snuggling close?" Tanner asked with a raised brow.

Stacy laughed. She darted around a chair and pointed at him.

"That was not a challenge."

"Challenge or not, this should be an interesting game," Tanner countered as he began to stalk her. Just as Tanner was about to catch Stacy, a knock sounded on the door.

Tanner looked rather perturbed over the disturbance, but Stacy claimed victory as she ran to answer it.

"Your grandfather is awake now and would like to see you," Peters told her as soon as she opened the door.

Stacy's heart swelled with pleasure. She had felt crushed an hour ago when they'd arrived and been told that her grandfather was sleeping. She had begged them not to disturb him, but her desire to see him now was so intense that she ached inside. Unfortunately, Tanner wanted her attention right now also. Hesitantly she answered, unaware of Tanner's approach from behind her.

"Peters, please tell my grandfather that I'll be down in a short while."

"Make that a few moments," Tanner cut in. Stacy swung around in surprise. "Lady Stacy and I will be down in a few minutes."

Peters nodded, and Tanner shut the door on his departure.

"Are you certain, Tanner?" Stacy immediately began. "I can tell Peters that—"

Tanner silenced her with a kiss.

"We'll go downstairs and see your grandfather. I'm looking forward to meeting him."

Stacy sighed, and her hand came up to stroke his cheek. "Thank you, Tanner."

Tanner sighed also, but for another reason. He was not used to putting his wants aside for others, but the look on Stacy's face when she'd found her grandfather asleep caused him to feel unusual compassion.

Tanner kissed Stacy again before taking her hand and holding it all the way downstairs, releasing her only when Stacy saw her grandfather and moved to hug him.

"Oh, Papa," was all Stacy could say as he held her. She always thought him a big man, and he was tall, but after Tanner's solid strength he seemed very thin, almost gaunt. Not that this mattered to Stacy. She was so content to be with her grandfather for the first time in months that for the moment nothing else really mattered.

"Good morning, your Grace," Peters greeted Tanner the next morning.

"Good morning. Have you seen my wife?" Tanner had wakened to an empty bed and no sign of Stacy or Rayna. Price had no information as he dressed, so as soon as he was decent, he'd made his way downstairs.

"Yes, my lord," Peters answered. "Lady Stacy and her grandfather have gone fishing. Would you like your breakfast now, my lord, or directions to the pond?"

Tanner, an expert at hiding his feelings, was struggling for the first time in years to keep his mouth closed. The man said his wife had gone fishing. *Fishing.* His statuesque, lovely bride was sitting on the banks of a pond, fishing. The idea was inconceivable.

These riotous thoughts invaded Tanner's mind for only seconds before he noticed Peters' patient stance, reminding him that he'd been offered breakfast. He was hungry, but his curiosity over his wife's fishing won the battle.

"I'll take those directions to the pond," Tanner said softly and listened intently as Peters spoke. Feeling like a vagabond, Tanner reached for several biscuits, eating as he walked toward the pond. He believed that his wife really was fishing, but the novelty of the idea forced a need in him to see for himself.

"Now that's five to my one," Stacy said with a sigh as Andrew brought in another fish. "I must have lost my touch."

"Indeed. It's the life of the idle rich that you now lead."

Stacy laughed in delight at the image his words portrayed, but then she grew very serious.

"It does take a little getting used to."

"I imagine it does. It must also make it hard to come here with all of our worn surroundings."

"Now that's where you're wrong," Stacy told him sweetly. "Morgan will always be in my heart, old furniture and all."

"I'm thinking of leaving it to Noel and Elena."

"I think that's very wise, but I hope you're not in any big hurry to leave us." Stacy's voice had been light, but Andrew did not reply.

"Is there something you're not telling me?" Stacy asked now, her voice fearful.

"It's nothing you don't already know. I just don't know what I'll have to live for if I lose my eyes completely."

"Oh, Papa," Stacy's voice was soft with pain. "I won't tell you I understand because I'm sure I don't, but please know how much I need you. If you can't keep going for yourself, then keep going for me. I can't stand the thought of your being gone."

Andrew took his gaze from the pond and stared intently at Stacy's tear-filled eyes. He was surprised to see those tears; he could hardly remember her ever crying. In fact the tears did not spill but sat pooled in her great blue eyes. Only one thought came to the old man. Was there a sweeter woman in all of England? Andrew was sure there was not. After a moment he reached and patted the hand she'd lain on his arm.

"Worry not, my dear. I shall keep on, if for no one else, then for you."

Stacy hugged his arm and brushed a quick hand across her eyes. They fished in silence until Stacy felt a mighty tug on her line. She stood with a shout, as did Andrew to watch as she worked the line and brought in the biggest catch of the day.

This was the scene upon which Tanner walked. He stood transfixed as he watched his wife laugh and unhook a good-sized trout from her line. Before he was noticed, he had time to take in the whole scene.

Andrew was bundled from head to foot, but Stacy was wearing only a dress, a dress that had been patched many times over and was too tight across her bosom. He wondered how many years she'd had it. Her hair was also coming down around her face, and there was a smear of mud under one eye.

"Oh, Tanner," Stacy suddenly spoke, and Andrew turned. "I didn't hear you come up."

Tanner hated the uncertainty he heard in her voice. His own voice was meant to soothe as he smiled and came forward.

"So when do we eat this catch, for breakfast or lunch?"

"Well..." Stacy began, still looking uncomfortable with a fish in her hand and a look of stark vulnerability on her face.

"We'll eat them for lunch," Andrew interjected, not noticing Stacy's hesitancy, or choosing to ignore it. "Why don't you run ahead to the kitchen, Stacy, and see that Mercy gets these."

"Yes, Papa," Stacy answered and moved to obey him, but Tanner caught her hand when she would have passed by him in silent embarrassment. He stood staring into her eyes. Stacy glanced over to see that her grandfather had begun to fish again, his back to them, so she spoke softly for Tanner's ears alone.

"You must be wondering what kind of woman you married."

"As a matter of fact I am."

Stacy looked crushed.

"I'm probably going to need the next 50 years to decide which woman I like better—the woman who has a wardrobe full of silks and satins and usually smells of flowers, or the adorable urchin before me, whose cotton dress looks like a rag and who smells of fish."

"You're really not angry or ashamed of me?"

"I'm furious and my reputation is shot." Tanner's tone was dry.

Stacy chuckled low in her throat and went on her way. Tanner sent her off with a smack to her backside and then joined the older man on the banks. Stacy's pole was nearby, but Tanner did not reach for it. Fishing held no interest for him.

"You don't fish?" It was the first time Andrew had talked with Tanner alone. Tanner genuinely liked his wife's grandfather and answered easily.

"No, sir, I don't."

"How about hunting?"

"Yes, I hunt. Do you?"

"Not with my eyes growing so unpredictable. My younger cousin, Noel, hunts. If you've a mind to be here awhile, you could go with him. He'd know all the best areas."

They were silent as Andrew pulled in another fish. Tanner watched him for a time, but then his gaze strayed across the pond to the beautiful area beyond. While Tanner studied the scape, Andrew, whose eyes were clear that day, studied Tanner.

There was plenty of temptation at a time like this to give speeches, but Andrew knew they would do no good. Either Tanner was going to take good care of Stacy or he wasn't, and Andrew sincerely doubted that anything he said would make a difference.

What he'd seen so far looked good, but Stacy had been raised in a different world, and her level of trust was very high, even when it ought not to be. As a duke, Tanner was certainly used to having his own way, and Stacy was a people pleaser. The old man shrugged mentally. It was out of his hands. As much as he'd like to wring a promise out of this young duke that his granddaughter would be well cared for, he knew better than to even try.

As it was, Tanner began to speak, cutting into Andrew's musings. He extended an invitation to Winslow, if ever Andrew wanted to make the trip, and then proceeded to tell him of the house and grounds. By the time they returned to Morgan for breakfast the older man was feeling much better about this young man.

In the next ten days that they visited, Andrew was given a measure of peace concerning Stacy's happiness. It wasn't anything specific, but Tanner proved repeatedly in the little things he said and did that he cared deeply for his new wife.

Because Andrew didn't know when Stacy would come again, the goodbyes at the end of their visit were harder than the ones in the spring had been. But from what he could tell, he believed Tanner was going to do right by Stacy. Beyond that Andrew could only hope.

Thirteen

STANDING IN THE DOORWAY of the master bedroom, Stacy was pleased that Tanner had warned her before they arrived. This room, the suite actually, was as massive as everything else at Winslow.

On one end were Stacy's spacious sitting room and large dressing room. From Stacy's tour, she knew that Tanner's sitting and dressing rooms were of the same size. Centered between these four smaller rooms was the bedroom itself.

The master bedroom was a room in which all the furniture played court to the huge bed that stood against the main wall. The headboard was over six feet high with pillared columns on the two corners. It was ornately carved in a rich cherry wood and inlaid with mahogany and ash. Large windows with beautiful smokey-gray hangings looked out over the perfectly manicured acres of Winslow.

If she leaned very close to the glass she could see the other wings, which housed dozens of rooms: bedrooms, private sitting rooms, small dining areas, a multitiered library, a music room, studies, lovely galleries, servants' quarters, and more than Stacy could keep track of.

The kitchen was at the rear of Winslow, off the first floor. Although Stacy had only gained a peek, her impression of hundreds of square feet of floor space and gleaming pots hanging and tables spread out was permanently stamped in her mind.

Her thoughts spun as she remembered the large number of kitchen staff alone. How would she manage all of this?

Stacy shook her head as the direction of her thoughts threatened to overwhelm her, and was relieved to see Rayna come to the edge of the room.

"I have your correspondence here, my lady."

"Oh," Stacy spoke with surprise, not having expected this. "Thank you, Rayna." She took the letters and glanced through them.

"I believe your aunt has been in touch with you," Rayna spoke respectfully. "She wrote to me also. If after you read your letter, my lady, and like the idea—my answer is yes. If there is nothing else, I'll continue your unpacking."

Stacy nodded, feeling confused as Rayna walked away, but she swiftly turned her attention back to the small pile of letters in her hand. After walking into her sitting room, she made herself comfortable in a chair and began to read. The first letter was from Lucinda. Stacy's eyes widened on two occasions, first when she wrote that Rayna could stay with her if the situation was suitable, and then again when Lucinda told of her upcoming marriage to Roddy.

Stacy's eyes slid shut in rapture at the latter news. They were so perfect for each other, and Stacy knew they loved one another deeply. A small smile played around the corners of her mouth when she considered the fact that she had probably helped things along when she'd talked with Roddy in the carriage. Stacy chuckled softly over how much fun it was to be a matchmaker.

The next letter was from a woman named Chelsea Gallagher, a neighbor apparently, and one whom Stacy hadn't met. She wrote to welcome Stacy to the area and to offer her congratulations. Chelsea also expressed her wish to meet Stacy soon.

Stacy pondered for a time as to whether she had seen this woman at a social gathering or at the wedding and decided that she simply couldn't recall. With a resigned shrug she opened the last note—it was from Sunny Hawkesbury. Sunny wrote to ask if she and her sister-in-law, Chelsea Gallagher, could call on her the afternoon of the twentieth. Stacy was smiling with delight at the prospect when Tanner entered the room.

"That's quite a smile," Tanner chuckled as he pulled his wife from the settee and into his arms.

"I got a letter from Sunny Hawkesbury. She and Chelsea Gallagher want to come to see me on the twentieth."

"That's this Friday. You'd better reply right away."

"How do I get word to them?"

Tanner, who had been bending his head to kiss her, straightened in surprise.

"You send a servant."

"Oh," Stacy said inadequately, feeling very young and gauche under his raised brow.

Tanner saw the color rise in her face. He bent and pressed a kiss to her brow and then spoke with his arms wrapped securely around her.

"I came up to ask you to go riding with me. Write your note, and I'll give it Price. If ever you have a question, see Price; he'll take care of you. After you've finished with your reply, you can slip into a riding habit and we'll get a ride in before dinner."

Stacy smiled gratefully and did as he asked. Within 40 minutes, she'd sent word to Sunny and was riding across the meadows of Winslow with her husband. Only once did she think of Lucinda's news and took a moment to share it with Tanner, who didn't seem surprised at all. As Tanner stepped up the pace to a gallop, Stacy wondered where her aunt and Roddy were now.

"Something is wrong, Cinda."

"No, Roddy, it's not."

"You're not being straight with me. Have I done something?"

"Oh, no," Lucinda shook her head, but she refused to look at him. They were at the new house on Bates Street, Brentwood. The painters had been there that day, and Lucinda and Roddy had come to see the results. The wedding was set for one month's time, and Roddy wanted to be certain that everything was just right.

Roddy did not press Lucinda as they continued their tour, but when Lucinda would have bid him goodnight at her front door, he came in without asking. She started toward the stairs, but he captured her hand and led her into the library. The fire burned warmly, and after they were seated on the sofa, Roddy spoke. Lucinda still had not looked at him, but Roddy told himself he wasn't leaving until he was sure he understood her silence.

"What's frightening you, Cinda?"

Lucinda drew a quick breath. He had so easily guessed her problem was fear. She wanted to deny it but couldn't find the words. Her throat closed with tears. Roddy's next sentence was her undoing.

"I'm not Aubrey."

Lucinda put her face in her hands and sobbed. Roddy's arms surrounded her. Her frame shook with harsh weeping, and Roddy let her cry. When it seemed that she was calming, he produced a handkerchief and Lucinda took it gratefully.

"I'm sorry," she said shakily, "I don't know what's come over me."

"I think I do. I think for years you've convinced yourself that Aubrey was unfaithful because of some deficiency in you. That's a lie, Lucinda. Aubrey wasn't faithful to you or to anyone, including himself. His infidelity was *his* problem, not yours.

"I'm not going to be married to you for a month and then go looking for greener pastures. If I'd been that kind of man, I would have proved it a long time ago. You're all the woman I want, and will ever want."

Lucinda was staring into his face, now close to her own, as though she were seeing him for the first time. He was so wonderful, more wonderful than she deserved.

"Do you believe me?" Roddy asked.

"Yes, I do," Lucinda said with wonder and then knew she had to be completely honest. "However, I may be plagued by doubts again."

"If you are, come to me, Cinda, just as soon as the fears surface."

Lucinda leaned forward and kissed him then, but Roddy held himself in check. They lived in an age and time where intimacy was a casual thing. Not so with Roddy Caruthers. Lucinda was precious to him, and even knowing that she would be his wife in a month was not enough to press him into doing something he felt was wrong.

Just a few weeks now, Roddy told himself as he exited. *She'll be mine to have and hold in just a few weeks.*

Stacy sat on the huge bed their first night at Winslow and tested the softness. She didn't lie back, but bounced a little on her seat and then got comfortable against the headboard. With the ease that years of practice afforded her, she then reached for her hair.

Rayna had brushed it smooth for her, but for as long as she could remember she'd braided it down her back at bedtime and did so now. It made her hair much easier to manage in the morning. Even though Tanner liked it hanging free, Stacy's mind was on other things and she acted out of habit.

She had just reached for a book on the nightstand when Tanner joined her. She watched him make himself comfortable against the footboard and then stare at her.

"How do you like Winslow?" he asked.

"Oh, Tanner," Stacy said, setting the book aside, her eyes

bright with enchantment. "It's the loveliest home I've ever seen. I can't think of what your impression must have been when we were in Middlesbrough."

"I was quite comfortable at Morgan, and I enjoyed your grandfather tremendously. Hettie tends to step out of place quite regularly, but since she doesn't live *here,* I think I'll survive."

"She's rather protective of me," Stacy returned apologetically.

"So I noticed. I've gained the fiercest looks from her. I don't know if she really believes we're married." Tanner's voice was dry.

Stacy laughed. "She's been like a mother to me, and even though she's negative and scolds a lot, I can't think of what I'd have done without her."

"Your parents died when you were young, didn't they?"

"I was little more than a baby. I don't remember either of them. It's always been Papa and Hettie and of course Peters. He's been like a father also."

"I have an ancestor that reminds me of Peters. His portrait is in the north wing. I'll have to show it to you sometime."

"Is the north wing always so cold?"

"Actually it is. It gets very little sun and has always been drafty."

"It's more than the temperature, though," Stacy said, her eyes on some distant spot. "The colors used in the decorating are cold too. It's nothing like the rest of Winslow. When I walked through there it felt like a completely different place."

"My grandmother had dreary tastes in decorating. Everything else has been remodeled. The north wing has what's left of her furniture. Feel free to redecorate."

"Is it used very often?"

"Almost never," Tanner answered her.

"Then I don't see any point in spending the money. If you want me to, I'll do it, but it seems like a waste."

"It's up to you," Tanner told her softly, but his mind was not on the north wing. It was on discovering that his wife was not a spendthrift. He didn't know a woman alive who didn't like to spend money on everything she could get her hands on. Tanner wondered how many years they would be married before she stopped being a surprise.

Fourteen

STACY PEERED INTO THE MIRROR for the fifth time and then paced the room some more. Sunny and Chelsea were scheduled to arrive in an hour, and Stacy was a nervous wreck. She so wanted to make a good impression, but she was convinced that they would find her out of place in a home as lovely and grand as Winslow.

Stacy stopped suddenly and mentally scolded herself. Her mind was headed off into all kinds of whimsical nonsense, and that was ridiculous. After a final glance in the mirror, she made herself walk calmly down the wide staircase to see if the parlor was in readiness. She met Tanner as he came from his study.

"Ah, here you are. I was just headed to see how you were doing."

"I'm doing fine," Stacy told him much too brightly, her face pale.

Tanner's voice was meant to be reassuring as he continued, "When do your guests arrive?"

"In 48 minutes."

Tanner had to hide a smile at her precision. She had obviously worked herself into a fine state and was on the brink of panic.

"I've known Chelsea Gallagher and her husband, Rand, for

years. She's a fine woman, and of course you've already met Sunny."

"Of course," Stacy agreed, feeling worse than ever. "I don't like my dress," she added absently.

"Then why are you wearing it?"

"Because it's part of my trousseau, and I can't let it hang there."

"Change your dress, Stacy," Tanner told her calmly.

"I don't have time."

Tanner gently took his wife's hand and began to lead her back up the stairs.

"You think I'm acting like a child, don't you?"

"No, I don't," Tanner answered her. "I think you're understandably nervous because this is the first time you've entertained here. Hating your dress only adds to the problem. Rayna!" Tanner finished with a shout to Stacy's maid.

When Rayna appeared, Tanner gave her orders and Stacy was amazed at how much calmer she felt from just listening to him.

"Lady Richardson does not like this dress, and quite frankly it's not my favorite either. Please see her into something more comfortable." With that he turned to Stacy.

"Do not rush. If your guests arrive early, I will keep company with them until you come down."

Stacy's chest heaved with relief. "Thank you, Tanner."

Tanner's long-fingered hand tenderly captured her jaw. "You're welcome, sweetheart, and trust me, you're going to do just fine."

Chelsea Gallagher was nothing like Stacy expected. She was older than Sunny, even though they were sister-in-laws. In fact, she was old enough to be Sunny's or Stacy's mother. She had a youthful air, however, and was beautiful in her own right. Stacy, who was at times rather uncomfortable with her figure, was quite pleased to find Chelsea more heavily endowed than she was herself.

Chelsea was not as tall as Stacy, but her overall figure was more filled out. Sunny was also on the tall side, but her figure was willowy. Her tummy was becoming nicely rounded, giving evidence of the child to come.

Sunny hugged Stacy as soon as she arrived, and Chelsea shook her hand so warmly that Stacy's fears melted. There was no lack of conversation in the time that followed as Stacy described how she and Tanner met and her honeymoon trip. The next two hours flew by, and Stacy couldn't believe how much she was enjoying herself.

It took some time, but Stacy suddenly realized how closely these women were related to Lady Andrea, Aunt Lucinda's friend.

"You haven't met my brother, have you?" Chelsea asked at one point.

"No."

"Well, where was Brandon that day we met in London?" Sunny interjected with a frown.

"I think he came just as our carriage was leaving," Stacy told them and then frowned herself. "Brandon is your brother?"

"That's right," Chelsea told her.

"Then Lady Andrea is your mother."

Chelsea smiled as she made the connection.

"I completely missed that. Will you tell me about the rest of your family?"

"Certainly. My youngest brother is Dexter. He's married with children. Miles and Holly are my own children. They're both grown and married, and they've made Rand and me grandparents three times over."

"You can't be a grandmother," Stacy interrupted.

Chelsea and Sunny exchanged a look, and then both laughed. Chelsea heard this comment often, and it was always a source of great amusement to her. She told Stacy that some days she felt like a *great*-grandmother.

The women did not stay much longer. Stacy walked them out to their carriage when they took their leave. Tanner suddenly appeared at her side to assist both ladies inside the coach.

"We would love to have you over for dinner in a few weeks," Sunny told the newlyweds.

Tanner glanced at Stacy for approval before turning back to the Duchess of Briscoe.

"We'll plan on it," he told her.

"Goodbye until then," Sunny called out the window as the carriage pulled away. When she settled back inside, Chelsea spoke.

"He's in love with her, Sunny. I wouldn't have believed it if I hadn't seen it with my own eyes."

"They seem very happy," Sunny agreed.

"But you're concerned about something," Chelsea interjected, watching the younger woman carefully.

"Oh, you'll only say I'm full of doom and gloom if I say it, but they are still newlyweds, and I know that Tanner's had some deep hurts. Brandon didn't go into detail, but he intimated that things have been pretty rough. Stacy couldn't be sweeter, but I can't help wondering whether Stacy will be able to stand the blow if Tanner's hurts do surface."

"We'll keep praying," Chelsea told her, and in fact they took time right then to lift the young couple to the Lord.

Two days after Chelsea's and Sunny's visit, Tanner made a fast trip into London. He spent more time in the carriage than tending his business, but he had several important matters to care for. One was a visit to his Uncle Edmond; the other was made with Stacy in mind. Both were attended to as swiftly as possible, but the day was long and he missed Stacy terribly.

Not for one moment, not even when he met with his uncle, could he dispel her from his thoughts. He wondered briefly if he was becoming obsessed but dismissed the thought immediately. He had no more determined to put her from his mind when he found himself wondering what she was doing right then.

Tanner would have been pleased and surprised to find that Stacy was digging in the garden just as Tanner had told her she could do. Not all of Tanner's staff was as friendly as Stacy would have liked, and there were times when she preferred to be out-of-doors and away from their watchful eyes.

Even though Joffrey was head of housekeeping, things seemed to be a little more finely tuned when Price was in attendance. Stacy couldn't help but wonder if Joffrey was rather remiss in his duties. It didn't seem possible, since even when in good humor Tanner was a demanding lord. But as Stacy thought about her weeks at Winslow, she realized the staff was not lax when he was present but only with her.

The thought caused her to frown, and she sat back on her heels. She didn't know what to do about the situation. Stacy knew that if it came to an out-and-out battle, she would wash her own clothes and get her own meals before she would confront anyone. Just the thought of confrontation made her stomach ache.

Stacy went back to her weeding, but her stomachache did not go away. It was then that she realized the sun had dropped low in the sky. It was dinnertime, and she was famished. Pushing herself off the ground, she moved toward the house.

Rayna was there to meet her, and Stacy, hungry as she was, enjoyed a leisurely bath. She knew the evening was going to drag with Tanner away, and a long soak in a tub filled with scented salts was just what she needed.

Supper was delicious, but by the time Stacy finished, she missed Tanner so much she didn't know how she would pass the evening. She opted for a book from the library and was headed that way when he came in the front door. Not caring in the least if the servants were watching, Stacy flew into his arms.

"I missed you," she told him as he bent so she could put her arms around his neck, pressing her soft cheek to his. It took Stacy a moment to realize she was not being hugged in return. He dropped a kiss on her nose before she moved back in order to stare up at him. She stood back and looked at her husband, whose arms were behind his back.

"I missed you too," Tanner told her as he straightened, but Stacy's mind was now on his arms.

"You're hiding something."

"Indeed I am."

Stacy tried to move around him, but Tanner simply moved with her and kept his secret concealed. Stacy finally stood still again and faced him.

"Is it for me?" she asked with a smile.

"Quite possibly," Tanner answered and Stacy saw how much he was enjoying this. She put her own hands behind her back and simply stared at him.

"Did you stay busy today?" Tanner asked.

"Yes," Stacy said simply, but couldn't stand the suspense any longer. "Do I get to see what it is?"

"Are your hands clean?" Tanner asked, sounding much like a parent. He ruined the effect, however, when his eyes lit with suppressed laughter.

Stacy, like an obedient child, brought her hands forward for his inspection.

"You've been digging in the dirt, haven't you?"

"Guilty as charged," she told him and joined his inspection of her chipped nails.

Tanner gave a deep, mock sigh and brought a large box out from behind his back.

"I'm not sure this is fitting for an urchin like yourself, but here it is."

Stacy's eyes widened in a way that Tanner loved, and he held the bottom of the parcel while she removed the lid and drew forth an exquisite gown.

"Oh, Tanner," Stacy breathed. "It's lovely."

"This is to replace the one you don't like."

Stacy held the dress out in front of her and stared. The dress was a very pale pink silk with snow-white lace. The skirt had multiple gathers at the waist before falling straight to the floor without ruffle or layer. The bodice and sleeves were both of bertha styling, and Stacy did not have another dress like it in her wardrobe. It was the most wonderful gown she'd ever seen.

Gently hugging it to her, she spoke. "I'm going to save this for something very special."

"Anything you wish," Tanner told her, feeling inordinately pleased at her response. He really had thought about her way too much, but she was obviously worth every reflection.

The evening turned out to be a wonderful surprise for Stacy since Tanner was home early and wanted to eat in the privacy of his sitting room. Stacy sat with him through the meal, and they talked of their day apart. When Tanner finished his meal, he dismissed the servants early and they were left alone until morning.

SEPTEMBER WAS DRAWING TO A CLOSE when Tanner told Stacy he was going to have to be away for a few days. Stacy listened in silent dismay as he told her casually that he would have to leave on the second of October and would not return until late on the third.

"Edmond insists that we go and see some breeding stock. I don't know why he doesn't want to part with his own brass for such nonsense, but he assures me this is an investment I can't pass up."

"Did you want me to come with you?" Stacy offered, hoping her voice sounded normal.

"Thank you for offering, my sweet, but I can assure you this trip will be dry-as-dust—strictly business. It's also going to be rather rushed because I want to be back home as soon as I can."

"I'll ask cook to prepare something special," Stacy said, a sudden idea springing to mind, "and we'll dine together when you return."

Tanner stood from his place at the breakfast table and came toward her.

"I love the idea, sweetheart," he told her as he stood by her place, "but I'll be very late that night. Hopefully I can slip into bed without disturbing you, and then I can tell you all about the trip the next morning. In fact, we'll take the day off. We'll sleep late and be very lazy all day and do anything you want."

Tanner kissed her cheek and moved toward the door, telling her over his shoulder that he had some work to do in his study. Stacy lifted her coffee cup very slowly to her lips. She simply didn't know how to tell her husband that his business trip was going to keep him away for her birthday, October 3.

"He's planning a surprise party," Stacy spoke out loud, causing Rayna to come back into the dressing room.

"Did you call me, my lady?"

"No, Rayna," Stacy told her with a smile. "I was just talking to myself."

Rayna nodded and Stacy settled back in the tub, a huge smile of contentment covering her face.

Two slow days had passed since Tanner had announced his plans to be gone. He had been busy and didn't notice anything out of the usual in his wife, but Stacy had agonized over whether or not to tell him.

Now there was no need. It was all a ploy to throw her off guard. Tanner was simply pretending not to be aware of her birthday so he could come home early and surprise her. Stacy lay back in the tub until her water grew cold. All she could think about was the wonderful man she had married.

"If I didn't know better, I would think you're glad to see me go," Tanner commented the morning he was scheduled to leave.

Stacy chuckled softly. "Don't be silly," she told him, straightening his cravat. "I even offered to go with you, remember?"

Tanner studied her soft, mischievous eyes and felt fear spiral through him. Leslie had never been sorry to see him leave. It took years before he learned that it was because she had never been without other men. The last one was his brother.

"Tanner, is something wrong?"

Tanner shook his head to dispel the images that had leapt into his mind.

"No," he forced the word as he turned toward the door. "I'd best be on my way."

"All right." Stacy's voice was uncertain now. He hadn't even kissed her goodbye. She followed him all the way downstairs and out the door, finally coming to a standstill on the porch to watch him stride away. When Tanner stopped just short of boarding the coach and turned back to her, Stacy spoke, her voice not able to mask her confusion.

"Take care of yourself, Tanner. Tell Edmond I said hello."

Tanner said something too softly to be heard and was back in front of her in six strides. He pulled her almost fiercely into his arms. Stacy was breathless when he released her, but she managed a few more words.

"I love you, Tanner."

He didn't speak, but his gaze softened and the back of his hand came up to stroke her cheek before he turned, strode to the carriage, and was driven away.

Stacy didn't stand on the steps for very long. She was too excited about her coming birthday. With her own long-legged steps she mounted the stairs to make certain her dress was perfectly pressed for the following night.

It was close to midnight before Tanner made his way up the stairs on the night of the third. Price, who had not traveled with him this time, was in attendance, and without a word Tanner undressed and moved soft-footedly into the bedroom and toward the bed. He was nearly on top of it before he realized that the covers had been turned down but the bed was empty.

With a feeling of dread, one that had hung with him since he'd left, he walked toward Stacy's dressing room. Finding it empty, he moved to the sitting room.

Stacy, dressed in her new gown, was seated by the fire, and sitting very upright in a chair. As he approached, Tanner saw that she was awake and staring at him. Upon seeing the new dress, anger rose within him so swiftly he thought he would explode. She had known he would not be home until late. For *whom* had she dressed?

"Why are you up and dressed like that?" Tanner was amazed that in his anger his voice sounded so normal.

When Stacy answered she did not sound guilty, only unhappy. "I thought you were giving me a surprise party."

A stunned silence followed this announcement as the anger drained out of Tanner.

"I am giving you a surprise party," he admitted after several heartbeats. "On your birthday, the thirtieth."

Tanner heard her sigh.

"Whom did you ask about the date of my birthday?"

"Lucinda," Tanner answered, feeling more confused than ever.

Stacy actually managed a small laugh. "Lucinda has never been able to get dates straight. My grandfather's birthday is the thirtieth, not mine."

The room was silent for a full 30 seconds.

"Anastasia," Tanner finally said, his voice deep and intense, "are you trying to tell me that today is your birthday?"

The question was no more out of his mouth than the clock on the mantel chimed 12 times. When it ended, Stacy answered him.

"It was yesterday, actually. I thought you knew, Tanner, and that your trip was a cover for a surprise party. That's why I didn't tell you."

Tanner's relief over the fact that she'd not been with another man was short-lived. He'd *missed* his wife's birthday. In just a few strides he was before Stacy's chair, taking her hands and pulling her into his embrace. Tanner's heart pounded with dread as he held her tightly against him.

"You're crushing my new dress," Stacy told him, but her concern was half-hearted.

"I'll buy you a new one—I'll buy a closet full of new dresses." The words came from above her as Tanner rested his chin on her head and continued to hold her close.

"I'm all right, Tanner," Stacy told him. "I wasn't all right before you came home, but I am now."

Tanner's eyes slid shut with pain. He hated the thought that she must have urged Rayna to do her best, and then sat in her room, looking beautiful and waiting for a party that never materialized.

"I'll make this up to you." Tanner now held her by the arms and tried to study her face in the small glow of the fire.

"There is no need," Stacy assured him. "I understand, and it wasn't your fault."

He ignored her words. "Would you like your present now?"

"You have my present?" Stacy was indescribably pleased. She told herself that it wasn't the day itself that mattered, but the celebration. At the moment it suited her fine that her birthday "party" was going to be just her and Tanner, sitting together while she opened her gift.

"Wait here," Tanner urged, and Stacy stood still for the minutes he was gone. It took a little time, but when he returned he was carrying a jeweler's box and a lighted lantern. He lit the other two on the mantel before presenting the box to Stacy.

"Happy birthday, sweetheart."

Stacy opened the top and gasped. Inside lay a necklace.

There didn't seem to be any more to it than gold and diamonds, seemingly hundreds of them.

"Oh, Tanner. It's simply breathtaking."

"I take it you like it?"

"I love it, but—"

"But what?" Tanner prompted her when she stopped and looked at him in horror.

"What if I lose it?"

Tanner made a low sound in his throat, one of complete disregard.

"I'll buy you another." This said he lifted the priceless object from its bed of satin and hooked it around his wife's neck. Stacy was trembling as she looked in the mirror that hung over the mantel.

"Oh, Tanner." Stacy didn't seem capable of other words. Without warning she turned and threw her arms around his neck. She tried to thank him then, but was interrupted by a huge yawn that she simply couldn't suppress.

"We'd better get to bed." Tanner's voice was amused.

Stacy yawned again. "Would you mind if I didn't come right now, Tanner?"

The change in him was instantaneous. "No." His voice was cold, belying the word. "What is it you need to do?"

"It's nothing," Stacy assured him quickly, startled by the change in him and the note of intolerance in his tone. "If you'll unbutton me, I'll get ready for bed."

It was as if a bucket of ice had been thrown on their celebration. Tanner knew he'd caused it with the tone of his voice, but her reluctance to join him in bed disturbed him no end.

In silence he unbuttoned Stacy. She reached for the back of her neck and unhooked the necklace. Standing still, necklace grasped in her hand, she watched her husband stalk from the sitting room. By the time she gained the bedroom, Tanner was in bed. For the first time there seemed to be a wall between them. Tanner told her goodnight but did not touch her.

"Thank you for the necklace," Stacy said from her side of the bed.

"You're welcome," Tanner answered briefly, leaving Stacy in the dark as to what she had done or how she was supposed to fix it.

An hour later Stacy lay listening to Tanner's even breathing and knew she was going to have to get up. It had all been so innocent. If only she had told him right away that she needed something to eat, he might not have grown angry. Stacy silently sighed at her own lack of courage, her own inability to stand up for herself.

With very subtle and quiet movements, she slipped from the covers. She didn't light a lantern until she'd reached her sitting room and then carried it out into the hall. If Tanner had been hungry, he'd have rung for a meal, but Stacy couldn't bring herself to wake someone just to wait on her.

She had just entered the kitchen and set the lantern down when her husband's voice sounded behind her. He was coldly furious.

"What are you doing down here?"

"Oh, Tanner," Stacy's hand flew to her throat. "You startled me."

"Answer my question." He ignored her fear. "What are you doing down here?"

"I'm sorry I woke you. I tried to go to sleep, I really did, but I'm hungry and I thought if I ate something, I could sleep. I'll come back up now so you won't be disturbed."

Stacy picked up the lantern, but Tanner didn't move. Stacy, afraid of angering him more, simply held her place.

"Why didn't you tell me?" Tanner was calming.

"I wanted to, but you seemed so upset. I thought I could wait until morning."

"Why didn't you ring for something?"

Stacy shrugged, feeling miserably inadequate to be a duchess. But that was not all. Things had not been completely right between them since they said their goodbyes for the trip, and Stacy, not really understanding the problem but assuming she'd done something wrong, didn't know how to put the relationship back on firm footing.

"Do you really need something to eat?"

"I can wait until morning," Stacy hurried to tell him, but Tanner just stared at her until she felt compelled to apologize.

"I'm sorry for whatever I've done wrong, Tanner. I think it must have started a few days ago. I'm not really certain, but whatever I've done to make you upset, I'm sorry."

Tanner couldn't take the way her eyes stared at him beseechingly or the sound of her sweet voice in misery. Thoughts of Leslie had ridden him hard since he'd agreed to marry Stacy, but never as roughly as in the last 48 hours. His black mood was terrifying his wife, and he was going to have to get a grip on himself. He was just about to say something when there was a rustling on the far side of the room.

"Excuse me, my lord, but I thought I heard voices." Winslow's cook stood across the room. "Is there something I can get for you?"

"My wife is hungry."

"Very well, I'll fix you right up." The rather plump woman was cheerful for the middle of the night. "Would you care for something, your Grace?"

"No. Just see to my wife."

Tanner left then, and Stacy felt utterly wretched. She stared at the door long after he exited, asking herself what she'd done.

"Now, my lady, if you'll just make yourself comfortable in the dining room, I'll bring something right in."

"I'll be fine here," Stacy told the older woman absently, missing the servant's shocked expression.

Cook watched Stacy take a chair at the small, crude table

and worked at keeping her voice level. The lord and lady simply did not eat in the kitchen! The kitchen was for servants, not the duchess; she deserved the best. However she simply said, "I'll just be a moment with your food."

Stacy sat, staring at nothing in particular until cook put a dish of sliced fruit on the table.

"There now. Why don't you start with that? I worried about you, my lady, when you didn't want your supper," she spoke in a motherly tone. "I'll have something more for you in a jiffy."

Tanner came out of the shadows at that moment and placed a heavy quilt around Stacy's shoulders. His hands were gentle and Stacy was thankful for the warmth, but she was decidedly uncomfortable when he sat down across from her.

"Why didn't you eat your dinner?"

Stacy swallowed a slice of apple before answering. "It was foolish of me not to."

"But why didn't you?" Tanner pressed her.

"I thought the surprise party would be a dinner party," Stacy admitted quietly, her eyes down.

Tanner's hand went to the back of his neck. Stacy still did not look up, or she would have seen the pain in his eyes.

You're a fool, Tanner Richardson, he told himself. *And you don't deserve this dear girl. She was honest with you and you took her head off.*

Stacy finished her meal in silence. Her stomach felt better, but her heart felt as if a giant hand was trying to squeeze the very life from it.

Tanner held her chair out when she was done and waited as she thanked cook. He escorted her up the stairs. When they were once again in the bedroom, he took her jaw in his hand, forcing her gaze to meet his.

"I've been in a wretched humor these past days, but things will be different tomorrow. You have nothing to be sorry about, and in the morning we'll celebrate your birthday properly."

Stacy, clinging to the tender, calm sound of his voice,

nodded with relief. She was still rather emotionally drained, but when they climbed into bed, she fell asleep just moments after the covers were settled around her.

Sixteen

STACY'S BACK RESTED against the base of a large tree, her legs stretched out in front of her. Tanner's head was in her lap, and thus far the day had been idyllic.

Both duke and duchess had slept late, eaten a leisurely breakfast, and gone for a long ride into the bluffs beyond Winslow. They had ridden for miles, and Stacy was amazed that they were still on Richardson land. Everything about Winslow was beautiful. Stacy said as much to Tanner.

"Including the mistress of the manor," Tanner commented. Stacy smiled at the compliment.

"Did I tell you that I saw Hawk while I was away?" Tanner asked suddenly.

"Hawk?"

"Hawk is Brandon Hawkesbury's nickname."

"Oh," Stacy said with surprise and then, "Is Sunny feeling better?"

"Yes. She was terribly disappointed that she had to cancel the dinner plans, but she's going to have you to tea soon."

"She didn't lose the baby, did she?" Stacy's voice was pained at the very thought.

"No. It was a nasty virus according to Hawk. The doctor has ordered her to take it easy, but the pregnancy is still strong."

Stacy sighed with relief. She was already excited about the arrival of this new little one and knew she would have mourned the loss. She had even started the baby's gift; it was a beautiful blanket in multiple colors appropriate for either gender, but secretly Stacy hoped Sunny would have a girl.

"I think I've lost you," Tanner commented as he sat up beside her and leaned against the tree.

"I was thinking about Sunny's baby."

Her voice was so wistful that Tanner stared at her. She sounded like having a child was the most precious thing on earth. Tanner frowned slightly. He did not have the heart to tell her that it might not ever happen for them.

He'd suffered a raging fever as a child, and the doctor had told his father that one of the long-lasting side effects might be sterility. In all the years he and Leslie had been married, she had never conceived. The fact had never really bothered him before, but now he wanted to give his wife a baby. His heart felt weighted down over what he assumed was an impossibility.

"I think I've lost you." Stacy echoed his phrase a moment later, and Tanner smiled down into her eyes before they began to talk of the coming winter.

The day ran on in a quiet and peaceful vein. Both bride and groom felt renewed in their relationship, and Stacy, although she had no answers to her husband's quicksilver mood changes, still believed Tanner loved her. She would work at this marriage for as long as it took him to say the words.

"I'm so glad you're feeling better," Stacy told Sunny as she hugged her. It was early the next week, and the women were finally getting together at Bracken for tea.

"I don't know when I've been so sick. Brandon said there were moments when I didn't even recognize him. He also told me that Sterling was frantic at times, having not seen me for so many days."

"Poor little thing," Stacy sympathized. "He must have been so confused."

"He was. I'm still taking it slow, but it's good to be up and around and spending time with both Sterling and Brandon."

"Is everything really all right with the baby?" Stacy's voice was anxious, and Sunny was quick to reassure her.

"Everything is fine. I wasn't able to eat for a few days, and that was a concern, but I'm back on track now."

Stacy's sigh was so heartfelt that Sunny smiled.

"Do you like children, Stacy?"

"Ever so much," she admitted, her eyes alight with pleasure.

"And Tanner, how does he feel?"

"I don't know," Stacy told her honestly. "We've never really spoken of it."

Sunny hesitated only a moment before asking her guest a very personal question.

"Do you think you might be expecting?" Sunny was ready to apologize if she'd been out of line, but Stacy's face was as open as ever. She shrugged slightly before answering.

"I don't think so. But I do wonder what signs I need to look for. Oh, not the obvious of course, but my cousin Elena is never ill when she carries a baby, and I thought that was one of the first warnings."

"It's different for every woman," Sunny told her. "I know that's no help to you, but I've known women who were not sure they were pregnant for several months and others who knew within days. Chelsea told me that she wasn't sick for even a day. However, my niece Holly was ill the entire nine months."

"That sounds awful," Stacy grimaced.

"It wasn't much fun," Sunny agreed. "But God gave them a beautiful baby, and Holly said it was worth every moment."

"I imagine it was." Stacy's voice was a bit dreamy, and

Sunny couldn't stop herself from hoping that God would give this couple a baby.

Keeping Sunny's recent illness in mind, Stacy did not stay long. However, their time together was sweet. The Richardson coach was coming around for Stacy when Sunny remembered she had a wedding gift for Lucinda and Roddy. The Hawkesburys were not going to make the special event, but Sunny sent best wishes through Stacy.

As the coach started for Winslow, Stacy fingered the neatly wrapped gift, her mind going to her aunt and Roddy. A smile of pure enjoyment broke across her face knowing that Lucinda would be preparing right now for the wedding. She and Roddy would be man and wife in one week's time.

"Is everything ready at Brentwood?" Lucinda asked her man, Craig, for the tenth time that day.

"Yes, my lady. All is prepared."

"And the groom's gift?"

"He's very comfortable in the stables." Craig's voice was calm.

Lucinda nodded but didn't answer. Her mind, moving from the magnificent horse she'd bought for Roddy, was already thinking on the clothes she'd purchased for their wedding trip. She simply couldn't decide which suit she should travel in. Maybe she would ask Roddy. But the thought no more materialized when she thought of something else for Craig to do. He was on his way out of the room when she stopped him.

"And, Craig, please see that Stacy's room is ready for her."

"I will, my lady, but I assumed the duke and duchess would be staying in Lord Richardson's town house."

"You're probably right, but I want the room ready just in case."

Craig left with only a nod of his head, and for the first time in days her mind slowed to a stop. It stopped on Stacy. Lucinda smiled.

They would be coming tomorrow, or was it the next day? *Well, no matter,* Lucinda thought. *I'm going to marry the man I love, and Stacy is coming.* Lucinda was so overwhelmed with peace and happiness that she simply sat, doing nothing, until Craig came and asked if she was ready for tea.

Tanner lay back in bed, reading some papers and waiting for his wife to join him. Just moments later Stacy entered the room, and Tanner smiled to see her hair down. He opened his mouth to speak, but as she neared the bed, he noticed that her expression was a bit strained. Tanner wondered if he might have imagined it, but knew better when she climbed onto the bed and not beneath the covers. He watched her kneel gracefully on her side of the bed, not actually keeping her distance, but just out of reach. Her expression was clearly preoccupied.

"Tanner," Stacy began, her voice telling of her distraction, "are you going to Lucinda and Roddy's wedding? I'm not sure if you ever said."

"Yes, I'll be there. Has that been bothering you?"

"Not exactly; I just couldn't recall if you'd told me."

Stacy fell silent then, and Tanner watched her, wondering at her mood. He didn't have long to speculate.

"Tanner, may I talk with you?"

"Of course," Tanner answered automatically.

"I heard from Elena," Stacy began, not even looking at Tanner. "She says the girls are fine and her pregnancy is going well. She writes that she's very large but feels good anyway."

Stacy glanced at Tanner then. He was not hearing a word she said. His eyes were back on his papers. Stacy sighed inwardly and resigned herself to keeping her feelings inside. She was moving to the side of the bed to draw the covers back and climb in when Tanner realized what he'd done.

"Is that all Elena said?"

"No," Stacy told him, still standing. "But I don't have to talk about it right now."

The pain in her voice made Tanner ashamed. He forced himself to shift against the headboard with a pillow at his back for comfort. Once settled, he gave her his full attention.

"What else did she say?" His voice was gentle, and Stacy, desperately needing a lifeline, sat down on the side of the bed.

"She said that my grandfather has lost nearly all of his sight. Even on good days he can see next to nothing." Stacy's voice told of her agony. "I've known this was going to happen for a long time, Tanner, but it's so hard. It's bad enough when he has poor days, but to lose his sight completely is almost more than I can take." Stacy's voice caught, but she didn't cry.

"Does Elena say how he's taking it?"

"Actually, she does, and she says that he's doing very well. It's just so difficult when I'm not there. I know Elena is giving me a straight story, but she doesn't live with Grandfather, and he's such a private man. I wish Peters had written to me. I'm going to get a letter off to both him and Hettie before we leave for London."

Stacy was silent for a moment after that. Tanner waited for her to speak. It took a little time, and she kept her eyes on the wall as she shared.

"He's always been there for me, Tanner, a tower of endurance. He's the only father I've ever known. I hate to see him vulnerable like this."

Stacy looked at her husband then. His eyes were intent on her and tender with caring. Stacy drew in a shuddering breath.

"Will you hold me, Tanner?"

His arms came out without words, and Stacy sighed deeply as he cuddled her against his chest.

"With or without his sight, your grandfather is still the same man. The man who took you to him when your parents died, and the man who still loves you today."

"Oh, Tanner," Stacy sighed.

"It's true," Tanner continued, his voice gentle. "He'll always be Andrew Daniels, and he'd probably resent any intimation otherwise."

Stacy nodded. She'd nearly forgotten her grandfather's pride.

Seventeen

"THE HOUSE IS SET UP for the ceremony and reception now, but as soon as Roddy and I leave for our wedding trip, the staff will move everything from both homes."

Closeted in Lucinda's bedroom, Stacy and her aunt talked about the wedding that would take place in approximately 48 hours.

"Did you have to let some of the staff go?" Stacy's voice was resigned.

"Actually, no," Lucinda told her with satisfaction. "Roddy has always had a very small staff. A few of my own were a bit frantic over being made redundant, but I assured them we would need them all.

"Now," Lucinda did a quick change of subject, "Roddy is due anytime, and before he comes I want you to come with me so I can show you the wedding gift I bought."

Lucinda rose and began to lead the way from the room.

"Where is it?" Stacy asked once they were in the hall.

"In the stables."

"The stables?"

Lucinda only laughed at her niece's look and proceeded to take her outside.

Stacy had never seen her aunt as nervous as she was just one hour before the wedding. It was a small affair, less than 70 guests, but Lucinda seemed unaccountably nervous.

Stacy stood beside her in an upstairs bedroom at Brentwood. The younger woman did not speak but offered support with her presence.

Maids came and went, but at one point they found themselves alone. The room was quiet for only a moment, and then Lucinda began to speak, as though to herself.

"Aubrey was not a kind husband. I'm afraid he was very selfish and he's left me with a rather negative view over certain aspects of marriage."

Stacy, without having to be told, knew what those aspects were.

"He didn't visit me very often, but when he did, there was no tenderness or caring. We never even spent the night together; Aubrey always went back to his own bed."

Stacy knew that it was time to intervene. Lucinda's voice had grown steadily sadder until Stacy feared she might cry. Stacy went to her and gently put her hands on the older woman's shoulders. Lucinda looked up at her, and Stacy spoke with a tender type of boldness that was totally foreign for her.

"Roddy Caruthers is the kindest man in all of England. He's also the most gentle. I've never seen a man more in love than Roddy. I can imagine that it's very hard to dispel Aubrey from your memory, but he's gone and Roddy's here. Aubrey made your life miserable while he was alive. Don't let him do it to you again in his death."

Lucinda stared at Stacy with new eyes. She was so right. Lucinda took a few deep breaths and made an effort to calm herself.

"Thank you, my dear," she spoke kindly, and then began to wonder aloud about her intended.

"I wonder how Roddy is doing?"

"Would you like me to go and talk with him?" Stacy offered and saw a relief on Lucinda's face that didn't need words. After kissing her aunt and telling her she'd see her downstairs, Stacy made for the door.

Once out in the hall she was spotted almost immediately by Tanner, who came up behind her and startled a small squeak out of her.

"Oh, Tanner!" Stacy's voice was breathless.

Tanner's arms had come around her.

"You look luscious in this blue thing."

"Thank you," Stacy told him, smiling up into his eyes both with love and the fact that he called her dress the "blue thing."

"When do I get my wife back?"

"Well, I have to go see Roddy, and then I'll come downstairs."

"That's not what I meant. I mean when do you stop playing wedding so I can take you back to Winslow?"

"Well, I told Lucinda I would handle things through tomorrow, but we could leave the day after that. Unfortunately, we have a weekend party at the Cradwells' almost as soon as we get home."

Tanner's eyes closed in long-suffering. "I'd completely forgotten about that."

"It would be fine with me if we didn't go," Stacy admitted, wanting very much to be alone with Tanner.

Tanner kissed her nose. "It would be fine with me as well, but we've turned down every one of their invitations, and because Price has already accepted for us, we had better be there."

Stacy did nothing to hide her chagrin, and the adorable face she pulled gained her another kiss.

"I've got to go," Stacy told Tanner after that.

He released her reluctantly and watched as she went to Roddy's door. Stacy knocked and turned to see Tanner's long-legged strides taking him back toward the stairs. He threw a smiling look in her direction just before he disappeared from view, and Stacy's heart skipped ahead a little faster.

Stacy was swiftly brought back to the present when Roddy's

door opened. His man, Carlson, stood beyond the portal, his expression solicitous.

"Carlson," Stacy began. "May I see Lord Caruthers?"

"Certainly, my lady."

The servant disappeared into the room. A moment later Roddy was at the door.

"Why, Stacy!"

"Hello, Roddy," Stacy spoke from her place in the hall. "I was just in with Lucinda, and she wondered how you were doing. I told her I would check."

"I'm fine. How is she faring?"

Stacy sighed gently. "She's a bit nervous."

"Over the wedding?"

"No," Stacy answered, her face heating slightly.

Roddy took in Stacy's pink cheeks.

"Tonight?" Roddy was always so perceptive.

Stacy nodded, her face still warm. "It might have been presumptuous of me, but I reminded her that you are not Aubrey."

Roddy's smile threatened to stretch off his face. He leaned forward and kissed Stacy's cheek.

"It sounds as though I couldn't have handled it better myself."

Stacy's smile of pleasure was genuine.

"I'd better get downstairs," she said a moment later.

"All right. But before you go I want to thank you. I'm not sure if you remember our day in the carriage, but your words changed my life."

"I remember. I was horrified at first, thinking I'd been completely out of line."

Roddy kissed her cheek again. "Lucinda is going to be my very own, Stacy, and I have you to thank for that."

Stacy took her leave then, walking on a cloud as she moved toward the stairs. Once she gained the lower level, several people wanted to talk with her, but she finally managed to slip into the seat next to Tanner.

Just minutes later the assembly was standing for the bride. Lucinda was resplendent in cream-colored satin and lace. Three tiers made up the skirt that fell so full from the waist that it touched either side of the double doors as Lucinda entered. The boat neckline was very flattering to Lucinda's face, and Stacy felt a surge of pride over how lovely her aunt looked.

The ceremony was short and tender. No one in the room could have missed the love that radiated from both bride and groom, and in a very short time the bishop was pronouncing them husband and wife.

A marvelous array of food was presented then, all prepared and eaten in their new home. There was no wedding dance, but the bride, groom, and all guests spent hours talking and eating. Lucinda had warned Stacy that she and Roddy would be slipping away without warning, so when neither one of them could be found, Stacy smiled and knew they were headed off on their trip.

The day finished in a whirl, and Stacy, in a near state of exhaustion, fell into bed that night. Tanner was tired as well, but they had a drowsy conversation before sleep came.

"Roddy sure knows how to pick wine. The champagne was excellent."

"Was it?" Stacy asked over a yawn.

"Didn't you have any?"

"No. I don't like champagne."

"What did you drink at our wedding?"

"Water."

"Even when we toasted?"

"Um hmm. If there wasn't a servant nearby, I just pretended to have something in my glass."

Stacy fell asleep to the sound of her husband's laughter.

Just three days after Stacy and Tanner returned to Winslow, they were on the road again, this time to the Cradwell estate. Stacy would have gladly remained at home, but Tanner had said they were going and she would never have argued.

They didn't have a long drive, no more than 90 minutes, but Tanner had chosen to ride for most of the way, so Stacy was in the carriage alone. It was not exactly a lonely time, but she didn't know the Cradwells well and wondered what type of weekend it would be. The very fact that it was a whole weekend and not just an evening or afternoon was taking some adjustment in and of itself.

Coupled to this was some very real anxiety as to how well she would fit in. She would have begged Tanner to turn the coach around if she'd had even the slightest inkling of how little she would have in common with her hosts and their other guests.

Eighteen

THE CRADWELL MANSION WAS BEAUTIFUL to Stacy's eyes, but she didn't care for the grounds. Tall hedges lined nearly every walk, blocking Stacy's view of the gently rolling hills she loved so well.

Tanner led the way up to the front door, which opened immediately. Stacy glanced around the grand foyer before their host arrived. The next few moments were a confusion to Stacy, but she remained silent.

"Tanner," Jeremy Cradwell spoke as he approached. "Welcome."

"Thank you, Jeremy." Tanner shook the younger man's hand, concealing his surprise over being greeted by Lord and Lady Cradwell's son and not the senior Cradwells themselves.

"I don't believe you've met my wife, Jeremy. Stacy, this is Jeremy Cradwell. Jeremy, this is my wife, Lady Stacy Richardson."

"It's a pleasure to meet you, Lady Stacy." Jeremy didn't care for the fact that she was taller than he was—it put him off terribly—but she was the duchess. Thus he did manage to make a suitable welcome and kiss the back of Stacy's hand. "You're sure to grace our weekend with your beauty."

"Where are your parents, Jeremy?" Tanner asked as soon as Stacy had reclaimed her hand.

The younger man did not meet Tanner's eyes. "They're not going to be here this weekend."

Tanner's own eyes narrowed, but still Jeremy would not look at him. He was certain the invitation had been from Lord and Lady Cradwell. Finally Jeremy shifted his gaze from beyond Tanner's shoulders to his eyes.

"You're not thinking of leaving, are you, Tanner? I've got a hunt planned, and I was counting on you."

Tanner was just a few years older than Jeremy, but at the moment he felt like a father figure. Jeremy had never been forced to grow up. This party in his parent's home, in their absence, was just a small example of a young man who had been pampered all his life and never told no.

Without even having to ask, Tanner knew that Jeremy's guests for the weekend would all be young and single. He made a quick decision, his manner gracious, but he was still very much in control of the situation.

"We'll stay, Jeremy, but I'll warn you, if there's any foolishness, we will leave without a word of explanation or apology."

Jeremy didn't care for the note of authority in his guest's voice, but still he nodded in acquiescence. What else could he do? He was counting on Tanner, with his knowledge of the land and excellent marksmanship abilities, to lead the hunting expedition.

Tanner also held a position of power that not even Jeremy's father, with all his wealth, could match. If Tanner wanted to leave, no one would gainsay him.

Moments later a servant led Lord and Lady Richardson to their rooms. A maid hovered nearby, hoping to unpack, but Tanner told her to come back later. Stacy spoke as soon as they were alone.

"Is there a problem, Tanner?"

"Not exactly," he told her as he began to peel off his dusty riding clothes. "It's just that I hadn't realized that Jeremy was hosting this party. He can be a little wild.

"I'm more than willing to join a hunt, but Jeremy and his

friends have been known to add drinking to their sport. I'm not about to hunt with a drunken bunch of kids and get myself shot."

Stacy couldn't stop wringing her hands. She was truly frightened by her husband's words. Tanner came to her, gently rubbing her arms with his hands.

"I didn't mean to alarm you. I won't let the situation grow out of control."

Stacy nodded but didn't look very happy.

"What are you thinking?"

"That we could be snuggled in at Winslow, just the two of us."

Tanner smiled and kissed her brow. "We won't be at Winslow, but we'll make our excuses as soon after dinner tonight as we can. I too would like to spend some time alone with you."

Nigel Stanley checked his appearance in the mirror for the fourth time. Perfect. She was actually here! Stacy Daniels Richardson, whom he had worshiped from afar for so long, was finally within reach. He had never had the nerve to approach her in London, but now he would wait no longer.

The fact that she was married made no difference to him. He knew that most London marriages were a farce—without love or caring, intended only to produce an heir. Nigel knew that if he could only gain an introduction to Lady Richardson, he could win her over. He hadn't lived in England very long, having grown up in France where his father was a diplomat, but he was certain, without ever having met the man, that her husband didn't care a wit for her. Nigel fully intended to take advantage of that. He was certain that as soon as Stacy saw the love and caring in his eyes, she would understand all he wanted to be to her.

With a final glance at his appearance, he moved toward the door, rubbing his hands together in anticipation.

"Your aunt was recently married, wasn't she?" a young woman questioned Stacy that evening before dinner.

"Yes," Stacy answered. "She married Roddy Caruthers."

"It was rather a private affair, wasn't it?" another young woman approached and interjected. She sounded offended, and Stacy wasn't sure what to say.

"You make it sound like you expected to be invited, Beth," the first young woman accused. "You don't even know Lucinda Warbrook."

Beth tossed her curls. "How do you know if I know her? Why just recently I was invited to—"

"Hello, ladies."

Stacy watched the faces of her companions as a tall man stepped into their group. In an instant all angry looks were gone, replaced with brilliant smiles and fluttering lashes.

"Hello, Nigel."

"You're all looking lovely this evening," Nigel smiled at them, thinking how easy it was to converse with people you didn't care for in the least. He hadn't even looked at Stacy yet, but he could already feel his heart pounding. Fear that he would be a tongue-tied fool when the introductions were made was escalating.

Stacy stood quietly and only half-listened to their exchange. She was not really heeding their words, so when they turned to include her, she forced her mind to attend.

"This is Lady Stacy Richardson," the kinder of the two girls began. "And this is Lord Nigel Stanley."

"It's a pleasure to meet you, Lady Stacy." Nigel bowed over her hand and let his gaze search her face.

Stacy, always kind, smiled with genuine warmth. The other women, watching the exchange, shared a swift glance when they noticed Nigel's besotted look. Stacy, on the other hand, only took his attention for kindness.

"I'm going to get something to eat," Beth tossed out belligerently, miffed over Nigel's attention to Stacy. The other girl said she would go with Beth.

Stacy, having been starved for hours, asked to join them. Both girls looked at her strangely but included her. Stacy made a polite farewell to Nigel, smiling at this kind stranger who was almost as tall as her husband. She had noticed that his build was slighter, and that he was quite handsome with his dark hair and mustache, but beyond that he was of little interest to her.

Trying to decide if she'd not noticed his signals or was just being coy, Nigel stood still after she left. He kept his place at the corner of the room, watching her until he saw her husband appear at her side.

Stacy was appalled over how hungry she was. The dinner hour was scheduled for no later than usual, but she felt famished. It wasn't like her to snack between meals, but when the hors d'oeuvres table was laid out, Stacy felt she could have attacked every dish.

She was on her second plateful when she popped something into her mouth that was so salty it puckered her lips. Stacy searched for something to drink, but the only thing laid out was champagne. No one was attending the table at the moment, and Stacy wasn't sure she could have spoken if she tried. In a move of desperation, she lifted a glass and downed the contents in nearly one swallow.

It didn't help in the least; in fact, Stacy thought it made things worse. Her mouth felt so dry she couldn't even swallow her own saliva. She lifted another glass and then another. Stacy was on her fifth glass when Tanner noticed her and moved in her direction.

"I thought you didn't like champagne," he commented, taking in Stacy's flushed face.

Stacy took another sip before answering. "I don't, but I ate something so salty that I had to have a drink."

Tanner watched as she finished her glass and reached for one more.

"How much have you had?"

"Quite a bit, I think." Stacy stopped speaking suddenly and giggled. Tanner, telling himself not to think of Leslie, moved away from her without warning. His intent was to get her some real food. He had only been gone a moment when Nigel appeared at her side.

"Oh, hello, Nigel. Have you had something to eat?" Stacy's voice was too loud and cheerful, but Nigel, having missed the champagne exchange, thought it was all for him.

Before he could answer, Stacy turned to look for some more food. She wavered a bit but would not have fallen; however, Nigel used her unsteadiness for an excuse and reached for her. His hands were carefully holding her waist when Tanner reappeared.

"Oh, Tanner, there you are. Have you met Nigel?" Stacy had been barely aware of his presence or his hands on her as she searched the table, but she remembered him when Tanner returned, and did not want to appear rude.

Tanner did little more than coldly nod in Nigel's direction before taking his wife's hand to lead her away. A minute later he sat her down at a table, and a plate was placed in front of her.

"Oh, Tanner, is it dinnertime? I'm so hungry."

With that Stacy began to eat with relish. She never noticed that they were alone or that Tanner, who was sitting beside her, did not have a plate. Her food was almost gone when she couldn't restrain a jaw-popping yawn.

"I'm sorry," she apologized. "I'm a little sleepy."

"Let's head upstairs."

"All right," Stacy agreed and reached for her plate.

"Leave that here."

Stacy put it down but looked longingly at the remains. Tanner thought she'd had enough so he urged her away from the table. However, Stacy reached forward at the last minute and grabbed her half-eaten roll. It was all Tanner could do not to shout with laughter as he led his beautiful, graceful, and usually dignified wife away from the party munching on a biscuit.

Once upstairs Tanner debated turning Stacy over to Rayna, but Stacy had become very preoccupied with the doors that led off of their room, and before she put herself back out in the hall or landed in a closet, he decided to put Stacy to bed himself. All went well until Tanner got to her shift, whereupon there was a gentle tug-of-war. Stacy had decided she wanted to sleep in it.

Tanner eventually let her have her way, and the moment she lay down, she curled on her side, happy as a child, and went to sleep. Tanner stood watching her for quite some time. He was certain that she wasn't even aware of the other man at the table, and he knew with a certainty that the drunkenness was an accident, but it was all so reminiscent of Leslie.

Tanner stood silently, knowing he was going to have to deal with this or ruin the entire weekend. As he stood still he remembered the way she had thrown her arms around him and with a loud declaration of 'I love you, Tanner,' given him a long, loving kiss. The only problem was that she had missed his mouth by a good inch.

Tanner began to undress himself, finally deciding not to rejoin the party. Most of the guests had been on their way to getting far more drunk than Stacy, and Tanner had no desire to join them. He slipped beneath the bedcovers and pulled Stacy against him. As sleep crowded in, his thoughts turned to Leslie one last time. Tanner pushed them away with anticipation of the hunt on Sunday.

Nineteen

THE NEXT MORNING Stacy squinted up into Tanner's grinning face, groaned, and pulled the covers over her head. She heard the laughter in his voice as he spoke.

"Aren't you going to come out and kiss me good morning?"

"My mouth tastes terrible, Tanner; you don't want me kissing you."

He laughed out loud then, and Stacy burrowed a little deeper into the mattress. Tanner sat down beside her on the edge of the bed.

"I promise not to say a word about your breath."

Stacy remained silent.

"Or the fact that you're sleeping away a beautiful morning."

Again Tanner was met with silence.

"Rayna brought you a pot of tea and toast."

The covers were slowly lowered until Stacy's eyes were peeking out.

"Did you say tea?"

In answer Tanner poured a cup and held it for her. Stacy shifted herself up against the headboard and took the cup from his waiting hand. Her first taste was a sip, but when she found the temperature to be perfect, she took a long drink before setting the cup back in the saucer with a sigh.

"I needed that."

"And I still need that kiss."

Stacy smiled and they leaned toward each other simultaneously. After they'd kissed, Tanner invited Stacy to go riding.

"I thought you were going to hunt."

"The hunt is tomorrow morning."

Stacy hid her disappointment. She had hoped that the hunt would be today and after Tanner returned, he would be ready to head home. She knew she'd made a fool of herself in front of the other guests last night, eating everything in sight and then drinking champagne as though it were water. If Tanner had gone hunting this morning, Stacy could have stayed out of sight until they were ready to leave for home.

But Tanner was already in riding clothes. Stacy mentally shrugged. At least going riding would get her away for a time. Maybe they would be alone and Stacy would have some time away from this group of strangers with whom she had yet to find something in common.

An hour later, Stacy got her wish. She and Tanner rode out, Tanner on his own horse and Stacy on a bay. They stayed away until lunchtime. To hear Jeremy Cradwell talk, Cradwell horses were the finest in the country. Stacy was not sure she believed that, but the horse she'd been given to ride was a good mount. Stacy was more pleased over having Tanner to herself than anything else.

They were just coming out into some open land when two riders approached—a man and a woman. As they neared it became obvious that one of the guests was out riding with a groom.

Tanner greeted the woman politely but impersonally. Stacy smiled at her but looked to Tanner in confusion when he let her pass with so little exchange.

"Tanner, why didn't you speak to her?"

"I did speak to her," he told his wife. "I said good morning."

"But beyond that? Why didn't you ask how she was doing?"

"Why would I do that?"

Stacy bit her lip, having a hard time believing that Tanner could be so cold to a friend.

"Stacy," Tanner went on patiently when he saw her face. "I don't even know that woman. She looks familiar, but I'm sure we've never met. Why would I speak to her?"

"Oh," Stacy said softly, wondering how she could have been so wrong. "I'm sorry. I thought she was the woman who was with you at the Royal Gardens."

It took a moment, but Tanner's eyes suddenly lit with amusement. "I'm sure you did see her at the Royal Gardens, but she wasn't with me."

"But I saw you," Stacy said softly, wanting desperately to understand.

"Yes you did, sweetheart. You saw both of us, but we were not together. I let you assume that we were, but I guarantee you we were *not.* I followed you to the Royal Gardens that day, and I can assure you I was quite alone."

Stacy's eyes rounded, but her mouth curled at the corners. "I wouldn't have thought you capable of such duplicity, my lord." Stacy's voice was dry.

"At least I don't jump to conclusions," Tanner reminded her just as dryly, and Stacy was suddenly very glad. She had thought of the woman from the garden on several occasions, hoping that she had not been painfully in love with Tanner but unable to feel sorry that she, Stacy Daniels, had been the one to marry him.

"What does that smile mean?"

"I'm not sure I should tell."

"Of course you should."

"I don't know, I read somewhere that a woman should always keep a few secrets."

Stacy heeled her mount forward on those words, so she missed the frown that momentarily covered Tanner's face before he kicked his own horse forward to join her.

After lunch, Tanner joined an afternoon round of cards while Stacy took herself off to the Cradwell gardens. Some of them were designed as mazes, and though they were interesting, Stacy soon tired of the high shrubbery walls. On her way back toward the house, she spotted what appeared to be a conservatory. Stacy walked to it with a sense of anticipation. She opened the door and called a greeting, but no one stirred or answered. Stacy went inside and closed the door, not at all unhappy to have the building to herself.

The conservatory was lavishly filled with plants and flowers. The day was cool, and the warm temperature inside felt lovely. Stacy had wandered around for the better part of 20 minutes when she heard someone enter.

"Hello," a voice called, and Stacy came out from behind a huge fern to find Lord Nigel Stanley. She couldn't remember his name but smiled kindly anyway.

"Hello."

"Having a look around?"

"Yes. Lady Cradwell has a wonderful array of plants. She even has them labeled. It's a help to me; I've never seen some of these varieties before."

Stacy spoke with her eyes on the foliage, but Nigel Stanley had eyes only for Stacy. It had taken quite a bit of following her and bolstered courage to get this close, but now that he had, he saw that she was even lovelier in the daylight than she had been the night before.

"I'm sorry," Stacy said, finally looking at the man beside her. "I can't remember your name."

Nigel hid his disappointment. "That's quite all right. I'm Lord Nigel Stanley."

"Of course. I'm sorry, Lord Stanley. I'm Lady Stacy Richardson. Are you having a nice time?"

"Yes," he returned, smiling secretly and wanting to laugh over the fact that he might not know her name. With his eyes intent on her face, he continued.

"My weekend seems to be getting better all the time. I was hoping I'd see—"

A gong rang out just then and anything else Nigel might have added was cut off.

"What was that bell?" Stacy asked.

"Oh, that's just the gong for the forage Jeremy has planned." Nigel's voice was bored, dismissive even. "I'm sure you're not interested in—"

"The forage?" Stacy spoke with surprise and started for the door. "I had no idea it was so late. I hope you enjoy the plants, Lord Stanley." Stacy added this last thought from the doorway, only just remembering her manners, amid worry that Tanner would be looking for her. In her hasty exit she never saw the way Nigel's hands balled into fists as frustration turned to rage.

Tanner was in his third garden and had just about given up locating Stacy when he heard voices on the other side of the hedge. He didn't recognize Stacy's voice or the voices of the two speaking, and was about to move off when he heard his wife's name mentioned.

"Lady Richardson?"

"Yes. I tell you Lord Stanley is smitten with her."

"Nigel? Who told you?"

"No one had to tell me. I could see it with my own eyes. Nigel *is* nice looking, but Lady Richardson would be a fool to leave a man like Tanner."

"I wouldn't mind," the other voice giggled. "If she did, I might try to hook Tanner myself."

Tanner, telling himself not to overreact, moved away to the sound of their high-pitched laughter. He came out of the hedged-in garden just as Nigel was leaving the conservatory. Tanner stood and watched him, suddenly remembering the way he'd held Stacy's waist the night before. Tanner was in the mood for a confrontation, but Nigel, without having seen the angry duke, turned and walked the other way.

Just as well, Tanner thought to himself, logic returning. *I don't think I could talk to either one of them right now.*

With that Tanner headed back to the stable. He ordered his horse and less than ten minutes later, set out on a ride, hoping to clear his head of the black thoughts that persisted.

Stacy sat in her room long after she was dressed, not going down to dinner even when she knew everyone would be sitting down at the tables. She had not seen Tanner since he went to play cards and she had gone to the gardens and the conservatory.

In truth she was now starving, but her worry of Tanner overrode her physical needs. Stacy had dismissed Rayna and was pacing on her own when he walked in. Stacy couldn't disguise her delight.

"They told me at the stables that you'd gone for a ride. Did you have a good time?"

Had Tanner not been wearing dusty riding clothes, he'd have crushed her in his arms. It had taken many miles, but Tanner had finally seen himself for a fool. It was none of Stacy's doing if a besotted young pup gawked at her. And since Stacy was as lovely as she could be, Tanner told himself he better get used to it.

"Yes," Tanner finally answered, "I did have a good ride."

Stacy stood staring up at him, her heart in her eyes.

"I'm late. Why don't you go down for dinner?"

Hungry as she was, Stacy declined. "I've waited for you."

Tanner tenderly stroked her cheek with one long finger before calling for Price. Stacy talked with Tanner as he enjoyed a quick bath and questioned her about her day.

"I didn't really care for the gardens, but the conservatory was lovely."

Tanner tried to push down the alarm he felt rising within him. "The conservatory? You were in there?"

"Oh, yes," Stacy enthused, having missed Tanner's hesitancy. "It's wonderful. I've never seen such a variety of plants and flowers."

"Were you alone?"

"Yes. Oh," Stacy suddenly thought, "no, not all the time. Lord Stanley came in, but the hour had gotten away and I wasn't able to talk to him very long."

Tanner was dressed now and moved to stand before Stacy. He looked into her guileless eyes and again called himself a fool. His own eyes lit with caring as he bent and kissed Stacy's brow and then her lips.

"Shall we go to dinner?"

Stacy nodded, wondering at Tanner's tender look even as he took her arm and escorted her downstairs.

IT WAS WITH A GREAT DEAL OF PRIDE that the Duchess of Cambridge saw her duke off on the hunt the next morning.

Talk around the dinner table the night before had been about the hunt. Not one man, not even those jealous of Tanner's position, could find a single fault in Tanner's expertise as a hunter. Stacy had had no idea. He was, from all accounts, one of the finest shots for miles around.

Tanner took all the comments in stride, but Stacy could tell that he was pleased, and when she took time to think about it, she wasn't surprised at his skill. Stacy was starting to see that Tanner excelled at each thing he did.

With her new knowledge of Tanner's ability, and knowing that he was going to lead the hunt, Stacy wondered if the buttons on her dress would hold as she watched him ride away at the front of the pack.

Stacy felt a little lonely when all the riders had gone and the dust had died down. She glanced around at some of the women talking among themselves, but felt no warmth or effort on their part to include her. She thought about the conservatory but was, in reality, in a mood to be alone with her thoughts. After a trip to the library, she made her way up to her room and settled in with a book until lunch.

Over lunch Stacy sat with four women she didn't know and Nigel Stanley. The women talked constantly of the things they read in the London social papers, and Stacy, being in complete ignorance, stayed quiet. She noticed Nigel's eyes on her from time to time, but he was across the table and quiet himself, so Stacy finished and left the dining room as soon as it was politely possible.

She had decided on a walk, but as soon as she was outside and spotted the conservatory, she changed her mind. With everyone else still at lunch, she knew she would find it empty. Her step quickened with anticipation, even as she hoped Tanner would be returning soon and they could leave for Winslow.

Nigel could barely hold his seat or his tongue once Stacy rose and left the table. The remaining women, vulgar cows in his estimation, began to talk of her in scathing tones. They started by declaring that she was a giant, was socially inept, and wouldn't hold the duke's attention for more than six months. Nigel secretly hoped they were right about the last item.

He knew that this was his last day to declare himself. Nigel sincerely doubted they could meet at length before the party was over, but if he could only tell her he was available, she would certainly jump at the chance to meet him later. He knew very well how busy most dukes were. It was just a matter of time before Tanner began to neglect his bride, and when Stacy began to look for attention elsewhere, Nigel determined that he would be in view.

With a move as casual as he could manage, Nigel rose from the table. He would go right now and find Stacy in order to tell her of his feelings. As Nigel made his way toward the door, he deliberately pushed away all he'd seen of Stacy and her husband over the weekend—every tender glance and every loving touch. He staunchly refused to believe that the duke and duchess might genuinely care for one another.

Stacy walked slowly through the glass building, amazed at how much she'd missed the day before. She thought she'd heard someone come in the door just a moment past, but no one called out and Stacy didn't even look. Whoever it was, she knew the structure was big enough so that they could stay out of each other's way. It only took a moment before Stacy had completely forgotten that anyone had come in, making it all the more startling when Nigel suddenly appeared at her side.

"I was hoping I'd find you here."

"Oh!" Stacy gasped, her hand flying to her throat. "You startled me."

"I'm sorry," Nigel's voice was tender. "I wanted to talk with you."

"Oh." Stacy smiled now. "What did you need?"

Now that he had her full attention, Nigel found himself tongue-tied. She was so lovely and tall. He could just imagine how well she would fit in his arms.

Nigel stood mute for so long, his eyes glazed over with passion, that Stacy's smile turned into a confused frown. Seeing that frown, Nigel thought she might be thinking of leaving. He acted in haste and grabbed her hand. When Stacy gave her hand a tug, Nigel would not release her.

"Lord Stanley," Stacy began, "please let go of me."

"No."

Stacy's breath caught. "I'm a married woman," she said on a gasp.

"That's all right," he declared fervently. "I need to touch you, and now that I have I know nothing matters except the two of us."

Stacy's eyes grew round at this announcement, and she tried in earnest to regain her hand. Nigel only transferred his hold to her wrist. Stacy began to panic.

"Please, Lord Stanley—"

"Call me Nigel. I'll call you Stacy, and you can call me Nigel."

Stacy shook her head and tried to move away, but with Nigel holding her wrist, it was impossible.

"Please," Stacy tried again, fear now pounding in her chest. "You're hurting me."

Nigel dropped her wrist immediately. Stacy reached for and rubbed the offended member, and then turned to run for the door.

"Please don't go!" Nigel's voice, now strangely high-pitched, stopped her. Stacy turned to him and began to back away, suddenly afraid to take her eyes from him.

"Stay away from me," she spoke with more calm then she felt, glancing behind her to see that the door was in sight. "I'm sorry if I gave you an impression to the contrary, but I am happy in my marriage."

"I love you," Nigel told her, "and I know that you love me too."

"No, Lord Stanley." Stacy's calm was deserting her, and she knew she was going to make a run for the door any moment. Nigel knew it too. The next time Stacy glanced to the exit, he grabbed for her.

Stunned to be grasped and pulled against this stranger's chest, Stacy did not immediately react. But only seconds passed before she put her hands against his chest in order to push him away. Stacy, no weak thing, did manage to put some space between them, but when she threw her head back in order to gain more leverage, Nigel put his lips against her neck.

Stacy begged him to release her and struggled in earnest, but he was too strong. The blood was just beginning to pound in her ears when she heard Tanner's voice. At least she thought it was Tanner's voice—she'd never heard him so angry.

"Get your hands off my wife!"

Nigel released her, and Stacy half-fell against one of the shelves. She righted herself and looked up to see a Tanner so furious, he terrified her. He had come at Nigel and was now holding him by the lapels. As upset as Stacy was over the attack, she suddenly feared Tanner's actions more, feared he would kill this man in anger.

"Tanner, please, don't."

He spun on her, still gripping the other man and pinning Stacy to the floor with his gaze.

"Protecting your lover?" he snarled.

"No!" Stacy denied breathlessly, aghast that Tanner could ask such a thing.

"Your wife and I are in love."

Both Tanner and Stacy turned to look at Nigel. Stacy couldn't believe her ears. Tanner had dropped Nigel's coat-front, but he truly looked capable of homicide.

Stacy opened her mouth to say something, but Tanner cut her off.

"Get out of my sight, Stanley. If I ever see you again, I'll kill you."

For the first time since he entered the conservatory, Nigel pulled himself out of his dreamlike haze. He looked at the fury in the duke's eyes and actually feared for his life. He ran for the door without a backward glance.

Wanting desperately to be taken into Tanner's arms, Stacy was jolted to the core when he turned his icy gaze on her.

"Get to the house and have Rayna pack your things. You have 15 minutes to be in the coach, or I'll leave without you."

Stacy could only stare at him. She saw the clenching of his jaw, a sign of pure fury, but seemed unable to move or speak.

"Did you hear me, Anastasia?"

His voice was calm now, deadly calm. Fear spiraled through Stacy as she ran for the door herself.

Twenty-One

THE 90-MINUTE RIDE HOME TO WINSLOW was the longest of Stacy's young life. Tanner was on his horse and she was alone in the carriage with her own torturous thoughts. Shudders ran over her frame repeatedly as she thought of the way Nigel had grabbed her in the conservatory.

At one moment Stacy glanced down to see a ring of dark bruises around her wrist. It was almost more than she could take. She had been bruised and manhandled, and Tanner obviously thought she'd welcomed Lord Stanley's attention. Stacy finally curled into a ball on the seat and tried not to think about anything the rest of the way home.

Two hours after they'd arrived at Winslow, Stacy lay in a steaming tub. She had searched for Tanner for over an hour, but he was not to be found. There was no doubt in Stacy's mind that this was deliberate.

The servants, never very congenial to Stacy, were extremely remote, and after an hour of their cold treatment, Stacy had sought out Rayna and a hot bath. She was not the least bit hungry for the food Rayna brought on a tray, so Stacy soon climbed into bed. It was early, but she was feeling so weak she was not even certain she could sit up in a chair.

Sleep did not come swiftly, but even as the time stretched into hours of restless tossing and turning, Tanner did not appear. It was well after midnight before exhaustion claimed Stacy, and even then it was not a relaxing night.

Stacy did not know until morning that Tanner had not been to bed all night. Feeling more tired than she'd ever been in her life, she dragged herself from beneath the covers and moved to her dressing room. Once over the threshold, Stacy saw something that stopped her in her tracks.

"Rayna?"

"I'm sorry, my lady." There were tears in the servant's voice. "Lord Richardson said I was to pack all of your things."

Stacy's hand came to her mouth. The action was almost too much for Rayna.

"Would you like some tea, my lady?" The servant's voice broke.

"No, Rayna, thank you. Please just help me dress."

This task was accomplished in some haste, and without a word to her maid, Stacy went in search of her husband. Her legs felt weighted, as did her heart, but she had to find out what was going on.

Stacy found Tanner in his study. There had been no answer when she knocked so she was surprised to find him at his desk when she opened the door and peeked inside.

"Tanner?" Stacy spoke softly, but he did not raise his head from the papers he was studying.

Stacy was trembling, but she entered the room anyway. After closing the door she stayed by the portal, hoping he would speak or at least look up. He did neither.

"Tanner, may I speak with you?"

"Has Rayna finished with your packing?" Tanner finally looked up, but his voice was so detached that Stacy found herself preferring his anger.

"I'm not sure. Where are we going?"

"*We* are not going anywhere. You are leaving."

"Where am I going?" Stacy's voice shook, but she somehow managed the words.

"I don't care where you go."

Stacy could not believe her ears. She knew that Tanner was upset with her, but nothing could have prepared her for this.

"Tanner," Stacy's voice spoke of her hurt and bewilderment. "Can we talk?"

"There's nothing to talk about," he stated. Some anger had entered his tone now, but his voice was controlled as he went on.

"I've been a fool to actually believe you were different, but you're not. You're as faithless as other women. You're better than most with your innocent eyes and sweet smile, but you couldn't keep the pretense up forever—the very reason I never wanted another wife."

"You didn't want a wife?"

"No." Tanner had finally stood, but his voice was still calm and cold. "Lucinda would never listen to reason. I never wanted you for a wife, only for a mistress. I was a fool to have agreed. Were you only my mistress, your little meeting with Stanley wouldn't have made a bit of difference."

"Tanner, I didn't meet Lord Stanley in the conservatory. I didn't ask him to kiss me or touch me."

It was the worst thing she could have said. Mentioning what Nigel Stanley had done turned Tanner's face a dull red. He was so furious that Stacy would have fled the room, but she couldn't make her feet move.

"Get out," his voice was low with fury.

Stacy managed to turn then. Her hands were trembling on the knob, attempting to open the door, when Joffrey pushed it toward her from the other side. Stacy stepped back and stood in surprise, but Joffrey barely glanced at her as he entered the room and spoke.

"Lady Richardson's bags are ready, my lord."

"Load them in the coach." This said, Tanner returned to his desk.

Stacy stared again at Tanner's bent head.

"Please, Tanner," she whispered, knowing he heard her. "Please let me stay so we can talk about this."

He never looked in her direction. Knowing that she could not take his disapproval any longer, Stacy waited only a moment. With her stomach churning so that she feared she might be sick, Stacy walked out of the study, leaving the door open behind her. The front door was open as well, and Price stood near. Rayna appeared out of nowhere with Stacy's cloak and ushered her outside; Price followed.

"The coachman will take you wherever you wish, my lady," Price informed Stacy.

"But I can't stay here." It was more of a statement than a question.

She sounded so much like a pitiful child being driven away from home that Price had to clear his throat before answering.

"No, my lady."

"The London town house?" Stacy asked, not thinking where else to go.

"No, my lady. I'm sorry."

"I don't know where to go." Stacy knew it was not normal to discuss this with a servant, but she had no one else.

"If I might make a suggestion," Price hesitated, but Stacy only looked at him. He went on gently, "I'm sure your Aunt Lucinda would welcome you."

"Aunt Lucinda? I don't think she and Roddy are back yet."

"I'm sure their staff would make you comfortable."

Stacy looked to Rayna, who nodded, certain of their welcome. "Come into the coach, my lady. We'll go to London and see your aunt."

Stacy had no idea how she looked. There was no color in her face, and the servants had watched her sway on her feet several times. If they didn't act quickly, they'd be forced to lift her unconscious body into the coach. Price knew that even if she did faint, it would not soften the master's heart.

Stacy finally nodded. She walked down the steps and turned to look back at the home she loved. She'd never seen anything to match its beauty and grandeur. Now with only a brief look, and hoping against hope that she would see it again some day, Stacy turned back, allowing Price to assist her into the coach. Moments later they were on their way to London.

"Stacy," Lucinda called to her great-niece from the edge of the bed, waiting for her to awaken. Stacy did stir, but very slowly. Lucinda's heart broke as she watched her smile, eyes still closed, clearly having forgotten the events of the last three weeks. Lucinda wanted to break down when the smile abruptly died and her eyes opened.

"I'm sorry to wake you, dear," she spoke quickly to cover her emotions. "I thought you would want to know that Tanner is in London." Lucinda knew this was abrupt, but believed it to be best.

Stacy pushed herself into a sitting position, her eyes intent on her aunt's face.

"Did he come here?" Stacy tried to keep her voice neutral, but Lucinda caught the note of hope.

"No, dear. Roddy was out last night and saw him at their club. You were asleep when he came in, and we thought it best not to wake you."

Stacy nodded, her gaze going to a distant point across the room. Prior to the last three weeks Stacy had never known the true meaning of pain. The coach ride from Winslow to Brentwood was made in a fog of disillusionment and hurt. The honeymooners had not arrived, but just as Price had predicted, the staff welcomed Stacy and made her comfortable.

A week had passed before Roddy and Lucinda made an appearance, and although they were upset over the fact that Tanner had sent her away, they were not at all upset that she had come to them.

The entire story emerged from both sides in the days that

followed. Stacy told Lucinda and Roddy everything that transpired and then asked Lucinda point-blank what Tanner had meant when he said he'd never wanted to marry her. The telling had been hard, but Lucinda started with all she knew of Tanner's first wife, including her infidelity and death. She then told of Tanner's offer for Stacy.

It had been the hardest thing Stacy had ever faced. For months, even before she and Tanner married, Stacy had convinced herself that this man loved her but just couldn't say the words. Now she knew that the words would never come because he didn't feel them.

"What are you going to do?" Lucinda broke into her reverie.

Stacy took a deep breath. "I've decided to return to Middlesbrough. I was going to tell you today. I'd planned to write Tanner about my decision, but now that he's in town, I'll try to see him."

"Are you sure you want to go all the way to Middlesbrough, dear?" Lucinda couldn't hide the pain in her voice. "What if you had a place of your own? I haven't done anything with my house, and Roddy still has his town house."

Lucinda would have gone on, but Stacy's sweet voice stopped her. "I can't take London, Aunt Lucinda. The gossip kills me. I don't feel I can even show my face. And there is something else."

Stacy hesitated, and Lucinda stared at her.

"I think I might be pregnant."

The older woman's heart sank in her chest. "Will you tell Tanner?"

"No" was Stacy's soft but immediate reply. "I have found that I don't really know Tanner at all, but I do know that even though we've been apart, he still won't want anything to do with me. There is a remote chance that by telling him I'm pregnant I might change his mind, but knowing that he wanted me back only for the baby would put me in agony for the rest of our marriage. I'm not even positive that I am expecting, but if there is a baby and Tanner ever wants me, I want it to be for me and not because of our child." This was all said calmly, but with conviction.

Lucinda nodded throughout Stacy's explanation and when she finished, urged her to follow her heart. Stacy had grown up so much in the last months, Lucinda couldn't have been prouder. When Lucinda left the room so Stacy could dress, the feeling of pride still lingered, but so did a feeling of loss, the loss of Stacy's innocence.

Two hours later Stacy stood in front of Tanner's town house and tried to breathe normally. She was so fearful of his anger that she wanted to climb back into the coach and return to Brentwood. One thing was stopping her. Almost everything had changed in the last weeks, but there was one fact in this whole ugly mixup that had been unfailing. Stacy was still head over heels in love with Tanner Richardson.

She wished it wasn't so, but wishing was not going to change her heart. So with a feeling of doom hanging over her head, Stacy went to the door and knocked. She nearly sagged with relief when Price answered the door.

"Hello, Price." Stacy's voice was hesitant. "Is he here?" Stacy's heart had leaped into her eyes, and even knowing how Tanner was going to react, Price could not turn her away.

"He's here," Price told her and drew her inside.

"May I see him?" Stacy asked as soon as the door closed.

"He doesn't really care to be disturbed." Price attempted to soften what Tanner had actually said.

"Oh, Price, I'm sorry to put you in this position, but will you please ask him to see me?"

Price nodded reluctantly, and Stacy stood still as he moved to a door off the entryway, leaving it open as he let himself inside.

"I told you I wanted quiet." Tanner's voice was little better than a growl.

"I'm sorry, sir, but Lady Richardson is here and would like to see you."

"Well, I *don't* care to see her. Tell her to get out."

Stacy had expected nothing more, but she still felt as if she'd been slapped. She remained still until Price reappeared, again leaving the door open. The loyal servant said nothing, only looked at Stacy and felt an urge to kick his long-time master.

"Maybe I could leave a message for Lord Richardson," Stacy suggested, trying to keep her voice from shaking. Price nodded and did nothing to stop Stacy when she moved toward the open portal. Stacy halted just outside where she could see Tanner at his desk. He never looked up, but she knew he heard every word. She spoke to Price without ever taking her eyes off her husband.

"Please tell Lord Richardson that I'm taking the train to Middlesbrough to my grandfather's. Tell him that if he wants to talk with me, he only needs to send word and I'll return immediately. I don't plan to come back unless he contacts me, but, please," Stacy's voice wavered and she hesitated before going on, "please also tell him that I love him."

Stacy stood for just a moment longer, but Tanner never looked up. Price, seeing that she had gone deathly pale again, gently took her arm and led her to the door and down to the waiting coach. He saw her on her way, silently holding his own anger in check over the way Tanner had treated her. How Lord Richardson could think that Stacy was anything like Leslie was beyond him.

Price hovered nearby for most of the day, hoping that Tanner would come to his senses and go after her, but the young duke never left the house. It was with great pain that Price received word the next morning that Stacy had taken a northbound train out of London.

Twenty-Two

MIDDLESBROUGH
SIX MONTHS LATER

STACY CAREFULLY LOWERED HERSELF into a chair and smiled at Elena's laughter.

"You can laugh, Elena, but I'm not sure I'm going to live through this," Stacy said good-naturedly.

"Trust me, you will. And you'll be so thrilled with the little person God gives you, you'll actually forget all of this discomfort."

"I hope you're right. I can't believe I've two weeks to go."

"You might not go that long," Elena said as she studied Stacy's huge abdomen. "You certainly *look* like the baby could come anytime."

"Tanner is a large man; maybe the baby is just big." Stacy gently rubbed her stomach as she spoke.

Watching her, Elena felt an ache beyond words for the pain Stacy had known these last months. But at the same time, she rejoiced, for it was because of that pain that she'd come to Christ. Stacy came home from London ill with grief and exhaustion. She'd been welcomed with open arms by her grandfather, and they were as close as they'd ever been, but it was to Elena that Stacy turned for comfort.

It was during some of the first days, when Stacy was beside herself with anguish, that Elena gently introduced her to the One who could fill the void in her heart and soothe the pain. In a quiet moment with both Noel and Elena present, Stacy surrendered her life and heart to Jesus Christ. She'd always heard of the death, burial, and resurrection of Jesus Christ, but she had never applied any of the facts to herself in a personal way.

Elena had pointed out in a tender way that the Bible, God's Word, says that all have sinned and need a Savior. Stacy read the Bible verses herself and realized for the first time what a supreme act of love God had displayed by sending His Son to die in her place. With a heart aching to be comforted, Stacy reached out in belief to accept Christ's gift of salvation.

"Any word from Tanner?" Elena asked gently, as she often did—not to pry, but so Stacy would know how much she cared.

"No, no word."

"Do you still write?"

"Every week."

"What do you usually say?" Elena voiced a question she'd never broached before.

"I tell him about village events and how grandfather is doing. Sometimes I talk about you and Noel and the children. I even tell him how I fill my days."

"But you never mention the baby."

"No. I've been tempted, Elena, I really have. But whenever I feel that I just *have* to tell him, I remember that he thinks I've been unfaithful. He probably wouldn't even believe that the baby is his."

"How about your newfound faith? Do you ever talk about Christ?"

"Not in so many words. Tanner can be so hard, and I'm afraid of his scorn. I'm sure he'll think I've turned into some kind of religious fanatic. I tell him I'm praying for him, but I never come right out and say I'm a new creature in Christ."

Elena nodded, thinking Stacy was the most amazing woman on earth. Elena had met Tanner Richardson only once, and now found herself having to fight the feeling that the man did not deserve a wife like Stacy. She knew that Stacy, a wonderful example to Elena, continued to show love to him even after he'd sent her away with a coldness that was frightening. Stacy's explanation of Tanner's first marriage was a great help, and although Elena didn't understand, neither did she hate Tanner. She continued to pray for him even as she was completely confused by his actions.

A sharp, indrawn breath from Stacy suddenly snapped Elena out of her musings. Elena looked over to see Stacy breathing hard, her face a mask of shock. As the contraction abated, she spoke.

"That hurt," she gasped.

Elena's voice was tender. "Yes, it does, but you really will be all right."

"I want to go home, Elena." Stacy's voice was just short of panic. "I want to see Papa."

Elena didn't answer because she was already ringing for a servant. Within five minutes Stacy was headed to Morgan, Elena by her side. Stacy had another contraction in the coach and another as she walked in the front door. Hettie was there to assist her, and her grandfather, who was almost completely blind now, hovered nearby. Elena spoke words of encouragement as they made their way upstairs, and all of them wondered if it was going to be a long day and possibly a longer night.

"She's lost a lot of blood."

The physician's voice came to Stacy as if through a fog. She wanted to open her eyes and ask whom they were talking about, but her body wouldn't obey. At least the pain was gone. Her brow furrowed when she realized she hadn't heard a baby cry. Wasn't all the pain supposed to give her a baby? Again she wanted to ask questions but couldn't seem to make herself speak. She floated on the brink of sleep for some moments before she drifted out completely.

It was a day and a half later, when Hettie was forcing water down her throat, that Stacy woke to coherency. It took a moment to find her bearings, but after just a second of awkwardness she lifted her head and drank with thirst. Hettie's eyes were suspiciously moist by the time Stacy lay back down with a sigh.

"Thank you." The younger woman's voice was little better than a croak.

Hettie had to clear her throat before she could speak in her matter-of-fact tone. "I thought we were going to lose you, love."

"My baby, Hettie." Stacy's senses were quickly returning to her, and she gave no thought to her own life. "Where is my baby?"

"He's in the cradle yonder."

"He?"

"Um hmm. A boy—the biggest I've ever seen."

"A boy." Stacy said out loud, but in her heart she prayed as a strange mixture of delight and sadness filled her.

I've given Tanner an heir, Lord. Will he ever know? Will he ever want us back? My little boy is the future Duke of Cambridge. Will the present duke ever acknowledge him?

Please give me peace. Please help me to see Your hand in all of this so I can go on and be the mother I need to be. Please cause Tanner to miss me and send for me.

A verse came to Stacy then, one from Philippians 4, exhorting believers to give up anxiety and put everything in God's care. She meditated on the words until she felt drowsy again. She would have dropped off, but the sound of a small cry brought her fully awake.

The little person in the cradle was at full volume by the time Hettie got to the cradle, lifted him into her arms, and brought him to his mother's side. Hettie jostled him gently as she spoke.

"Do you feel up to nursing, love? I've a girl here from the village, a nice clean girl named Felicity whose baby is a month old. She's let him nurse since she's plenty to spare, but I thought you might want to do it yourself."

Stacy could only stare at the longtime servant. What was she talking about? Had she really been asleep that long?

"What day is it, Hettie?"

Hettie saw the confusion in her mistress' face and kindly explained.

"The baby was born late Wednesday night and this is Friday morning. We had to get him some nourishment."

Stacy nodded, her face clearing. She wouldn't have believed she could sleep that long, but then she realized how achy her body felt. Suddenly the doctor's comment about the loss of blood made sense. The thought of another woman feeding her baby was a bit disconcerting, but she was glad someone had been found.

"Well, love," Hettie went on, "do you want to give it a go? I've no doubt you'll have plenty of milk, but it's a full commitment once you start."

Every inch of Stacy's body ached, but at the moment all that mattered was the howling infant just out of her reach. With the rise of Stacy's arm, Hettie moved. She gently laid the little lord in the crook of his mother's arm and fought tears once again.

Stacy took one look at the screaming infant and laughed. He was red with fury, his face balled up in anger, and Stacy didn't know when anything was so precious or so funny.

"Shhh," she spoke softly, laughter still filling her voice. "Don't cry, my darling. Mummy's here."

To Stacy's delight and amazement, the baby stopped crying and turned yet unfocused eyes toward her voice.

"There now," she continued tenderly. "Everything is going to be fine. Hettie and I are going to take very good care of you." Stacy spoke for a few minutes longer, but the infant's fascination with the voice was quickly overridden by hunger. Once again he began to howl.

With a bit of maneuvering Hettie helped Stacy into a position on her side so she could nurse her baby. Her body screamed at her to lie still, but she ignored its demands and stared in fascination at the child who finally lay quiet at her breast. He was beautiful, with a head full of blond hair and skin like the petal of a rose. In fact he was pretty enough to be a girl. Stacy said as much to Hettie.

"It might be better if he had been" was Hettie's negative comment.

"Why do you say that?"

"If his father gets wind of his arrival, he'll probably come and take the boy."

Hettie did not stick around after she spoke these depressing thoughts, and Stacy, who suddenly had much on her mind, was glad for some moments alone.

"What are you going to call him?"

The question came from Andrew Daniels as he sat at Stacy's bedside. After feeding the baby she had slept for a time, but now she'd had some lunch. Even though she was as yet unable to sit up, she felt much refreshed and was thrilled with her grandfather's presence.

"I was thinking on that just before I fell asleep. He's going to be Andrew." Stacy watched as a look of delight came over the old man's face. "Andrew Tanner Richardson, and I'll call him Drew for short."

Andrew cleared his throat a few times. "It's a fine name. He's a fine boy."

"He is, isn't he?" Stacy's voice held the tone of a child desperately needing approval. Again Andrew cleared his throat.

"We almost sacrificed you to have him, and I wouldn't have cared for that, but I'm glad he's here."

"Are you really glad he's here? I mean, I made such an awful mess of my marriage. I wasn't really sure you'd be pleased about my having Tanner's child."

The viscount's face tightened in anger. "The breakup of your marriage was not your fault, and I don't want to hear you say such a thing again. It's your husband who's the loser. He's got a beautiful wife and now a son, and it's *his* loss for not claiming either of you."

Stacy had grown very quiet in the midst of his anger. When the old man was done, he turned fading eyes to her face. He could barely see her, but the serenity in her gaze was unmistakable. She had changed so much since coming home and spending time with Elena. At first it had been hard for Andrew to see her turn to Elena so often, but then he watched her go from despair to hope and he could no longer find it in his heart to begrudge her the help.

And if the truth be stated, Stacy's relationship with Elena had caused no distance between her and the man who raised her. Grandfather and granddaughter were as close as they had ever been.

"Are you going to write Tanner and tell him he has an heir?" The question came after just a moment of silence, but Stacy answered immediately.

"No. I seriously doubt that his knowing would change anything, and it would only feel like one more rejection."

"But you will continue to write to him?"

"Yes. As soon as I'm on my feet again. I tried to get Hettie to take down a letter for me, but when she found out it was to Tanner, she refused."

Andrew nodded. Hettie had muttered to herself for an hour after Stacy's request, and it wasn't at all hard to figure out what had set her off. The older woman had never taken to Stacy's marrying someone from London, no matter who he was. Then when she'd met him, she thought him too good-looking and smooth to be real. Once Stacy returned to Middlesbrough, and Hettie had heard the entire story of the way she'd been sent away, dislike had turned to loathing.

Andrew's reflections were interrupted when Stacy yawned. "I'd better let you get some rest," he commented.

Stacy smiled sleepily. "I could use some sleep. Hettie said that Felicity has been wonderful, but Drew can be rather demanding and I want to continue feeding him myself." This was punctuated with yet another yawn as Stacy's eyes slid shut.

She was almost asleep when her grandfather rose to leave and was uncertain later if he tenderly touched her hair and cheek or if she only dreamed it.

Twenty-Three

More Than
Two Years Later

"Would you like something, Lady Stacy?"

"No thank you, Mercy. Grandfather should be here any minute, and I'm really not hungry."

Stacy fell silent then and continued to watch her son eat. He was working on bread with jam. A cup of milk sat at his elbow, and he already sported a milk mustache. Completely unconscious of the adorable picture he presented, Drew sat staring out the kitchen window at the half-dozen ducks that waddled complacently across the grass.

"You look miles away," Mercy commented as she sat down beside Stacy and studied the younger woman's face. Stacy knew that this type of familiarity with servants was unheard of at Winslow or even at Roddy and Lucinda's, but this was all Stacy had ever known.

"I just can't believe he's two," she told Mercy with a voice of wonder. "I don't wish the months back, but I do wonder where the time has gone."

"It flies, it certainly does. Did you say Lord Andrew is going with you today?"

"Yes. Drew misses him terribly when he doesn't come to the pond, and that was all Grandfather had to hear to be

"Drew." Stacy's voice was stern without being loud. "You will go with Peters immediately, and you will not fuss about it!"

Drew stood for just a moment, and Stacy watched a look of acceptance come over his face. She spoke again. "Kiss Grandpapa and then come and kiss me."

Drew did as he was told, and just moments later he was skipping off with Peters, chattering fifteen to a dozen. The two remaining fishermen were quiet for a time, but Stacy was fairly certain she knew what her grandfather was thinking. She was correct of course, and when he spoke, it was confirmed.

"You should have let the boy stay."

"I appreciate your not saying that in front of Drew, but you're wrong. He needs his nap."

Andrew chuckled. "I wouldn't have believed anything could change you so much, but becoming a mother certainly has."

"I will admit that becoming a mother alters everything, but the greatest changes in me have little to do with motherhood."

"You mean this thing between you and God?" Andrew's skeptical voice spoke volumes.

Stacy sighed very quietly. Her grandfather refused to believe that a person could have a personal relationship with God or his Son, but at least he was talking. This was the first time he'd brought the subject up. Stacy was usually the initiator, and when she did talk of her beliefs Andrew changed the subject very quickly. Seeing an open door for the first time, Stacy chose her words carefully.

"I believe the Bible, God's Word, to be true. And in His Word, I've read how much I mean to God and how much He wants to mean to me. My belief is a choice, Papa, one that I'm more than satisfied with."

"What about the church?" It was a sore subject between them.

"The bishop never has answers to my questions," Stacy explained as she had before. "I don't think he studies the Bible at all. I haven't given up on the bishop, but it concerns me that he only stares at me in dismay when I ask questions and tells me that I must not take the Bible too literally. Well, that's absolute rubbish." Stacy's voice was very earnest, but not accusing or angry. "Noel and Elena have spent enough time in God's Word to help me. If they don't have an answer to my questions, they at least know where to look.

"The Bible is our standard and if we shift our foundation, we're going to fall. It was in the Bible that I read that because I was a sinner without a Savior, I was headed to a lost eternity. But I've now met that Savior, and I know where I'm headed.

"I love you, Papa, but I think the very reason you argue with me is that you're afraid. You have no peace about your eternity, and that terrifies you; it would me also. I have peace, and if you would let me read the verses to you, I could show you how to have it too."

"Does your Bible also teach you how to speak disrespectfully to your elders?"

Stacy wanted to cry, but now was not the time. She hadn't been disrespectful, and they both knew it. Her voice was gentle when she went on, and unbeknownst to her, somewhat defeated.

"I'm sorry if you find me disrespectful, but if that's all you got out of what I just said, I'm even more sorry for what the future holds for you."

A heavy silence fell between them, and Stacy prayed. She asked God to give her patience and not to say things that would antagonize her Papa or drive him further from the truth. She loved him so much, and it was at times like this that she had to remind herself that God loved him more.

You are not the one who saves, Stacy, she said to herself.

"I'm ready to go in now," Andrew said then.

"All right," Stacy answered simply and rose to help him. In the past she would have apologized for what she said, but just in the last few days she had realized that was a mistake. She needed to be bold for Christ. She had spoken the truth, and she couldn't possibly be sorry for that.

That her grandfather expected an apology was more than obvious by the time they arrived at the house. He stood just inside the kitchen, his face turned toward her, a look of confused anticipation in his eyes. Stacy did not satisfy him.

"Would you like me to get Peters or ask Mercy to fix you something?"

Andrew was silent for a moment, and Stacy knew he would opt to go to his room.

"Peters, please." His voice was low, and Stacy had all she could do not to throw her arms around him and beg his forgiveness. It was so hard to admit that the man you have always loved and respected was wrong. She swiftly moved from the room before she could change her mind.

"Does Grandpapa love Jesus?"

Stacy smiled. It was bedtime, and Stacy had just read Drew a Bible story about Jesus and His disciples. What a question to come from her son the very day she'd laid things on the line to her grandfather!

"I'm not certain how he feels right now, Drew, but we can pray that he'll understand how much God loves him."

"God loves me."

"Yes, He does," Stacy agreed and wrapped her arms around his sturdy little form.

He was the image of his father, and at times it pained Stacy to look at him. He was tall for his age, which was no surprise, and other than Stacy's straight, thick, honey-blonde hair, he was every inch Tanner Richardson's child.

Because Drew lived in a houseful of adults, his speech habits and vocabulary were rather advanced. She read to him from the Bible every night and was amazed at how much he retained, and how excited he became whenever Jesus was in the story. Stacy believed his understandng of the Scriptures was a gift from the Lord.

It had been a temptation to sugarcoat the truth of Christ's death and resurrection, but Stacy had not yielded. She knew well that this was the foundation of all she believed. The sooner Drew understood, the sooner he could make his own decision and commit himself to Christ. Stacy prayed for his belief every day as she did for her grandfather's and everyone else's at Morgan.

She also prayed for Tanner. She asked God to prepare his heart for acceptance. Stacy was beginning to believe that she would never see him again, but still she prayed. Each and every time she considered writing about Drew, she knew it would be a mistake. But at some point Stacy knew she needed to explain to Tanner about what had happened to her concerning Jesus Christ.

Tanner had always been cynical about things concerning the church, something that had never bothered Stacy before to any great degree, but now it made her fearful of how he would respond to her beliefs. "Religious fanatic" was sure to be the nicest thing he would have to say.

The thought gave Stacy no peace, and she wrestled inside of herself often as she tried to give her husband to the Lord. At times she would lie in bed and dream about their first weeks together, when he made her feel treasured and cherished. Stacy ached for her husband's love, but knowing how godless their life had been cast something of a damper on her memories.

Tonight as Drew fell asleep, Stacy remained by his bed and let herself remember. After a time she prayed.

"Please save Tanner, Father, and bring us back together. I know You love him, and I believe You would want us to raise Drew together. How long do I wait, Lord? He never acknowledges my letters. I know unless he sees him, Tanner will never believe Drew is his son, but You can work this out, Lord. You can move in hearts and lives so that Your will is done and You are glorified."

The day ended, but Stacy's faith and hope did not. Days and weeks passed. She continued to pray, committing her life and loved ones to God. But time moved on, and before Stacy's eyes she watched her son blossom toward his third year. At the same time, she watched her grandfather wither as he approached his last.

Twenty-Four

DREW GALLOPED ALONG BESIDE HIS MOTHER on the way to the pond, pausing now and then to inspect a stone or watch a bird. It took some time, but eventually he turned and noticed that Peters was not following with his grandfather.

"Where's Grandpapa?"

Andrew had not fished with them for several weeks, but Drew still asked after him every time they went.

"He wanted to rest today." Stacy's line was becoming standard. "We can go to his room as soon as we're done, however, and show him our catch."

Drew seemed content enough with this, and Stacy was glad when he did not chatter on. Her grandfather's ill health was a source of great concern for her these days, and some quiet hours at the pond were just what she needed. However, Drew had other ideas. He was quiet only until he remembered the special event of the next day.

"Are we going to have cake?"

Stacy smiled. He knew they were because Mercy had talked of nothing else for days, but she answered him anyway.

"Yes, we're having cake."

"And surprises?"

"Surprises too."

"When?"

"Oh, maybe a little bit all day."

"I'll be two."

"No, you're two now. Tomorrow you'll be three."

"Please show me the fingers."

Stacy placed her pole on the ground and used both of her hands to carefully position Drew's tiny fingers until three stood in the air.

"This is three," he stated.

"That's right. Tomorrow you'll be three."

"How old are you?" the small boy suddenly asked.

"Very old," Stacy told him with a twinkle in her eye.

"Two hundred?"

Stacy laughed and grabbed for him. She tickled him and laughed at his small giggles until they both lay spent on the ground. After just a moment Drew heaved a great sigh and sat up in order to peer down into his mother's face.

"I love you, Mumma."

"I love you, Andrew."

"I'm Drew."

"I love you, Drew."

The little boy smiled, and Stacy smiled in return. They didn't fish again for a time because Drew wanted to hear a story. Stacy told him all about Noah and the ark God told him to build. Before Stacy could finish naming the animals that came two by two, her almost three-year-old had fallen asleep in her arms.

"It's a train, Grandpapa! Look at it, look at it."

Drew shoved his favorite birthday present into his great-grandfather's hands and waited for him to respond. They were sitting around the fire in the main salon, for Morgan was cold until midsummer.

"Well, now," Andrew spoke with proper seriousness. "An engine. Who's going to drive this fine train?"

"Me," Drew nearly shouted and proceeded to make the sound of a train so his great-grandfather would be convinced.

"And who will you take on your train?"

"Mumma and Mercy and Hettie and Peters."

"What about Grandpapa?" his mother wanted to know.

"Oh, yes!" Drew shouted as he climbed into the old man's lap, never seeing his grimace of pain. "Grandpapa will be up in the engine with me, won't you, Grandpapa?"

"Of course I will." Andrew's voice sounded strong, the only thing that kept Stacy from removing her son from his lap. Drew was not a tiny child any longer, and Stacy knew how frail her grandfather's legs had become. His color was better today, however, and Stacy took that as a sign of hope. Just four nights past he'd labored for breath for several hours. They had thought it the end.

"What else did you receive?" Andrew asked of Drew.

The child named a few items, but his concentration was on his train and he didn't really answer. Believing that respect was important, Stacy would have said something, but her grandfather looked so content to have Drew now leaning against him and playing with his train that she went ahead and told him herself.

"He received a pair of long britches from Hettie. They're dark brown and fit him perfectly. A red flannel shirt came from Mercy. It's trimmed with brown cord and looks wonderful with the trousers. Peters gave him a wooden whistle, and Noel, Elena, and the children gave him the train. The train is red with black wheels and trim and printed on the side are the words 'London and Birmingham.' I bought him a new comb, and I knitted him an afghan for his bed. It's every shade of green and quite large—wide enough to cover his entire bed."

This said, Stacy placed the edge of the blanket in her grandfather's lap so he could feel the weave. Drew had moved to the floor, so Andrew took a moment to handle the blanket.

"Very soft," he approved. "You always do nice work."

"I'm glad you think so, because I'm working on one for you."

"Do I have to wait for my birthday?"

"No. I'm over half done; you should have it sooner than that."

Andrew nodded. "Drew?" he spoke softly.

"Yes, Grandpapa?"

"Come up here a minute. I want to give you my present."

The word present was enough to shift Drew in a hurry. He put his train aside, and by the time he stood before Andrew he was squirming with excitement.

"This gift belonged to me when I was just your age. I'm going to give it to you, and I want you to take very good care of it. Do you promise?"

"Yes, Grandpapa."

Stacy had no idea what the gift would be, and both she and Drew grinned in delight when Peters suddenly appeared with a child's wooden rocking chair.

"Oh, Mumma," Drew exclaimed. "It's for me!" With that he plopped his small bottom into the seat and began to rock. His mother's voice came to him very softly, but with warning.

"Andrew."

"Oh," he jumped from the chair and moved to Andrew. "Thank you, Grandpapa. Thank you for the rocking chair."

"You're welcome. Does it fit you?"

"I fit," he told him and sat back down to prove it, even though the old man couldn't see.

Watching her grandfather, Stacy felt something tug inside of her. He suddenly looked older and more tired than Stacy had ever seen him, but there was also a contentment about him. Stacy wondered if maybe the rocking chair had been quite special to him and giving it to Drew, his only great-grandchild, was more significant than any of them realized.

"I believe I'll rest now," Andrew told them and stood to go. Drew hugged his legs before he got away, and Peters began to lead him from the room.

"I'll bring you a tray later," Stacy called to him.

"All right," he said and kept walking. Stacy watched, unable to decide if he was moving more stiffly or not. She prayed then as she always did that he would understand his need for Christ while there was still time. Her prayers had been increasing lately and held a special urgency. It seemed clear that Andrew's time with them was coming to an end.

Two days later, in the middle of the night, Peters wakened Stacy from sleep. She had been dreaming about Tanner and Drew, and her first thought was for her small son.

"Is it Drew?"

"No, Stacy. Your grandfather is asking for you. He's having trouble breathing again."

Stacy's wrapper went around her as she ran, and within seconds she was at her grandfather's bedside.

"I'm here, Papa," Stacy said and watched his eyes open. She knew the lamplight made no difference to him, so she turned the wick higher in order to see him.

"Stacy" was all he said before staring sightlessly in her direction.

"I'm here, Papa. Don't try to talk."

The old man's eyes closed, his breathing labored on. Stacy's own breath came in gasps as she realized he might be slipping away before her eyes. Suddenly his eyes opened.

"I need to tell you something."

"Please don't try to talk," Stacy begged him, thinking he needed to conserve his strength.

"I talked to God, Stacy. For the first time, I really talked to God. I've lived my life for myself, but when I almost died last week, I knew I wasn't ready to meet Him. I think I took care of it, but tell me again, Stacy. Tell me how you come to God."

Stacy's voice shook with emotion and she didn't know how she would speak, but the words came. "The Bible says believe on the Lord Jesus Christ and you will be saved, Papa. I simply told God that I need to be saved from my sins and that I believed His Son could save me. I asked Him to be the Lord of my life."

Andrew's eyes closed again. "It's taken care of then. I was certain that it was, but I needed some reassurance from you. I'm not afraid to die now. I wish I could be here with you and Drew for years to come, but my body is tired and I'm not afraid to go. God will take care of both of you. I'm sure of that for the first time."

"It might not be time, Papa." Stacy was so overcome with emotion she could barely talk. "Just rest now. I'll be here."

The old man nodded and slept for nearly an hour. Stacy sat in a chair right by his side, her heart so full she could hardly move. Her grandfather had come to Christ! Her heart was overflowing with thanksgiving. She wanted to shout and dance.

He's Yours now, Lord. I would love to have more time with him, but even if tonight is the night, he's Your child and You've given us both your peace. Stacy, whose throat was clogged with tears, couldn't pray anymore. She sat trembling, half with fatigue and half with joy, her heart too full to form thoughts.

Stacy had just began to doze when Andrew woke. He asked Stacy to read to him. She chose the Twenty-third Psalm, a psalm she'd read all her life, but one that had taken on new meaning in the last three and a half years. She was now certain it would be new to her grandfather as well.

She read and then prayed, and Andrew listened as best he could. The night moved on in such a manner—Andrew and Stacy dozing for a time and then waking to share the Scriptures again and again. Andrew said little through this, speaking only once to thank her for showing him the way, to tell her of his love and to ask her to tell Drew of his love also.

In her exhausted, emotional state, his words were almost more than Stacy could bear but she praised God for hearing them since this was in fact Andrew's last night with her. He fell asleep just before dawn, and this time he did not waken.

Stacy had no more than let Drew finish his breakfast before she scooped him up and headed to the pond. She sidestepped all of his questions concerning his grandfather and didn't really start to talk to him until they were seated by the big willow that sat at the edge of the water.

"Where are the poles?"

"We're not going to fish today, Drew. I need to talk with you."

"We can't show Grandpapa our catch."

"No, we can't, but our having a talk is more important right now." Stacy stopped then. Where to start? He was so little, but she knew he had to be told. He was much too aware of Andrew's movements to hope that he wouldn't notice or miss him.

"I talked with Grandpapa last night, and he told me something wonderful," Stacy began as Drew sat in her lap and looked trustingly into her eyes. Her voice wobbled only slightly, but she continued. "Grandpapa told me he loves Jesus. Isn't that wonderful?"

"We love Jesus too. And God," Drew told her with big eyes.

"Yes, we do," Stacy said with a smile, knowing he did not yet understand that God and Christ were one.

Stacy glanced up at the tree, wondering how she should continue. She had to tell Drew that his Grandpapa was gone, and she simply didn't know how.

"I think that fish is dead."

Stacy's head snapped down in surprise. She thought he'd been watching her, but she now saw that his attention had begun to wander. Stacy's own eyes drifted to the dead fish that floated on the water, and suddenly she had the words.

"How do you suppose that fish died?"

"I don't know," Drew answered, his eyes intent on the already decomposing fish.

"Things do die, don't they, Drew?"

"Um hmm. Mercy and I saw a dead mouse in the kitchen."

"I remember that. Drew," Stacy called his name and waited for him to turn to her, "people die too. Did you know that?"

The small boy didn't answer, but only stared at her. The subject was new to him.

"Everything dies—mice, fish, and even people, but when that happens we know that it's all a part of God's plan. He gives life, and He says when it's time for someone or something to die."

Stacy hesitated. Drew still watched her. Tears filled her eyes when she said the next words. Drew had never seen his mother cry.

"Grandpapa died this morning, Drew. His body was old and tired, and God said it was time for Grandpapa to leave this earth. Before he died though, he told me he loved Jesus, and that's why I'm certain God took him to heaven to be with Him.

"He also told me that he loves you, but that he knows and trusts that God is going to take care of you and me. We won't have Grandpapa here with us anymore, Drew, but God is going to take care of us."

It was not surprising that Drew had no questions. She knew that much of what she said had been too old for him, but she would just keep telling him and reassuring him until he understood.

Stacy had already thought out the aspect of Drew seeing Grandpapa's body and decided she would not subject him to that. The man he knew—the loving, alive, vibrant man—was gone. She saw little or no point in showing Drew his cold, white, earthly shell.

They took a long walk before going back to Morgan. In that time Drew did not mention his great-grandfather. Not until he was going down for a nap did he say he wanted to see him. Stacy had to remind him that the old man was gone, and Drew cried because he wanted his grandfather and didn't understand why his mother would keep him away.

Stacy allowed him his tears and lay next to him long after he slept. Stacy's own tears finally came. Not a torrent, because her wonder and joy over Andrew's salvation was too wonderful for it to be a time of complete sadness. She joined Drew in his nap while she was still praising God for His saving love.

Twenty-Five

THE MOURNERS AROUND THE GRAVE were few. Andrew Daniels was an old man, and many of his friends had passed on before him. The bishop was present, but Stacy had asked Noel to officiate the ceremony. He did a wonderful job, and Stacy nearly broke down several times as Noel honored and praised God for His love and mercy. That, as well as the way Drew's little hand clung to her own, made her aware of just how vulnerable Drew was right now. She felt him tremble at times.

She knew that this had little to do with the actual death, because he did not fully understand the word, but his world had been turned upside down with the "disappearance" of his great-grandfather, as well as the appearance of strangers in the forms of Roddy and Lucinda.

They were positively taken with the child, but he was still feeling a bit overwhelmed with the events of the last days to get overly close to them. They wisely did not push their attention on him, but Lucinda broke down on several occasions over what she exclaimed was the most precious child in all the world. Such actions were unusual for her, but Stacy believed it had much to do with the passing of her brother.

Everyone gathered back at Morgan when the funeral service was over. The staff was visibly upset, but all rallied and prepared a large meal for the mourners. Stacy acted as hostess, seeing to it that all were comfortable. It never occurred to her to have someone else take over. Lucinda would have been the logical choice, but she was too distraught to do much of anything.

At one point, when there was a lull in the activities, Stacy and Elena found themselves alone. They embraced warmly.

"Did Noel tell you about Papa's decision?" Stacy asked.

"Yes." Elena's eyes were glowing.

"Oh, Elena." Stacy's voice was awed, her own eyes wide with wonder and joy. "I've been selling my Lord short. I never dreamed He would save Papa so near the end, but He did. I already miss him so much, but God has given me such a peace that I can hardly—"

Stacy had to stop. Sometimes words weren't necessary between close friends; this was such a time. Elena hugged Stacy again before they finally made themselves comfortable and really began to talk.

"Roddy and Lucinda have already talked to me about coming back to London with them."

Elena nodded. "Roddy spoke with Noel. What are you going to do?"

"I'm not sure yet. The thought of leaving you is dreadful, but what if this is God's way of repairing my marriage? I know that Tanner is never going to come here; he's had over three years to prove that. Maybe if I was back in London, he'd want to see me."

"And that's what you want?" There was no censure in Elena's tone, only caring.

"As frightened as I am of Tanner, I would like my marriage back. I would desperately love for Drew to know his own papa. When Lucinda mentioned our coming to live with them, she also offered to get us a place of our own if we preferred that, so I know we'll be taken care of. I just don't want to do anything that's going to be harmful to Drew. Tanner can be so hard, and the London gossips can be ruthless."

"You could always give it a try," Elena told her.

"What do you mean?"

"I mean that Noel, the children, and I are going to move here to Morgan just as we all decided, but Noel would never get rid of our place. It's not very big, so if things don't work out for you and Drew in London, you can move back here, either to Morgan or our house."

"Oh, Elena" was all Stacy said. Such a thought had never occurred to her. For weeks now she'd prayed about some way to open a door between her and Tanner, and now this might be it. She knew she was going to have to be the one to reach out, and although her faith was small concerning the outcome, she was willing to try.

The image of Tanner's angry face, as he'd been in the conservatory and then at Winslow the day he'd sent her away, flashed through her mind. The fear she felt took her breath away.

"Stacy, what is it?" Elena had watched her pale.

"I was thinking of Tanner. He still has the power to terrify me, but I've got to do this, Elena. I don't know how I'll be when we're finally face-to-face, but I've got to try to save my marriage."

"It's going to be all right, Stacy." Elena's voice was soothing. "I've already gotten a letter off to Sunny about Andrew's death, knowing you would be too upset to write. You've had lots of contact with her in the last few years, and I know she'll be there for you if you return.

"I certainly can't predict what Tanner will say, but knowing that Sunny will be there, a sister in Christ, comforts me over your leaving."

"In all the uproar, I'd forgotten about Sunny and Brandon," Stacy admitted. "It does make it easier to go, knowing how close they live."

"So you think you'll be back at Winslow?"

Stacy nodded. "I don't know why, and I don't think it will be easy, but, yes, I think I will end up back at Winslow. The only thing that would stop me is if Tanner refuses to let Drew come with me. If that happens I'll return here."

"Drew is the image of his father. How could he turn him away?"

Stacy's smile was sad. "By not seeing him at all. You don't know Tanner, Elena. He can be very hard. He thinks I've deceived him, so I dare not hope that he will even want to see Drew."

Elena could only stare at her. This had never occurred to her. Stacy didn't notice her look. Her mind was running from one person to the next. First she saw Drew, and then she saw Tanner.

If it comes down to proving Drew's parentage, Stacy thought, *I won't need to say a word. Tanner need only see his son's face.*

"I won't let her tell me no, do you hear me, Roddy? I tell you I won't leave here without them."

Roddy did not answer from his place in the bed, but continued to lean against the headboard and watch his wife's agitated movements. Her voice wobbled with unshed tears.

"I had no idea they had so little. Did you see the furniture in the salon? It's a mess. All this time they've been living like paupers, and I've had so much." Lucinda broke down then just as she'd been doing for days.

"Come on, Cinda," Roddy called to her and pulled the covers back on her side of the bed. Lucinda moved with leaden steps and climbed in, sobbing all the while.

"Did you see Stacy's dress?" Lucinda wailed as Roddy pulled the covers around her. "It's one from her wedding trousseau. She hasn't had anything new in all this time. I just can't stand it." The tears increased for a time before subsiding into huge shuddering breaths. Roddy waited for just such a time to speak.

"I think Stacy will come with us."

"You do?" Lucinda's voice held hope.

"Yes, especially if you let me handle it. Now, don't be hurt," Roddy added when he felt her stiffen in his arms. "Stacy and I have always been able to talk, and I think she will be honest with me. If you really want her and Drew to come home with us, you'll let me handle it."

"I do, Roddy. I desperately want them to come." All anger had drained from Lucinda in the light of wanting Stacy and Drew with them. Lucinda was willing to try anything.

"I do also, but there are some things we need to talk about." Roddy paused before going on firmly. "Lucinda, you must let Stacy mourn as she wishes."

"What do you mean?"

"I mean, no balls, no teas, and no shopping unless she wishes to do so. This will be nothing whatsoever like her first visit. She's been married and now has a child. The growing up she's done in the last three and a half years is remarkable.

"Since we've arrived, I've watched how she handles Drew. A more devoted mother I've yet to see. Carlson has talked to the servants here at Morgan and tells me that motherhood is what it took to make Stacy bold. She will brook no interference with the way she raises her son, and from what I can see she needs no outside help.

"Cinda, you must examine why you want them to come with us. If it's to play mother to that boy, then it won't work; he's already got a mother. If it's to mother Stacy or run her life, then it still won't work. She doesn't need a mother or anyone to tell her what to do. She needs a friend with a listening ear, even if you don't agree with all her decisions."

Lucinda stared up into her husband's face. He knew her so well. She did like to run other people's lives and took it for granted that they wanted her to, but Roddy was right about Stacy. She was a different person now. She'd even gone to calling them by their Christian names without using aunt or uncle. It was yet another sign of her maturity.

Lucinda suddenly realized that it had been Stacy who had been the pillar of strength for everyone at the funeral and then downstairs in the large salon. This young woman, whose only parent-figure had just died, was the one to see that all were taken care of and comforted in this time of loss. She had become an independent and capable woman in her own right. Lucinda wasn't certain that she was even needed, but she still wanted Stacy and Drew with them more than she could say.

"What if Tanner wants her back?" Lucinda voiced the thought as soon as it surfaced.

"Then that will be her decision." Roddy returned logically. "It doesn't seem likely. They've had no contact and he hasn't even asked about her in all these years, but nevertheless, Stacy will make her own choice and we will support her no matter what."

Lucinda sighed. Again he was right.

"Will you speak with her in the morning?"

"Yes, as soon as I'm able."

Lucinda was quiet for a time. "Is my face all puffy?"

"It's just terrible. I can barely stand to look at you."

Lucinda tried not to smile, but it didn't work. "I love you, Roddy."

"I know," he said with a wide, cheeky grin. "And you know the feeling is quite mutual."

Hearing those words, Lucinda sighed again, this time with pure contentment.

"Uncle Roddy and I would like to talk. Can you find Mercy and see if she needs some help?"

"I want to stay here," Drew told his mother.

Stacy glanced over his head at Roddy, who was sitting patiently across from her in the library. She didn't want to send Drew away because he wouldn't understand and he'd been rather clingy that morning. Stacy understood completely; still, she did want to speak with Roddy.

"Why don't you see what Aunty Lucinda is doing?"

"Aunty Lucinda cried."

"Yes, she did. But she's not crying now. She would be very happy to see you."

"You can ask to see her jewelry. It's very pretty," Roddy put in. Even though Drew was considering the idea, he was clearly not convinced. To Stacy's relief, Mercy chose that moment to ask Drew to test some cookies in the kitchen.

"Can I bring some in here?" Drew wanted to know before he left.

"In a while," Mercy told him while Stacy was still trying to frame a reply.

"All right," he said, but he didn't look very happy. Stacy gave him a silly smile on his way out the door that wrung a small laugh from him just before he disappeared from view.

"He's a fine boy, Stacy."

"Yes, he is," she agreed, her eyes still on the closed portal. "He's more precious to me than I can say."

"You've done a good job with him."

"It's a lot of work, but he's a delight to be with."

They fell silent for just a moment, Stacy wanting to tell Roddy that she and Drew would come to London but waiting in case he and Lucinda had changed their minds about the offer.

"I think you know what I want to ask you, since we've already talked of it," Roddy began, "but before you give an answer, I want to tell you a few things. I've reminded Lucinda that this will not be like your first visit. We are not going to take over your life or Drew's life. We want you to come and stay as long as you like, but we aren't going to parent you; we realize you don't need that."

Stacy smiled so widely that Roddy stopped.

"What are you thinking?" Roddy's eyes widened comically in mock anticipation.

"I was going to tell you, yes, I would like to come, but then I was going to ask you if Lucinda realized that it would be different this time." Stacy's voice was so relieved that Roddy laughed.

"She'll be thrilled with your answer, Stacy, as I am."

"I appreciate the offer, Roddy. It feels as though we've been thrown a lifeline." Stacy paused then and went on slowly. "But there is something you should know. I'm hoping above all hope that if I return to London, Tanner will be willing to see me. He certainly hasn't been an exemplary husband, but if there is hope for my marriage, I'm willing to try. I would also like Drew to know his papa."

"Have you ever told Tanner about him?"

"No. I'm sure you understand why."

"Indeed, I do. It doesn't matter to us why you're coming; we just want you there." Roddy stopped for a moment and looked unsure. Stacy understood his expression when he continued.

"I see Tanner now and then, and I'm sorry to say that he's never asked about you. Please don't get your hopes too high, my dear."

Stacy sighed deeply, but it was no more than she expected. "Thank you, Roddy. If the truth be known, I'm feeling rather pessimistic about the whole thing. If at any time I feel there is any threat to Drew, I'll leave immediately, but I must try. For the sake of Drew and my marriage, I must try."

"Lucinda won't be thrilled, but I know she'll stand by you."

Stacy thanked Roddy, but beyond that she didn't reply. She knew that should they disagree on some issue, she was finally ready to face her aunt without fear, but she wasn't so confident about her husband. The thought of his anger was still enough to make her physically ill.

Twenty-Six

LONDON

"I'VE GOT NO BUSINESS running halfway across the country at my age."

Stacy ignored Hettie's grumbling just as she'd done for the last hour. They were all exhausted from the train ride and even though Stacy had told Hettie to leave the unpacking for the next day, she refused. Stacy was going to give the other woman just a few minutes more, and then she would shoo her out so Drew could sleep.

The train ride had seemed endless. Saying goodbye to Elena and the staff at Morgan had been a draining experience. Stacy half-believed that she would be with them again soon, but leaving the security of their love and heading into a future that was all a mystery had hurt.

At least Stacy had Hettie along. Hettie was not the easiest person to live with, but she loved Stacy and Drew to distraction, and she never said a critical word concerning Stacy's faith in Christ. This had not been the case with Peters or Mercy. Both of them had struggled with the change in her. It had taken Stacy quite some time to finger the reason, but she eventually deduced that her conversion was threatening to them. Things eased after a time, but neither one was open to the gospel.

Now she was in London. No real doors, not even on the train, had opened up for Stacy to talk with Roddy or Lucinda, but Stacy hoped that even if they disagreed, they would take on Hettie's attitude and not Mercy's.

Thinking of Mercy right then made Stacy want to weep, a sure sign that she was too tired. Drew had eaten and was now playing with his train, but she could see that he was drooping. Fighting the urge to bathe him, she decided to put him to bed immediately. With surprisingly little fuss she convinced Hettie to abandon her unpacking, and within minutes Drew was tucked up for the night, with Hettie going to bed as well.

Stacy bathed herself, pleased to have Rayna assisting her after three and a half years apart. In a reasonably short time, Stacy was ready for her own bed. She'd made one final check on Drew and wasn't at all surprised to find Hettie on the sofa in his room. She had a room of her own, but old habits die hard, and Hettie was used to guarding over Drew like a mother bear with a cub.

It was with a smile that Stacy finally placed her head on her own pillow, able to hear the old woman snoring all the way from Drew's room. Just before sleep came, however, Stacy's thoughts turned to Tanner. She tried to push them away, but didn't succeed. In her dreams she was almost certain that she could feel his arms surrounding her.

"Andrew Tanner Richardson, *what* are you doing?" Stacy asked her son two mornings later.

"Sliding. Aunty Lucinda said I could."

Stacy turned unbelieving eyes to her aunt, who was standing nearby. "Did you really give him permission to slide down the banister?"

"Yes," Lucinda answered meekly and then hurried on excitedly. "It really is all right. There aren't many things for Drew to play with here, and I really don't mind."

"Lucinda." Stacy's voice had turned patient. "The buttons on some of his trousers will scratch the handrail."

Lucinda shrugged helplessly, looking much like a child caught in the act. "I want him to have fun, Stacy, and that's difficult in a houseful of adults."

"He has never known anything but a houseful of adults," Stacy reminded her aunt, and stared at her until she nodded. She then turned to Drew.

"You may slide down the banister. But," Stacy added when his face lit and he started toward the stairs, "an adult must be with you, and you must be wearing the right pants."

"Are these?" Drew shoved his stomach out until it seemed he would topple. Stacy hid a smile.

"Yes."

The word was no more out of Stacy's mouth when Drew went charging for the top of the stairs. Both she and Lucinda watched as he slid down the banister, giggling all the while. He was allowed to slide four more times, and then it was time for breakfast.

Roddy, Lucinda, Stacy, and Drew all ate together in the small dining room. The day before, their first real day at Brentwood, had been very low-key with meals taken in their rooms. This was the first meal where Drew had eaten with his elders. Roddy and Lucinda were so fascinated by Drew's manners and eating habits that they barely talked to Stacy.

It was at this time that Stacy realized they would never have grandchildren; Drew was as close as they would ever come. She suddenly saw her son through their eyes. He was immeasurably precious to her, but in the eyes of a "grandmother," he was a treasure without equal. A treasure who could slide down the banister and even scratch it, play in her expensive jewels, or eat chocolates for breakfast. A treasure who never really did anything wrong, at least not intentionally.

"Aunty Lucinda."

"Yes, my darling."

"I don't like red grapes."

Stacy was proud of the way Lucinda opened her mouth, closed it, and looked to her without answering.

"I want you to eat your grapes, Drew," his mother intervened.

"I like green grapes," he told her.

The table was silent as Stacy reached for Drew's plate and swiftly cut some of his grapes in half.

"See. They're a little green inside. Now try one and if you still don't like them, you only need to eat the grapes I've cut in half."

Drew did as he was told and ended up eating them all. Lucinda was finishing her coffee when the little boy wanted to get down, so she gently washed his hands, making a great game of it, and took him away to see the garden.

More coffee was poured for both Roddy and Stacy, and they began to talk with the ease of old friends. Roddy shared some London events, what the Queen and Prince Albert had been doing and the latest battle in Parliament, but for some reason Stacy's mind strayed to the last time she was in this home.

Lucinda and Roddy were just married, and she had just been sent away from Winslow. Suddenly Stacy pictured Nigel Stanley's face and asked a question that had long been on her mind.

"Has anyone heard from Nigel Stanley in all of this time, Roddy?"

"No, actually. There were various rumors after you left. Some said he sailed for America, wanting only to escape with his life. Some say that Tanner tracked him down and had it out with the man, and that's why he's not been seen again."

Roddy's last statement so alarmed Stacy that she paled.

"Stacy," Roddy admonished her softly. "The gossip mongers love a sensational story. You don't really believe Tanner capable of murder, do you?"

Tanner's livid, almost unrecognizable face swam before Stacy's eyes. He'd told Nigel that if he ever saw him again, he would kill him.

"Stacy?"

"I don't know," she admitted. "He was so angry, and he did threaten Nigel before we left the Cradwells'."

"Oh, I heard about all that, but that hardly makes him a murderer. Men say strange things when they're enraged."

Still Stacy did not look comforted. She didn't want to even consider that Tanner could do such a thing, but that was exactly the way she was thinking. She said as much to Roddy.

"I understand why you might feel that way, Stacy, but try to put it from your mind. I really don't think there is any validity to it. And if you do plan to see Tanner, suspicion is the last thing you need clouding your judgment."

Stacy's shoulders sagged with relief. Roddy was right. The whole idea was nonsense. Her hand covered his where it lay on the table.

"Thank you, Roddy. I need your level-headed logic."

"No thanks necessary, my dear. It just shows what a wonderfully compassionate person you are that you would be concerned about the man whose actions caused you such pain."

"I have prayed for Nigel from time to time, and I'll continue to do so when he comes to mind."

Roddy stared at her, simply amazed. He wouldn't have believed that Stacy could be any more tranquil or compassionate than she had been the summer of 1853, but she was. There was a peace and tenderness about her that was nearly irresistible. Roddy was very drawn to her, not romantically, but as a loving father who delighted in her company. He also had the feeling that if Tanner ever got within close proximity, he would be as overpoweringly drawn to her as Roddy was himself.

"Have you thought about contacting Tanner yet?" With thoughts of Stacy's husband, Roddy asked the first question that came to mind.

"I've thought about it but not decided on anything definite. Do you have any ideas?"

"Would you rather be in London or go to Winslow?" Roddy needed to know.

Stacy thought. "I don't want to see Winslow again unless I can stay. I loved our home, and going out there only to be sent away might be more than I could take. I guess I'll bide my time and hope he comes to London."

"I think that's wise. I don't believe I would try to surprise him; men don't like that. If he comes to town, I would send a note asking if you could call or if he would like to meet you somewhere. Who knows, he may even be willing to come here."

"Do you think so, Roddy?"

Roddy patted her hand and shocked Stacy speechless with the next words out of his mouth. "Even if he doesn't, my dear, you just keep praying. God will take care of you."

"God made flowers," Drew told Lucinda as they sat on a bench in the garden and ate the cookies that someone had delivered to them from the kitchen. "He made the whole world, even the animals and birds."

"Did He now?" Lucinda murmured absently, not really hearing Drew's words, just feeling delight that he was becoming more comfortable with her. He was such a gift, a balm of sorts, applied directly to the ache inside of her over her brother's death.

"May I have another cookie?"

"How many have you had?" Lucinda was making a genuine effort not to spoil him.

"I think 200," he told her with a great smile.

Lucinda laughed and hugged Drew. This was the scene Roddy came upon.

"Well, it looks like you two are having fun."

"Indeed, we are," Lucinda told him, her arm still around Drew.

"Where is Mumma?" Drew was looking beyond his Uncle Roddy, his brow lowered in concern.

"Your mother is inside. Did you want to go and find her?"

Drew nodded with relief and jumped down from the seat. He ran along the path to the house. Roddy and Lucinda followed more slowly.

"Oh, Roddy," Lucinda spoke when he was out of earshot. "He's so dear."

"That he is, just like his mother."

"What is Stacy doing?"

"I'm not certain. We were discussing Tanner. She might be writing to him."

"If he comes," Lucinda said after a rather pregnant pause, "he'll take them away, and we won't have Drew."

"We can always go see them."

"What if Tanner doesn't allow that?" Lucinda felt panicked over the thought.

"Tanner has never had any argument with us, and too, Stacy is different. She's stronger now. I don't know how she'll be with Tanner, but I just can't believe that she wouldn't allow us to see her or Drew."

"I hope you're right, Roddy." Now Lucinda's voice was wistful. "I truly hope you're right."

Twenty-Seven

"HOW DOES A TRIP to the Royal Gardens sound?" Stacy posed the question just two days later and stunned nearly everyone at the breakfast table. Not knowing what she was talking about, Drew went on eating his toast. Lucinda was clearly uncertain, and Roddy put his newspaper down to look at her.

"We wouldn't need to make a great show of it," she explained. "But I would like to get out, and I know Drew would enjoy the paths and flowers. If you'd rather not join us, I'll understand. Hettie will be with us. I'd like to go right there and come back. We wouldn't stay overly long, but mourning or not, I *need* to get out."

A silence that lasted an entire minute fell over the table.

"I think it's a good idea," Lucinda finally said, her voice serene. "I'm going to stay in for now, but I do think you should go. Roddy, will you be joining them?"

"Unless you'd like me to stay."

Lucinda smiled at him, and Stacy saw a glimmer of the aunt she remembered. Since she'd arrived in Middlesbrough, she had not been the same.

"Thank you for offering, but I shall be quite fine alone. Now, Drew," she added, "you're going to be visiting the Royal Gardens, one of my favorite places. You must come back and tell Aunty Lucinda everything."

Drew nodded. "Mumma, what is Roll Gardens?"

"Royal Gardens," Stacy corrected him with a smile. "They are much like Aunty Lucinda's gardens, only larger and with more flowers."

And so they were off. Roddy wisely ordered a closed carriage for the ride, and Hettie joined them inside. Drew was allowed to look out the window, and his questions were nonstop from beginning to end of the journey.

The gardens were all that Stacy hoped they would be—a riot of springtime color that was so glorious to see and smell that she wished they could stay all day. Drew had inherited his mother's love of the outdoors, and just as she knew he would he ran and skipped until his face was flushed with exertion and pleasure. At one point he spotted a fountain and nearly turned inside out with excitement.

"Oh, Mumma! We can fish! We can fish!"

"No, my darling, we can't. This is a fountain, not a pond."

Drew looked crestfallen for just a moment, but then he spotted a bird and once again they were off. Hettie trailed after him, this time with Roddy and Stacy coming in their wake. The paths had not been crowded in the section they traveled, but whenever they did pass someone, Stacy averted her face. Roddy was sensitive to this and did what he could to aid her privacy.

Stacy was not ashamed, just desiring as little publicity as possible. The desire for solitude and the beauty of the day reminded her of Morgan, naturally turning Stacy's thoughts to her grandfather. She couldn't help but think how much he would have enjoyed this stroll with them.

Then Stacy remembered her last hours with her grandfather as well as the last time she was here. The last time she'd been to the Royal Gardens she had not yet understood her need for a Savior, but God had reached down and rescued her, just as He had her grandfather. She continued her walk with a heart filled with joy and prayers that her life would be a testimony of God's saving grace.

Roddy, Stacy, Drew, and Hettie had only been home from the gardens for two hours when Craig came to Stacy's bedroom door. As usual, his manner was formal, but Stacy knew he genuinely cared for her.

"You have a visitor, Lady Stacy."

Stacy had written a letter to Tanner but had not sent it. Still she wondered if it might be him. Her heart pounded in her chest before Lucinda's head servant continued.

"The Duke and Duchess of Briscoe are waiting for you in the large salon."

Sunny and Brandon.

"Thank you, Craig." Stacy beamed at him and nearly ran down the stairs when he held the door for her. She didn't stop to school her features or fix her hair, but burst into the room like a small child at Christmas.

Sunny rose as soon as she saw her, and the women met in the middle of the room in a huge hug. They separated long enough to laugh and stumble over each other's words before hugging again. When Sunny released Stacy at last, Brandon was there to take her place. Tears stung at the back of Stacy's eyes at the feel of his solid arms. He was so like Tanner in height and build.

"How are you?" Sunny asked when she'd finally claimed Stacy's hand and pulled her over to sit beside her on the settee. "I'm all right," Stacy smiled at both of them. "Did Elena tell you in the letter?"

"About your grandfather? Yes!"

The women hugged again.

"Tell us about it," Brandon urged, and Stacy did. There were tears swimming in Sunny's eyes when she was done.

"I miss him so much," Stacy admitted. "But knowing where he is gives me such a peace. I keep seeking out verses that talk about heaven, so I can try to imagine how wonderful it must be."

"Study verses about God too, Stacy." Brandon spoke now. "Heaven is God's home, and when we know Him, I think heaven and our time with Him becomes clearer. There is even a verse in Revelation, chapter 21, that says there is no sun or moon in the new Jerusalem, which is heaven, for God's glory illuminates that holy city."

"Thank you, Brandon." Stacy's voice was awed and humble. "There is so much I don't know. Thank you for telling me that."

He smiled at her, and Stacy's heart turned over. *Oh Father,* she prayed silently. *Please save my Tanner. Please give us a marriage like this one—one that's built in You.*

"Have you seen Tanner?" Sunny's question cut through Stacy's thoughts.

"No. I don't think he's in London right now. I've written him a letter asking him to see me, but I haven't posted it. I'm afraid I don't have high hopes. He hasn't wanted me in over three years, and I doubt if that has changed."

Sunny reached for and squeezed Stacy's hand. "We're still praying."

"Thank you. Brandon, do you ever see him?"

"From time to time."

Stacy couldn't disguise the love in her face or her voice. "How is he?"

"I think he's fair," Brandon answered honestly. "He was quite thin for a time after you left, but he's filled out again. He doesn't smile much, but he always wants to talk. I think he gets lonely."

Stacy drew in a shuddering breath as pain squeezed around her heart. She was silent for a moment, praying again about what she should do. She decided suddenly not to do anything. God might have something special planned, and if she went rushing ahead on her own she could ruin everything. With this decision came such a peace that Stacy knew she was doing the right thing.

"Are you all right?" This came from Brandon, who along with his wife had been carefully watching Stacy's face.

"As a matter of fact, I am." She told them simply that she was not going to mail her letter but would keep praying.

"Well, there's one thing you won't need to pray about any

longer," Sunny said. "You are going to join my Bible study with Andrea."

"Oh, Sunny," Stacy breathed. "Are you certain? I mean, won't Lady Andrea mind?"

"It was her idea. That way when I can't be there, the two of you can meet."

Stacy's eyes closed in relief. She had felt rather adrift with her separation from Elena and Noel.

"I don't know what to say."

"Say yes," Brandon told her, making it sound so simple.

"Yes," Stacy said and was still beaming at both of them when the door opened.

"Mumma?" a small voice called, sounding on the edge of tears. Stacy turned in surprise.

"Come here, Drew," she called to him. He'd been down for over an hour, and Stacy had planned to be there when he awoke. She wondered what woke him early. Brentwood was larger than Morgan, and he was still a little confused by all the doors and hallways. In fact, Stacy was surprised that he'd found her at all. Hettie must have fallen asleep, or he'd have never gotten downstairs.

Both Sunny and Brandon watched the small boy approach, his hair on end, his face flushed from sleep. Stacy pulled him into her lap. After he laid his head against her chest, he closed his eyes again. Stacy glanced over to find her guests' eyes glued to his small face.

"I know what you're thinking," Stacy spoke softly, referring to Drew's resemblance to Tanner. "Since you're going to be praying, the first thing you might ask of God is that He would move in Tanner's heart so that he'll see this child."

The Hawkesburys nodded, but no one said anything for a time.

"Would you like me to pray right now?" Brandon suddenly asked, his voice hushed.

Stacy glanced down to see that Drew was sound asleep before motioning with her head.

They didn't join hands, but Brandon's soft, deep voice surrounded them as he committed Tanner, Stacy, and Drew to God. He asked for wisdom on Stacy's part as well as their own, and then believing it to be God's will, he prayed for Tanner Richardson's salvation.

Twenty-Eight

NOT UNTIL THE FOLLOWING DAY did Stacy learn that her trip to the gardens had been a mistake. Brentwood sat on a quiet street and until she went out, her presence in the city had been undetected. Well, such privacy was over; she and Drew had been spotted and were now public news.

Roddy had been to his club that morning so he was able to report that the Duchess of Cambridge was on everyone's lips. She had even made the papers. Stacy found herself staying close to Drew all that day as if he somehow needed protection. Drew wanted to go out into the yard, but although the garden was surrounded with a high stone wall, she kept him inside.

Stacy wasn't sure if she was overreacting or not, but she didn't know what else to do. The temptation to mail her letter to Tanner was nearly overpowering. She wanted to know where she stood. If she mailed the letter and Tanner still wanted nothing to do with her, she could return to Middlesbrough.

If there had been any dread in returning to London, it had been for this reason. Knowing that Noel and Elena's house was available to her and that her grandfather had left her a small legacy made her want to walk away from all the gossip and scandal, but she knew such an action would be hard on Lucinda and Roddy.

When Stacy took a moment to consider the idea she realized she'd been giving in to impulse and emotion. Maybe the gossip would die down and she could live a normal life. She tried not to let it bother her, but even the servants who weren't as familiar with her began to watch her with speculative eyes.

"How are you, my dear?" Lucinda had found Stacy in Drew's room. She wasn't hiding exactly, but neither did she feel like wandering the house.

"A little shy of the windows and yard, but doing well."

Lucinda sighed. "The gossip mongers of the town can be such a trial. I'm glad he's too young to take much notice," Lucinda said, nodding her head in Drew's direction. He was sitting on the floor with his train and a small stuffed bear.

"The only problem is his complaint that I won't let him out in the yard."

"I think you're wise. We really are quite protected and secluded here, but you're big news." Lucinda's voice was dry, and this wrung a smile from Stacy.

"I came up because I wanted to remind you that Roddy and I will be away for part of the day tomorrow. Roddy has some property he must check on, and I said I would go with him."

"We'll be fine. Roddy found a trunk of old toys. Hettie is cleaning them, and by tomorrow Drew will have more treasures than he'll know what to do with."

"Good. I've asked cook for a special meal tonight to shake off your feeling of captivity. We won't be around until late afternoon tomorrow, so this will be your official welcome-to-London feast."

Lucinda's voice was so dramatic that Stacy had to laugh. Drew, not to be left from the festivities, wanted to be in his aunt's lap. Lucinda cuddled him close and sang a silly rhyme in his ear. The three of them passed a fun hour before Craig came to say that lunch was served.

Tanner had been in London for two days, and everywhere he went, people gawked in his direction and whispered. He was not one who paid the slightest attention to gossip, even when it concerned him, but this was affecting his purpose for being in town and that was getting on his nerves.

He had come to London on business just the day before, and within the hour had learned that his wife was in town as well. The gossip mill also said she was accompanied by a small boy.

Planning to stay about a week, he was swiftly changing his mind. He had nearly decided he would tell Edmond to finish the business and take himself back to the solitude of Winslow when the questions began.

Could he really leave London knowing she was here? Could he have Stacy this close and not see her? What did she look like now? How could she come back to London with another man's child? Tanner felt such a mix of emotions that it staggered him. One minute he was livid with remembered pain, and the next moment he thought he must talk to her before he could possibly go on.

It was early afternoon when he made his decision. After all she was his wife; he would see her if it pleased him to do so. Her presence in London was disrupting his whole life, and he had rights. Maybe he would send her out to Winslow until life could right itself again. His mansion was huge; he never had to see her if he didn't want to.

Tanner suddenly remembered the boy. Rumor had it that he looked like a Richardson, but that was ridiculous. No doubt the boy would prove to be nothing but trouble. But if he knew Stacy, and he believed he did, she would never consent to giving the child up.

Tanner ordered his carriage and found himself consumed with thoughts of Stacy all the way to Brentwood. He finally admitted to himself that he had missed her. He hated himself for the weakness, but it was true. To fight the feeling, he grew angry.

By the time he arrived at Brentwood he knew exactly what he would do. He would send Stacy to Winslow, but this time he would be in control. If he wished to see her, he would send for her, but outside of that she was only his wife. She would do as she was told and live where he told her to live. Right now he wanted her at Winslow. The boy came to mind one last time, but Tanner pushed him away. He would deal with the brat when the time came.

Drew's attitude had been poor at naptime. He had been nearly delirious with the toys Hettie had produced, and by the time he needed to eat lunch and nap he was totally spent. He had been quite cross with his mother when she wouldn't allow him to sleep with every toy Hettie had cleaned. When he spoke back to her repeatedly, Stacy had been forced to paddle him—something she hated to do. Drew had been quite repentant afterward, and they'd prayed before he'd fallen asleep.

Now Stacy was in her own room, much in need of rest herself. She didn't lie down but made herself comfortable in a chair that sat by the window. She gazed out the window at an area that was nearly like a forest. It was one of Stacy's favorite views, so unlike many parts of London with its sewer-lined streets and filthy houses.

She pondered the view for a time, but she was tired. Her eyes were sliding shut when her doorknob turned. She looked up in surprise. No one had knocked. Thinking it was Drew, she began to rise. Stacy was standing in front of the chair when Tanner pushed the door open and walked in. She froze in place when he pinned her to the spot with his dark, compelling eyes.

Before either of them could speak, Craig appeared and

hovered anxiously in the background. Stacy glanced toward him in an effort to tell him she would be all right. She wasn't certain herself, but she knew that Tanner would only send him away, and none too gently.

"My lady?"

"It's all right, Craig." Stacy found her voice and watched as the elderly servant exited reluctantly. He closed the door soundlessly behind him.

Stacy looked back at her husband and forced herself to breathe.

"Hello, Tanner."

"Stacy." His disinterested voice belied the way his heart leapt at the sight of her. "What brings you to London?"

"My grandfather died."

This gave Tanner pause. This particular bit of information had not reached him.

"I'm sorry for your loss."

"Thank you."

"But that still doesn't answer my question."

Stacy, unable to take her eyes from him, finally shrugged rather helplessly and then stared at the floor.

"Lucinda and Roddy wanted me to come, and I felt it was best at the time."

Stacy heard footsteps, and her eyes flew up to find him approaching. If he was trying to intimidate her, it was working. He stopped just scant inches in front of her and stared down into her face. Stacy was amazed at what she saw. Tanner still cared. He tried to show her otherwise, but Stacy had caught the slightest glimpse of caring.

"What are you thinking, Anastasia? Afraid I'll kiss you?" Tanner's deep voice questioned softly.

Stacy couldn't answer.

"You are my wife," Tanner told her as if she was the one who'd forgotten. "I will kiss you whenever I feel like it. Do you understand?"

Stacy could only nod.

"Tell a maid to pack your things; you're coming to Winslow." Tanner's voice had turned curt as he abruptly turned away.

"You want me at Winslow?" Stacy found her voice.

"Did I not say as much?" His impatience was evident. "A carriage will be here for you in two hours."

Two hours! Stacy nearly panicked. She said the first words that came to mind.

"I have a son."

Tanner, who had been heading toward the door, stopped in his tracks. He turned with maddening slowness and stared at Stacy.

"I'd heard as much," he said in a voice that was stone cold. "I suppose you may bring the child, if he causes me no trouble."

Stacy was horrified at his words and tone. She was on the verge of refusing him as it was, but he went on and Stacy completely lost control.

"Who knows," Tanner said with a negligent shrug as he again turned to the door, "maybe I'll grow to like the boy and get rid of you."

"No." The word was spat out, and Tanner turned in amazement. No longer was Stacy standing frightened before him. Her hands were balled so tightly in front of her that they were white. She was trembling from head to foot, her face flushed with rage.

"You'll not take my son. He needs me, and I won't let you take him. I won't go with you. You can't make me. You'll not take my son from me." Her voice was furious and desperate, and in just a few strides Tanner covered the distance between them, his own anger completely gone, replaced by something he could not define.

"Stacy," he spoke with more calm than he felt, his hands grasping her upper arms. "I won't take the boy."

"No, you won't!" Stacy was still beside herself.

"I won't separate you from your son."

"I won't let you. I won't let you hurt him."

"I won't hurt the boy or take him from you."

Stacy stopped long enough to listen to him and study his eyes. She went on, still boldly, but her tone was calming.

"Promise me, Tanner. Promise you'll not take him from me."

"I promise, Stacy." He gave her a little shake to make sure she was listening. "He can come with you to Winslow, and I'll not hurt him."

Stacy took a deep breath and tried to relax and believe him. Tanner felt her nearly violent trembling under his hands and grew angry at himself for wanting to enfold her in his arms. He had thought it would be such a pleasure to hurt her as she'd hurt him, but it was not turning out that way at all.

With another abrupt movement, he dropped his hands and turned away. "You and the boy will be ready to leave in two hours."

Stacy's hand flew to her mouth.

"Tanner." Her voice was now fearful and subdued.

"What?" He turned back with his hand on the door, his brow lowered menacingly.

"I'm not certain I can leave just now."

"Are you telling me no, Anastasia?" His voice was so low and angry that Stacy could barely force the words from her throat.

"No, it's just that I need to tell Roddy and Lucinda goodbye and explain where I'm going. They're not here right now."

Tanner seemed to consider the idea. "When will they return?"

"Not for several hours."

Again Tanner paused. "A coach will be here at 8:00 tomorrow morning. Be ready, Stacy. I don't want to have to tell you again."

He didn't wait for an answer this time, and since Stacy's legs gave out as soon the door closed, she was glad the chair was directly behind her.

"He terrifies me just as he always has," Stacy said out loud to the Lord. "I haven't changed at all. I was going to be so strong, Lord, and I was terrified."

Defeat washed over Stacy as she prayed and tried to calm herself. She had asked God to open a door, but she never dreamed it would be like this. This door had brought the north wind. As Stacy quieted, God reminded her of His sovereignty. Tanner's arrival was no mistake. This was the door God intended, cold wind and all. Believing that, Stacy would meet the challenges beyond that door with hope.

She sat for only a moment longer until she realized how much work needed to be done. She gathered both Hettie and Rayna in order to explain the situation. Hettie was to travel with her, but not knowing what Tanner would want, Stacy did not feel at liberty to ask Rayna to accompany them. Both women were clearly disapproving of the move to Winslow, but Stacy, needing both of them to pack for her and Drew, ignored their looks. Her husband wanted her back. She had no illusions of paradise, but at least Tanner wanted her at Winslow.

Tanner suddenly found himself with nothing to do. For over an hour he paced the study floor at his town house. He would not leave London until he was certain that Stacy was on her way to Winslow. He now wished he'd forced her to leave on the spot so he could get on with his life. He was a fool for letting her change his mind.

The smell of her skin and bath oil suddenly assailed his senses, and Tanner looked down at his hands. She had felt as wonderful as ever. Her eyes, so huge and blue, had been just as he remembered—with a mixture of wonder and innocence. Not wanting to dwell on this, he forced his mind to move on.

Her reaction to a comment he hadn't meant scared him. He'd never seen her that way. He'd heard that motherhood could do that to a woman the way nothing else could, but he had not been prepared for her response.

"She must have loved the boy's father," Tanner heard himself say out loud and stood still as rage and agony ripped through him. He knew then that he would have to be very careful. The last thing he wanted was another's man child beneath his roof, but if that's what he had to put up with to have Stacy, he would do it. He had seen her, and that was all it had taken to make him admit to the truth, infuriating as it was. He wanted Stacy. Right now nothing else mattered.

Twenty-Nine

THE NEXT MORNING LUCINDA STOOD STILL and forced her hands to her sides. The sight of Drew coming down the stairs with his train and bear was enough to make her wring her hands.

She had come home the day before from a marvelous but tiring day with Roddy, only to be met with Stacy's news. Lucinda cried herself dry before falling into an exhausted sleep. She woke early, before 6:00, knowing that Stacy would be up and readying herself to go. And now, even though it was just a little before 8:00, she felt utterly drained.

Stacy had shared about her faith in God, but Lucinda was too angry to trust. What kind of God took a person's family away? She had been planning to visit her brother that very summer, but God had taken him in the spring. Lucinda would never have admitted to herself that her own selfish lifestyle had kept her from visiting Andrew more regularly.

Now Drew and Stacy were leaving, and after just a few days too, making Lucinda more bitter than ever. They needed her, she was certain of that. And she needed them.

Roddy stood beside her while all of this ran through Lucinda's mind. He shared Lucinda's grief, but he would not say anything that would stand in the way of Stacy's happiness. Lucinda was quite certain that Tanner would not do right by his son, but Roddy believed differently. Just as he'd known that Tanner would once again be taken with his wife—after all, he'd ordered her to Winslow just moments after he arrived—Roddy also believed that one look at his son and Tanner's heart would be lost.

"Well, we're ready," Stacy said as she finally gained the foyer. "Thank you for everything, Roddy and Lucinda. I don't know when we'll be back to London, but I hope you'll come and see us."

"No one can keep us away," Lucinda stated as she put her arms around Stacy. Each knew that her *no one* referred to Tanner.

"Goodbye, my precious." Lucinda's voice wavered as she hugged Drew, and she didn't tarry long with her embrace.

Lucinda stood at the door with her sodden handkerchief, but Roddy scooped Drew up in his arms and walked them down to the carriage. Hettie climbed aboard with a sour comment about her old bones, and Stacy turned to her dear friend.

"Will Lucinda be all right?"

"I think so. It might take some time, and we will need to visit or she'll be miserable."

"Please do, Roddy. I don't want to fight with my husband, but if Tanner isn't going to let me see my family, I won't stay." Stacy paused and then looked chagrined. "Of course, I say that now, but the minute he looks at me I'll shake."

Roddy smiled at her words. "You'll do fine, and we will come to visit even if we have to charge the castle gate."

"What castle?"

Stacy looked stunned. At times it was so easy to forget that Drew was present and taking in every word.

Roddy kissed the little boy's cheek and handed him over to his mother. Stacy passed him in to Hettie and then turned to embrace Roddy. They didn't say another word to each other, but Stacy waved from the window as soon as she was inside. She couldn't be certain, but it looked as if Roddy's eyes were wet. Stacy smiled into his eyes as the carriage moved away to Lucinda's cries of goodbye and I love you.

Stacy had completely forgotten how long the ride to Winslow could be. The carriage stuck in the mud on two occasions, and each time it took considerable maneuvering to get them moving again. These interludes were a delight to Drew, who was rather bored with the bumpy ride and had nothing to play with save his train and bear.

Stacy wouldn't have minded the ride so much, except that she'd been under the impression that Tanner would be with them. When he hadn't been with the coach that morning at 8:00, Stacy thought they would be meeting him. Now they were only about 45 minutes from Winslow, and there had been no sign. Stacy decided to sit back and not worry about it.

Just short of an hour later, Winslow came into view. Not even Hettie could find a negative word for its grandiose beauty. Stacy's chest heaved with pleasure at the sight of it. She had truly loved their home.

Let this be a beginning, Father. I don't know why Tanner came ahead of us, but let this be a time of repair for this damaged marriage. Help Tanner put his pride away and accept Drew so we can be a real family.

"Mumma."

"Yes, dear."

"I'm hungry."

"All right, darling. We'll be inside in just a moment."

And indeed they were, but it was not the warm welcome Stacy had expected. It was Joffrey and not Tanner who was at the door to meet them, and his manner was even more frigid than Stacy had remembered.

"Hello, Joffrey. Is Lord Richardson here?"

"No, he is not."

"Oh." Stacy was starting to feel alarmed. "Is he out riding?"

"No." Joffrey's voice clearly said it was none of her business, but he still explained. "Lord Richardson is still in London. When he plans to return I do not know. I did receive word that you were coming, but since his lordship is not here, maybe you should return to London."

"My orders were to bring her ladyship here," a gruff voice spoke up from behind Stacy. It was the grouchy old carriage driver. Stacy smiled at him gratefully, but he didn't return the smile.

He had not come inside for Lady Stacy, but for himself. He was tired and nothing could make him drive all the way back to London right now. Knowing Joffrey as he did, he'd come inside just to make certain that the self-seeking head of staff didn't talk the duchess into returning.

"Very well," Joffrey stated with a sigh, as though Winslow were his own and he alone was put out by their presence. "I'll show you to your rooms."

Ignoring Hettie's dark looks, Stacy followed, thankful to be going to her room and getting a chance to be alone. She glanced over her shoulder and sighed with relief to see a footman handling their trunks. For a time she felt certain she would have to lug her own.

Her pleasure over the trunks was short-lived. Stacy's heart sank when she saw that Joffrey was leading them toward the north wing. Her heart begged God to give her strength and to calm the resentment rising within her that Tanner would be so thoughtless.

"Will two rooms be enough?"

Stacy stared at Joffrey, amazed at his daring. He clearly hated her and was doing nothing to hide it. She knew Hettie wanted her to take the servant down a peg, but surprisingly enough she felt too much compassion for that. They were all taking their cue from the duke, and he despised her. Stacy told herself not to be a quitter, but she knew if the coachman was willing she would leave immediately.

"Two rooms will be fine," Stacy answered finally and entered the room with Drew. She nearly balked when she felt how cold the air was once she passed over the threshold.

The three of them stood still as the trunks were placed on the floor and the servants left. Joffrey started to leave but turned back. His manner said that it caused him great pains to do so.

"Dinner will be served at 6:30 in the main dining room." This said, he left, closing the door behind him.

Stacy looked over at Hettie to see that the old woman's jaw had actually swung open. Had Stacy not felt so miserable, she would have laughed.

"Mumma, I'm hungry."

Stacy quickly knelt in front of him. She hugged him before answering, more for her own need of comfort than his.

"Joffrey left before I could tell him that we haven't eaten. I'll get you something, all right?"

"I'm cold."

"Well, Hettie can warm you up—"

"I'll see about the food," the old servant cut in, her voice odd. Stacy stared at her, thinking she must be very tired, and then nodded.

As soon as Hettie left, Stacy changed Drew into warmer clothing and played a game with him, intended to warm them both. She was hungry herself, and the feeling that no one outside of London cared for them was pressing down on her with every passing second. Stacy would have been greatly cheered if she could have seen Hettie downstairs in the kitchen right then. At least she would have been certain that someone at Winslow cared for her.

"I told you earlier," Joffrey said with his nose in the air, "dinner will be served at 6:30. As a servant, you may eat when the duchess is through."

"Don't you try your uppity ways with me," Hettie nearly hissed at him. "Now you've got ten minutes to have a tray up to Lady Stacy—a nice full tray for all three of us."

"I do *not* take orders from elderly servants who do not know their place."

Hettie's thin chest heaved, and her eyes narrowed. "I mean what I say. You've got ten minutes to have that tray ready. If you don't, I'll tell Lord Richardson everything. He can't stay away forever, and when he comes I'll tell him every word you said." Hettie turned and started away, but paused and looked back.

"And you'd best remember one more thing. That's the duchess you're serving up there, and that boy is the future Duke of Cambridge."

Joffrey looked uncertain for the first time. Hettie left, and cook erased the smug expression from her face just before Joffrey turned to look at her. She began putting a tray together without being asked, determining then and there that she would be the one to deliver it.

Four days passed before Tanner returned to Winslow. Stacy found out quite by accident that he was back when she ran into Price in the hallway.

"Hello, Price." Her voice told of her genuine pleasure at seeing him, but Price read the strain in her face.

"Good morning, my lady."

"Are you just back from London?"

"Last night," he told her gently.

"Is..." Stacy began and hesitated. "Is Tanner with you?"

"Yes, my lady, he's here."

Stacy did not want to keep him, so she thanked him and moved back to her rooms. It was like living as a prisoner. She was afraid to let Drew make any noise for fear of disturbing someone. The notion was ridiculous since they were so far away from the rest of the house, but Stacy was not coping very well. In fact, the strain was beginning to tell on both of them. Stacy knew she was losing weight, and Drew's tan little face was growing pale and drawn.

Stacy hoped all of that might change with Tanner's arrival, but this was not the case. Two more days passed, and in that time he never sought them out or even saw them. Stacy was totally confused as to why she'd been brought here. He wanted nothing to do with her. She reminded herself how much she was hated. He was trying to humiliate her, and unfortunately it was working. Stacy felt more downtrodden then she ever had in her life. Thankfully, Drew's sneezes changed all of that.

He and Stacy were playing on the floor where they spent much of their time. They had tried going out of doors, but both the gardener and the stablemaster had made it quite clear with their looks and actions that their presence was not wanted. Stacy could not rest under their frowning looks and shaking heads.

Now this morning Drew began to sneeze as he played. Stacy felt his forehead and found it cool, but his little hands were so cold she felt frightened. She gathered him into her arms and held him almost fiercely. Drew let out one more sneeze, and Stacy realized this was the very thing she had feared—but she was doing nothing about it. She could handle the fact that Tanner didn't care about her, but Drew was another matter.

"Hettie," Stacy announced as she put Drew back on the floor and rose. "I need to see Lord Richardson. Will you please see that Drew stays warm?"

Stacy's color was high as she said this, and Hettie nearly cackled with glee. The old woman had wondered how much more Stacy was going to take.

"Bye-bye, Mumma."

"I'll be back soon."

"Hettie?" Drew spoke when his mother had left.

"Um hmm?"

"Why are you smiling, Hettie?"

She didn't answer his question. "Come over here, Drew, close to the fire. Sit in my lap, and I'll tell you a story."

Tanner Richardson, a man of tremendous willpower, had been struggling for days to forget that his wife and her son were in the house. He hadn't gotten a thing done in all that time, but this morning was different. He had finally forced his mind to the task at hand and had put in several productive hours of work on business matters. He was not happy to have someone knock on the study door.

He opened his mouth to say that he did not want to be disturbed, but hesitated. Stacy, never far from his mind, might be seeking him out. He sincerely doubted it, but on the chance she was he wanted to hear what she had to say.

"Come in," he called and watched with satisfaction as his wife came tentatively through the door.

"I'm sorry to disturb you, Tanner, but I need to ask you something."

"What is it?" His voice sounded more impatient than he felt, but it had its usual effect. Stacy's hands came together in a nervous gesture, and her voice turned hesitant.

"Would it be possible for us to move out of the north wing?"

Tanner frowned. "I was under the impression that you chose the rooms yourself."

Stacy didn't know how to reply to this. It wasn't true, but she couldn't bring herself to tell of Joffrey's actions, reprehensible as they were.

"What seems to be the problem?"

Stacy nearly sighed with relief that he cared enough to ask.

"The rooms are rather cold."

"Well you can certainly ask Joffrey to supply you with extra blankets." His voice was that of a parent addressing a simple child.

"We're not cold at night, just during the day."

Tanner's mouth twisted cynically. "Now, that's the problem, isn't it. You have no business keeping that boy in all day. You've probably coddled him until he's a monster. Get out during the day, Stacy, and you won't be cold in your rooms."

This said, Tanner bent his head back over his papers. She had been dismissed with his tone and gesture. She stared at the top of his head for a moment, but the fight had gone out of her. She turned and let herself back out the door. Once outside, she stood for a moment in misery.

"That was telling him, Stacy. You really set things straight."

"Were you speaking to me, my lady?"

Stacy hadn't even noticed the faithful servant.

"No, Price," she told him softly.

The servant watched for long moments as she moved up the stairs with a heavy tread. When Stacy was out of sight, Price moved into the study.

Thirty

PRICE MOVED ABOUT THE STUDY VERY QUIETLY, not wanting to disturb his lordship but sensing he might be needed. He delivered the coffee he'd been carrying and prepared it just as Lord Richardson liked, but the cup was not touched. Tanner sat with his eyes on some distant spot, his papers in front of him, forgotten.

"Did you pass my wife when you came in?"

"Yes, sir."

"How did she seem?"

Price hesitated, and Tanner finally looked at him.

"She seemed," Price hesitated over the words, "she seemed somewhat defeated, my lord."

Tanner wondered why this brought him no pleasure. Again he had believed it would be good to see her humbled and miserable, but he hated this.

"It isn't like Stacy to complain." Tanner said this more to himself than anyone else, but Price still answered.

"I believe that her concern might be for the child's well-being."

Alarm slammed through Tanner. It didn't matter that he wanted nothing to do with the boy; the thought of his becoming ill was not to be tolerated. And then there was Stacy. She had not been happy with the way he'd treated her, but there was something more.

"Did Lady Stacy look all right to you?"

"She seemed thin, my lord, but I have not seen her of late and am probably not the one to judge."

But Tanner was one to judge. She did seem thinner, even since he'd seen her at Roddy and Lucinda's.

And why wouldn't she? Tanner asked himself in disgust. *You treat your animals with more kindness than you've shown your wife.*

"Have Lady Stacy, her maid, the boy, and the boy's nurse, moved down the hall from my room."

"Her maid, sir?"

"Yes, her maid." Tanner's voice was testy.

"Oh, Hettie," Price clarified. "Of course, sir." Price would have moved to the door then, but Tanner's face was that of a thundercloud.

"Are you saying my wife has no maid?"

"No, sir, but she does have Hettie."

"That's all? Just Hettie?"

"I believe so, sir. There is no other staff of which I am aware."

"Who takes care of the boy?"

"I believe Lady Richardson and Hettie do it themselves, my lord."

Tanner wasn't sure what to do with this. He had sent Stacy away, too angry to care if she had anything to live on. And by the time he had wondered about it, she had moved back to Middlesbrough where he knew her grandfather would take care of her. But now the old man was dead. He'd seen Morgan. Andrew Daniels had not died a wealthy man. What was Stacy living on?

"Would you still like Lady Richardson moved, my lord?" Price asked. Tanner was glad of the interruption.

"Yes. Have Joffrey arrange it. Have him see that they're made very comfortable. On second thought, see to it yourself. Do you know the rooms I want?"

"Yes, sir. Down the hall from yours. I was going to put the

child and Hettie in the two adjoining, and Lady Stacy directly across the hall."

"Good. And Price," Tanner began when the servant began to move away, "tell Lady Richardson that I will expect her to join me for dinner tonight. Seven o'clock."

"Yes, sir."

Price left, and Tanner finally reached for his coffee. He brooded for a long time on the situation in his home, a situation of his own creating. He asked himself many questions, ending with whether or not he should have left Stacy in London. He didn't have answers for each question that came to mind, but to his last, it was an unqualified no.

Stacy moved toward the north wing but did not return immediately to her room. She stood in the massive hall down from the door and looked out the window. It was a cloudy day, and Stacy thought it fit her mood.

"I thought I could do this, Lord, but I'm failing miserably," she whispered out loud. "What is my responsibility here as a wife? Do I stay no matter what? Do I honor Tanner's wishes, no matter what he expects of me? I wish Elena were here to talk with. It's not as if we have no place else to go. This is not a fit place with us tucked away all the time and the servants glaring at us when we make work for them.

"Tanner has done everything in his power to kill my love, Lord, but it's not working. My heart still turns over every time I see him. I need some help, Father. I need something to tell me if I should keep on here. I can't do this on my own."

Drew began to cry from inside the room. It was the best thing Stacy could have heard. As she moved to see to the trouble, she realized she was not more restful over the situation, but Drew needed his mother and that was all that mattered at the moment. She felt that she'd utterly failed him by coming here and keeping him shut away like so much excess baggage. He trusted her to see to his best, and up until now Stacy had been too afraid of Tanner to do that. Well, no more.

As she opened the door to the bedroom, she determined that as soon as she could figure a way to return to London and then Middlesbrough, she would do so. Tanner hadn't wanted her for three and a half years, and even though it looked for a time like things had changed, he didn't want her now. As much as it pained her to admit it, there was no reason to stay.

"You're moving us?" Stacy questioned Price just 30 minutes after she'd made her resolution.

"Yes, my lady. Lord Tanner has selected rooms for you in the other wing. If you'll come with me—"

Price cut off when Drew came from behind his mother to see whom she was talking with. He had been behind her skirts, thinking this all a game, when he popped his little face out and then moved his whole person to stare up at the unfamiliar servant in their room.

Price cleared his throat and opened his mouth to speak, but nothing came. He couldn't seem to take his eyes from the child. When he finally looked up, it was to find Stacy smiling at him, her heart in her eyes.

"Thank you, Price."

"For what, my lady?" The man's voice was hoarse.

"For reacting as you did."

Price's expression told her he understood, but he still looked as if he couldn't believe his eyes. He had never doubted Lady Richardson's faithfulness to her husband, but the face of this child was enough to stop him in his tracks.

Price had been employed by Tanner's father to serve as Tanner's valet; he had been 12 years old at the time. Tanner had been four and a mirror image of the child before him. Price found himself wanting to let out an emotional shout for the first time in years. His lord had an heir, a beautiful male heir.

Price cleared his throat and slowly said, "If you'll come with me, Lady Richardson, I will see that you, young Lord Richardson, and Hettie are settled comfortably."

"Maybe I should have Hettie pack our things."

"Lord Richardson's orders were clear—a maid will take care of that. He also wanted me to tell you that he'd like you to join him for dinner this evening at 7:00."

"Thank you, Price."

And so it was that the small band of neglected visitors followed Price out of the north wing to their new rooms. Stacy ignored Hettie's comment about it being long overdue; she was just glad that Tanner had not been as indifferent as he'd acted.

Drew skipped along, holding Hettie's hand and trying to take in parts of Winslow he'd never seen. Hettie kept him moving fairly fast, but Price noticed the child's interest and asked Stacy to contact him if she wanted young Lord Richardson to have a tour.

"I appreciate the offer, Price, but since Tanner hasn't met Drew, I think we should wait."

"As you wish, my lady. This will be your room."

Price opened a door, and Stacy entered with relief. They had been heading in the direction of the master bedroom, and her mind was put to rest to be given another just now.

It was a bedroom she remembered, and in fact was one of her favorites. Done completely in navy and a deep shade of rust, it was one of the warmest bedrooms in all of Winslow. There was a sitting room off the bedroom and a huge dressing room. Everything was spotless, and a maid stood in attendance, preparing to pour tea.

"Please wait for Lady Richardson's return," Price told the maid before leading them across the way to Hettie and Drew's rooms. They were as marvelous as her own, but other than having Drew wash his hands in the basin they did not linger. They quickly moved back across the hall to enjoy tea in Stacy's sitting room.

An hour later, Tanner, on the way to his own room, was stopped in the hall when he heard a child laugh. For long moments he stood. Another giggle sounded, and with it all doubts about moving them closer evaporated. He knew he was going to have to meet the child eventually, but not just yet. Hearing that laugh and knowing he'd done right by Stacy and the boy was enough for now.

Thirty-One

For the second time in just weeks, Stacy found herself rushing down the stairs to see Sunny Hawkesbury. Joffrey had put her guest in the main salon. Stacy would have chosen a smaller, cozier room for their meeting, but she was glad to see her anywhere. The friends embraced warmly and then sat close together on the settee to talk in quiet tones.

Sunny wasted no time in asking questions, telling Stacy to tell her if she was out of line.

"First of all, are you all right?"

"I think so. The events of the past week have been rather hard, but I think things might be turning."

"Can you tell me about them?"

"When we arrived Tanner wasn't here. I wasn't prepared for that, but the worst thing that happened was that we were given rooms in the north wing."

"What were the problems?"

"It's oppressive, cold, and dreadfully dreary. I thought Drew might be catching something so I went to Tanner about moving, but he said no. However, he must have had second thoughts because he did move us. We're in lovely rooms just down the hall from the master bedroom."

"What did he say about Drew?"

"He hasn't seen him yet."

Sunny glanced around the cavernous room. "That's not hard to believe. Winslow is larger than Bracken. I take it Tanner doesn't see much of you, either."

"No, but he has asked me to join him for dinner tonight."

"Will you go?"

Stacy's smile was self-mocking. "You don't tell Tanner no—at least I don't."

"Stacy," Sunny's voice turned urgent. "Is he hurting you?"

"No, not the way you're thinking. My heart feels rather battered, but he doesn't touch me."

"Should you be staying here?"

"I believe so, yes. I was ready to leave, although I don't know how I would, when he moved us to more comfortable rooms. I rather took that as an indication that I should keep on here."

"Stacy, what did you mean, you don't know how you would leave? Surely you can order a carriage for yourself."

"I'm not sure. You see, the servants don't really care for me. Some of it's my fault because I'm not very assertive, but I feel as if—"

Joffrey chose that moment to enter with the tea tray. He had not knocked but simply entered of his own accord.

"I assumed my lady and her guest would care for tea?" Joffrey's voice told them how much he knew he was appreciated.

Stacy glanced at Sunny, who indicated no with a slight shake of her head.

"No, thank you, Joffrey, not just now." This came from Stacy.

Joffrey's face and body movements communicated his deep affront, and Sunny could only stare at him. Stacy, being used to such things, did nothing. Collecting the service, Joffrey caught the shocked look in the Duchess of Briscoe's eyes. He swiftly schooled his features into humble servitude before leaving the women alone.

"Is that normal?"

"I'm afraid so."

"I can't believe Tanner puts up with it."

"They don't do it to Tanner."

Sunny stared at her friend and thought furiously how she could help her. This was awful, but what should she say? She was still thinking when Stacy asked, "Should I stay here, Sunny?"

"Are you afraid to stay?"

"I am afraid, but not for the reasons you might think. I'm afraid of being swallowed up by Tanner because I won't stand up to him. I'm afraid he'll take Drew from me. Oh, not actually remove him from Winslow, but take his affections until he won't remember that he has a mother. I think I can stand many things, Sunny, but not that."

Sunny was about to reply, but the door opened again. Sunny was ready herself to tell the servants to leave them alone, but it was Tanner. He crossed the room in long-legged strides so like Brandon's that she smiled to herself.

"I'm sorry to bother you, ladies, but Price told me Sunny was here. Would you mind giving these to Hawk? Tell him I'll be over in the next few days to discuss them."

"I'll make sure he receives them."

"Thank you, Sunny." Tanner's tone was congenial, his eyes kind, but as he transferred this gaze to his wife, his look became intense.

"Did you need something, Stacy? Shall I send Joffrey in?"

"No, thank you, Tanner. We're fine."

"All right." The words sounded like he was through, but he continued to stand and study his wife's face.

"Did you get my message from Price?" Tanner's voice had changed and become intimate and low.

"Yes, thank you. This evening, seven o'clock."

"Good." Tanner spent another few seconds studying her as though to memorize her features, then bowed to both ladies and went on his way. It had appeared as though he was searching for something in her expression. Both women wondered if he found what he'd been looking for.

"I didn't know what to tell you before he came in here, Stacy, but right now I think you should try to stay."

Stacy was beginning to agree, but she still asked, "What changed your mind?"

"His face, more specifically, his eyes. He still believes you've duped him in some way, but he's so drawn to you he can't stand it. I believe he would have joined you on this settee had I not been here."

They continued to talk for another 20 minutes and then Sunny said she had to be leaving. Stacy hated to see her go, but she praised God for the visit. Sunny left her with some words of encouragement.

"Read the third chapter of First Peter, Stacy. Please don't mistake it for saying that you should stay here no matter what happens to you or Drew, but it might help you to know how to pray.

"If you need to talk and you can't come to me, send word with a servant. I'll come to you. Outside of that, pray, and I hope God will lay it on my heart to come to you."

"Thanks, Sunny. I hope I can come to Bracken soon. Drew would love to play with your boys."

"Oh, Stacy," Sunny sparked. "I didn't even think of it! Please come sometime soon. I know my boys will love Drew."

The women hugged, and Stacy stood in the front yard even after the Hawkesbury carriage was out of sight. Wishing she could go for a walk, she gazed out over the landscape and then realized there was no reason she couldn't. Drew was somewhere with Hettie, and a stroll, even a short one, in the springtime sun would do her good.

Watching her from the study window, Tanner wondered at her thoughts as she walked slowly toward the garden. He was still studying her when a small boy darted out from the side of the mansion. That Stacy was surprised and thrilled to see him was obvious with the way she scooped him into her arms and began to swing around. Another woman, presumably Hettie, had come behind the boy, and Tanner saw the three of them heading off into the gardens and out of sight.

How did a man tell his wife that he was willing to forgive her past indiscretion, but that he wanted nothing to do with her illegitimate child? He wanted her back in his life, but not the boy. He would have to tread carefully for a time. Tonight probably would be too soon, but in time he would find a way to have Stacy again and on his own terms.

Stacy's dinner with Tanner was on her mind as she put her son to bed, and even though she read him a story, she was terribly preoccupied; preoccupied until Drew decided to pull one of his question-and-answer sessions.

"How tall will I be?"

"I'm not sure."

"Taller than Hettie?"

"Probably."

"As tall as you?"

"You might be."

"Will my hair get long?"

"Well, we'll have to keep it cut. Do you want it to get long?"

"No, I don't like it on my neck. Do you like it on your neck?"

"I don't mind too much, unless it gets very hot. You need to go to sleep now."

"Where is Grandpapa?"

"In heaven. Remember we talked about that just yesterday. When we believe in Jesus Christ, we die and go to heaven and live with God."

"Tell me about heaven, Mumma."

"You are stalling, Andrew. Now go to sleep."

"What's stalling?"

Stacy shook her head. "Sleep." She couldn't stop the smile that threatened, however, and Drew grinned back at her when it burst into full bloom on her mouth. She cuddled him close for a time, kissing his soft, warm cheek and telling him he was her little love. He was nearly asleep when she rose.

Hettie went to the door with her, and Stacy paused, knowing that something was on the woman's mind.

"Drew asked me about dying just the other day. Do you want me to tell him what you just said?"

"I tell Drew that, Hettie, because it's what God's Word says, so he can believe it's true. So to answer your question, yes, I would. Would you like me to show you the verses in the Bible that tell us that?"

Hettie nodded. "Sometime, yes, but I'm tired tonight."

"All right. Goodnight, Hettie."

"Will you be in your room in the morning?"

"What do you mean?"

"I mean, should Drew come and find you if you're not in your own room tomorrow morning?"

Stacy didn't know how to answer her. Suddenly the way Tanner looked at her earlier that day gave her pause. Why hadn't it occurred to her before? Not until Stacy had gained her room did she remember she hadn't answered Hettie's question.

"If you're not in your own room."

The words kept sounding in Stacy's head as her hands fluttered nervously over her hair. She checked her dress, a peach silk creation covered in thin black stripes that she had saved for special occasions, repeatedly before going down the stairs. Even though she looked wonderful, her stomach was in knots. She adjusted the lace at her wrist and neckline at least six times, acting as if this was her coming out and not merely dinner with her spouse.

Stacy had almost convinced herself to calm down when she spotted Tanner waiting for her at the bottom of the stairs. He looked gorgeous and larger than life in black evening dress. Stacy was so busy gawking at him that she missed the last step.

Her eyes were the size of saucers when she found herself falling and then caught up tight against Tanner's chest. Stacy looked up into his passion-filled eyes and couldn't speak. She felt panic coming on. She was not ready for this.

"I'm hungry," she suddenly blurted, her eyes still huge in her face.

Stacy's vulnerability touched that spot in Tanner's heart that was so often affected when Stacy was near.

"Shall we go into dinner?" Tanner asked softly as he set her gently away from him.

"Yes, please." Stacy's voice was quiet with gratitude, and Tanner offered her his arm and led her to the dining room. Stacy had no idea what the evening would bring.

Thirty-Two

HOURS LATER STACY LAY ALONE IN HER BED and recounted her dinner conversation with Tanner. It had been a disaster.

"I saw you walking toward the garden today."

"I couldn't resist. After Sunny left I was drawn almost against my will." Tanner was being his most charming, and Stacy was fairly relaxed. "Your gardeners do a wonderful job."

"They would probably appreciate your praise."

Stacy was thinking that they wouldn't want her anywhere near them when Tanner asked, "How is your meal?"

"Everything is delicious, thank you."

"Are you settled in your room?"

"Yes. It's a beautiful room."

"Well, I hope you don't get too comfortable."

Stacy's eyes flew to her husband at the other end of the table, but he was bent over his plate and didn't notice. Stacy took a deep breath and forced herself to speak.

"If you don't plan on my staying at Winslow very long, maybe it would be best if I left right away."

Tanner frowned at her for just an instant. When his face cleared, he explained.

"I wasn't referring to your moving from Winslow, only from your bedroom."

Suddenly Stacy wasn't hungry anymore. It didn't matter that half of her meal was still on the plate, she knew she was through. Stacy still loved her husband, but she was having a hard time forgetting that he thought she'd had another man's child. With this in mind, she found it hard to believe that he desired her at all. Even if he did, would it last? Or would he grow angry again and push her away at a moment's notice.

"Doesn't the idea appeal to you?" Tanner asked, having carefully watched Stacy's face.

"It's not that."

"What is it?"

Tanner's tone had become slightly impatient, and Stacy wished she'd kept her mouth closed.

"I asked you a question, Anastasia."

"You've made it quite clear that you desire me, Tanner, but I doubt if desire is enough to build a marriage on."

"Meaning?" He was angry now, and Stacy's stomach churned.

"Meaning that as soon as you think I've betrayed you again, I'll be sent away once more."

It was the worst thing she could have said. Tanner was so furious his face flushed.

"You make it sound as though I imagined the events at the Cradwells'."

Stacy couldn't answer.

"I was there, Stacy." Tanner now stood, his voice tight with rage. "I saw Lord Stanley's hands on you." He stopped and tried to control himself before going on in a cold voice. "I think you might be right. Whatever is left between us is probably not enough to work with."

He had left the room then, and after a moment Stacy herself had gotten slowly to her feet.

Now Stacy lay and tried to think of how she could have handled the evening differently. After just moments she realized that it would have happened no matter what. Maybe her comments had brought it on a few weeks early, but there was no way that this arrangement was going to last. Tanner still carried too much bitterness over something he wasn't even willing to discuss.

Knowing she was not going to sleep, Stacy rose and decided she would start her packing. She lit a lantern and moved around the room collecting things, not bothering to put on her wrapper. The maid Price had sent to do her unpacking had done a wonderful job of laying her things out and making everything feel "homey," but now Stacy was forced to search every drawer and surface for her belongings.

She had worked along steadily for close to an hour when her bedroom door opened. Stacy was startled by the intrusion and then alarmed when Tanner came through the portal. He was still wearing his dinner slacks. His white shirt, now without the tie, was open at the throat.

Without a word, he moved to Stacy. She wanted to step away from him and the intensity in his eyes, but she was too stunned to move. For all Tanner's severity, his touch, when he finally stopped before her, was extremely gentle. He reached for and grasped her upper arms, pulled her close and then bent to kiss her.

Stacy was so unprepared that she didn't at first react. Tanner's kisses were a homage to her loveliness, and within just seconds he'd made her feel like the cherished wife of old. Stacy was so confused she couldn't think. At last he raised his head and spoke. His voice was gentle.

"You're not leaving Winslow, Stacy. You're my wife, and I want you here. If I said something that intimated otherwise, disregard it."

Tanner glanced around the room, already having summed up the situation.

"Do not put all of these things away tonight. Go back to bed; someone will see to them in the morning."

Stacy opened her mouth to speak, but Tanner went on.

"Do as I tell you. You look too tired and thin for my liking. Now into bed and sleep."

Stacy could hardly believe it when he turned her and gave her a small push toward the bed. She climbed beneath the covers. As she lay on her back, Tanner bent over her.

"Go to sleep," he said one last time and kissed Stacy again. He turned the lantern down, and in the remaining glow Stacy watched him leave. She fell asleep as she was asking God what she was going to do with this man who so confounded her.

Tanner finally sought his bed. He'd been in the study earlier when Price came in. It was quite late, and Tanner, surprised to see him still up, had told him to go to bed. But Price had not come to serve his lord.

"There is a light burning in Lady Richardson's room, my lord. Would you like me to send a maid to her or check on her myself?"

Tanner had not immediately told Price that he would check on Lady Richardson himself; there was suddenly too much on his mind. The very fact that Price would ask him such a thing spoke volumes. No one it seemed, least of all the staff, knew Stacy's status at Winslow. Oh, she was the duchess; that was clear. But he saw for the first time that they didn't know what to do with her.

It suddenly became apparent that this had to do with the boy. He had told Stacy, in so many words, to keep the child out of his way. She had taken him a little too literally. He'd been half hoping to see the child up close at some point, but Stacy, fearing it would cause a disturbance, wasn't going to let that happen. He saw then that he was going to have to go to them in order to prove to her that he would not harm the boy.

Their conversation over dinner came back to him at that point. He hadn't meant to mention their separate bedrooms, nor had he anticipated Stacy's fearful response when he did. When he'd calmed down, her reaction made perfect sense.

As Tanner settled the bed covers around him he reached for the empty side of the bed and simply let his arm lie. She had actually intimated that she'd been innocent at the Cradwell party. Tanner didn't believe that for a moment, but maybe he had overreacted three years ago. She had seemed sorry for her actions, and Leslie never had been. Stacy had acted as if she wanted to stay; Leslie had been happier when he was miles away.

Tanner didn't sleep for many hours that night. He was too busy plotting how he would romance and woo his wife. He told himself that she didn't deserve it, but if that was the way it had to be, he would at least give it a try. His only regret at this point was that he was probably going to have to befriend the boy to do it.

"Now, this shoe is an island, so you must sail your ship far around it, Drew."

Stacy and her young son were on the floor of her sitting room two nights later. Drew's face was still flushed from his bath, and he was all ready for bed. Since it was still a bit early, he and his mother were playing "boats" with several of Stacy's shoes.

"This is the pirate boat, Mumma. It's coming to get you."

"I'm going to sail away, Captain Drew. You can't catch me."

Drew let out a shriek of laughter and jumped up to move one of the other shoes.

"This is a pirate too," he cried. "I've got you. You have no cannon and I—" Drew abruptly halted, and Stacy looked at him. He was staring at something behind her. He then moved quite close to where she was half-lying on the floor. Stacy's heart began to pound even before she sat up and turned to see Tanner.

What she saw nearly broke her heart. All color had drained from Tanner's face, and his eyes were locked on Drew. He moved to sit in the nearest chair, one by the door, without even looking at it.

"Mumma?" Drew whispered softly to his mother. It was just what Stacy needed to open her mouth.

"Drew, this is Lord Richardson."

"Richardson?" He was too bright not to recognize the name.

"Yes. He's letting us stay here at Winslow. Please go and introduce yourself."

Drew scrambled immediately to his feet and went to stand before Tanner.

"Hello, sir," he bowed from the waist. "I'm Drew—"

"Andrew," his mother started him again."

"Andrew Tanner Richardson."

With that, Drew put his small hand out, and Tanner, in a near state of shock, shook it.

"You're tall," Drew said when he regained his hand.

"Yes." Tanner's gaze had softened, and Drew's fascination with this tall stranger bubbled to the surface.

"Mumma is tall."

"Yes, she is."

"Are you taller than Mumma?"

"Yes, I am."

"I might be tall."

"Yes, I think you might be."

"Grandpapa was tall. He's in heaven."

Tanner had no reply to this, but he was content just to sit and stare into Drew's captivating little face.

"Drew," his mother called to him after just a moment. "It's bedtime now."

As if on cue, Hettie came to the door.

"Go with Hettie, and I'll come and kiss you later."

Drew threw his arms around his mother and kissed her exuberantly. Stacy cuddled him close for as long as she dared before releasing him to go with Hettie. He was nearly to the door when she called his name.

"Andrew."

"Oh," the little boy stopped, facing the large man in the chair. "Thank you for meeting me, sir. Goodnight, sir."

Stacy was so proud of him she could have sung. When the

door closed, however, and she found herself alone with Tanner, she couldn't remain on the floor. She rose and gathered the shoes they'd been playing with, returning them to her dressing room. When she came back into the sitting room, Tanner was just as she'd left him.

Stacy couldn't quite bring herself to look at his face, so she took a seat on the sofa, taking some time to adjust her skirt before she looked into his eyes. To her utter relief he was not angry.

"Why didn't you tell me?"

Stacy took a breath. "After all that has passed between us, I wasn't sure you would believe me." She paused and then went on with her eyes in her lap. "And in truth, I wanted you to want me back for *me*."

Nothing had ever rocked Tanner's world the way events of the last ten minutes had, and for Tanner Richardson, that was saying quite a bit. He had a son. *A son!* He was a man who had believed he could never help create a child, and here he had a beautiful boy who sported his high cheekbones and dark brown eyes. Except for Stacy's straight, thick, honey-blonde hair that fell so perfectly across his forehead, Drew looked just like his own childhood portraits.

"He's a fine boy," Tanner managed at last. "You've done a good job with him."

"He is a good boy," Stacy agreed, now able to look up at her husband.

"How old is he?"

"He was three last month, the tenth of April."

"And you call him Drew?"

"Yes. It was easier since we were living with my grandfather, and now he prefers that to Andrew."

"You should get him out more," Tanner said, but it was not a criticism.

"I didn't want to do that until you'd met him and seen what a well-behaved boy he was. He can be rather rambunctious at times, and I didn't want him to disturb you."

"Winslow is his home; he can go where he likes."

Stacy nodded, trying to hide how crushed she felt inside with the way he'd said "his home." She tried to push it away before she read too much into it and put herself into agony.

Tanner stood, seeming almost anxious to be away. "I'll leave you now. I have some things to do in my study. Goodnight, Stacy."

"Goodnight, Tanner." Stacy said the words automatically, uncertain that it was going to be a good night at all.

Tanner locked the door of his study before turning the lamps high and moving to the safe. He spun the dial effortlessly and in moments the door swung open. However, his hand shook when he looked inside and reached for a thick bundle of papers. A moment later he sat at his desk, every letter Stacy had written placed in front of him.

When the letters first arrived he had never read them; not for months did he even open them. Price would always announce that one had arrived, but Tanner would tell him he didn't want to see it.

Then about six months after Stacy left, the letters stopped. Tanner didn't know what to think. He questioned Price. To his relief the faithful servant had saved every bit of her correspondence. Tanner had read through them all in an evening and then sat in agony when it seemed that she would write no more.

What if she's dead? he'd asked himself. He had said he didn't care, but he was lying to himself. This and many more questions had tormented his confused mind for two weeks. Then a letter arrived. She hadn't missed a single week after that, and Tanner read each one as it arrived.

Now he carefully looked at the date of each letter. It only took a few minutes to see how the dates matched. Stacy had not written those two weeks in April because she was having his baby. Again questions swarmed his mind. Had it been hard? Had she been sick? Even though she'd been in bed, couldn't she have written? Had Drew been a difficult or sickly baby? It wouldn't seem so now, but three years was a long time.

And what would the next three years bring? This was the last question Tanner allowed himself to ask, because he couldn't stand not having answers.

Thirty-Three

AFTER DRESSING THE NEXT MORNING, Stacy went in search of Drew. He usually came to her while she was still in bed. Stacy wondered this morning if he wasn't sleeping in. She was met by a disapproving and worried Hettie, who said that the duke had come for her son just moments earlier.

"Didn't even ask—just told him to come and of course Drew followed like he'd known him all his life."

Stacy told herself not to be alarmed, and in truth she wasn't, but she did feel curious as to where they might have gone. She was on her way down the stairs when she saw Drew ahead of her, still in his nightclothes, sliding down the banister and giggling with all his might.

"Andrew Tanner Richardson." Stacy's voice was firm but not harsh. "You asked me when we arrived if you could slide on this banister, and I said no."

"Come now, Stacy," Tanner said before the boy could say a word. Stacy had gained the foyer but hadn't even seen him as he lounged against one wall watching his son's antics. "What's the harm?" he went on critically. "You're acting like a silly old woman."

"Silly old woman," Drew echoed, and Stacy turned to her son in outrage.

"*Andrew Richardson!* You will not speak to me in such a way or ever call me names. Do you understand?"

The little boy was crushed. "Yes, Mumma."

"Go right now and find Hettie so you can get dressed."

Drew, very subdued, moved to do as he was told. Stacy waited until he'd met Hettie at the top of the stairs before turning to Tanner. He had pushed away from the wall and now stood alert. The betrayal he saw in Stacy's eyes was almost his undoing. Her pain-filled voice made it worse.

"Obedient children do not just happen. They are the result of months of hard work. As you can see, Tanner, you can undo all of that work in a fraction of that time." Stacy's voice caught, but she went on. "You promised not to take him."

She turned then to run up the stairs, but Tanner caught her on the third step. His hands held her waist, but Stacy would not turn around.

"My promise still stands. I won't take him."

"I wish I could believe you," Stacy admitted. It was easier to be honest when he wasn't looking at her.

"I grew up without a mother, Stacy. I would never separate the two of you, not even emotionally, especially now that I'm aware."

Stacy turned then. The difference in their heights was removed because Stacy was on a higher step. She looked directly into his face as she said, "I didn't know your mother died when you were young."

"She didn't. She just didn't want me."

Stacy looked into his wonderful, dark eyes and slowly shook her head. "How could she not want you?"

Tanner shrugged. The pain in his eyes was only slight. The years had dulled the ache. "She never wanted any of us, not my father, my brother, or me. Sometimes I can still hear her telling my father she was a fool for having married him and an even greater fool for giving him sons."

"Oh, Tanner" was all Stacy could say.

"It's not going to be that way for Drew. This is your home now, our home. I don't know if I can ever forgive you for what you did, but Drew's going to have his mother and father with him."

Stacy sighed. "You still believe the worst, Tanner, even after seeing Drew?"

"Drew is obviously my son, Stacy, but we won't speak of the other." His voice said there would be no argument and, as usual, Stacy acquiesced.

When Stacy looked defeated, Tanner's hands gently stroked her waist. "Come have breakfast with me. Bring Drew if you'd like."

Stacy saw it for the olive branch that it was. She hated living under this false accusation, but for now she was going to have to let it drop. It wasn't ideal, but maybe in time he would come to see that there had never been anyone but him.

"What is it?"

"It's an egg dish. Now I want you to try some."

The three-year-old's face was so comical that Tanner had to raise his napkin to his mouth to hide his smile. If he wanted to provoke his wife at that moment and probably earn himself a tongue-lashing, all he had to do was laugh. He certainly admired her way with Drew, especially when she must have been tempted to laugh herself. Tanner knew he would never have made it.

The duke was correct about his wife's desire to laugh. When Drew started to eat, Stacy sent a warning glance in Tanner's direction, but not even she could hide the twinkle in her eye before turning to her own plate.

Tanner was just starting on his third cup of coffee when he realized that a nanny or nurse should have been doing Stacy's job. He pondered on the different women who had been in charge of him and his brother over the years, and then knew it would be years before Drew appreciated having his mother there instead.

While most women were sewing or visiting with friends, Drew's mother was teaching him to eat correctly and to respect his elders. It suddenly occurred to him why. There would not have been money in the viscount's household for a luxury such as a nurse. Tanner determined to ask Stacy if she wanted to hire a nanny, but he knew what the answer would be.

"Tanner," Stacy cut into his thoughts, "would it be a problem if I visited Bracken today?"

Tanner's brows rose to his hairline. "You certainly don't need to ask permission to go calling, Stacy. Just order the carriage and go."

"Thank you, Tanner," she said softly. He almost told her that wasn't necessary either.

"Am I going to Racken?"

"It's Bracken," his mother corrected him, "and, yes, you are. You can play with Lady Sunny's little boys."

"Do they have toys?"

"I'm sure they do," Stacy answered absently and reached for her cup of tea. She wouldn't have been quite so calm if she'd seen Tanner's shocked look.

He had a sudden image of his son playing with shoes on the floor of his mother's sitting room. Something painful tore inside of him at the way his wife and son had been living for the past three years. This was his family home; all of his childhood toys must be here somewhere.

Tanner excused himself a very short time later. Stacy was surprised to see him go so suddenly, but she was thankful for their brief time. She would have been even more thankful if she'd known that he was ordering the house servants at Winslow to ready the nursery for Drew while he and Stacy were at Bracken.

"Oh, Sunny, you should have seen his face when he saw Drew. I thought my heart would break."

"He didn't question his parentage at all?"

"No," Stacy answered and went ahead to tell her the entire story. "God is so good," Stacy said as she finished.

"How about the verses; were they an encouragement?" Sunny's voice said she hoped they had been.

"'Likewise, ye wives, be in subjection to your own husbands that, if any obey not the word, they also may without the word be won by the conversation of the wives, while they behold your chaste conversation coupled with fear; whose adorning, let it not be that outward adorning of plaiting the hair, and of wearing of gold, or of putting on of apparel, but let it be the hidden man of the heart in that which is not corruptible, even the ornament of a meek and quiet spirit, which is in the sight of God of great price. First Peter 3:1-4.'"

"I can't believe you memorized those verses," Sunny said in amazement.

"I cling to them," Stacy told her, "and it's been such a comfort. But my favorite verse isn't with those. It's at the middle of chapter three. 'For the eyes of the Lord are over the righteous, and his ears are open unto their prayers; but the face of the Lord is against them that do evil.'"

"You challenge me, Stacy. I haven't memorized a verse in several weeks."

"Oh, Sunny, I think God understands. You said that Preston had a cold and then you and then Sterling. I think at times like that you have to concentrate on the verses you already know."

Sunny's brow drew down in a mock frown. "I thought when we studied that I would be teaching you. I really needed to hear that, Stacy. Thank you."

Stacy smiled. "There is so much I don't know, Sunny, and I'm still too timid. I haven't even told Tanner about my conversion. I need boldness."

"Has there been an opportunity to tell him?"

This gave Stacy pause. "Now that you mention it, I'm not sure if there has. Maybe I need to give it more time."

"It sounds like you'll have the time. And don't forget your verses so fast. Your life will show him better than words."

"Yes, it should. My pride rears its head, and I want to shout at Tanner and defend myself. His words about not forgiving me were hard to take, so I concentrated on his wanting a real family. I've prayed about that for so long."

"Speaking of families, did you want to check on the boys?"

"Yes. Drew will be growing hungry soon."

"As will Sterling and Preston. We can have tea when they're settled with lunch."

"Oh, Mumma," Drew cried when his mother appeared at the nursery room door.

"Hello, my darling. Having fun?"

Drew ran to hug Stacy. "They have real boats!" His voice was breathless with excitement. "Lots of boats!"

Stacy's grin was as large as her son's eyes.

"How about some lunch?" Sunny asked the gang, and they responded loudly.

Stacy studied them as they moved out of the room and down the hall. Sterling was a most handsome young lad, sporting his father's dark hair and eyes. He was just short of his sixth birthday. Preston was less than a year older than Drew, and his hair was as dark as Drew's was fair. They were of the same build, Preston being an inch or so taller, and both were the picture of young health.

Since he was a little older, Sterling was inclined to be more serious, whereas both Drew and Preston were in some ways little more than babies. Sterling was wonderfully patient with all of their antics, and Stacy had not as yet heard a cross word between them.

After seeing that they were nicely settled, the Hawkesbury nanny in attendance, Stacy and Sunny went to the small salon for their tea.

They made themselves comfortable and talked as if Stacy had been back for years instead of weeks. The Duchess of Cambridge had a small sandwich halfway to her mouth when her husband and Brandon walked into the room. Stacy, suspecting she might choke if she took a bite, replaced the sandwich and sat still while Tanner approached.

He bent as soon as he was near, grasped her jaw, and kissed her. Stacy stared up into his face a moment, her own face still cupped in his hand, before speaking.

"You could have ridden over with us." Stacy prayed that he was not checking up on her.

"In truth I was in need of a ride. My horse has been getting fat of late. If you don't mind my company, however, I'll go back with you."

"All right," Stacy smiled sweetly, the first real smile since her husband had come for her. It was so reminiscent of their first months as husband and wife that Tanner had a hard time taking his eyes away. Only Brandon, coming to greet Stacy, moved him on.

In the next few minutes, the men took seats and were served tea. The conversation ran from one subject to the next until Parks, head of housekeeping at Bracken, came to the door.

"I'm sorry to disturb you, my lord," he said to Brandon.

"That's all right, Parks. What is it?"

"Nanny reports that young Lord Richardson bumped his head while playing and is quite inconsolable."

Stacy began to rise.

"I'll go," Tanner told her. He moved to the door, Brandon behind him.

"You look thunderstruck," Sunny commented when the men left.

"I'm just surprised that he wanted to go."

"I guess I'm not. Whenever he visits here and the boys are present, he always speaks to them with genuine interest. I think he really loves children."

Sunny talked on, cutting off only when the men reappeared, Drew in his father's arms. He was not crying, but his fair head lay on Tanner's shoulder and the evidence of tears was on his cheek. Tanner deliberately took the settee next to Stacy and as soon as Drew saw his mother, he reached for her.

Stacy took him on her lap but looked down to see that he was smiling back at Tanner.

"You certainly don't look any worse for wear," Stacy commented and looked for the bump. Some tears filled Drew's eyes, but they did not spill.

"I believe it was quite minor." Tanner's voice was dry. His son might have overreacted, but he was adorable while doing it.

"I think what you really need is a nap," Stacy said.

Drew's lip quivered, but Stacy's voice was firm.

"You will not fuss about it, Drew. Now let's say goodbye to Lord and Lady Hawkesbury."

Tanner came behind his wife and son to say his own goodbyes, but he was rather preoccupied. Why hadn't it occurred to him that Drew cried harder because he was tired? He decided he could learn a lot about parenting from Stacy.

Tanner would have laughed at his own seriousness if he could have seen Brandon's and Sunny's amused expressions after he left. Of course, they would have been the first to admit that they had no idea what it was like not to meet your son until he was three.

Thirty-Four

AS USUAL, STACY WAS STARVING. She had eaten a large dinner and even enjoyed Tanner's presence in the process, but that felt like hours ago. She tried to sleep, but it just wasn't going to work. After fighting the urge for just a few minutes, she decided to go to the kitchen. She knew the feeling and was certain it would not go away.

With a decisive move, she threw the covers back and reached for her wrapper. It came to her as she was leaving her room that Tanner would simply ring for something, but Stacy's relationship with the staff was only just slightly warmer now than it had been when they first arrived.

Cook, Price, and of course, Hettie were the only servants who did not act as if they were doing Stacy a favor every time she called on them. It was only when Drew needed something that she was bold enough to speak up, which of course was the very reason Stacy was walking toward the kitchen this late at night, feeling rather clandestine about fixing herself a snack while the rest of the mansion slept.

Tanner climbed the stairs rather late that night. He'd had some figures to go over concerning a land deal he and Brandon were involved in, and he'd not been satisfied with the outcome. They had already talked of it several times and were going to talk of it again in another few weeks. Tanner had wanted the paperwork out of his head so that he could once again concentrate on Drew and Stacy.

As was swiftly becoming his habit of the last few weeks, Tanner moved to Stacy's door. Each night before he went to bed he would check on both her and Drew. He'd have much preferred Stacy to join him in his own room, but that had not yet happened. She was growing less wary of him each day, and he felt that given time they would once again live as man and wife.

This didn't immediately erase all the past, but Stacy had a good memory; she would not forget his reaction last time and play him for a fool again. Tanner wondered briefly if she'd had other men while in Middlesbrough and then realized that such thoughts were dangerous. He shifted his mind away from such visions as he soundlessly opened Stacy's door.

Tanner did not like finding her bed empty, but he remained calm as he moved across to Drew's room. His heart was silently telling Stacy that she had better be there. When she was not, he decided to wake the entire house to look for her but refrained from doing so until he checked the upstairs and then made his way down the stairway.

She was not in the library or the gallery. He wondered if he'd missed her somewhere on the second floor and was actually halfway up the stairs when he thought of the kitchen. He almost laughed. If Stacy were hungry she would never ring for a servant. With a smile on his face he moved toward the kitchen.

Lady Richardson had just finished an apple and was starting on a piece of pie when Tanner came in the door. She froze, a crumb of food at the corner of her mouth, and watched him approach.

"It seems we have mice—tall, blonde mice."

"I was hungry," Stacy told him unnecessarily, still trying to decide if she was in trouble.

"I can see that." Tanner used his handkerchief to wipe her mouth and then stood staring at her.

"Don't stop on my account," he told her. "Go ahead and eat."

Stacy did so, but it was not easy with Tanner staring at her. His gaze was warm as he watched her. He even pulled a chair up, so his eyes were level with hers.

"Would you like something?" Stacy asked.

"To eat? No, thank you."

Stacy finished her pie. "You're making me nervous," she admitted, a small quiver in her voice.

"You're not afraid of me, are you?"

"I'm not sure what to say to that."

"You are afraid," he stated.

"Of our being together, no, but of my having you for a time and then your pushing me away again, that terrifies me."

Surprisingly this did not anger Tanner. He looked as though he understood. Unfortunately he felt no guilt over the way he'd sent her away. In his mind he had been wronged. If Stacy would only comport herself faithfully, he would care for her all the days of her life. He felt whether or not she stayed was all up to her.

Suddenly Tanner held out his hand. "Come here, Stacy" was all he said. It was hardly an explanation, but Stacy went to him when he reached for her. They kissed in the kitchen, and she had no protest when Tanner lifted her and carried her upstairs.

She had prayed long and hard about this time, wanting with all of her heart to do what God would have her to do. *Maybe,* Stacy reasoned, *this will be one more way to show Tanner that my love has always been constant.*

The next morning Tanner eased quietly out of bed, careful not to wake Stacy. He stared down at her, thinking there wasn't a lovelier, more giving woman in all of England. At this moment he could almost believe her when she claimed that he had misunderstood the scene at the Cradwells'.

With feather-soft movements he reached for his robe and left the room. Stacy had come in with just a light wrapper on the night before, so Tanner was headed to her room to find her a robe. He didn't want her feeling at all uncomfortable when she awakened.

Stacy's bed was as he'd seen it, covers thrown back and left. There was no sign of her robe, so he lit the lantern and went into her dressing room. He paid little attention to her dresses but quickly spotted a thick, white robe and took hold of it. He was on his way out when he spotted an envelope. He would normally have given little notice to such a thing, but it was addressed to him.

Tanner set the lantern down and looked at the front of the letter. "Lord Tanner Richardson" was written out in Stacy's hand. Tanner removed the folded letter without a moment's hesitation.

"Dear Tanner," it began. "I'm not sure if you knew I was back in London, but I arrived just this week. I am staying at Brentwood with Roddy and Lucinda. I would like to see you. I know I told you I would not return unless you sent for me, but my grandfather has died and I've come at Lucinda's bidding.

"I would like to see you, Tanner. I would like to talk about the Cradwell party and explain about Nigel Stanley. I made a terrible mistake, and if we could only talk, I feel we might resolve this painful thing between us."

There was more, but Tanner stopped reading. He had been ready to believe it had all been a mistake—that he had misunderstood. This was harder to take than Leslie's betrayal. Stacy's sweetness wove its way into his heart until he felt like a snared bird. He had loved that snare when they had first married, but after Stacy's betrayal, he'd felt like it was strangling him.

Tanner threw both the letter and Stacy's robe to the floor and exited the wardrobe and bedroom with long, angry strides. He dressed with Price's help, giving terse orders all the while.

"Pack my bag; I'm leaving. See to it that my *wife*"—it cost him just to say the word—"does not get too comfortable in my bed."

"You do not want me to accompany you, my lord?"

"No. I shall be gone at least a week, but that's no one's business. Handle my correspondence as best you can. No social engagements at all."

"Yes, my lord."

Just 20 minutes later Tanner was in the coach and headed to London. He was not entirely certain what he needed to do there, but he had to put some space between himself and his adulterous wife. He thought he could put it behind him, but right now that didn't seem possible—the letter had finally told him that what he'd believed all along was true.

The night they had spent together ran through his mind, and Tanner knew he would always desire his wife. His next thoughts were of his son, the precious little boy he was just getting to know. Tanner's head fell back against the squabs. He would never break his promise, but agony ripped through him that he could not live in peace with the boy's mother.

Stacy woke slowly and smiled. Surprisingly, she didn't feel any disorientation waking up in the master bedroom. She knew exactly where she was and, with the smile still on her face, rolled toward Tanner's side of the bed. A lopsided frown replaced the smile when she found the bed empty.

"Tanner," Stacy called softly, hoping he was in his dressing room.

"Tanner," she tried again and sat up when the door opened. She lay down swiftly however, quickly covering herself with the bedclothes when Price appeared instead. She grinned at him from the pillow, even though she was somewhat embarrassed, but her smile slowly faded at Price's serious face.

"Is Lord Richardson dressing, Price?"

"I'm sorry, my lady, but Lord Richardson is not here."

"By not here, do you mean not upstairs?" Her tone was almost too much for the man.

"No, my lady."

"He's left Winslow?"

"Yes, my lady. Would you like me to send Hettie to you?"

"No, Price, that's all right. I'll get up as soon as you go."

Price bowed his way out, and Stacy lay still for a moment. If he had left money on the pillow beside her, she couldn't have felt any cheaper.

Five minutes later Stacy was standing in her dressing room. She bent slowly and picked up the robe and crumpled letter. It didn't take long to figure what had happened. Stacy's eyes closed in agony.

"Oh, Tanner," she whispered. "What have you done?"

Thirty-Five

STACY WAS SORRY SHE CONFIDED in her aunt. Lucinda was so angry she could hardly see straight. Tanner had been gone three days now, and her aunt and uncle had arrived that morning. They were in the large salon at Winslow. Drew was on the huge Persian carpet that covered the floor, but Roddy had brought him a toy and he was not listening to the adults.

"First he takes you from us," she raved, her voice soft but venomous. "And then leaves you here like so much excess baggage. He's an absolute beast. I want you to pack your things immediately. You and Drew are returning with us."

Stacy only shook her head, calm in the face of her aunt's ire.

"How can you stay here?" Lucinda was incredulous.

"Because I want my marriage to work. Running away will accomplish nothing."

Lucinda sat back in utter defeat. Roddy studied his wife and then commented.

"Unless you fear for your safety, I think you're wise, Stacy. What you've told us is heartbreaking, but I think Tanner is confused."

"Confused!" Lucinda snorted scornfully, but a look from Roddy silenced her.

"If he is confused," Roddy continued, "then maybe you can work it out when he returns."

"I thank you for the vote of confidence, Roddy, but he'll probably be angry when he returns. And as you know, Tanner's anger has a way of intimidating me."

"But you don't fear he'll harm you?"

"At times I feel emotionally spent, but no, I don't fear Tanner that way. I think Tanner is wrong to react as he does, but part of the problem is mine because I'm not bolder when I know I'm supposed to be. I decided a few days ago that leaving cannot be an option, or every time I'm upset I'll want to run."

"So you'll stay here no matter what?" Stacy could hear tears in Lucinda's voice.

"I won't go so far as to say that, but I will stay on just as long as I can and hope that means I'll be here for the next 60 years."

It was not what Lucinda wanted to hear, but Stacy believed she was making the right choice. The first time Tanner growled at her she knew she'd be tempted to hide, but for now, for her sake as well as Drew's, she must stay.

The subject was dropped when Drew wanted to go upstairs. Stacy rose to accompany him, but Lucinda, her eyes alight with adoration for Drew, offered to go instead. Stacy was happy to agree. Not until after they'd gone did Stacy take her seat and notice a very thoughtful look on Roddy's face.

"My, but you look serious," Stacy commented lightly. To her surprise Roddy did not laugh at his own somber demeanor.

"How did you come to this decision, Stacy? I mean, to stay here with Tanner?" Roddy asked.

"I believe it's what God wants me to do," she answered simply.

"But how do you *know?*" Roddy's face was filled with yearning. "Has God spoken to you in some way?"

"Through His Word, yes. I believe God speaks to His children through the Bible. I've matured through my study; in fact, I'm a different person now, Roddy, and that's because of the time I've spent in God's Word."

"And you really believe that the Bible is the inspired Word of God?"

"Yes, I do, Roddy."

"But what if you simply can't find the answer you're looking for? Then what do you do?"

Stacy smiled. "God has never let me down, Roddy. If I truly need to know something, He shows me. I don't mean going off on some tangent in order to disprove whether or not Jonah really was swallowed by a fish and lived to tell about it. I'm talking about real-life issues that apply directly to my heart and change me forever."

Roddy nodded slowly and admitted softly, "I'm still working through the cross."

Stacy's smile was tender. She wasn't exactly sure what he meant, but she could hear Drew and Lucinda coming back to join them. "I'll be praying for you, Roddy, and if there is anything I can help you with, please don't hesitate to ask."

Roddy thanked her and then spoke softly before they were interrupted. "*Do* you believe that Jonah was literally swallowed by a huge fish?"

Again Stacy smiled. "With all my heart."

Stacy was ready to change her resolve over staying almost as soon as Tanner came back a week later. She knew he would not seek her out, and she had no intention of mentioning the letter, but Stacy forced herself to see him in order to know where she stood.

"Welcome back, Tanner," Stacy ventured hesitantly from her place just inside the study door, glad to have even gained entrance. "Did your trip go well?"

"Sufferably," Tanner answered without ever looking up from his desk.

"How was your birthday?"

This got the duke's attention. His head came up, and he looked at her in surprise. Stacy began thinking she'd mistaken the date all these years.

"It was your birthday two days ago, wasn't it?"

"Yes." Tanner's voice was cold. He seemed to be angry that she remembered when he had not.

"It doesn't sound like you celebrated." Stacy tried to be cheerful. "Shall I ask cook for something special for lunch?"

"I'll be busy."

"Dinner then?"

"No. I have work to do, Stacy."

She watched his head go back down and knew she had to ask the next question if it killed her.

"Tanner, would you rather we leave?"

Brown eyes burned into blue, and Stacy held her breath.

"Do as you like." Again the head went back down.

"So we can stay?"

"I don't—" Tanner stood and began to shout, but cut off when he saw his wife blanch.

He was still angry enough to throw her out, but thinking about it and actually doing it while looking into Stacy's vulnerable, strained features were far different.

"You're welcome to stay." Tanner's was calmer now. "But I am a busy man, so I would appreciate being left alone."

Stacy nodded and turned to the door. Her hand shook as she tried to open it, forcing her to try again. She exited the room without once glancing back to see her husband watching her, an unreadable expression on his face.

"Here we go." Stacy swung Drew back up onto the bank and they started their trek home.

Two weeks had passed since she'd talked to Tanner in the study. He rarely spoke to her, although there were times when he sought Drew out and talked with him.

Just when she didn't think she could bear up under the strain, the Lord used Drew to rescue her.

"Mumma, can we fish?"

It was on Stacy's lips to say no because there was no water, but she suddenly remembered a creek that she and Tanner had passed years ago while out riding. It would take some legwork, but Stacy was sure they could walk it.

Today was their sixth trip. Stacy did not say yes every day, but in truth she needed the outings as much as Drew did. The servants, with the exception of Price, were more unpleasant than ever, and Winslow had become an oppressive place for Stacy. Hettie had come down with a summer cold that went straight into her chest, so Stacy and Drew were on their own much of the time.

"I'll carry the fish," Drew now said, and Stacy gave him the string. She knew he wouldn't last long with the heavy line, but she let him try. They were both tiring as they neared the rear of the Winslow stables, but Drew still had energy to chatter. He made Stacy laugh on several occasions, and she was still laughing when Drew cried out.

"Oh, look, Mumma, it's Lord Richardson. We can show him our catch."

This was the last thing Stacy wanted to do, but Tanner was standing ahead of them in the path, watching their approach. The twosome had no choice but to walk right past him.

"We fished," Drew said as soon as he was in close proximity. "See our catch, Lord Richardson!"

Stacy had stopped, and Drew now took the fish and ran from his mother's side to hold up the string of trophies. Tanner moved toward his son and hunkered down to Drew's level.

"It looks as if you've been busy."

"Mumma caught them, and I helped. Someday I can fish with a hook too."

"I'm sure you'll do very well."

Drew chattered on, and Tanner paid close attention. Stacy would have been surprised to know that he was watching her as much as listening to Drew.

She was dressed in a worn day-dress, looking more like a scullery maid than a duchess. Not that it mattered; Tanner found her lovely whatever her attire. Her face was flushed and her hair a mess, and Tanner suddenly realized they had come from behind the stables and not through them.

"Where did you fish?" He stood in one easy movement, his voice nonchalant.

"At the creek."

"Did you walk?"

"Yes," Stacy answered slowly, sensing for the first time that he might not be too happy about that. "It really isn't far, and we needed to get out."

"I don't want—" Tanner began, his tone severe.

"Mumma?"

"Andrew," Stacy turned to her son when he cut in, "Lord Richardson is talking. Do not interrupt." Stacy turned back to Tanner, but he was staring down at Drew. Stacy followed his gaze to find her son standing with his legs close together and a look of near panic on his face.

Oh my, Stacy thought, thinking that if she took care of Drew's needs, Tanner would be angry. To her surprise, Tanner stepped in. He swiftly scooped Drew into his arms and headed into the bush off the path.

Stacy heard low voices beyond the shrubs and shook her head in wonder. One moment her husband was completely unapproachable and then next he was taking his son into the bushes. Although, if Stacy thought about it, Tanner was always kind to Drew. It was to her that he was unapproachable. He didn't seek Drew out very often, but his face and voice were very gentle when they were together.

Drew marched out of the bushes then, Tanner on his heels.

"Mumma, can Lord Richardson eat our fish too?"

"Of course, darling; we have plenty."

"I'll tell cook," Drew stated and started toward the mansion once again. Stacy thanked Tanner for seeing to Drew's needs and moved along the path. She wasn't certain if Tanner followed or not, but right then she couldn't make herself stay and be scolded over the fishing trip. Feeling every inch a coward, she rushed along behind Drew to the kitchen.

Three hours later Tanner came from his study in time to see a maid taking a tray upstairs. The unmistakable smell of fish wafted through the air. Tanner frowned at the woman's back. Hadn't Drew wanted to eat with him, and hadn't Stacy agreed?

"Did you need something, my lord?"

Tanner turned to find Price in attendance.

"When is dinner?"

"Seven o'clock, unless of course you wish to change the time?"

Tanner knew it was just now six.

"And what is cook serving?"

"I believe Lord Drew requested that you enjoy some of his fish."

Tanner nodded. He'd assumed that they would be eating together and realized then that he should assume nothing. His disappointment was keen. He had looked forward to eating with his son and seeing Stacy. His anger was wearing off, and even though he was in no mood to allow her any foothold in his life, she was still a delight to the eyes, and because she didn't chatter constantly, a very restful person to be with.

"Please tell cook that I wish my dinner now, and served with my wife and son."

Price bowed and left to change the arrangements. Tanner, not bothering with a coat, took the stairs two at a time to find Stacy and Drew.

Stacy had just seated Drew at the table in her sitting room and was about to serve him when Tanner knocked on the door. Stacy stared up at him, uncertain about his presence until Tanner's brows rose almost mockingly.

"Come in," Stacy quickly invited, feeling flustered.

Tanner spoke once he was inside.

"I thought I'd been invited to eat fish with you."

"Oh!" Stacy said. "I'm sorry, Tanner, I didn't realize. Please sit down."

She rushed to pull up another chair to the small table and serve him. Tanner frowned at her actions, looking around for the kitchen maid. He would have questioned Stacy about this, but there was another knock at the door.

Each evening at 6:00, a tray was delivered by a kitchen maid to Drew and Stacy. The maid never stayed to serve them in any way, but now that Tanner was present, not only one maid came to attend him, but three. The plates uncovered from Tanner's tray were filled with sumptuous foods and added to Drew and Stacy's meager fare. Stacy and Drew never received any more than one piece of bread each—Tanner had an entire loaf. He had butter—they never saw the stuff. They felt blessed if they received one vegetable—Tanner's tray had four.

Stacy, fighting resentment over the way she and Drew were treated, busied herself with her son's plate, filling it with the best food they'd eaten since arriving. Then she cut his fish and got the spoon into his hand. He bumped his water at one point, but Stacy caught it. It wasn't until that moment that she glanced up to find Tanner's gaze on her.

He'd been talking with Drew, and Stacy, who was still in turmoil inside and had not said a word, only listened. She thought she'd been hiding her feelings but realized now that her color must be high with her agitation. She was more angry at herself than anyone else for not telling Tanner on the spot that this was the best they'd eaten.

As soon as Drew was well ensconced with his food, Stacy lowered her eyes and dug into her own plate. She didn't care if she was being watched or not, she was suddenly so hungry she was shaking.

"Mumma," Drew suddenly said. "We didn't pray."

Stacy took a deep breath and praised God for this gentle reminder. "You're right, my darling. Shall we pray now?" Where Stacy found the courage to suggest this without even looking at her spouse, she didn't know, but pray she did.

"Father in heaven, we thank You for this food and all Your blessings. Please keep us this night that we might wake tomorrow to know You and serve You better. In Your name we pray. Amen."

"Amen," Drew echoed and picked up his spoon once again. Stacy retrieved her own utensil and only then did she look up to see Tanner staring, but this time he was looking at Drew, contentment etching his handsome face.

"It's good that children pray," Tanner finally commented. Stacy nearly dropped her fork. She recovered swiftly, however, and put in her own gentle oar.

"I find that prayer is also good for adults. That, along with time spent reading God's Word."

Tanner's attention turned to her, his eyes thoughtful. "I wondered at your having a Bible near your bed."

"I read it every day." Stacy spoke calmly but was amazed that he'd even noticed.

"Why?" he asked bluntly, as if doing such a thing was only for the weak.

"I have a yearning to know more. I have a relationship with God through His Son, Jesus Christ, and I want to know Him better."

Tanner clearly did not know what to do with this answer. He didn't believe that God involved Himself in people's daily lives. That type of thing was reserved for the Old Testament times, when God spoke through a burning bush or met Moses on the mountain to give him the law. And yet Stacy was so sincere. She was not the type to go off on some emotional religious experience, and the serenity in her eyes as she'd answered him was unmistakable.

Tanner went back to his plate, and Stacy knew the discussion was over. It hadn't been much, but he'd at least listened to her without ridicule. Stacy continued to eat as well. Drew started to chatter right after that, but Stacy's mind was praying and she did not attend.

Thirty-Six

THE STUDY DOOR BURST OPEN, and Tanner, having been disturbed, came out in a dreadful humor. Stacy and Drew had been on their way to the front door, and Stacy, thinking Tanner was away again, was chasing Drew and making him giggle loudly. They both shrank back when he stood before them in a towering rage. Stacy, fearing he would shout at Drew, called to Hettie.

"Drew," she told him when the old woman appeared, "go on to the coach with Hettie; there's a good boy. I'll be out shortly."

"I'm sorry, Tanner," Stacy said when Hettie and the boy were gone. "We didn't realize you were here."

Tanner's mood was not improved by her apology. Stacy, thinking it best that she just leave, took a step away.

"Do they not have dressmakers in Middlesbrough?"

The question was not lost on Stacy. She was wearing a dress of dark blue satin with matching bows and white lace on the bodice and neckline. It was one from her wedding trousseau—in fact all of her dresses were from her wedding trousseau.

"Well, actually I gained quite a bit of weight when I was carrying Drew, and I wasn't able to wear many of my gowns. Some of them are virtually new." Stacy stopped, thinking this explanation enough, but Tanner still scowled.

"You're leaving?"

"Yes. We're going to Bracken. I hope it will be quiet for you then."

Tanner didn't even bother to acknowledge her statement. Without so much as a by-your-leave, he turned on his heel and walked back to the study.

"So you think things might be a little better?" Sunny asked.

"Well," Stacy tried to explain, "Tanner's moods are usually pretty black, but he's been very attentive to Drew and sometimes he's very kind to me. One night—" Stacy began and went on to tell Sunny what had happened over the dinner table with Drew, the prayer, and their discussion afterward.

"It was very brief, but then a few nights later Tanner showed up at Drew's bedtime. I always read Drew a Bible passage, and Tanner actually stayed to listen. It was the parable of the prodigal son from Luke 15. Tanner seemed fascinated. Now he looks at me as if he doesn't know me, but it's not in a negative way. Does that make sense?"

"Yes. You think he might be warming up?"

Stacy shrugged ruefully. "He wasn't too happy when I left this morning. I always seem to underestimate Tanner. I've been so relieved on several occasions that he hasn't seemed to notice my clothing, and then this morning I discovered he hasn't missed a thing."

"Upset, was he?"

"Yes. I know my clothes are all out of date; Lucinda made that quiet clear, but it just hasn't been important, Sunny. When you think of all that's gone on in my world in the last few years, you can probably see why having the latest outfits was not a priority."

"It's a matter of pride."

"You think I'm being prideful?" It was hard for Stacy to hear this, but she needed to be made aware.

"Not you, Stacy. Tanner. He's a duke, a wealthy one. He wants you dressed in the finest attire money can buy."

Stacy's look was comical. "I've never thought of it that way."

"It might be best if you did, because I wouldn't be too surprised if he suddenly decided to do something about your wardrobe."

Stacy nodded in understanding. They both knew that "something" meant a shopping trip to London.

"Thank you, Sunny," Stacy said softly, and for the moment the subject was dropped. It was time to go upstairs. Earlier, the boys had asked their mothers to have tea with them in the nursery.

For the second time since Stacy returned to Winslow, Tanner "followed" her to Bracken. She had been other times on her own, so she knew he was not checking on her, but the emotions she felt when he appeared were riotous. Actually they were the same emotions that occurred nearly every time he sought her out—some fear, but also some hope that maybe he had come because he'd missed her.

The women were still in the nursery when Tanner and Brandon came in. Tanner did not immediately speak to her beyond a short greeting but talked with Brandon, Sunny, and the boys. Stacy noticed the way he studied the children, and something in his expression made her wary. She didn't have long to wait. Tanner refused tea and just ten minutes after he arrived, he turned to Stacy.

"I want us to leave for London."

"Right now?"

"Yes."

"All right," Stacy stood. "Would you like me to go home and pack?"

"You and Drew are already packed. Hettie is waiting with the carriages." His voice was not harsh, but Stacy could tell that he was not feeling overly patient.

"Oh." Stacy was not certain how to reply to this, but she knew she needed a moment of privacy. "Drew and I will just take a minute to prepare, and we'll be right down."

Tanner's nod was almost curt as he told them he'd be waiting downstairs and abruptly left the room. Stacy made swift thank-you's, and Sunny took her and Drew to a retiring room. Stacy's heart sank when Drew decided he needed to sit down on the commode. Stacy knew it would do no good to rush him, but she could almost feel Tanner's impatience from downstairs.

When they finally started to rush down the stairs, Drew got it into his head to examine everything they passed. Tanner was in sight when he stopped the last time to look at a bronze statue.

"Andrew!" Stacy's voice was sharp with panic. "Lord Richardson is waiting for us. Come now."

Afraid of his fury, Stacy kept her head lowered as they passed. Sunny walked Stacy and Drew to the carriage, and Tanner and Brandon followed more slowly.

"Come again when you can stay," Brandon told the other duke.

"I'll do that, Hawk. Thank you."

"I might be out of line," Brandon continued as they walked, "but Stacy gave Sunny the impression that you've accepted Drew as your own."

"Of course I have." Tanner frowned darkly at him, but Brandon was not so easily intimidated.

"Then why the Lord Richardson?"

"I don't know what you're talking about."

"Your son calls you Lord Richardson, and Stacy calls you by your title when she's speaking of you to Drew."

Tanner's air left him in a rush. He hadn't even noticed. He'd had a formal relationship with his father, never calling him anything but "sir," but not even he and his brother had been expected to call him by his title.

"It's your choice, Tanner," Brandon said softly. "And the last thing I want to do is interfere. It's just that Drew obviously thinks quite a lot of you, and I think he's a fine boy."

"Yes, he is," Tanner admitted, looking his friend in the eye. "I'll see you later, Hawk."

"Goodbye, Tanner."

The two men shook hands, and Tanner covered the remaining distance to the carriage and pulled himself inside. Stacy and Drew waved briefly from the window before settling back for the long trip to London.

Tanner could not get Sterling and Preston from his mind. He'd come to Bracken determined to take Stacy away and dress her in London's finest, and then he saw his son with the Hawkesbury boys. Tanner had not even thought about Drew's clothes. In all fairness, Stacy had done an admirable job with their son's wardrobe, but next to the smart outfits and fine fabrics of the other boys' clothes, he looked dressed in homespun cloth. It didn't take more than a second to know that he wanted better for his son, a son who chattered nonstop for the first 15 minutes of the ride before falling into an exhausted sleep in his mother's lap.

Stacy settled him on the seat beside her and gambled a look at Tanner. He'd been in no mood for chitchat when he'd come into the carriage, and other than an occasional comment to Drew or an answer to the boy's questions, he had been quiet. Stacy knew she would find out sooner or later what was on his mind, but not having been privy to his conversation with Brandon, it came as a complete surprise when he finally told her.

"I don't want Drew to call me Lord Richardson. I want him to know who I am."

Stacy blinked at him. "All right," she replied slowly. "Would you like to tell him?"

"What do you think?" Stacy had never seen Tanner humble; it was a little hard to grasp.

"I think he'll be thrilled."

"That isn't what I meant. I meant should I tell him, or would he take it better from you?"

Stacy thought. "Why don't we tell him together? He's awfully little, but I think I can make it clear for him. If you were there also, you would know firsthand if he understood."

"At bedtime then," Tanner said, but Stacy feared it would only excite him and cause an hour of work to get him to sleep.

"I think dinnertime would be better."

Tanner stared at her. It was such a surprise to have her contradict him in any way. There had been no heat, but he could see that she was adamant. Not for any other reason did Stacy stand up to him. He suddenly remembered how much trouble he'd been in over the banister, and for the first time in weeks knew a desperate urge to please his wife.

"Dinner it is. What time would you say is best?"

"Drew usually eats at six."

"Six o'clock then."

Drew began to stir, so the adults fell silent. Stacy kept her eyes on her son until he settled again, but the conversation did not resume.

"Lord Richardson asked me to give you this, my lady."

Stacy took the paper from Price's hand. It was an itinerary laid out for the next few days. According to the schedule she had an appointment with Madame Angelica for the following day. She was to be fitted for a summer, fall, and winter wardrobe.

Drew had an appointment with the tailor two days after

that, but Stacy thankfully saw that the tailor would be coming to the town house.

"If you have any questions, my lady, just ring for me. I would be happy to explain."

"How long will we be here, Price?"

"Probably not as long as you might think," he took the liberty of telling her. "Your clothing can be picked up by one of the coachmen and delivered to Winslow."

Stacy breathed a sigh of relief and thanked Price. He had read her concern so accurately. London was always a trial for her, and if she had needed to wait for three wardrobes, they could have been there for weeks.

Price went on his way after that, and Stacy settled down to write Lucinda. If she'd read the schedule correctly, she had a day between her own fitting and Drew's. With a bit of maneuvering she could get a visit in with her aunt and uncle.

The meal that evening was very relaxing. Tanner was most charming, and he made Stacy and Drew laugh on more than one occasion. When it seemed that Drew was finished with his dinner, Stacy petitioned God for help one last time and plunged in.

"I have something special to tell you tonight, Drew," Stacy began, knowing she had to do this in her own way. Only her fear that Drew would be hurt in some way by the news gave her the boldness to handle it as she saw fit.

"Do you remember my telling you about baby Moses?"

"He went in the water."

"That's right. Did Moses have a mother and a father?"

"I think so."

"Yes, he did, because that's God's way. How about Adam and Eve in the garden? They had children, didn't they? A mother, a father, and children make a family.

Stacy paused when Drew needed a drink, and then asked, "Who is your mother, Drew?"

"You, Mumma." He smiled as though she were making a game.

"That's right. Who is your father?"

Stacy didn't know which was more heartbreaking, the confusion in her son's eyes or the yearning in her husband's.

"Lord Richardson has the same name as you, doesn't he, Drew?" The little boy looked at Tanner and then back at Stacy. "His name is Tanner Richardson and your name is Andrew Tanner Richardson. That's because Lord Richardson is your papa."

"What about mumma?"

"I'm still your mumma," Stacy swiftly assured him. "I always will be, but now you have a papa too."

When Drew looked back at Tanner, the duke smiled at him. Drew smiled in return, and Tanner reached forward and brushed the hair over his forehead. Drew's grin broadened, although Stacy wasn't certain he actually understood. Stacy doubted that Tanner was as calm outside as he appeared, but she was thrilled with the way it had gone.

Conversation started up again among the three of them, and whenever Drew started to call Tanner sir or lord, someone would gently correct him. Stacy wasn't certain as to how much he was beginning to understand until it was bedtime.

"Would you like Papa to carry you to bed?" she asked.

Drew's eyes flew to Tanner's, and Stacy's smile was huge as he swung his small son up into his arms.

"Off we go, son." It was as if it happened all the time.

Stacy nearly floated into Drew's bedroom. They were going to be a family! Tanner was not what you'd call warm to her, but he didn't seem quite so angry.

Thank You, Lord, Stacy silently prayed. *Thank You for giving us another chance. Please help us to make the best of it.*

Thirty-Seven

MADAME ANGELICA, LONDON'S PREMIER DRESSMAKER, rattled off a string of sentences in rapid French to Tanner. Stacy had to hold her mouth shut as Tanner replied back in French. When pleasure and something akin to greed lit the woman's eyes, it wasn't hard to figure out that Tanner had told her what he sought.

"Come in, my lady," Angelica nearly cooed. She had dozens of seamstresses and assistants, but this was a duchess, and for this reason Angelica would see to the fittings herself.

"Thank you."

Stacy and Tanner followed her, Stacy noticing as they walked that she had the disconcerting habit of muttering to herself in French. Stacy wondered what the dressmaker was saying as they were led into the private dressing room.

"I need my tape," Madame Angelica explained briskly and rushed off still muttering to herself. Stacy looked to Tanner.

"She's quite taken with your figure, but she says your dress, one of her own magnificent creations, is sadly out of date." Tanner's voice was so bored as he recited this that Stacy blushed.

She found herself wishing that Sunny had never mentioned Tanner's pride. He was only doing this for himself, because it was shaming his reputation to have his wife seen in outdated clothes. Stacy felt resentment rising within her.

"Now then." The dressmaker was back. "I will help you out of this gown," she began, and then the rest was in French. Just moments passed before Stacy found herself in her underclothes, being measured from head to foot.

"Now, I have a dress, the latest style and almost complete, but the fabric, you see, is flawed. I would like you to try it just for fit."

Stacy agreed with a nod of her head, and the older woman was gone and back in record time, carrying a gold creation over her arm. The dress was slipped over Stacy's shoulders, settled around her hips, and buttoned up the back. Madame Angelica had forgotten yet one more thing, and as she rushed off, Stacy was given her first full look in the mirror. She was horrified by what she saw...why not even her shift was that low!

Stacy told herself not to overreact; maybe there had been a mistake. But as she studied herself in the mirror, she knew there had been no error. Her hand came slowly to her mouth as her stomach churned.

Oh please, Stacy silently begged her husband. *Please don't make me go into public this way.*

Stacy was so shaken that tears filled her eyes. Knowing that Tanner was somewhere behind and to the side of her, Stacy carefully moved her face away from him as well as her own image in the mirror. She racked her brain for a solution, but she was too much in a panic and none came. Tanner would be furious if she made a scene in the dress shop.

A chance glance in the mirror told her that Tanner had moved until he could study her face in the reflection. Stacy swiftly turned her tear-filled eyes away, but the hand she'd placed over the missing material told Tanner all he needed to know.

"Now then." Angelica was back.

"The dress is too low," Tanner interrupted before she could say another word.

"But Lord Richardson," Madame Angelica replied, clearly

shocked, "it is the latest style, and your wife's figure, ooh la la—it is perfection. How can—"

"It's too low," Tanner stated again, and this time his voice did not invite Angelica to argue.

With a heartfelt sigh, she asked, "What is it you wish?"

"Lady Richardson will show you."

Stacy was still shaking, but she managed to show Angelica what she had in mind. The plump dressmaker was not at all happy, but she gave no further argument.

Just a short time later Stacy was back in her own dress, and the process of choosing patterns and fabrics began. She learned that Tanner had magnificent taste, and Stacy had to do little more than nod while he, Angelica, and all her helpers sorted their way through patterns and bolts of cloth.

It wasn't until they were back in the carriage that Stacy was given a chance to thank Tanner. He frowned at her as though the words were not necessary, so Stacy let the subject drop as well as her eyes.

"I've never been tempted toward criminal actions before," Lucinda told her husband. "But I want to steal this child."

Roddy laughed. He certainly knew how she felt. Drew had been spending the day with them, and even though they had known he should have a nap, the time had just flown. Now he was asleep in Roddy's lap, and the two adults present could not keep their eyes off of him.

"I love the way his face flushes when he sleeps," Roddy murmured.

"I've missed him so much. I was even hoping things wouldn't work out between Stacy and Tanner so he could come back here."

"Cinda." Roddy's voice was a soft rebuke. "That's a horrible way to think, and besides, Winslow is closer to us than

Middlesbrough, which is where I suspect Stacy will go if Tanner ever sends her away again."

Lucinda's brow furrowed. She had thought of this, but it was not something of which she approved. Roddy saw the stubborn look on her face and frowned in concern. Lucinda had been running people's lives for years, and even though she said little to Stacy, Roddy knew she still wanted to run hers as well.

From time to time Roddy had worried over his wife's busyness, but never like he did now. When it came to Stacy, and most especially Drew, she was like a woman possessed. Roddy had tried to talk with her on a number of occasions, but she always grew very agitated and he would let the matter drop.

He contemplated bringing it up now but hesitated, feeling a coward. Another hour passed. Just as he was finally ready to say something, Tanner and Stacy arrived. Even though he was grateful, he felt cowardly for his relief.

The day after the dress fitting, a Richardson carriage pulled up in front of Featherstone. Stacy glanced out the carriage window to see Lady Andrea waiting for her. The first day in town, after Price had given Stacy the itinerary, she had been on the verge of sending her note to Lucinda and Roddy suggesting they have tea. However, a note arrived from Brandon's mother before Stacy could do anything.

How she had known that Stacy was in London, Stacy could not imagine, but she was thrilled to be able to accept. The note she had finally sent to Lucinda and Roddy asked them if they would like to have Drew while she was at the dressmaker's and with Lady Andrea. Stacy felt a twinge of guilt at not spending the following day with them, but wanted very much to see Lady Andrea and felt her family would understand.

"My dear," Andrea said warmly as she came forward and embraced Stacy. "I'm so glad you came. Come inside. I've a splendid tea laid out. Is Drew with you?"

"He came to London with us, yes, but right now he's at Brentwood."

Andrea smiled. "Lucinda must be thrilled."

Stacy moved inside with her hostess and when she'd laid off her things, she asked Lady Andrea how she'd known of her presence.

"I was in need of some papers from Bracken," the older woman told her. "Brandon sent them by coach yesterday, and when they arrived I found that Sunny had added a letter telling of your visit."

"I'm so glad she did. I don't care for London all that much, and it's nice to come here where I can forget the gossips and even the dressmaker."

"Was it so bad?"

Stacy pulled a face. "I hadn't realized the necklines had gone so low."

Andrea nodded understandingly. "I'm afraid they become barer every year. Is that what Tanner wanted for you?"

Stacy sighed gently, still feeling very thankful. "No, he didn't. I was quite nearly in tears in the dressing room, and he didn't push me. I know Madame Angelica thought we were mad, but at least my dresses will be modest."

"It's amazing isn't it? I mean, the little ways God takes care of us?"

"Oh, my," Stacy agreed fervently, "I certainly found that out this last year."

Andrea poured the tea then, and Stacy shared some of the ways God had worked in her heart and at Winslow. Andrea's eyes filled with tears as Stacy shared how thankful she was for the little things, like being moved from the north wing. Then she told of the great things, such as Tanner's wanting Drew to know of his parentage.

Andrea's handkerchief was in her hand when she told Stacy she would be praying that Tanner would continue to grow closer to her and Drew. They fell silent for a time, and then Stacy spoke thoughtfully.

"I could have a better attitude about the fittings. Lucinda adores shopping and fittings, and when I lived with her she finally despaired of ever changing me."

"Sunny positively hates shopping, so do you know what she does?"

"No."

"She sends her measurements to Madame Angelica. She's been doing it for years. When the wardrobe is completed, it's all sent to Bracken. When the gowns arrive she needs an occasional tuck here and there, but she has a marvelous maid who can do that for her. She dresses in the latest with none of the pains of fittings."

"What a marvelous idea! I might ask her about that when I return. Of course I won't need anything for a time, but it's certainly a handy idea."

The next two hours flew by as the two women shared about everything under the sun. Stacy had a few questions about the passage of Scripture she was studying in Romans 12. Lady Andrea proved a great help. Stacy's own words to Roddy came to mind as the coach moved toward Tanner's town house.

God has never let me down. When I truly need to know something, He always shows me.

Thirty-Eight

BY THE TIME TANNER, STACY, HETTIE, AND DREW arrived back at Winslow, Stacy was so tired she could hardly move. The ride seemed to lengthen every time she made it. She let Hettie feed Drew while she bathed, and as soon as she'd read to him and tucked him in, she took herself off to bed. She slept dreamlessly all through the night but woke earlier than she would have liked.

Stacy rolled to her stomach, determined to go back to sleep, but a sudden tenderness in her breasts caused her to open her eyes. She lay for some time thinking on the fact that this tenderness wasn't so sudden; she just hadn't given it any heed. It had been this way with Drew also. Long after Stacy should have given attention to the other signs, she would not let her heart face the evidence before her. Stacy sat up slowly. She and Tanner had only shared one night. Was it possible?

"Of course it's possible."

Stacy reached for her Bible. She read about Sarah, Abraham's wife, and how she had a child when she was 90. Sarah wasn't perfect, but she had faith in God. Stacy turned to Hebrews 11:11 and read that Sarah found God faithful to the promise He made to give her a child.

"You've given me no such promise, Lord, but You have said that You will never leave me or forsake me. If there is to be another child, help me to see Your sovereignty in its conception.

Tanner is so difficult to live with, but I don't have to answer for his actions, only for my own response.

"I'm afraid to tell Tanner, Lord. Please be with me. Please give me boldness. Please use this to soften his heart, and if it doesn't, give me the right words."

Stacy waited three more days before approaching Tanner, carefully monitoring the condition of her body. He was in his study as usual, and Stacy could see that he was not happy to be disturbed. She'd prayed long and hard about this conversation, however, so she stepped forward with more boldness than she ever had before to take a chair in front of his desk.

"I'm sorry to disturb you, Tanner, but I need to speak with you."

Tanner placed his papers back on the desk and sat back in his chair; his face a study in indifference. Stacy cleared her throat.

"I'm pregnant, Tanner. I must be some weeks along, but I just now realized it."

Nothing. She was met with absolute silence; his face never changed expression.

"Tanner, did you hear me?"

"Yes, I heard you."

Stacy sat nonplussed.

"Are you worried the child isn't yours?" she asked, desperately trying to gauge his true feelings.

"Is it mine?" Tanner's voice was still unresponsive.

"Yes."

The duke shrugged, and Stacy realized she had been prepared for anything but his indifference. She stood slowly, thinking that if she stayed in the room she might break down, but something stopped her from exiting. At the door, Stacy turned and faced her husband again. He had not gone back to his papers, so Stacy was able to speak with her eyes holding his.

"When you came for me at Lucinda and Roddy's, I came back to you because I was afraid to say no, but there was more, Tanner. I also came because I believed it might be God's way of repairing my marriage.

"I've never stopped loving you. When you wanted me back, even before you knew that Drew was yours, I took that as a good sign. But it hasn't been good. You despise me, and the staff takes their cue from you. I would love to stay right now and work on our marriage, but I must think of our unborn baby. Drew and I will be leaving for Lucinda and Roddy's as soon as we're packed." Stacy paused, seemingly out of energy, but an unprecedented boldness came over her.

"I never really stood a chance, did I, Tanner? Leslie saw to that. Well, I'm not Leslie. I'm Stacy. The letter is still in my dressing room, Tanner. You're welcome to go and get it. This time I hope you read the whole thing."

Tanner never moved from his chair as the door closed. He knew Stacy would actually leave, and because he thought the distance might do them some good, he did not try to stop her. He was surprised, however, when she left without seeking him out again. Two hours later the carriage pulled away, and she hadn't even brought Drew in to say goodbye.

You just want her because she's not here. All this time she was right beneath your roof, and you ignored her. Now that she's gone you want to talk to her. The feeling will pass.

Tanner knew he was lying to himself. He had said all of this to himself and more, but Stacy had only been gone one week and he had never known such loneliness. Tanner had held himself in check most of the time Stacy had been there, watching her from down the hall or from a window when she wasn't aware. To let her know that he thought of her and Drew constantly would not do. If he became vulnerable to her, she would only hurt him again. Or would she? Tanner was beginning to doubt his own sanity.

Almost of their own volition, Tanner's feet moved toward Stacy's bedroom. Her dressing room was nearly empty, but just as she'd said, the letter was there. Tanner started at the beginning again.

> Dear Tanner,
>
> I'm not sure if you knew I was back in London, but I arrived just this week. I am staying at Brentwood with Roddy and Lucinda. I would like to see you. I know I told you I would not return unless you sent for me, but my grandfather has died and I've come at Lucinda's bidding.
>
> I would like to see you, Tanner. I would like to talk about the Cradwell party and explain about Nigel Stanley. I made a terrible mistake, and if we could only talk, I feel we might resolve this painful thing between us.
>
> There has never been anyone but you, Tanner. I was very naive concerning Lord Stanley, and I didn't understand his intentions quickly enough to allow me to escape him, so when you came in, it looked as though we'd met. I don't know what possessed him to tell you we loved each other because I'd never seen him before the party, and, aside from that, I was already in love with you. Please send for me, Tanner, and give me a chance to explain.
>
> Always yours,
> Stacy

He balled the letter in his hand, but not out of anger. For weeks now he'd kept Stacy at arm's length, never letting her close to his heart. He had been ready to believe her innocence, but when he'd read the first part of the letter where he thought she'd all but confessed, he'd gone back to keeping her as far from him as possible.

Leslie's face swam through his mind. For the first time he pushed it away with barely a thought. Stacy herself reminded him that she was not Leslie. That fact was never more evident to Tanner than it was right now.

His anger had been putting distance between him and Stacy even before they were married. If he was going to get his wife back, Tanner knew he was going to have to get a grip on himself. He'd ask her first. If that didn't work, he'd *tell* her she was coming back so he could prove he was ready to be the husband and father he needed to be.

Tanner knew he couldn't take one more day without her at Winslow. Even though the shadows were long, Tanner ordered his carriage. Price packed and accompanied him, and the next morning he was at Brentwood, ready to see his wife.

"What do you mean she's not here?"

"Just what I said," Lucinda told him unsympathetically. "She's not here, nor is Drew. They've gone to stay with friends in the country."

Tanner frowned. The only friends Stacy had in the country were their neighbors around Winslow, and outside of Brandon and Sunny, he knew she wouldn't visit them. Even without asking, Tanner knew she was not at Bracken.

"When do you expect them back?" Tanner was keeping a tight grip on his temper.

"Oh," Lucinda said airily, covering the fact that they'd only just left, "Stacy desperately needs a rest. She'll probably stay until the baby is born."

Tanner would tolerate no such thing. It was the second week in October and he'd already missed her birthday. There was no way he'd let anyone keep him from his wife and son until sometime the next year.

"Tell me where she is, Lucinda."

"No."

"Did Stacy ask you to hide her?"

Lucinda hesitated just long enough for Tanner to realize she was lying. "Yes, she did. She's tired of the way she's treated at Winslow and tired of you. You're despicable and cruel, and you don't deserve her! She never wants to see you again!"

It was quite obvious that Lucinda was verbalizing her own feelings and those she wished were Stacy's.

"You have no right to play with people's lives, Lucinda." Tanner's voice was calm, and Lucinda looked uncertain for the first time. "Now tell me where she is."

The older woman looked as if she might be considering it, but then her chin came out and she slowly shook her head. Tanner's eyes bored into hers, but still she did not flinch. Without a word, Tanner turned on his heel and walked out.

"You deliberately waited until I was gone, and then you sent them away," Roddy railed at his wife. "How could you, Lucinda? You cannot run other people's lives."

"Now you sound like Tanner." She spat the words.

"Tanner was here?" Roddy was incredulous, but Lucinda, having regretted telling him, would not look in his direction. He'd returned an hour earlier with flowers for both Stacy and his wife and a hat for Drew, only to be told they been sent away, and no one except Lucinda knew where. All of their own coachmen and coaches were present, telling Roddy that Lucinda had hired someone else. Roddy had no one to question.

"Lucinda, did you tell Tanner where she is?"

"No, and I won't tell you. You're too soft, and I know you would tell him. I'll not give Tanner Richardson another chance to hurt my girl."

Roddy sat down in absolute defeat. He'd never seen Lucinda quite this consumed. When Stacy arrived he'd been troubled about the relationship. But when Tanner came looking for his wife—in Roddy Caruthers' book that meant he cared.

Oh, Cinda, he thought as he watched her try to ignore him. *What have you done?*

They didn't speak of it again, and after a few days Lucinda began to believe that Roddy had come around to her way of thinking. There was a strain between them, but Lucinda refused to acknowledge it, smiling a little too brightly when Roddy was in the room and suggesting one party or tea after another. She would have been livid if she'd known that Roddy was investigating Stacy's whereabouts each morning when he left the house.

Tanner stayed in London for a week but came up with nothing. He considered calling in the police, but Lucinda was Stacy's aunt, and he wanted to avoid that at all costs. He was on the verge of hiring an investigator when he thought maybe he should check with Brandon and Sunny. He knew Stacy wouldn't be there, but he hoped that with all the time Stacy spent with Sunny, the duchess would know something.

He arrived unannounced at Bracken near dinnertime, but the Hawkesburys made him feel welcome. Soon he was sitting down to eat with them. Tanner had no idea how drained he appeared.

"Did you know that Stacy left Winslow?" he asked partway through the meal.

"Yes," Sunny answered. "I just received a letter."

"A letter? Does it say where she is?" Tanner nearly rose from his chair.

"Why, she's in London with Roddy and Lucinda. Didn't you know?"

Tanner sighed deeply and explained. Sunny's emotions were wrung out once again by this unsettled couple. Just when it seemed that Tanner was finally ready to be a husband to Stacy, Lucinda had to pull this.

"Did she ever say anything to you, Sunny, that might tell me where she is?"

"I don't think so. I mean, Lucinda has friends everywhere, in the country and all over London. Maybe someone on her staff would know something."

"Or you might try questioning your own staff, Tanner. They might be of some help."

"I doubt that," Sunny said softly, but Tanner had heard.

"What did you mean, Sunny?"

"Your staff is not very close to Stacy, so I doubt if she would confide in any of them."

Tanner studied her and knew there was more. "Is there anything else you'd like to tell me?"

Looking uncomfortable, the duchess suddenly knew what Stacy was at times afraid of. There was an intensity about Tanner that could be unnerving, but she knew she had to be honest.

"Some of the staff at Winslow make things pretty hard for Stacy."

"In what way?"

Sunny explained what she'd seen and the little Stacy had shared with her. "Stacy isn't the type to complain. In fact, if it wasn't for Drew, she probably wouldn't have said a word, but Drew naturally brings out the mother in her. She talked to me out of concern for him."

Tanner was quiet, but a hardness entered his eye. He remembered his fish dinner with Stacy and Drew and how little food they'd had on the table before his trays arrived.

Just looking at him, Brandon could see that his friend was developing a plan. After a moment he asked, "What will you do?"

Tanner answered immediately. "I'll go back to Winslow

and dismiss the staff. Then I'll have Price start interviewing for replacements, people who understand that their sole duty is to make my wife and son comfortable. After that I'll go to London and hire an investigator to find Stacy."

Thirty-Nine

STACY WANDERED THROUGH THE GALLERY, her round tummy preceding her, and studied the portraits of generations of Blackwells. Some looked stuffy and old before their time, and some looked like they had lived life to the fullest.

Of course it wasn't fair to judge a person by his portrait, but Stacy felt as if she had to examine them all before seeking out the one she came to see, the one who reminded her of Tanner.

Lord and Lady Blackwell were no relation to her husband whatsoever, but one of their ancestors bore a striking resemblance to Tanner. It certainly wasn't the same as being with him, but it was nice to look into brown eyes so like his and to study that firm chin that even Drew was beginning to sport.

Stacy now stood before the portrait. It was as she remembered it, but today she didn't enjoy it as much because she missed Tanner terribly and ached over the fact that he hadn't sought her out. It seemed that things really were over between them. Stacy thought maybe she should return to Middlesbrough. Lord and Lady Blackwell couldn't have been kinder, but Stacy was starting to lose hope.

With Stacy's feelings about London, Lucinda had had no trouble coaxing her out into the country. However, she had been here for weeks with almost no contact from Lucinda and none at all from Roddy. The letters that had come from her aunt were so bland, never addressing Stacy's questions, that she felt completely out of touch. Stacy missed everyone so much she was considering returning to Brentwood for a visit before leaving on her way north, but the first time she had mentioned a possible trip, Lady Blackwell had acted oddly.

Stacy had thought little of this and decided to stay put for the time. But then the previous night, when once again Stacy mentioned going to see her aunt and uncle, Lady Blackwell stumbled all over her words until Lord Blackwell gently explained that they were rather busy right now and maybe another time would be best.

Stacy couldn't believe her ears. Surely they understood that she could go without them. Not to mention the fact that this was the first time they'd denied her anything. Up until now they couldn't do enough for her. She and Drew had been lavished with gifts to meet every possible want or need. Meals were centered around them and so sumptuous that Stacy thought she might be putting on more weight than necessary.

She mentioned it to Hettie at one point, but Hettie only shook her head.

"You're swollen with child. How did you expect to look?"

"I guess you're right," Stacy sighed. "But if Tanner ever does come for me, he won't be able to get his arms around me."

"Are you still hoping for that?"

"You know I am."

The older woman snorted.

"Now what does that mean?" Stacy wanted to know. In all of the weeks that Stacy had been waiting for Tanner to come Hettie had never said a word against him.

"It means that even if he is looking for you, I wonder if he'll be able to find you."

"What are you saying, Hettie?" The duchess' voice became firm.

"I'm saying I don't like the way we left London. Your aunt was so nervous she jumped at the slightest noise. And it seemed strange to me that a hired coach and driver brought us here."

Stacy stared at her, and understanding dawned. *You knew, Stacy,* she said to herself. *You've known for days that all was not right here, and you've wondered for weeks why Lucinda and Roddy never visited. Tanner didn't come, and that's all you've cared about. Instead of drowning in self-pity, you should have been more aware.*

"What are you going to do?" Hettie asked.

"Nothing right now. I'm going to sleep on it and then confront the Blackwells in the morning."

"You make it sound as if it were bedtime."

"I know it's just past lunch, but I think better in the morning. If the Blackwells won't help me, I'll have the day to decide how to get us back to London."

Hettie finally agreed that it was a good plan. Both women would have been filled with joy had they realized that even as they spoke, help was on the way.

If Roddy had ever thought there was anything dimwitted about his wife, he now knew better. He would never have believed that she could so completely cover her tracks. It seemed as if Stacy and Drew had vanished off the face of the earth.

Not a single coach company would admit to having done business with her, nor would any of the coachmen. He racked his brain for every family they knew, even the slightest of acquaintances, and had them all checked out, but to no avail. Weeks later, he'd finally written to Noel and Elena, not wanting to upset them but desperate to find Stacy.

Elena had written back, stating that they had heard from Stacy. She had misplaced the letter, but remembered that she and Drew were doing fine and staying with someone named Blackmore or something similar.

It had been all Roddy needed. Little wonder he'd never considered the Blackwells. Decades before, Lady Blackwell and Lucinda had quarreled. Lucinda hadn't spoken to her in 30 years.

Now as Roddy's carriage took him deep into the country, he let his heart feel all the ache he'd tried to squelch. Never had he been so disappointed in anyone as he was with Lucinda or himself, for he knew he was partially to blame.

Lucinda had been running the lives of others for years, and Roddy had allowed it with nary a word. He realized now that he should have been bolder on countless occasions. He could have and should have told her to mind her own business.

Roddy wondered if perhaps this was why Stacy was so special to him. They both feared confronting the people they loved the most. Stacy had been so heavy on his mind in the last weeks that the thought of getting this close and being wrong made him a bundle of nerves. He also began to know panic at the thought that Stacy would be there, but the Blackwells would forbid him entrance.

"Please help me, God," Roddy prayed, not for the first time. He knew it was a selfish prayer and that finding her was partly selfish also. He had questions he needed to ask, and he believed with all of his heart that the only person who could answer them was Stacy.

Stacy heard voices from her place in the library. They were not raised in anger, but something was not right. She was able to come to the door without being spotted and did so to eavesdrop shamelessly.

"I tell you she's not here." This came from Lady Blackwell.

"And I believe that she is." Stacy heard Roddy's voice but kept still.

"I don't know where you've gotten this ridiculous notion, but I must ask you to leave."

"I will not leave until I'm certain Lady Stacy and her son are not here."

"Please—"

"No." Roddy's voice was firm. "Now tell me the truth; tell me where—"

Roddy cut off when Stacy suddenly stepped into view. The sigh that escaped his chest was heartfelt. Stacy came forward, but Lady Blackwell wouldn't look at her, even when she spoke.

"Lucinda asked me to keep you and hold all of your letters to Brentwood. It had been so long since she and I had—" The older woman stopped and looked helplessly at Stacy. "I'm sorry."

Both Stacy and Roddy watched her walk away, head down, steps laden. It was a posture that Stacy would have normally pitied, but the import of Lady Blackwell's words were pressing in upon her. All these weeks, months actually, she'd waited to hear from someone or dreamed of looking up and seeing Tanner approaching, but no one had even known where she was. No one but Lucinda.

"Roddy, what has Lucinda done?"

Roddy took in her flushed features and doubted his wisdom in coming.

"Where can we talk?"

Stacy took a breath. "The morning room."

She led the way. Once inside Roddy saw her comfortable on the settee. Her color still worried him, but he knew he had to take this all the way.

"Did Lucinda really hide us?"

"I'm afraid she did."

"And she didn't tell you?"

"No. It's taken me this long to learn of your whereabouts."

"Has Tanner been to Brentwood, asking for me?"

"A week after you left Winslow." Roddy's tone was regretful.

Stacy eyes slid shut in agony. The fingers of one hand came to her mouth, and Roddy watched in amazement as tears slid out from beneath her closed lids. She was trembling all over, and the earl was becoming frightened.

"Please, Stacy, please don't get so upset. I know what a shock it must be, but I'm thinking of the baby as well as you."

"How could she, Roddy?" Stacy whispered. "All this time I thought he didn't care. I was going to the Blackwells in the morning to tell them I would be returning to London and then Middlesbrough. How could she, Roddy?"

"I don't know." Roddy's voice was sad. "Tanner has always reminded her of Aubrey, and she's still very bitter over his memory."

"I can't begin to tell you how I've longed for my husband," Stacy went on. "I left because of his indifference. The servants were very hard to take, but I could have stood almost anything if only he would have shown me he cared. Did he just come to see if I was there, or to take me back to Winslow?"

"I wasn't there, but he told Lucinda he *would* find you."

"Maybe he didn't actually look."

"Yes, he's looking. He even hired a private investigator to locate you."

"Oh, Roddy! How do I get word to him? How do I tell him where I am?"

"I'll get word to him, Stacy, but I wish—" Roddy paused.

"What is it, Roddy?"

"I wish you would pray for me."

Stacy was dumbfounded.

"Not about Tanner; he'll be very pleased to hear from me," Roddy explained. "But I've got to go home and face Lucinda with this. Things have been pretty strained between us, but she's never shown remorse. When she finds out that I've learned of your whereabouts, she'll be livid."

"Of course I'll pray for you, Roddy," Stacy told him, but

then she paused. "There is something more, isn't there, Roddy? You have something on your mind."

Roddy opened his mouth once and then closed it. Stacy waited.

"I want what you have," Roddy admitted softly, his eyes searching hers. "I'm trying to pray and be like you, but something is missing."

Stacy smiled so tenderly that Roddy's heart began to pound. He knew she would have the answers; he knew she would not turn him away.

"Tell me, Stacy. Tell me about Jesus Christ."

So Stacy began. She assumed Roddy knew nothing and started at Christ's birth. She explained that His birth had been prophesied for years, and that it had been the fulfillment of a promise.

She told Roddy about God's promise to Simeon that he would see the Savior before he died, and how Joseph and Mary took Jesus to the temple in Jerusalem where Simeon saw him. Stacy explained about the second trip when Jesus was 12, and how his parents had found him in the temple amazing the elders with his knowledge.

"He began his public ministry when He was 30, and He called 12 men to work alongside of Him. One of those men, Judas, would betray Him, but even this was used of God so that Christ could be our Savior.

"After three years of public ministry Christ was arrested, beaten horribly and then died on the cross, but He didn't stay dead, Roddy." Stacy was growing very animated, and Roddy hung on her every word. "They buried him in a tomb and covered the entrance with a huge stone, but an angel came and the stone was rolled away. The grave was empty, and burial clothes lay discarded.

"Every church I've ever been in sports a crucifix; not an empty cross, but one with Christ hanging there. But Christ isn't dead. The Scriptures say he rose again the third day and now sits at the right hand of God the Father. He has bridged the gap between a holy God and sinful man."

"I can't begin to tell you how you've helped me," Roddy replied. "I thought you would say it's too late, that I've lived too much of my life without God."

Stacy shook her head and smiled. "My grandfather was nearly on his deathbed when he confessed Christ, and I know he's in heaven because God is faithful to His promises. You can have that same assurance, Roddy."

Roddy took Stacy's hand and held it gently. He was so anxious he was trembling, and Stacy was reminded of the way she felt when Elena and Noel sat with her and led her to Christ. It was much the same now.

Stacy sat quietly as Roddy prayed. His voice faltered on several occasions, but she just held his hand and prayed for him as he spoke in his heart to God.

Roddy raised his head, and Stacy saw peace in his eyes.

"It's taken care of now."

Stacy threw her arms around Roddy and tried to squeeze the life out of him. He hugged her in return and then spoke, his voice fervent.

"I meant what I said to God, Stacy. I truly want to live for Him."

"Oh Roddy, I can see that you do."

"I'm just worried about sin. I told God I want to put Him first, but what if I do sin?"

"I'm afraid it's not if, Roddy, but when. But there is hope. First John 1:9 says, 'If we confess our sins he is faithful and just to forgive us our sins, and to cleanse us from all unrighteousness.'

"Sin never pleases God, but it's going to happen. What we do with that sin makes all the difference in our relationship with God."

"So there is a chance I won't go to heaven when I die?"

Stacy shook her head vehemently. "No, Roddy. Nothing could be further from the truth. Read Romans 8. That whole passage is to believers in Christ. It says that nothing can separate us from the love of God. That's not a promise to the whole world, Roddy—just to believers like you and me.

"When I said it's what we do with that sin that makes all the difference, I was talking about confessing that sin and turning away from it, thus restoring a right relationship with God through his Son."

Roddy took a deep breath. He was not discouraged, just overwhelmed with joy. They talked until Hettie sought Stacy out, telling her that Drew was looking for her. Drew was thrilled to see Uncle Roddy, but on this particular day, Stacy did not allow him to stay. She and Roddy talked through dinner until they were both spent. They also talked again in the morning before Roddy left.

"Does Lucinda even known you were looking for me?"

Roddy shook his head regretfully. They were standing outside Roddy's carriage, and he was headed to see Tanner at Winslow.

"I was afraid she would do something to try to move you. Are you sure you won't come with me?"

Stacy shook her head. "No, I'll stay here in case he doesn't want me back."

"I know he does."

Stacy tried to believe that.

"You will come for me if he doesn't want me, won't you, Roddy?"

"You don't even need to ask."

With that Roddy kissed her cheek and climbed into the carriage. Stacy promised to pray for him and he for her, and then she waved until he was out of sight.

Forty

THE EVENING OF THE THIRD DAY was upon Stacy, and still she had had no word from Tanner or Roddy. It occurred to her that she didn't really know where the Blackwells lived. It had taken a day's carriage ride to come from London; maybe it took longer than that to come from Winslow. She had no sense of direction as they'd come from London and not fearing anything underhanded, she had not bothered to pay attention.

"I'm too tired to think about this right now."

Stacy spoke this to no one, having dismissed her maid and sent Hettie to bed. The older woman had not felt at all well lately, and Stacy knew that the job of trailing an active three-year-old was starting to tell.

After sitting on the side of the bed, she bent over her swollen stomach to strip off her stockings and then let her hair down. It felt good to shake it free. Wearing nothing but her nightgown, she stood to scratch first her head, where the pins had sat, and then her tummy, which seemed to itch constantly.

She drew the covers back, too tired to even read. She sat down on the edge of her bed and was in the process of turning the lamp low when the door opened.

"Hettie?" Stacy called as she squinted toward the dim doorway.

"No, it's not Hettie."

The air rushed out of Stacy at the sound of her husband's

soft voice; she was thankful to be sitting down. Stacy's eyes, now growing accustomed to the darkness, watched as he entered, shut the door, and approached. Tanner stopped just a few feet in front of her and simply stared down.

Stacy swallowed. "Did Roddy talk to you?"

"Yes. I would have been here yesterday, but he had trouble tracking me down."

Stacy didn't know quite what to say to that. Tanner looked wonderful to her, but the expression on his face was unlike anything she'd ever seen before. She couldn't gauge what he might be thinking.

"How is Drew?" he asked, his voice still rather hushed.

"He's doing well."

"Good. Here," Tanner continued as he bent low and adjusted her pillow. "Lie down. You need your rest; we're leaving for Winslow in the morning."

Stacy did as she was told, never taking her eyes from his face. His look was serious now, and after he'd adjusted the covers around her he placed his hand against her cheek and just left it there for a moment. Stacy's lids were growing heavy, and as much as she wanted to stay awake and talk with him, sleep was crowding in. She felt his hand stroke her hair, but she was deeply asleep when he pulled a chair close, turned the lamp a little higher, and just stared at her.

"We're not going to be separated again, Stacy," Tanner whispered. "I promise this was the last time."

It didn't matter to him that she didn't hear. He felt better having just voiced his thoughts. He let his eyes move over her and felt something squeeze around his heart at the extent of her pregnancy. Had she missed him? Was she able to travel to Winslow?

Tanner could have questioned these things for hours, but he made himself stop. He was here now, and if appearance could be trusted, Stacy was doing very well. Outside of that, little else mattered.

Stacy did not awaken early as was so often the case. This morning, light was streaming through the windows when her eyes opened. She woke up facing away from her side of the bed, and one of the first things she noticed was the indentation in the other pillow. Tanner! Stacy sat nearly upright. Tanner had come last night; she hadn't just dreamed it. He'd really been here, *and* in bed with her. Stacy wouldn't have believed that she could sleep that deeply, but now that she thought back, a vague impression of a warm presence came to her.

Stacy lay back, tempted to stay in bed for the next hour and just think about her husband. However, Tanner and Drew had other ideas. They burst through the door with barely a knock.

"Mumma! Look who's here."

Stacy's mouth dropped open as she saw her son so elevated. She never imagined where Drew's head would be if he sat on his father's shoulders, but he was high. Tanner swung him easily to the floor, and Stacy hugged him close when he scrambled onto her bed.

"How did you sleep?" Tanner had come near to the edge of the bed and stood staring down at Stacy.

"Well. Thank you."

"Are you up to traveling today?"

"I think so. Is it far?"

Tanner nodded. "With your condition we'll have to make a stop tonight and won't arrive at Winslow until late afternoon tomorrow."

Stacy noticed that his face and voice gave nothing away. She wished she could tell if he found this an inconvenience or possibly a duty. Stacy felt so perplexed with her thoughts that she transferred her attention to Drew.

"Where did you leave Hettie this morning?"

"She's in bed," Drew told her. Stacy felt alarmed. It was much too late for Hettie to still be abed. Stacy shifted Drew to the side and eased from the bed.

"I need to check on Hettie," Stacy spoke as Tanner stepped back and allowed her to reach for her robe. She glanced up to find his eyes on her stomach and self-consciously pulled at the fabric over her swollen waist. Tanner's eyes came to hers, and Stacy wished once again that she knew his thoughts. Stacy tried not to believe that he found her repulsive, but the thought did enter her mind.

Tanner would have continued to watch Stacy, but Drew captured his attention. Stacy was in her robe and out the door before he knew it.

"Where is Hettie's room?" Tanner asked his boy as he swung him back onto his shoulders.

It had taken quite a bit of tactful negotiating, but Tanner had finally convinced Stacy that she should leave and Hettie should stay put. He had followed his wife to the older woman's room and found her very ill indeed. Naturally, Stacy had wanted to stay and nurse her, but Tanner had put his foot down.

The next suggestion had been that they all simply stay until Hettie could go with them. Tanner was gentle, but adamantly against this also. With much talk between Stacy and Lady Blackwell, it was finally decided that Tanner would take his family home and send a carriage back for Hettie in two weeks' time.

When Stacy and Drew were finally ready to go, Tanner made one last trip to the sickroom. He could tell that Stacy was still apprehensive, and he wanted to be able to reassure her that he'd checked on Hettie again. To his surprise, Hettie had gained enough strength to take him on.

"You will have excellent care. In two weeks," Tanner was speaking from where he stood by the bed, "a Richardson carriage will be here for you." Tanner did not go on to say that he'd greased a few palms to see that she would be treated like a queen while at the Blackwells'.

"Who will see to Stacy and Drew?"

It irked Tanner that the old woman used their Christian names, but he held his tongue.

"They'll be well taken care of."

"Like they were before—with not enough food and living like prisoners? They couldn't even walk in the garden without the gardeners coming out to glare."

This was the first Tanner had heard of the gardeners being rude as well, but he continued to assure Hettie.

"All of that is changed now. My wife and son will have the best of care."

"What if the baby comes?"

"The baby's not due for weeks."

"Drew was early. Stacy nearly died; did you know that?"

Tanner's heart slammed in his chest, and he could only stare at the sick old woman.

"I've never liked you," Hettie went on, her voice growing weak. "And I know that you think I'm out of line to be saying this, but there's no one to care for Stacy without me."

The words completely taxed her. She lay, chest heaving, her eyes angry, but also pleading with the duke. Tanner wanted to go to Stacy on the spot, but something in Hettie's face compelled him to console her one last time.

"It is as I've said." This time Tanner's voice did not allow her to argue. "All that is changed now."

Tanner's intense gaze held Hettie's for just an instant, and then he was gone.

Stacy squirmed in the seat and told herself to go to sleep, pray, or do anything that would take her mind off of how badly she needed to relieve herself. They had been traveling for over two hours without a stop, and Stacy thought she might burst. Had he been in the coach with them, Tanner might have noticed her discomfort, but he'd opted to start the journey on horseback.

Drew had fallen asleep almost as soon as they had left, and even though Stacy had shifted his head from her abdomen for some relief, she was now growing desperate. Suddenly Drew stirred.

"Mumma," he said in a sleepy voice. "Mumma, I need to be excused."

Stacy's fist flew to the top of the carriage, and seconds later the coach slowed to a stop. When the door opened, Tanner stood there.

"Drew needs to be excused."

"All right." Tanner's voice was calm. "I'll see to him."

"I'll take care of him!" Stacy nearly shouted in his face. Tanner blinked at her tone before stepping back quickly when she barged her way from the carriage. Understanding was only seconds in coming, and he was calling himself every kind of fool as he followed her into the privacy of the woods.

"Here, Stacy, I'll see to Drew."

Tanner didn't give Stacy time to argue as he lifted Drew in his arms and went in the opposite direction. Stacy wasted no time but shot behind some bushes to see to her own needs. Some minutes later she made her way comfortably back to the carriage. Tanner and Drew were already there, and Stacy saw instantly that Tanner's horse was tied to the rear of the carriage.

"Lady Blackwell sent a large hamper along. Would you like to stop now?"

"I'm really not hungry," Stacy told him. "Would you like to stop?"

"No, we can wait." Tanner's voice was cordial as he ushered her and Drew into the carriage. Drew sat in his father's lap then and entertained the older lord for the next two hours. Stacy lasted only 20 minutes before she let her head fall against the side of the coach and went to sleep.

❦ ❦ ❦

"The White Stag" was the sign above the inn door as Tanner saw his family into the public room that evening. The great room was clean and sparsely occupied, making the duke and his party all the more conspicuous.

Stacy stood holding Drew's hand as Tanner had a few words with Price. Every head in the place was turned in their direction, but Stacy kept her eyes on Tanner. Some minutes passed before the innkeeper led the way upstairs.

The room the man opened for them was clean, but small. It sported one full bed, and Stacy wondered about the sleeping arrangement. She didn't wonder long, however. As soon as the innkeeper left them, Tanner explained in a soft voice while Drew stared at his reflection in the glass of the window.

"We'll have our dinner up here, probably delivered in a few minutes. Price is going to be across the hall, and Drew will sleep with him."

"I thought Drew would be in here with us."

"There really isn't room. And," Tanner went on when Stacy opened her mouth, "do not even suggest that the two of you stay alone because I won't allow it. Price has one of my pistols, and I have the other. This is the safest arrangement."

"If the inn is not safe, why are we staying here?"

Stacy's voice was as low as Tanner's, but he could read the panic in her eyes. His hand came up to touch her cheek as he answered.

"The White Stag is one of the more reputable roadside inns, but since our clothing and coaches spell money, they all carry a measure of risk. I assure you, no harm will come to Drew when he's with Price, and any man coming to this door will have to go through me."

Stacy had little choice but to agree. She wondered if they should have stayed on the road. When she said as much to Tanner, he adamantly shook his head.

"You are nearly out on your feet, and we all need to eat."

"I need to eat." Drew had left the window and now stood looking a bit anxious at his father's side; it had been a long day. Tanner lifted him into his arms.

"Our food will be here at any time, and then you're going to spend the night with Price."

Drew's eyes rounded. "Price?"

"That's right, and then in the morning you'll come back in here for breakfast and we'll head home."

"To Roddy's?"

"No, my darling," Stacy interjected, her heart turning over for him. "We're going to Winslow."

Drew looked uncertain.

"You know Winslow," his father said. "Your room is brown and gold and you have a huge nursery to play in."

Now it was time for Stacy to share Drew's confusion. Mother and son stared at Tanner until he frowned fiercely.

"You were never shown the nursery, were you?" Tanner's voice was tight, but Stacy could see that he was trying to control his anger and that it was not directed at her.

In answer to his question, she only shook her head and tried not to think about going back to Tanner's difficult staff. More might have been said on the subject, because Stacy truly believed it needed to be discussed, but there was no more opportunity. Someone knocked then, and their food was delivered.

Because they left the inn early and the roads were fairly dry, they made good time going home. The coaches pulled up just after noon, and Tanner held Stacy's elbow as they went inside. Standing ready to greet them was a man Stacy had never seen before.

"This is Reece," Tanner explained. "He is the new head of housekeeping. He will introduce you to the rest of the staff as needed."

"Hello, Reece," Stacy, in a state of shock, spoke to the kind-looking man.

Reece bowed low, his posture and very expression begging to serve her. "Welcome home, my lady. I hope we can serve you well. This is Juliet." Reece brought forth a young maid. "She will be your personal maid until you wish to choose another. Would you like Juliet to go with you now?"

"No," Tanner answered for her. "I'll see my wife upstairs and will send for you later."

"Yes, my lord." Reece bowed again and backed away so they could pass. Several other staff members were present, all complete strangers to Stacy. Their faces were all wreathed in smiles, however, and the young duchess had the impression that any one of them would hand her the shirt off his back.

Once Tanner and Stacy gained the upper floor, Stacy questioned her husband.

"I take it you've replaced some of the staff?"

"Not some of them, but the whole."

Stacy stopped in the hall. "Even cook?"

Tanner gently shook his head. "Let me amend that, I've dismissed everyone but Price and cook."

Stacy just stood and stared at him. She would have continued to do so, but he reached for her hand and led her through a door. Not until that moment did Stacy realize it was the master bedroom suite. With a heart pounding with unidentified emotion, Stacy allowed herself to be led through her old sitting room, past the dressing room, and into Winslow's spectacular master bedroom. Tanner brought them to a halt but didn't turn to Stacy or even look at her. Stacy hated to question him and break the sweet communion that had existed between them since he came for her, but she had to know.

"Tanner, if you're going to change your mind about my being in here with you, I'd rather start down the hall."

"We've slept in the same bed for the last two nights." Tanner's voice betrayed none of his feelings.

"I realize that," Stacy spoke evenly. "But you didn't really have much choice."

This time Tanner didn't answer. He reached for the small satchel in Stacy's other hand and tossed it onto the bed. Stacy knew that would have to be answer enough.

Forty-One

THE FORK IN STACY'S HAND felt weighted as she tried to eat the lunch set before her. She had been quite weary for several days before Tanner came for her, and frankly she was tired of being tired. But what could she do? It must be the pregnancy.

A glance at Drew told her he was equally exhausted, and Stacy knew it was also the carriage ride home. She was looking forward to putting him to bed and climbing in herself. However, it wasn't that simple.

At Roddy and Lucinda's or at the Blackwells', she would have taken Drew right into bed with her, but she didn't feel as free to do that here. Her bed now was also Tanner's, and she didn't know if he approved of such a thing.

At the moment, Stacy missed Hettie terribly. Irrepressible Hettie, with her sharp tongue and stubborn ways, would have taken Drew off to his bed, put herself in the fireside chair in his room to sleep, and allowed Stacy to find her own rest. Stacy had just about decided to go to Drew's room with him when Tanner came to her rescue. He entered the small dining room and bent to speak closely into her ear.

"I've asked Price to put Drew down for his nap so you can rest."

"Oh." Stacy was surprised and uncertain. "I don't mind putting him down."

"I know you don't, but he and Price are getting along well, and Drew will do well with him until other arrangements can be made."

This statement sounded somewhat cryptic to Stacy, but she was too tired to argue. She watched her son carefully as Tanner broke the news to him, waiting for him to cry for her or complain. Once his face and hands were clean, however, he kissed his mother and skipped off with Tanner's man as if it were an everyday occurrence.

Juliet was waiting for her in her sitting room, and although Stacy felt a bit awkward in her presence, Juliet's manner was kind and matter-of-fact. Within minutes Stacy was down to her shift and tucked into bed. The sheets were cold at first and caused her to become quite wide awake for a moment, but it didn't last. Very soon, while praising God for bringing her home and for Tanner's efforts to take care of her, Stacy fell sound asleep.

Two hours later, she was just beginning to stir. She rolled to her back, feeling fully refreshed and contemplating rising when Tanner came in from his dressing room. He sat down on the edge of the bed and leaned over her. Stacy stared up into his face, wishing again that she knew his thoughts.

"I'm glad to see you looking so rested. When I came into the dining room I thought I might need to carry you upstairs."

"I doubt if you could lift me at this point."

One of Tanner's brows flew upward. "Your face is just starting to fill out so you look like the girl I married, Stacy."

Stacy's eyes widened, and Tanner shook his head.

"I suppose you've got some silly notion that I find you repulsive while in your present state."

Stacy blushed at his perception. "The thought did cross my mind."

"Oh, Anastasia." Tanner's voice was low. "Nothing could be further from the truth."

Stacy watched his eyes move warmly over her, his scrutiny ending with her stomach and the way it rounded the blankets. For the first time, he touched her. Stacy lay still as he placed his hand gently on her distended abdomen and splayed his long fingers wide.

"You might get kicked," Stacy whispered, as if a louder voice might break the spell.

The baby moved as though on cue. Stacy watched her husband's face as he moved his other hand to his wife's stomach and stared in wonder.

"Will you be cold if I draw the covers back?"

"No."

Tanner did so, anxious to feel the baby through just the light fabric of her shift, but it seemed that the little person inside had settled once again.

"Does he move often?"

"All day."

"Does it bother you?"

"Only when I'm trying to sleep."

"Your stomach is hard." Tanner's hands were still spanning her middle.

"Harder sometimes than others."

"Am I hurting you?"

"No," Stacy chuckled. "Drew climbs all over me. Speaking of Drew, I should get up and check on him."

"He's been up a few minutes, and he's still with Price. Before you go to him, I want to talk to you about something."

Tanner's hands came away from her now, and after he replaced the covers, Stacy lay watching him.

"I've hired a nanny."

Stacy's entire frame stiffened. Alarm covered her face as she half sat up.

"Tanner, I—"

"Just a minute," he cut her off, but there was nothing dictatorial in his tone. "Let me explain."

"Hettie—" Stacy started again.

"Will come back as ornery as ever, I have no doubts about that." Tanner's voice was dry. "But her recovery will not erase the years. She's getting too old to be shadowing a boy as active as Drew."

The words so echoed Stacy's thoughts of late that she lay back to hear him out.

"The nanny's name is Mrs. Maxwell, and she was recommended to me by Sunny." Tanner let that sink in a moment before going on. "She is not here to take yours or Hettie's job, but to give you both a hand. She will have no other responsibilities here at Winslow other than to see to Drew. She will be free to help at a moment's notice."

"Is Drew with her now?" Stacy's voice was accusing, but Tanner did not take offense.

"No, as I said, he's with Price. I honestly think he will fall for her as soon as they meet, but I didn't want that to happen without talking to you."

"How old a woman is she?"

"Mid-fifties."

"Where is her husband?"

"She's a widow. Her children are all grown. She has two grandchildren, who, I have assured her, would be welcome to visit here if you approve her staying."

Stacy took a deep breath. She was a little surprised that Tanner had done this after he'd gone to so much trouble to fire and rehire the staff for her. Stacy hated to admit it to herself, but Tanner's hiring a nanny without first talking to her felt just a little sneaky. Such thoughts flew out of Stacy's mind, however, on Tanner's next sentence.

"She shares your beliefs."

"She what?" Stacy could hardly believe her ears.

"Mrs. Maxwell believes as you do, that you can have a personal relationship with God. I think if you meet her, you'll find her most suitable for Drew's needs."

Stacy momentarily found herself without words. With the exception of Price, Tanner was not in the habit of becoming well acquainted with any of his servants. Stacy couldn't help wondering how he'd come by this knowledge.

"Will you meet her?" Tanner pressed, his expression giving nothing away as he watched Stacy's face.

"Yes, I will. I've been concerned about Hettie for some time. She's been with me for so long she seems more like a mother than a servant. I know you balk at our familiarity, but I can't cast her aside."

"I think I understand. I have a feeling that Hettie will do some balking herself over any changes we make, but on the inside she's bound to be relieved."

Stacy could hardly argue with that. *And who knows,* Stacy thought to herself. *If Mrs. Maxwell is a sister in Christ, maybe she'll have some positive impact on Hettie.*

Mrs. Maxwell was all Stacy could have prayed for. She was gentle-mannered and soft-spoken, and her humble willingness to please put Stacy immediately at ease with her. Stacy was present when she met Drew, and just as Tanner had predicted, he took to her right away.

It took a number of days for Stacy to recover from the long carriage ride, and during that time Mrs. Maxwell was invaluable. She seemed highly sensitive to Stacy's fatigue and would, with the most gentle of urgings, distract Drew from talking overly much or making unreasonable demands.

Stacy couldn't have been more grateful, as word came to them just a few weeks after they'd arrived home that Hettie would need to stay where she was. Lady Blackwell assured Stacy that Hettie was not on her deathbed, but that she was still very ill. Stacy wanted to go to her, but in her condition Tanner had to refuse.

To relieve Stacy's mind, however, Tanner sent a servant to check on Hettie and return with a report. It was just as Lady Blackwell had said. She was not dying, but neither was she ready for the long journey home to Winslow.

Drew cried when he learned that she would not be home for Christmas, and in fact Stacy felt close to tears herself. It was the first time they'd been apart during the holidays.

Forty-Two

STACY FOUND SOUTHERN ENGLAND in January to be warmer than usual as far as the temperature went, but the "weather" inside Winslow was still on the cooler side. Stacy, thinking her relationship with Tanner was finally on solid footing, found herself confused. After spending much time in prayer concerning the matter, however, Stacy was reminded just how intense Tanner's personality could be.

He was throwing himself into a business deal at the moment, and other than at the dinner table, Stacy wasn't seeing much of him. He came to bed long after she slept and was up before she woke. He wasn't even taking time out for Drew. Stacy found herself keeping her son quiet once again for fear of disturbing Tanner and incurring his wrath. He had been a bit on edge lately, and Stacy knew his temper was close to the surface. It seemed too that he was distancing himself again, but Stacy prayed that she was only imagining it.

However, Stacy was not imagining Drew's despondency. The little boy had quickly come to love Mrs. Maxwell, just as Tanner had predicted, but he was missing Hettie's and his father's attention terribly. His little face was solemn most of the time, and he simply wasn't his old chattery self. It was this melancholy, the quiet his mother was imposing on him while in the house, and the overall upheaval of their life in the past months that caused Stacy's heart to melt. For several days

Drew had been asking to go fishing, and Stacy had simply not had the energy. He never fussed or made a sound when she said no, and in some ways this made it all the harder.

"Can we go fishing today, Mum?" Drew would ask. He'd taken to calling her Mum most of the time now, and his sweetness when he said it made her want to give him the world on a silver platter.

"Oh, Drew," Stacy would reply, "I don't know if I can manage it today."

"All right, Mum." He would smile at her just a little. "After the baby has come, could we then?"

So when Drew sweetly asked Stacy again if they could fish, she agreed. The baby was due in a month, and she was feeling tired and huge, but she said yes anyway.

Stacy informed Mrs. Maxwell in the middle of the afternoon, when she would have normally taken Drew for a few hours. "Mrs. Maxwell, if anyone is looking for us, Lord Drew and I have gone fishing. We will be back in a few hours."

The nanny never blinked or commented beyond a respectful "Yes, my lady," but Stacy could feel her surprise. At the moment, however, she didn't care. She walked out to the stable with her son to collect the poles, all the while asking herself if she could drive a pony trap over her enormous stomach. One look at their small size, however, and she changed her mind. She couldn't bear the thought of a pony pulling her or of having to control one of the larger animals.

Drew had actually had a nap that day. Often these days he did not fall asleep, but after nearly two hours of sleep he was in rare form. Stacy had to call him back several times. He was so excited to be out and making noise that he simply forgot himself.

They both worked up something of a sweat on the way, but because the air near the creek seemed cooler to Stacy, she was thankful they had both dressed warmly as they settled down to fish. In no time at all they caught several. The smell, which usually never bothered Stacy, was a bit strong to her today, but

Drew was so helpful and entertaining that she determined not to let it spoil their time.

The beginning of the walk home wasn't much fun for Stacy. Drew carried the fish himself, but Stacy's legs felt like lead as they trudged through the fields toward Winslow. However, Drew, who was still feeling like he'd been set free, managed for at least part of the time to pull Stacy's mind from her painful body and legs.

"I'm going to eat a whole fish by myself."

"Are you now?"

"Yes, and then I'm going to share with Papa and Mrs. Maxwell."

"I'm sure they'll enjoy that. Will I get some fish?"

"Oh, Mum!" Drew's huge eyes were comical. "You'll get the first one because you caught the most. Remember that big one?"

Stacy laughed when Drew stopped on the path and made fish lips. She roared when he moved his lips and crossed his eyes. She was still laughing when Winslow came into view. Drew was beginning to stagger under the weight of the fish, which only added to his hilarity. Stacy was so glad they'd gone that she swooped suddenly and caught Drew in her arms, fish and all.

"I love you, Drew."

"Oh, Mum, I love you too. Papa!" Drew, while still in his mother's embrace, spotted his father. He was coming toward them on the path, his face expressionless but his stride purposeful.

He bent and lifted Drew as soon as he was beside them. He then reached for the string of fish without looking at Stacy and led them back to Winslow. Stacy sighed gently to herself. He was coldly furious. As tired as she felt, she knew she would be in tears if he shouted at her.

Drew talked to his father nonstop on the short walk inside, and Stacy realized how much she missed his joyful, happy moods. He was so rarely solemn that it had been like watching a different child.

Mrs. Maxwell was waiting for them, as was Reece. The fish were handed off to Reece, who immediately retired them to the kitchen. Drew was still in his father's arms, but Stacy didn't wait for Tanner to give the orders.

"Drew, please go with Mrs. Maxwell now. She will give you your bath. I'm going to eat in my room tonight, Mrs. Maxwell. Will you please bring Drew to me when he's ready for bed?"

"Certainly, my lady. Come along, Lord Drew. We'll have you cleaned up in no time."

"I caught fish, Mrs. Maxwell. I used a hook."

"Did you now?"

Stacy watched them for a moment and then without even glancing at her husband took the stairs herself.

You're a coward, Stacy, she rebuked herself as she walked away, knowing that Tanner was still standing at the bottom of the stairs. But try as she might she could not make herself go back down or even find the energy to turn around and face him.

Thankfully, Juliet was waiting for her in her sitting room. For a young woman she was certainly competent, and in a very short time, Stacy was luxuriating in her bath. The aches in her body and even the coldness in her husband's eyes gradually receded. She soaked for nearly an hour before Juliet brought her a lovely peignoir. It was voluminous, something Stacy's shape welcomed.

"Would you like a dressing gown, my lady?"

"Yes."

When she was warmly covered, Stacy sat at her dressing table and let Juliet brush her hair. Since it was wet, the maid left it down so Stacy could sit before the fire to eat and let her hair dry.

Dinner was quite the feast, but Stacy was not overly hungry. She felt thoughtful, meditative even, over her outing with Drew. Tanner would not seek her out, she was certain of that. And even if he did bring the subject up, Stacy realized she was not sorry for her actions. In fact, the joy she saw in her little boy's face was enough to convince her that she would do it again should he ask.

A knock at the door interrupted Stacy's musings, and a moment later Drew and Mrs. Maxwell came through. Drew sat in what was left of his mother's lap, and Mrs. Maxwell took a chair out of the way.

"Are you going to read to me tonight, Mum?"

"Well, now," Stacy spoke softly, her eyes on his precious face. "I'm rather tired. How would you like to tell me a story?"

Drew's eyes rounded with delight.

"All right. How about the story of Ruth? Would you like to hear that one?"

Stacy was telling him yes when Tanner came soft-footedly into the room. Drew did not notice his presence, and Stacy, although surprised to see him, did not give him away.

"Ruth was married, but her husband died," Drew began. "She lived in Moab with her mother, I think." Drew didn't understand about in-laws, so Stacy let it pass. "Anyway, they went back to where Naomi lived, and then Ruth went to work in the fields. Bozus—"

"Boaz," Stacy corrected him.

"Boaz," Drew started again, "owned the field, and when he saw Ruth he told his servants to be kind to her. They were, and then Naomi sent Ruth to Boaz, so Boaz would know he could marry her. They were married and had a baby named Jesse."

"Obed," Stacy corrected gently.

"Oh, that's right, Obed. And then Obed had Jesse and Jesse had David and then," Drew's voice grew as triumphant as Stacy's whenever she told the story, "a long time later, Joseph was born, and he was married to Mary, and Mary had *Jesus*. Jesus was not Joseph's son, because He was the Son of *God*."

"Oh, Drew." Stacy's voice was soft with wonder. She had talked to him about these things almost from the time he was born, but Stacy had not realized just how much he had taken in. She could feel Tanner's eyes on them in the dim light of the fire, but she kept her own gaze averted. A jaw-popping yawn from Drew reminded Stacy of how late it was getting.

"You best head off now, my darling."

"All right, Mumma. Good night."

They kissed sweetly, and then he crawled from her lap and moved toward Mrs. Maxwell. Tanner chose that moment to come out of the shadows.

"Come along, old man," he said as he swung Drew up onto his shoulders and moved to the door. "I'll cart you off to bed."

"Good night, Mum," Drew managed one last time. Mrs. Maxwell followed her young charge, and Stacy found herself alone. She was growing more weary by the second, so she took herself toward the bedroom before she fell asleep in the chair.

Knowing it would be disastrous at this point to lie down, Stacy sat on the edge of the bed to read her Bible. She read from Jeremiah 9, verses 23 and 24.

"Thus saith the Lord, Let not the wise man glory in his wisdom, neither let the mighty man glory in his might, let not the rich man glory in his riches, but let him that glorieth glory in this, that he understandeth and knoweth me, that I am the Lord who exerciseth lovingkindness, judgment, and righteousness in the earth; for in these things I delight, saith the Lord."

These were the verses Lady Andrea had shared with Stacy concerning Romans 12. Stacy had been worried about her attitude. She feared that she might be thinking of herself more highly than she ought to by telling people how God was working in her life and heart. The verses in Jeremiah gave her peace, as long as she gave God the glory, she was moving with a right attitude and heart. The verses also gave her a direction for prayer, something she would have spent some time doing right then, but she was growing very weary.

She stood and removed her robe, absently wondering when Tanner would come to bed. She had just turned the lantern down low when he entered. Stacy turned from the bed where she'd been ready to climb in and watched him. He stood for a moment, his eyes seeming to assess her before moving to turn the lantern higher. Stacy said nothing to the cold anger in his eyes, and Tanner, obviously expecting something, began to pace. Stacy watched him in silence. Finally he stopped and pinned her to the floor with furious eyes.

"It is beyond me, Anastasia, how you could go fishing in your condition."

He began to pace again, and quite suddenly Stacy was overcome with anger, rage actually. Her hands fisted in front of her. When Tanner stopped and pointed a finger at her, ready to go again, Stacy cut him off.

"Don't you say a word to me, Tanner Richardson! Don't you even so much as scowl in my direction!"

Tanner was so taken aback by this outburst that the anger was surprised right out of him.

"Drew's entire life has been turned upside down in the last year. His grandpapa, the only father he'd ever known, suddenly leaves, and he can't talk to him or play with him anymore. Then we move to London where everything smells and he sees water but he can't fish. You come on the scene when he's finally beginning to adjust to Brentwood, and we're whisked out here to Winslow where we're treated like so much baggage—and unwanted baggage to boot!

"He no more finds out that you're his father, then we go away again. Now his mother is starting to rival his pony for size, and his father is so busy with work that he doesn't have a moment to give him.

"I *will* take Drew fishing if he asks me, and *no one* will gainsay me! I will take him until my pains begin, if that's what it takes for him to know that he's loved and cared for."

Stacy was trembling from head to foot. She turned and walked on shaking legs to the window and simply stared at the glass. Never had she felt so angry and alone. She heard Tanner come up behind her but didn't move or speak, not even when his arms came around her and he rested his chin on top of her head.

"You're trembling." His voice was a whisper.

Stacy didn't reply.

"I must admit to you that I've never looked at it from Drew's standpoint. Suddenly your actions make complete sense."

"I meant what I said, Tanner."

"I know you did."

"Drew needs me to be as normal as possible."

"I understand."

They fell silent then, and Stacy felt bone weary without being sleepy. She thought her body could melt with exhaustion, but her mind was still moving like a team out of control.

"I need to lie down, Tanner."

He didn't reply, but immediately lifted her and moved to the bed. She landed softly against the mattress where his hands gently tucked her in and made her comfortable.

"Can you go to sleep now?" he asked.

"I'm not sleepy, just weary."

Reaching to turn down the light, Tanner suddenly stopped. He sat on the edge of the bed and stared at Stacy.

"You've been busy lately," Stacy commented, not able to read his thoughts through his eyes.

"Yes" was all he said.

"Tanner," Stacy spoke, feeling suddenly brave. "Should we talk about the Cradwell party now?"

"No." Tanner's answer was immediate, but not angry.

Stacy looked disappointed, so he explained.

"I realize now that Stanley was out of his head, and that you were innocent of all he claimed, but I'm not ready to hear what happened."

Stacy nodded, and a weight that she had become accustomed to suddenly lifted from her shoulders. He believed her. After all this time he knew she had been faithful. *Thank You, Father; thank You, Holy God.*

"How was your delivery with Drew?"

The question was so far from Stacy's own thoughts that she didn't immediately answer him.

"Was it hard?" Tanner became more specific, thinking she'd misunderstood him.

"I think most deliveries are hard, but when you see the baby, you tend to forget all about the pain."

Stacy saw that he was not satisfied with her answer. She tossed around in her mind for what he needed, and suddenly Hettie's face came into view. This was why Tanner had put distance between them, why he had been working so hard. Hettie had talked and scared him about the birth. Stacy was as certain of this as if she herself had heard the conversation. With a voice tender with compassion, she asked, "Are you worried about something, Tanner?"

He didn't answer. Stacy knew she had to be honest.

"They tell me I nearly bled to death after Drew was born. I was rather out of it, so I don't recall everything. Drew was over 24 hours old before I was even coherent enough to learn that I'd had a baby boy."

Tanner licked his suddenly dry lips. "And do you not dread the coming birth?"

"No, I guess I don't. I was down for two weeks—"

"I know," Tanner cut her off. "You didn't write."

Stacy stared at him, confounded by the fact that he would know this.

"I interrupted you; go on."

After just an instant, Stacy did. "I did lose a good deal of blood and was down for two weeks, but after that I never looked back. I have a peace, Tanner. I certainly have no guarantees concerning life, but if I had to make some type of guess concerning the future, I would say that I'll be here to be your wife and a mother to the children.

"If in fact God's plan is quite different from that, I still have peace. I know where I'm going, and I trust that He will take care of the three of you in my absence."

Tanner refused to believe in something he couldn't feel or see. Her peace and trust were a mystery to him, but he admired her tremendously. At one time he'd thought of her as weak, but now he saw that Stacy's faith made her stronger. However, he had no desire to discuss any of this with his wife. He knew she would gladly talk of it at any time, but the subject made him uncomfortable, and so he turned his attention to the baby. Stacy saw his eyes go to her stomach.

When Stacy first arrived back at Winslow, and Tanner seemed so fascinated with her shape, Stacy thought he would be taking a more consistent interest, but this was not to be. She finally understood the reason he had put space between them; he'd been afraid of losing her.

Without asking this time, Tanner lowered the covers just enough. The fabric of Stacy's gown was sheer, but even this was too much. With tender movements and eyes centered wholly on Stacy's extended abdomen, he moved the garment aside, baring her stomach for his touch.

The baby had been quiet for quite some time, but Tanner's gentle touch roused a response. Soon the baby was kicking and making Tanner's face light with wonder. Tanner thought he could stay in such a position all night, feeling Stacy's soft skin and the child within her, but a glance at her face stopped all movement. She was sound asleep.

Tanner stared at her a moment and then bent and quietly kissed the skin of her stomach before softly restoring her gown and the bedclothes. He quickly readied himself for bed and climbed in beside her. Stacy moved only slightly when he shifted close and put his arm around her. He didn't know when anything had felt so good as to lie beside her and hold her close.

Oh, Tanner, he said to himself as sleep crowded in. *How much you've missed.*

Forty-Three

"May we go fishing today, Mum?"

Stacy's attention was elsewhere, so she did not answer her son. Tanner, who was breakfasting with his wife, heard Drew's question and simply waited to see how she would respond.

"Mum?"

"Yes, darling," she now acknowledged him.

"May we go fishing today?"

"Oh, I think that would be fine. This morning?"

Drew nodded anxiously, and Stacy smiled at him before glancing at her husband. Tanner's look was a bit stern, but Stacy met his gaze, her chin rising in the air ever so slightly. Tanner quickly lowered his gaze to his own plate before she could detect the gleam of amusement.

He'd wondered from time to time what it would take to make a tigress out of his wife, and now he certainly had his answer.

"When exactly will you be going?" This came from Tanner. Even though Stacy's heart was pounding, she answered calmly.

"In about an hour."

Stacy sounded like she was addressing a servant. Tanner felt like laughing, but kept it well hidden. He simply nodded and went back to his breakfast.

Stacy contemplated his bent head for a moment and then speared a slice of tomato from her plate. The last three days together had been incredible. Tanner couldn't have been more attentive. He ate every meal with Stacy and Drew and even lay down with Stacy when she took her nap. She knew he never slept, but he was there when she drifted off and there when she woke.

One such afternoon, before Stacy fell asleep, she questioned him as to his recent business deal. His answer surprised her.

"I've turned the entire thing over to Edmond."

"I didn't think you trusted Edmond with business details."

Tanner shrugged. "It's his money as well as mine. If he wants to mess it up, he'll be out as well."

"But what about your money?"

Again Tanner had only shrugged, causing Stacy to stare at him until he kissed her and told her to go to sleep. She had given way to slumber, but the memory came back so strongly now that she paused in her eating.

"Is your food all right?"

"What?" Stacy gave him a blank look.

Tanner stared at her and stated the question again.

"I said, is your food all right?"

"Oh, yes. I was just wool gathering."

"Are you in pain, Stacy?" Tanner's voice was low.

"No," Stacy answered in surprise and wondered what her expression had been. A glance at Drew told her he was attending every word, so she smiled to reassure him.

"If you're done eating, Drew, please go with Mrs. Maxwell. I'll come for you when I'm ready to go."

"Should I change into fishing clothes?"

"Yes, Mrs. Maxwell will know the ones."

Tanner spoke as soon as Drew had left the room.

"I'll meet you in the foyer when you're ready."

"You're going with us?" It had crossed Stacy's mind that he might, but she had immediately dismissed the idea.

"Yes. I'll drive you out and bring you back."

"Thank you, Tanner," Stacy said with a smile. Tanner's gaze warmed noticeably in the light of her pleasure.

Tanner went back to eating, but Stacy was thoughtful. What a strange marriage they'd had thus far, but it seemed to be coming around. Stacy thought of how many other times she had expected her marriage to improve only to be disappointed, but swiftly pushed the thought away. This was here and now, and this was what she would work on and pray for, not dwelling on the aches and mistakes of the past.

Husband and wife parted soon after with plans to meet and go fishing. Stacy took herself back to her room, and Tanner, after ordering a small, enclosed buggy, told Price he needed warm hunting gear. Less than an hour later, Tanner stood wearing knee-high suede moccasins and buckskin pants and shirt as he stared out the window at the pouring rain.

He wasn't completely convinced that the sudden rain would deter Stacy and Drew's plans. They were, he realized, a hearty pair, and Stacy was most determined to please her son. With a sudden, brilliant idea that he hoped wouldn't land him in trouble, he moved toward the door.

Stacy moved toward the nursery, ready to find Drew and start on their way. She knew it was pouring but told herself it could stop anytime. If Tanner had ordered a covered coach, they could just wait out the rain. The thought of being outside in the rain at all gave her a sudden chill, but she pushed it away and told herself to buck up.

Knowing that Tanner would be waiting, she walked on to the nursery, a long, narrow room done in all shades of green and filled with every conceivable type of toy. When she arrived, however, she found that Tanner was not downstairs but had reached the room ahead of her. He and Drew were in deep conversation on the rug. Tanner was stretched out on his side by the fire, seemingly miles of him, and Stacy for once was able to sit down and listen.

"What is it called?" Drew asked again, as he ran a hand over his father's shirtfront. He was sitting cross-legged near the older man's chest and speaking directly into Tanner's face.

"Buckskin. Made from the hide of a deer."

"It's soft. Do I have buckhide clothes?"

"Buckskin," Tanner corrected him. "I'm not sure that you do. Would you like some?"

"Yes." Drew's eyes stared into Tanner's. "Then I could wear them fishing."

"Do you and your mother fish in the rain?" Tanner's voice was a study in casualness.

"Oh, yes," he answered simply. "Sometimes you catch more fish."

Tanner nodded. "I think that sounds like good fun, but you know your mother needs a little extra care these days."

Drew nodded. "She has a baby in her tummy." He held out small hands, about ten inches apart, to show his father the baby's size.

"Yes, she does," he said with a smile. "And until the baby is born, which will be very soon now, she needs to take extra rest. Most of the time fishing is fine, but in the rain she could catch a chill."

"And then the baby would catch a chill. The baby feels what Mum feels and eats what she eats."

"That's right, so maybe for today we had better not fish."

"All right." Drew sounded neither happy nor sad, but accepting.

Stacy watched Tanner scrutinize Drew, knowing that he was trying to read his son's thoughts.

"So what shall we play instead?"

Drew's mouth dropped open in a way that shamed Tanner. "You're going to play with me?"

"Anything you'd like," Tanner stated softly.

Delighted with his father's offer, Drew made a lunge for Tanner's neck, and a moment later they were wrestling on the nursery room rug, something Tanner had never done with his own father.

The morning passed in great fun that went from wrestling to trains, boats, pretend fishing, and back to trains again. They included Lady Richardson in their play, and although she didn't wrestle, both of Stacy's "men" laughed when Tanner helped her to the floor and she groaned all the way down. The three were not disturbed until just an hour before lunch.

"I'm sorry, my lord." This came from Reece as he soundlessly opened the door. "Lord and Lady Hawkesbury and their sons are here to see you."

"Sterling and Preston?" Drew had come to his feet.

"Yes, Lord Drew."

"Go ahead with Reece, Drew," Tanner told his ecstatic son when he looked to his father. "And tell them your mother and I will be right down."

Tanner helped Stacy to her feet and then to their room so she could freshen up.

"You can go ahead, Tanner. I'll be right down."

"I'll wait for you," he told her simply and sprawled in a chair while she sat before the mirror and repaired her hair. After just a moment, Stacy caught Tanner's eye in the glass.

"That was quick work on your part when the rain began."

Tanner grinned. "I'll admit it was impulsive, but after your outburst a few days ago, I thought I stood a better chance with Drew."

"You make me sound like a shrew." Stacy's voice was dry.

"Maybe it would be easier if you were."

This comment made Stacy take her hands from her hair and turn to her husband. She watched him for a moment but didn't know what to say. Tanner finally shrugged.

"Don't mind me. It certainly isn't your fault that at times I forget I have a wife and son."

"Are you trying to tell me you *want* me to nag you?"

"Maybe just a gentle reminder now and then."

Stacy knew this needed no reply, so she turned back to the mirror and just moments later stood.

"You could have called your maid to do that," Tanner commented as they moved out the door.

"True. But I didn't mind doing it myself."

"Are you really up to seeing anyone today?"

"Certainly. I feel fine."

They were at the top of the stairs when Stacy looked up to find Tanner studying her.

"What is it that you expect to see, Tanner?"

"If only I knew," he admitted. "You will tell me when your pains begin?"

"I think you'll know."

Tanner slowly shook his head. "You rarely ask for help, and you never complain. I'm afraid you're going to excuse yourself from the dinner table some evening, and by the time I get upstairs it will be all over."

Stacy put a hand on her husband's cheek and stroked softly. "You probably won't want to be anywhere near me when I'm giving birth, but I will tell you when things begin. If you're not here, I'll send word if I know where you are."

"I'll be here," Tanner assured her in a voice that only a fool would argue with before he captured the hand on his face to lead his wife downstairs.

"How can you believe the Bible to be God's Word? What in your opinion gives it merit?" Tanner asked Brandon after lunch, when both men had settled in the study. The children were with Mrs. Maxwell, and the women were in one of the small upstairs salons.

Brandon could not say how they'd come onto this discussion of God and the Bible, but because it was a first, he wanted to remain amicable and keep the door of inquiry open.

"I'm rather glad you asked that Tanner," Brandon complimented him.

Tanner stared at him in surprise. Knowing Brandon's stand on the Bible, he'd been expecting some sort of attack or rebuke for questioning the Bible's validity. Brandon's openness caused him to wait almost anxiously for a reply.

"If the Bible is not entirely from God, then the basis of authority for most of what I believe is cracked and unreliable." Tanner was clearly listening to every word, so Brandon went on.

"You asked what gives it merit; I'll tell you. Some 3000 times the Bible specifically, directly, claims to be from God—not man's word about God, but God's word about man.

"I'm also amazed how so many prophecies made hundreds of years before their intended fulfillment actually came to pass."

"What does that prove?"

"Have you read the Bible, Tanner?" Brandon challenged him quietly. "Written by many men, each author agrees about problems and themes that are very controversial. For instance, the world culture in Old Testament days overwhelmingly believed in many gods; yet the Old Testament authors unanimously affirm the existence of one God and creator of all.

"They also affirm the universality of man's sinfulness and the need for the blood of an unblemished sacrifice to remove the guilt of sin. One author's theology never contradicts another's—all contribute to one single system of belief."

This was new to Tanner, and he took time to think about what Brandon was saying, but he was still not persuaded. After a minute he asked a question that had long disturbed him.

"What about the inconsistencies?"

"What inconsistencies?" Brandon pressed him.

"Stacy told me once that she takes the Bible literally when it talks of the whole earth being flooded or Jonah being swallowed by a huge fish, but the Bible also says God has feathers. Am I to believe He's a bird?"

Brandon smiled and answered gently. "The charge that the Bible is strewn with inconsistencies is hardly a new one, Tanner. But I have found it necessary to distinguish between inconsistencies and problems. There are many problems, to be sure, but I've found that with objective bias and careful research, the apparent inconsistencies dissolve in the face of honest study."

Tanner could not argue with this because he had never put in any time of "honest study." He was deeply impressed by Brandon's knowledge, but the real impact came from his deep conviction and the way he'd spoken of it. However, Tanner was not convinced. He believed himself more than capable of handling his own affairs and taking care of his own. Why would he need God? It was a question he wouldn't have been so comfortable with if eternity had come to mind.

Had Brandon been able to read his thoughts he would have questioned him on that very subject. But as it was he could not read his friend's thoughts, and when Tanner changed the subject, Brandon felt he had little choice but to let the matter drop.

"You look wonderful," Sunny commented as she took in Stacy's healthy glow and round figure.

"I look huge," Stacy corrected her. "Sometimes I find Drew staring at me, and I know he's trying to decide which is larger, his mother or his pony."

Sunny chuckled, well able to remember how Stacy felt. At this point in any woman's pregnancy, it felt as if her condition was going to last forever.

"I'm so glad you felt free to come by," Stacy told her friend. "As you can imagine, I'm not getting out these days."

"We knew you were back, but I wasn't certain if we should call. Suddenly I couldn't stand it any longer. Was it pretty awful?"

"Yes and no. I never really expected Tanner to be in touch, so I wasn't surprised when I didn't hear from him. And then after I'd learned that he didn't even know we were staying at the Blackwells', it was torture. Roddy told me he came to Brentwood a week after I'd left."

Sunny nodded. "He came to Bracken, looking beside himself. We talked for quite some time. I don't know if you'll be upset, but I told him about how badly the servants treated you."

"I'm not at all upset, but do you know what he did?" Stacy asked.

"He told us what he had planned. Did he do it?"

"Yes. Price is still here, and so is cook. That's it. Not even the stable hands stayed. Sometimes I feel wretched about it, but then I remind myself that they all made their choices."

"That they did," Sunny agreed, not at all afraid of sounding harsh. She'd been waited on her entire life and honestly believed that both lord and servant could make the best or worst of it. Knowing what an undemanding person Stacy was, Sunny knew that the original servants at Winslow had been completely out of line.

"What do you hear from Roddy and Lucinda?" Sunny asked.

"From Lucinda, nothing, but Roddy came to Christ when he came to see me at the Blackwells', and we've had quite a bit of communication."

"Oh, Stacy," Sunny exclaimed and hugged her friend. "You must be thrilled."

"I am that. God had certainly prepared his heart for our time together. Roddy was so eager to let God fill the void he felt inside. Now he's like dry ground in the rain with the way he's reading the Word and growing."

Stacy had no desire to gossip, so she did not go on to say that he was also doing amazingly well considering that he and Lucinda were not living together at the moment.

"But you say that Lucinda has not been in touch?" Sunny inquired.

"I've written her twice," Stacy explained, "asking her to write to me so we can talk this out, but I've not heard a word. I love Lucinda and I've already forgiven her, but I did tell her I want some answers. She's obviously not ready to give them to me."

"Another thing to pray about."

"Yes," Stacy agreed.

Much to everyone's delight, Sunny and Brandon ended up staying for the greater part of the day. However, Stacy found it taxing. In fact she was so tired that Tanner had to hold a surprise he had been keeping over until the following day. The look of delight on Stacy and Drew's faces when he brought Hettie into the breakfast room the next morning was worth the putting aside of his own feelings about the old servant.

Forty-Four

LUCINDA KNEW THAT ALL OF LONDON was talking about her and Roddy. It was not the gentle variety of gossip as when they'd been married or what a handsome couple they made, but it was the vicious type, the type Lucinda herself had often engaged in. Minds and tongues were speculating everywhere as to why the Earl of Glyn's wife had chosen to move from their home.

Some said it was because they'd ruined a beautiful relationship by getting married in the first place. Others said that nothing could last forever, and some even said that the affections of both parties had drifted and each decided to seek out greener pastures.

Lucinda knew better than anyone how far the rumors were from the truth. The fact that the Blackwells lived so far distant from London was the only reason the duplicity of Lucinda's actions toward Tanner and Stacy were not on every tabloid in the city.

Lucinda kept telling herself she didn't care. She staunchly put aside all emotions and went shopping and to the theater whenever she desired. She did not see other men, but she had determined to be as worldly as ever, a facade she couldn't quite manage in the lonely confines of her own room.

This morning she was feeling every one of her years and so

lonely for Roddy that she wanted to weep. Their last conversation, the one she managed to submerge so deeply within her mind that she hadn't thought about it in all these weeks, came back to her now so sharply that Roddy could have been standing in the room with her.

"How could you?" Lucinda spat in anger.

"How could I what? Go after Stacy? Return her to her husband?"

"How could you go behind my back?"

Roddy stared at her in disbelief. He'd returned from his search for Tanner to find that Lucinda had received word of his actions and had moved from Brentwood to one of London's finest hotels. She was beside herself when he sought her out at the hotel, but her worry had nothing to do with Roddy's well-being in the last four days, only the exposure of her subterfuge.

"How can you possibly accuse *me* of going behind *your* back?"

"You don't understand," Lucinda railed. "He's going to hurt her again, just like he always has. She thinks she wants him, but she doesn't really. She was probably completely over him by the time you got there, but you've sent Tanner to her and now he'll give her no choice but to return."

"You couldn't be more wrong." Roddy's voice told his wife he was growing furious. "She was miserable and lonely without him. You can ask her yourself."

"How could you?" was all Lucinda would say.

"Your line of reasoning frightens me. In fact, *you* frighten me," Roddy told Lucinda coldly. Lucinda's eyes widened with shock. However, Roddy went on without mercy. "You wait until I leave, and then you sneak Stacy and Drew away, and now you stand there and ask me how I could go behind your back. Like I said, you frighten me." Roddy turned to the door but paused just before leaving. "When you're ready to come to your senses and talk about this, Lucinda, you know where to find me." With that Roddy had walked out. They hadn't spoken since.

Now the words, the entire scene, unfolded so clearly in Lucinda's mind that she felt a stab of pain around her heart. He had been so right. At the time she had refused to see her own wrong. She had accused him so she didn't have to face her own actions. But now...

Lucinda could not finish the thought. It had been weeks since she'd seen him. What if it was too late? What if Roddy had given up on her and begun to look for another?

Lucinda found this thought so unbearable that without care for how she looked, she snatched her cloak and ordered her carriage. She was at Brentwood before she really had time to think about what she would say, but she needed to see Roddy so badly that she didn't care. It felt strange to come to the door as a guest, but Roddy's man, Carlson, greeted her warmly and, thankfully, told her that his lord was in.

Carlson tried to show her to the parlor, but Lucinda declined. She was still standing in the entryway, taking in the sights and smells of her beloved home, when she heard Roddy's footsteps. He stopped just two feet away from her and drank in the sight of her flushed face and messy hair. She was wearing a simple day-dress, with no jewelry or special fixings, and Roddy thought her beautiful.

Lucinda was feeling quite the same way. Roddy had never looked more wonderful. He was jacketless, but his shirt was very white and crisp and his necktie was the same color as his eyes. He stood tall, with his back straight and every hair in place. Lucinda's eyes ate up the sight of him.

"Hello, Cinda," he said gently and in the next instant she quite nearly threw herself into his arms. She sobbed without disgrace and was still sobbing when Roddy led her into his office, gently helping her get comfortable on the sofa. When Lucinda's sobbing had subsided, he began to question her gently, his arms still tightly around her.

"Why have you come?"

"I missed you so."

"I missed you too. Are you back to stay?"

"If you'll still have me," Lucinda hiccuped.

"There was never any question of that, Cinda. My love for you is constant, but if you haven't apologized to Stacy then you need to do that."

"She wrote me twice, but I was too angry to write back."

"And how do you feel now?"

Lucinda sniffed. "I still think Tanner will hurt her, but I feel just wretched for hiding her. It was so foolish of me. Do you think she'll forgive me?"

"I'm sure she will."

"And you, Roddy? Can you find it in your heart to forgive me?"

"I already have."

Lucinda let herself be cuddled against his chest for a long moment. She was no longer crying, but she felt weak and shaky all over. Some minutes passed in silence, and then Lucinda sat up suddenly.

"I'll go to her, Roddy. I won't write. I'll go to Winslow and make things right."

"I think that's a wonderful idea, my darling, but the baby is due very soon now, and I wonder if maybe you should wait."

Lucinda's face was a mask of horror. "The baby! I'd almost forgotten about the baby. Oh, Roddy, what have I done?"

Roddy thought that her tears were spent, but he was wrong. She was off again on a flood of weeping that took some time to calm. When Roddy was certain that Lucinda was ready to listen, he told her she could write to Stacy, but that they would not visit until sometime after the baby was born. Lucinda agreed without argument.

There was something different about Roddy. He was taking charge of things in a very soothing way, and Lucinda, only too happy to be back in his care, was for the first time in her life thrilled to let him lead.

Tanner thought that if Stacy shifted one more time in her chair, he was going to come undone. It was obvious she was uncomfortable, but she was not at the moment going to say anything.

Tanner's eyes kept straying to Hettie, who was knitting in a chair but whose eyes constantly drifted to her mistress. He was trying to read in Hettie's face what Stacy would not admit to. All at once, Tanner could stand no more. He stood and nearly accused his wife.

"You're in pain, aren't you? I wish you would just tell me."

"But I'm not, Tanner." Stacy's voice was reasonable. "I'm not feeling the best, sort of achy, but I'm not in labor."

Tanner's seat hit the chair very hard. He really thought this was it.

"I think I would like to go to bed, however," Stacy continued. "I know it's early, but I'm tired."

Tanner nodded and rose, trying hard not to dread the next days or weeks. He was certain the baby was coming tonight, but he was not excited, only anxious. This was all new for him, and he simply wanted to get it started and over with. He knew that Stacy wouldn't appreciate his feelings, so he kept them to himself.

Five hours later, he wished he'd voiced his thoughts, if for no other reason than to have them off his chest. Stacy had fallen asleep immediately, but not Tanner. He had still been awake at midnight and at one. At any other time he'd have gone off and done some work, read, or even taken a walk, but his need to be near Stacy right now put him in bed at nine o'clock and kept him there even when all he did was stare at the ceiling.

Tanner finally drifted off somewhere around two in the morning, which was the cause for all sorts of confusion when Stacy woke him at three.

"Tanner," Stacy called softly, but her husband did little more than stir.

"Tanner, can you wake up?"

"Um."

The response was slightly more than the first time, but not enough.

"Tanner, I need you to get Hettie."

Her voice was louder this time, and Tanner finally stirred.

"What did you say?"

"I need Hettie."

"What do we need Hettie in here for?" His voice sounded very crabby, and Stacy had all she could do not to laugh.

"Things are starting, and I want Hettie."

"Things? What things?"

Stacy did laugh this time, but another contraction hit and her breath was cut off in a sharp gasp. Understanding finally dawned, and Tanner flew out of the bed. He didn't bother with his robe. If Stacy had been able to speak, she would have told him to cover up for poor Hettie's sake.

The sun had been up for hours when Stacy, feeling utterly spent, lay back against her pillows. She knew she had less than a minute before she would need to push again, but right at the moment, she didn't know where she would find the store.

"Is this one worse, Hettie?"

"Than Drew?"

"Yes."

"I can see you're not going to bleed as badly this time, but the pains are all 'bout the same, I 'spect."

Stacy would have replied, but another pain was on top of her. Tanner had been with her for most of the time, but when he'd become shaky, Stacy had finally sent him away to eat something. He was just coming in as the pain subsided.

"I feel like I can't keep this up," she admitted softly, and Tanner looked into her exhausted eyes with tenderness. He thought she was the most amazing woman on earth.

"I'll be here for you."

"What if I can't do it, Tanner? What if I can't push again?"

Tanner did not need to answer because another pain racked Stacy's body. He supported her back as she pushed.

"I see the head," Hettie cried, and new strength seemed to pour over Stacy. She waited anxiously for the next contraction, ready to do whatever was asked of her in order to meet this baby.

"Here it comes, Hettie," Stacy gasped, and the old woman stood ready.

A long minute passed.

"One more and we'll have it," Hettie crooned, and she was right. The next contraction hit, and the old woman cackled with delight.

"A girl! A big, healthy girl with a head full of black hair!"

Stacy lay back and laughed weakly with relief. She wanted to reach for the baby, but her arms felt weighted. A glance at Tanner made her chuckle again. He was staring at the squalling red infant in Hettie's hands as if he were in a trance.

Tanner Richardson had never seen anything so miraculous as the birth of his daughter. She was a mess, all red and curled up and howling at the top of her voice, but he thought she was the most precious thing he'd ever seen.

I love her, he thought to himself. *She's my daughter, and I love her. I love her the way I loved Drew the first time I set eyes on him.*

The magnitude of his thoughts was overwhelming. He glanced down at Stacy, her own eyes now back on their daughter, and thought about what she'd just given of herself. She'd been in agony to accomplish this wonder, and now she was smiling and talking to their baby.

"Don't cry, my darling. Mumma's here. Don't cry. May I have her, Hettie?"

"Just another minute, and she's all yours."

Hettie finished the cleanup, and after wrapping the baby in a soft warm wrap, she handed her to her mother. Stacy crooned softly into the baby's face and after a moment, the tears stopped. She couldn't rock her very well, but she moved her arms just enough. Within moments, the baby was asleep.

"Would you like to hold her?"

Tanner's eyes flew to Stacy's. He'd been so intent on the baby that he hadn't immediately realized she was speaking to him. He shook his head.

"Another time" was all he said.

"All right." Stacy watched him for a moment. "Are you disappointed that it's not another boy?"

"Not in the least," Tanner told her. There was so much more that he wanted to say, but none of it would come. Had they been alone he might have tried, but Hettie's presence along with that of three housemaids caused him to keep still.

He was suddenly very tired. Tanner opened his mouth to tell Stacy that he was headed off to get some rest, but her eyes were already closed, the sleeping baby still tucked in the crook of her arm. Seeing this, Tanner made his way from the room to find his own rest.

Three hours later Tanner returned to the bedroom to find Stacy awake and partially sitting up. He strode confidently into the room, but slowed somewhat when he saw the baby at her breast. That Stacy planned to nurse the baby herself had never occurred to him. He wasn't certain how he felt about this. He loved his daughter, but he'd had the distinct impression that when she was born, he could have his wife back. Selfishness was beginning to rear its ugly head.

"Hello," Stacy greeted him and watched as Tanner came to the bed, sat down, and leaned against the footboard.

"How are you feeling?"

"I'm fine. Did you get some sleep?"

"Yes. I was just in with Drew. He wants to see you."

Stacy nodded. "I asked Hettie to wait until I'd fed the baby."

"Did you nurse Drew?"

"Yes," Stacy answered, and for the first time understood the odd expression on Tanner's face. It was on the tip of Stacy's tongue to ask Tanner if he objected, but she knew she couldn't do that. She had already made up her mind.

"I'm sorry you don't care for the idea."

Tanner noticed that she did not offer to stop. "It's not that I don't care for the idea as much as it takes a little getting used to. I know I'm being selfish, but I thought I would be getting my wife back."

"I think you will be getting me back, but I won't tell you that she'll never interfere. We've created this child together, and I think my care of her is important. It would be easier if we'd been living together all these years, but in truth it isn't all that much time to sacrifice. Drew stopped nursing before he was nine months old. In fact, he tapered way off around six months."

Tanner nodded. He was not overly upset and, in truth, the idea was becoming easier all the time. He stared down at the baby and then shifted to his stomach so he could watch her.

"I think she's done."

Stacy gently bounced her a few times, and she began to suck again.

"She keeps falling asleep, so I have to give her little wake-up calls."

"Does it hurt?"

"Not hurt exactly, but it will take some time for my skin to toughen up and grow accustomed to the sucking."

Tanner was silent as he watched for the next few seconds. When the baby seemed to be sleeping again, he asked, "What are we going to call her?"

"I don't know. Have you any ideas?"

"Was your mother's name Alexa?"

"Yes. How did you know that?"

"While we were at Morgan I was studying her portrait. Your grandfather's man—"

"Peters?"

"Yes, Peters. He came by and said it was your mother and that her name had been Alexa Catherine."

"Alexa." Stacy tried the name on her tongue. "I don't think I would have thought of it, but I like it."

"Alexa it is then. Alexa Anastasia Richardson."

Stacy grinned in delight and felt amazed over how painless it had been. She'd heard that people could go for weeks with great struggles and quarrels over names, but this one was so perfect.

Alexa was done eating, so Stacy shifted her to her shoulder, covered herself, and gently rubbed the baby's back. Tanner continued to watch her, and after a moment Stacy asked if he wanted to hold Alexa.

Tanner sat against the headboard this time and carefully took the baby. She was sound asleep and even though he jostled her slightly, she never stirred. She was so tiny in his hands. Her head was slightly pointed at the top, but Stacy had assured Tanner this was from the birth and would change with time. Alexa's lashes were long and dark and lay like tiny fans against her cheeks. She was round and soft, and Tanner couldn't decide which he enjoyed more, the feel of her soft skin or her fragrance, which reminded him of a forest after the rain.

After a few minutes he shifted Alexa around until she lay in the crook of his arm. Stacy was silent as he stared down into the baby's face. Suddenly Tanner turned to her, his voice low, but almost fierce.

"If a man offered to make her his mistress, I'd call him out—but that's exactly what I did to you."

Stacy said nothing, but the pain of those days when she thought Tanner would never be hers and when he admitted that he'd never wanted her for a wife, came flooding back.

"I should have been pilloried for such a thing."

"It's over now, Tanner." Stacy's voice was gentle.

"It might be over, but I've never told you how much I regret my actions and words. I'm sorry, Stacy."

Stacy could hardly believe her ears as her husband apologized for the first time in their relationship. She stared at him, unable to frame any type of reply.

As it was she didn't have to. Tanner, still holding the baby, leaned toward her. It was the most tender of kisses, and when they parted Tanner looked into her eyes for a long time.

She didn't know what he was thinking and wasn't sure if she should speak. For the moment they were content to be silent in each other's company, a silence that lasted only briefly as Drew was finally allowed to come and meet his baby sister.

Forty-Five

"THREE MONTHS OLD TODAY," Stacy whispered quietly to her baby daughter. "What a big girl you are."

Just the sound of Stacy's voice was enough to send Alexa's body into a tempest of leg kicks and arm swings. Her small, round face was wreathed in smiles. She was a most delightful baby, and Stacy grinned down at her as they sat before the fire in the nursery. The warmer winter had made their cool spring feel all the colder, but Stacy didn't mind being forced indoors when the company was so delightful.

"Aunt Lucinda and Uncle Roddy will be here any time. Did you know that?"

Alexa, who didn't understand a word of it, smiled and kicked some more. Watching her, Stacy knew how amazed Roddy and Lucinda would be. She had only been a month old, still sleeping most of the time, when they'd last visited. Now her world was expanding, and she was turning into a real person. At the moment, however, her world was her mother's face. Alexa's eyes followed Stacy's every move.

"Mum," Drew called from the doorway. "Is Alexa awake?"

"Yes, she is. Come in."

"Alexa," Drew said to her in a voice that sounded like a growl as he bent over her and rubbed noses. Stacy watched. The baby grinned as if on cue. This was Drew's latest voice with his sister. The first month he always said her name in a very high pitch. The next month he drew the name out in a singsong way—Aaaalexaaa. Now he sounded like a bear. His sister loved it.

Drew had turned four just a month back, and he was a wonderful older brother. Already showing signs of being quite responsible, Stacy even allowed him to carry the baby at times. He took this job very seriously, even though Hettie nearly fainted whenever she watched him.

"When will Uncle Roddy be here?"

"Oh, soon, I expect. Which reminds me, I'd better feed your sister now so we can go for a time without being interrupted."

Stacy came off the floor in an easy movement, and after lifting Alexa into her arms, she took the rocking chair. Drew stayed to visit with her, and when Alexa was more than halfway through, Tanner also came into the baby's room. He bent low to kiss Alexa's head, scooped Drew into his arms, and then took a chair.

"I have to go to London at the beginning of next week." Tanner's tone was regretful.

Stacy frowned slightly. They had only just began to enjoy married life again, and right now they felt like honeymooners.

"How long will you be away?"

"Four or five days. A week at the most."

Stacy was not thrilled, but she was accepting. Tanner watched her face and smiled inwardly. He would have said something very intimate to his wife just then, but his children were present. He hadn't wanted to be away from her for a moment in the last few weeks, and her frown over his news told him she felt the same way.

"May I go with you?" This came from Drew, and Tanner looked down in surprise at the little person in his lap. His first response was to say no, but when he took a moment to think on it, he wondered if it might be a good idea.

"Let me talk it over with your mother," Tanner told him, having already decided to take Drew along.

"All right." Drew naturally took this as a good sign, and his look became very hopeful. He was going to ask where they were going to stay, but Reece came to the door at that moment to announce Roddy and Lucinda's presence.

Having gained permission, Drew joined Reece when he went back downstairs. Stacy rang for Hettie. After the baby had been taken to her room, Tanner stood up. Stacy did also and caught his hand before he could move away.

"I really wish you would see her."

Tanner's eyes grew hard. Stacy was forgiving; Tanner was not. When they had come a month after the baby was born, Tanner refused to see Lucinda. He'd spent some time with Roddy, but if Lucinda was in the room, Tanner was not.

"She is really sorry."

"You can't give Lucinda an inch, Stacy. Give her half a chance, and she'll try to control your life again."

"I'm not going to let that happen."

"I don't see how you'll stop it."

"I take it you're planning to send me away again."

Tanner's arms were around her in an instant, and he brought her hard up against him. His face was so close when he spoke, she felt his breath on her cheek.

"You know I'm not."

"Then what are you worried about?"

Tanner had no answer, but as he stared into Stacy's eyes, remembering the way Lucinda had kept them apart, he knew he couldn't take it ever again.

"I think you like holding onto your anger," Stacy spoke solemnly. "I know she was wrong, and Lucinda knows it too, but I think you've made up your mind not to forgive her. You're holding onto that bitterness for no good reason."

"Do not," Tanner's voice had grown very cold, "talk to me as if I were Drew."

"Then stop acting Drew's age!" Stacy shot back at him and stepped from his embrace. Her voice shook when she spoke, but she did not look at him as she headed toward the door.

"You're angry and since your anger always scares me, I'm leaving now."

She got no more than three feet away before Tanner was pulling her back into his arms. He didn't kiss her but held her tightly against his chest. Stacy lay agreeably in his arms, telling herself not to apologize for speaking the truth. Tanner said after some minutes, "I'll try to come down, but I make no promises."

Stacy lifted her head to look at him. "Thank you, Tanner."

"You look marvelous," Lucinda exclaimed the moment she saw Stacy. "I thought you would have the baby with you."

"Hettie is changing her, and then she'll bring her down."

"Oh, good. I brought her a little something, and I want to see what she thinks."

"Something tells me she'll love it." Stacy's voice was dry, and Lucinda laughed when she realized what she'd just said.

"Hello, Roddy."

Stacy finally turned to hug this man who was so dear to her. After embracing, they stood for just an instant and stared at each other. Things were so special now that he'd come to a saving knowledge of Christ. He had always been a kind, gentle man, but there was a warmth and peace about him now that Stacy could not even begin to describe.

"How are you?" she asked.

"I'm fine. How about you?"

"I'm well."

"Is Tanner taking good care of you?"

Stacy's smile was tender, causing Roddy to reach out and gently squeeze her hand. No words were needed.

Lucinda had sat down to hold Drew on her lap and called to her husband.

"Come and sit beside me and see this little man."

Roddy complied. "You look more like your father every time I see you, Drew."

Drew smiled at Roddy, who was one of his favorite people, but an odd expression came over Lucinda's face. When Drew climbed from Lucinda's lap onto Roddy's, she said softly, "Will he see me this time, Stacy?"

"I honestly don't know, Lucinda. I asked him if he would, but I'm not sure what he will do."

"I've been telling Lucinda she must keep quiet, even if he does make an appearance."

"Is he right, Stacy? Should I really not bring the subject up?"

"Well," Stacy answered slowly, wanting to say the right thing. "You did write him?"

Lucinda nodded.

"And in the letter you already apologized?"

Another nod.

"Then I think I would stay quiet about the Blackwells unless the subject comes up. Tanner might be ready to put it behind him, and if he is it will only irritate him to belabor the point."

Lucinda was more than ready to comply with any suggestion. The three of them spoke of it for a few minutes more, and then Hettie appeared with Alexa. Lucinda and Roddy were both captivated with her. Alexa sat on her mother's arm and stared at the strangers with huge, dark eyes.

"She's adorable," Lucinda breathed.

"Would you look at those eyes," Roddy added.

"Alexa," Drew growled, and a huge smile broke across the baby's face.

If Roddy and Lucinda had found her cute before she smiled, they now thought her enchanting. They watched as she kicked her legs and smiled at her brother's antics. Lucinda came near and Stacy passed Alexa to her. Alexa smiled engagingly through the transition, even when she realized that she was no longer in her mother's arms.

She then proceeded to charm the stockings off of her Aunty Lucinda. She smiled and drooled with charm, before sticking a finger in her eye and causing great tears of self-pity to roll down her round, flushed cheeks. She was passed to Stacy, who had only just calmed her down when Tanner walked in and made her forget all about her eye.

Unless Alexa Richardson was eating, her father was her favorite toy. She smiled as he neared, and the legs that had been calm began to kick with delight. Tanner, his eyes alight with amused pleasure, made straight for his wife and daughter. He took Alexa into his arms, bussed her once on the cheek, and then turned to his guests.

"Hello, Lucinda, Roddy. How was the trip out?"

"Not bad," Roddy answered. "The roads are a bit wet."

Tanner nodded, and Stacy prayed.

"I'm headed out for a ride," Tanner continued. "Would you care to join me, Roddy?"

Roddy answered with a smile in his voice, "Your daughter is stiff competition, but I could use some exercise."

Tanner chuckled and spoke to the baby in his arms. "Are you working your wiles on your Uncle Roddy?"

He received a toothless grin for the attention, and Tanner couldn't resist kissing her again.

"Papa?" Drew spoke. Tanner looked down to find him standing at his feet and asking to hold the baby. He waited until Drew was settled in a chair and placed Alexa in his small arms.

Tanner seemed anxious to be on his way, so he and Roddy left just after Drew took the baby. Lucinda brought out her gifts for the children in the next few minutes, and as much as Drew enjoyed his new sweater and hat, and Stacy, holding Alexa, exclaimed over the new dress and shoes for her, the younger woman could tell something was wrong.

Lucinda's features were oddly strained, but not until Hettie had taken Alexa away and Drew had gone off with Mrs. Maxwell did Stacy ask. Lucinda's reply was so surprising that all Stacy could do was listen.

"She would never have reacted that way if Tanner was a stranger. Alexa's whole face lit up at the sight of him. All this time I thought he had forced you back here, that you were being treated like before.

"Tanner cares for you; he truly does! I thought he was just like Aubrey, but he loves his children—I can see it in his face. He was so tender with both Alexa and Drew.

"Oh, Stacy, all this time...What have I done?"

"It's over, Lucinda," Stacy knew it was time to cut in. "I won't say that Tanner hasn't hurt me, but, God willing, the worst is over. I'm not exactly a saint myself, I hope you realize, but I believe we're both committed to making this marriage work."

Lucinda drew in a shuddering breath. "Thank you for being so understanding. Roddy said that you were, and I know you've forgiven me, but I don't feel I deserve it. It's all a little hard to take in."

Stacy nodded understandingly, thinking this had been a long time in the coming, but well worth the wait.

"Stacy," Lucinda said after a moment, her voice a bit reluctant, "Roddy has been talking to me about his," she hesitated over the words, "experience with God."

Stacy hid a smile. "What did he tell you?"

"Quite a bit, actually. He's very excited. He says that you helped him."

"Yes, we discussed it at the Blackwells'. Roddy was really feeling rather empty inside and—"

"But we've patched everything up now," Lucinda cut her off, thinking she understood.

"I know you have, Lucinda, and I'm thrilled that you're back together, but the emptiness Roddy was experiencing was not physical or emotional. It was spiritual."

Lucinda stared at her niece. Never had she felt so left out as she did when Roddy and Stacy talked about God. At the same time she was interested. Lucinda had gone to church all her life, but she also had too many bad things happen to her to believe that God really cared about her. However, the change in Roddy was remarkable.

Stacy would have commented on Roddy's conversion then, but Lucinda began to look very uncomfortable.

Lucinda changed the subject by asking about Brandon and Sunny. Stacy let it go, but her heart was deep in prayer for Lucinda's salvation. However, the subject did not come up again, but God's care was evident in the marvelous evening they all shared.

Tanner finally seemed willing to put the past behind him and was a wonderful host. After the children were put down for the night, the four adults dined and talked. It was very late when the duke and duchess climbed the stairs for bed, but knowing Roddy and Lucinda would be with them for only a few days made it worth the loss of sleep.

Forty-Six

STACY WATCHED TANNER, whose expression was serious, and debated whether or not she should intrude into his thoughts. Drew was not with them now, but just minutes before he had been in Stacy's lap. The two of them had been discussing the upcoming weekend at Bracken.

At the mention of the event, Tanner had become pensive. Stacy wanted to respect his moods, but she knew she would be miserable if they went when he didn't really care to.

"Tanner?"

"Yes?" He looked at her, his expression now open.

"Would you rather we didn't go to Bracken?"

Tanner almost smiled. Unless he worked at it, Stacy could usually read his thoughts just by looking at his face.

"I have no objections to our going to the party."

"But given your choice, you'd rather stay here?"

Tanner reached for her hand. "It seems that I am often having to share you. Roddy and Lucinda were here, and now we're headed off to a weekend of being separated by friends and activities." Tanner stopped when he saw amusement in his wife's face.

"Roddy and Lucinda left a month ago." Stacy's voice was dry.

"True." Tanner's voice had turned just as wry. "But then there's your time with Alexa. You knew from the beginning that I was going to be jealous of that."

"She does like to eat," Stacy admitted. The duke and duchess smiled at each other as they both visualized their butterball daughter.

"Seriously, Tanner—" Stacy had to go back to the subject at hand. "If you don't want to go, I know that Brandon and Sunny will understand."

Tanner kissed the back of her hand. "We'll go. I'm just being selfish."

"Drew certainly will be pleased," Stacy told him, feeling well pleased at the way Tanner was putting his own wants aside. "He's talked of nothing else for days."

"Well, he doesn't have long to wait now," Tanner commented as he went back to his book. "We leave tomorrow."

"When do Stacy and Tanner arrive?" Chelsea asked Sunny.

"Tomorrow. They live so close that it seemed silly to stay over, but it's more fun that way, so I talked Tanner into it."

"I haven't seen Tanner Richardson in years," Miles Gallagher commented.

"Well," Sunny told him, "he's doing fine, and you're going to love his wife and children. Oh, Miles," Sunny spoke suddenly. "I've written up a family tree. Will you look at it for me?"

"Sure."

Sunny moved to the small writing desk in the corner and returned with a small roll of paper.

"I haven't added the dates, but will you check and see if I have all the names down?"

Miles took the roll and his mother, Chelsea, leaned over his shoulder as they read.

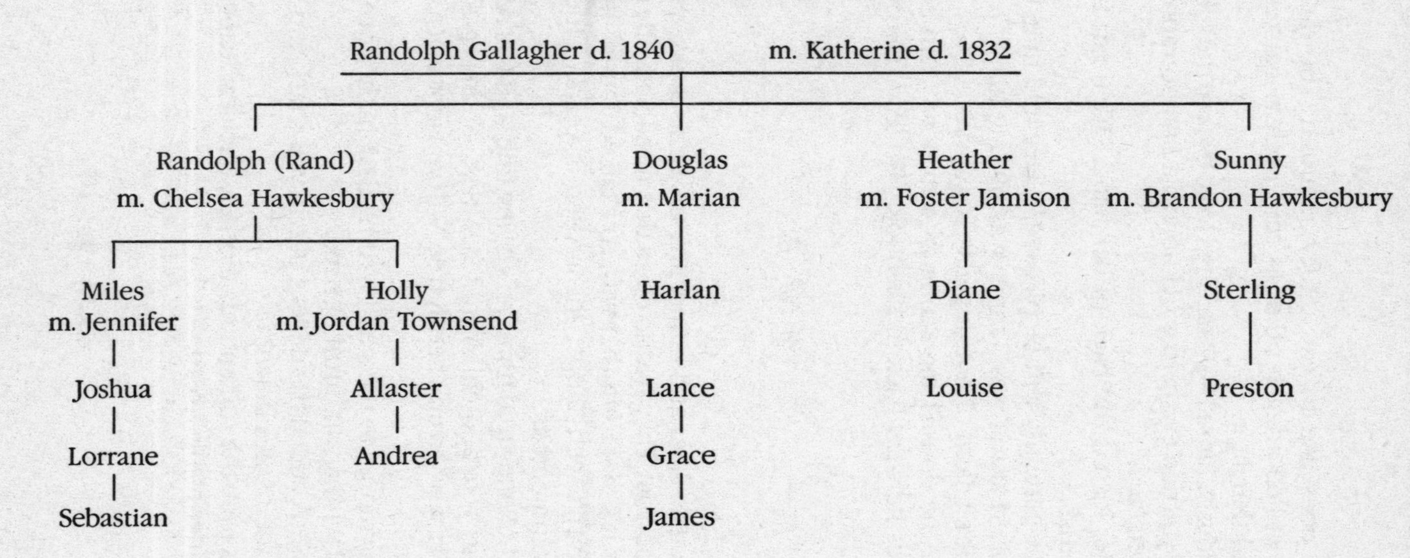
Gallagher Family Tree
Randolph Gallagher d. 1840
m. Katherine d. 1832
Randolph (Rand)
m. Chelsea Hawkesbury
Douglas
m. Marian
Heather
m. Foster Jamison
Sunny
m. Brandon Hawkesbury
Miles
m. Jennifer
Holly
m. Jordan Townsend
Harlan
Diane
Sterling
Joshua
Allaster
Lance
Louise
Preston
Lorrane
Andrea
Grace
Sebastian
James

Hawkesbury Family Tree

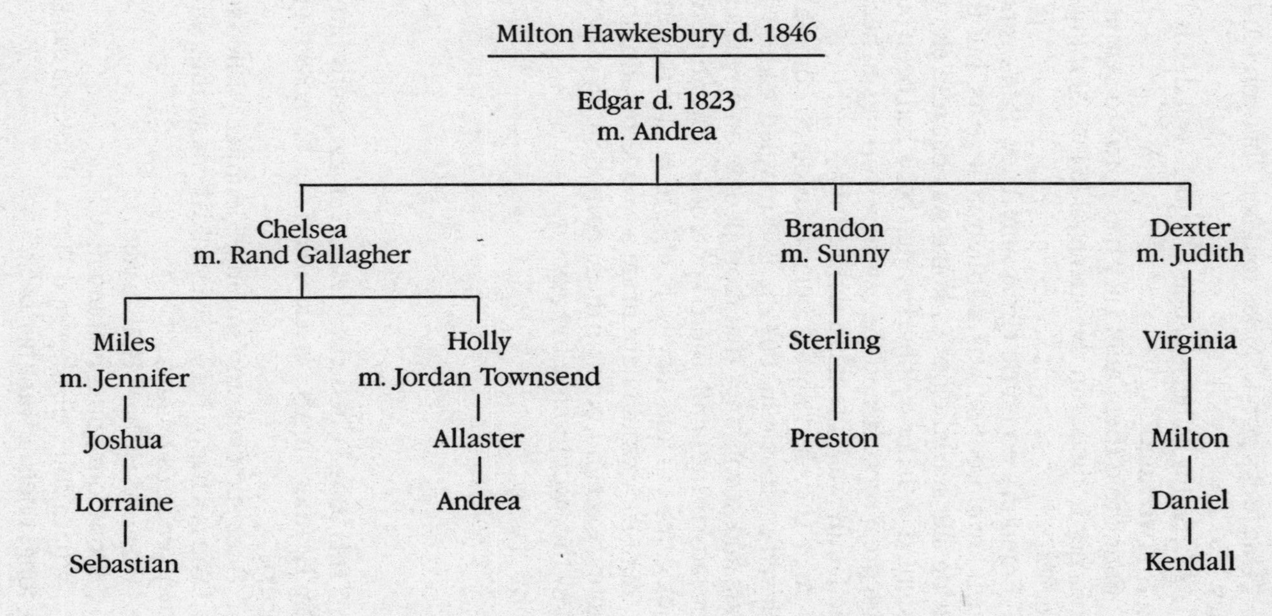

"This looks good," Miles told her, "but you left out Aunt Lucy."

"Oh, Sunny," Chelsea added, "I guess you did. Is she coming this weekend?"

Sunny told them Aunt Lucy had opted to stay at Ravenscroft, her home set in the countryside just 20 minutes from Bracken.

Brandon's eccentric Great Aunt Lucy didn't venture out much anymore. She was getting on in years, but the main reason she stayed close to home was because she was still occupied with her writing. Her first book had been published with great success, and she was now working on her second. The family was still amazed over this.

Aunt Lucy had always been considered something of a beloved scatterbrain, but she had traveled widely over the years and seen things that most people only read about. In fact, most of the family didn't know of her adventures until her book came out and they were able to read it themselves.

Aunt Lucy would have made a wonderful addition to the hunting weekend, but with the huge mob Sunny expected, she knew they would have fun anyway.

"This baby," Chelsea exclaimed as she gently lifted Alexa from Heather's arms, "is adorable. Look at those round, rosy cheeks!"

"Does she ever stop smiling?" Jennifer wished to know.

"She is a happy baby," Stacy told them, smiling with pride at her precious daughter.

"How old is she?" Holly asked.

"About four and a half months."

"What a doll," Heather said. "Don't think you can keep her for long, Chels. I want her back."

The women had been visiting nonstop for what seemed like days. Stacy was having the time of her life. She had never been around so many believers at once, and found it to be the most encouraging time she had experienced in many months. Tanner seemed to be enjoying himself too.

The men were all out hunting and had been gone for hours, but Stacy was so involved with the children and the other women that she hadn't had time to miss Tanner. Both Brandon and Rand had a way of making Tanner feel at home, and even though all the men were believers who made no secret of their faith, Tanner had not put his guard up as usual.

When it was time for lunch and the men were not back, Stacy began to wonder. She tried to take her cue from the other women, however. When none of them seemed concerned, Stacy relaxed somewhat. She tried to remember how long Tanner had been out with the hunting party at the Cradwells', but it had been so many years ago that she simply couldn't recall.

"I wonder what's keeping the men?" Chelsea ventured out loud when lunch was over and the women retired to the upstairs salon.

"Did they say how far they were headed?" Sunny asked.

"I didn't hear anyone say," Holly replied.

"Well, Foster has closeted himself downstairs in the library. Shall I ask him?" This came from Heather, who was more than willing to check things out. But almost as soon as she offered, Brandon walked in.

Sunny's face lit for just an instant before she saw that his face was as pale as death. All the women watched as he walked straight to Stacy.

"There's been an accident, Stacy," he said without preamble, his voice breathless. "Tanner has been shot."

Stacy stood. "Is he alive?" she barely managed.

"Yes. We were closer to Winslow, so we took him there."

Stacy started moving for the door, but stopped abruptly and faced the room. "What about Drew and Alexa?"

"The children will be fine, Stacy," Sunny told her. "Just go," she urged. "We'll get them home to you as soon as possible."

Stacy nodded, still in shock. Sunny gave her a swift hug, and Brandon ushered her to the door and downstairs.

The coach had been traveling at full speed for nearly ten minutes before Stacy spoke.

"Where was he hit?"

"His upper chest, the left side."

So near the heart, her mind cried. She swallowed hard to keep from sobbing.

"Has he lost much blood?" she asked next.

"Yes."

Stacy didn't want to know any more. It didn't matter how it happened or who was involved, only that she was there in time. Stacy prayed as the horses' hooves ate up the ground between the estates.

I don't know what I'll see when we arrive. Please help me to be prepared for the worst, Lord. I know he hasn't come to You, Father, and for this I would ask You to spare him. Your will is perfect; help me to believe this with all of my heart. Help me to trust You even in this time of hurt.

Maybe this will be the turning point, Father. Maybe Tanner will see his need for You because of this. Please give me some assurance. Please let me talk to him before You take him to You.

Stacy realized then that she was praying as if she knew he was going to die, which was ridiculous. She began to alter her prayer, asking God to help her fight the numbness that seemed to be pervading her limbs, knowing she would be needed as soon as they arrived.

By the time they had pulled into the courtyard of Winslow, Stacy felt more in control. The ride had seemed to take ages, but doors opened seemingly of their own accord as the duchess's presence was made known. Stacy hurried indoors. With no care for watching eyes, she picked up her skirt and took the stairs two at a time.

She entered the master bedroom on swift, silent feet and stared down into the pale features of her husband. Both Rand and Miles Gallagher were present. Tanner's shirt was off, and a wrapping of sort had been bound around his chest. The side directly over the wound was soaked with blood. Stacy stared down at him and felt an amazing calm come over her.

"Has someone sent for the doctor?" she asked, her voice soft and in control.

"Yes. Jordan and Dexter have ridden to find him."

"I need Hettie," Stacy began. "Oh, that's right, she's with the baby. Eden," she said to a maid standing nearby, "bring me some more dressings and hot water, and please be quick about it."

Brandon, whose gun had caused the damage, now stepped forward. He'd been in a state of shock up until then, but seeing Stacy in charge propelled him forward to assist her. In just a matter of minutes he was carefully lifting Tanner so Stacy could change the wraps.

"Do you think the bullet is still in there?" Her voice was hushed, as though afraid to wake her patient.

"No. It went clean through."

"Good. Let's pad the back here. Reece?" Stacy called quietly to the faithful servant who came immediately to her side.

"Yes, my lady."

"Check as to whether a coach is bringing Hettie and Price. If not, see to it. I need them both immediately."

"Yes, my lady."

"Tanner," Stacy now spoke to her unconscious mate. "I'm going to take care of you, but you need to wake up and tell me how you feel."

Stacy felt better having said the words, but Tanner lay mute, his eyes closed, his skin almost clammy with cold.

"Let's get this sheet up around his chest now, and then a light blanket," Stacy went on. Again Brandon's hands were there to assist her.

The men in the room watched in some fascination as she worked. Stacy herself could not have told them where she had learned to do such things, but her husband needed her, and at the moment that was all that mattered.

The doctor showed up some time after Stacy and Brandon had washed their hands. Stacy stayed very close as he checked the wound. She took no offense when the doctor assumed Brandon had done all the work or when he addressed all of his questions to Lord Hawkesbury. Stacy was content to silently observe until the doctor reached for his bag and spoke.

"I'm going to have to bleed him."

"What did you say?" she asked.

"I'm sorry, my lady. I'm going to have to ask you to leave so I can bleed your husband."

"But he's already lost blood, more than he can spare." Stacy's voice was reasonable, but she felt panicked inside. Andrew Daniels had always been against this practice, and some of his beliefs had carried on to his granddaughter.

"It's still necessary," the doctor said, his voice resigned.

"No," Stacy told him.

The doctor did not look overly surprised. His gaze swung to Brandon. "Will you please take Lady Richardson from the room?"

Whether or not Brandon would have done such a thing, Stacy would never know. She didn't give him a chance to move.

"Reece!" Stacy used a voice none of them had ever heard before. "Remove this man at once!"

The doctor's mouth opened in shock, but Reece, surprised as he was by her tone, promptly came forward to do as he was told.

"You'll kill him," the man sputtered as Reece lay hold of the doctor's arm.

"You will *not* bleed my husband," Stacy told him, her eyes shooting sparks.

"He'll die otherwise." The doctor had pulled himself from Reece's grasp and was coming back to the bed. Stacy stood between Tanner and the doctor like an enraged warrior. The fact that she stood many inches taller than the doctor caused the man to stop.

"I said you will not bleed him, and if that is all the treatment you can offer, then get out." Stacy's voice was deadly cold.

The man was so flustered he could only stare at her. Brandon, Rand, and Miles had moved in such a way that they seemed to flank Stacy. The doctor glanced into their eyes and knew he would find no help from any of them. With a deep sigh he said, "I think you're making a grave mistake, and I won't be held responsible."

"Then by all means go," Stacy told him reasonably, not at all fearful of the responsibility.

The doctor sighed again. "I do have a poultice," he said, knowing he could not leave without doing something. "I can apply that to the wound if you'd like."

Stacy nodded, her voice soft but not apologetic. "Thank you."

The doctor was watched like a hawk as he bent over Tanner and applied the poultice and wrap. He left another poultice with Stacy and gave her instructions as to how to apply it before taking his leave. He was not a heartless man, but he honestly believed that Lord Richardson would be dead by morning.

Forty-Seven

"I WANT TO TELL YOU WHAT HAPPENED, STACY," Brandon said softly when he, Stacy, Rand, and Miles were alone in the room. The doctor had been gone just minutes, and now Stacy stood next to the bed, staring down into Tanner's pale face.

"It doesn't matter, Brandon," Stacy looked up and told him. "I know whatever it was, it was an accident."

"You're right, it was," Brandon agreed with her, his voice tight with pain. "But it was my gun, and I want to tell you."

Stacy's heart turned over when she saw tears in this man's eyes. She was not shocked or angry to learn that it had been Brandon's gun. She preferred that over it being the gun of one of the boys who had gone on the hunt and who might never get over such a mishap. Still, his obvious pain made Stacy ache for him. He cared deeply for Tanner, and she could well imagine how he must feel. On Stacy's nod, Brandon began to speak.

"I've never done anything so foolish in all my life. I pointed my gun—that is, I gestured with it to a place behind me—and my finger was on the trigger. I knew that Tanner was behind and to the side of me, but I thought it was the other side.

"The gun seemed to go off of its own accord. I know that can happen to anyone. My deepest regret is that I used the gun to point at all. I have two good arms for that. I can't think what possessed me. I'm sorry, Stacy."

Brandon's voice broke then, and Stacy went to him. She hugged this man who was so like her husband in size and listened as a sob caught in his throat. It never even occurred to Stacy to be bitter or unforgiving, and after a few moments they broke apart and Stacy smiled gently at Brandon.

"God is only good to us, Brandon. I know that He is going to use this in a mighty way in Tanner's life."

Brandon drew in a deep breath. He didn't know where Stacy found the strength to do it, but she was actually ministering to him. Rand and Miles came close at that point, and the men hugged Brandon and Stacy also.

"Now," ever-practical Rand spoke when everyone had their emotions under control, "what can we do for you, Stacy?"

Stacy had just opened her mouth to answer when she heard Alexa's cry in the hall. Her milk came down in a rush, and when she did speak, it was with her arms tightly folded across her chest. She spoke as calmly as she could.

"Please ask Hettie to give Alexa to Juliet, and then I would like to speak to Hettie." This was all accomplished in competent haste, and just minutes later Hettie stood before her.

"Hettie, Rand is going to take you to the village. I want you to find a wet nurse. You know the kind of woman to look for. If you need to bring several women for me to meet, then do, but I want to speak to whomever you bring *before* she goes to Alexa. When you leave, tell Juliet to bring Alexa to me."

"Yes, my lady." Hettie's voice was humble. She had thought to come back and find Stacy a mess, but Stacy's control was a comfort to everyone near her. Mrs. Maxwell, who had Drew, was just as calm. Hettie knew that she and Stacy shared the same faith and wondered if there could be a connection.

Five minutes later Stacy had cleared the bedroom so she could feed her daughter. She did this while sitting next to the bed, her eyes more on Tanner than her daughter. She fed Alexa only long enough to bring herself some relief and temporarily satisfy her baby.

Not until she'd returned Alexa to Juliet and changed her

clothing did she have time to think about where everyone was. Miles had gone with Hettie and his father. Brandon had gone down to Tanner's study to write letters to the family. Brandon's first letter was to Roddy and Lucinda, and the second was to Uncle Edmond.

Now Price, who had come in when Alexa was given to Juliet, was the only one in the master bedroom with Stacy. Price was the consummate gentleman's gentleman. As he stood on the opposite side of the bed and stared into Tanner's pale features, however, his emotions were starting to win the battle. Thankfully Stacy glanced at Price just then and recognized his plight better than he did himself. Stacy compassionately dismissed him.

Stacy was glad for a few solitary moments with her husband. He was so still it was alarming, but the gentle rise and fall of his chest told Stacy that it was not yet God's time for Tanner to leave this earth. Tanner had been placed on her side of the bed, so it was easy for Stacy to reach her Bible from where she sat. She turned to Psalm 135 and read quietly to her spouse.

"Praise ye the Lord. Praise ye the name of the Lord; praise him, O ye servants of the Lord. Ye who stand in the house of the Lord, in the courts of the house of our God, praise the Lord; for the Lord is good. Sing praises unto his name; for it is pleasant. For the Lord hath chosen Jacob unto himself, and Israel for his peculiar treasure. For I know that the Lord is great and that our Lord is above all gods. Whatsoever the Lord pleased, that did he in heaven, and in earth, in the seas, and all deep places. He causeth the vapours to ascend from the ends of the earth; he maketh lightnings for the rain; he bringeth the wind out of his treasuries."

When Stacy finished, she set her Bible aside and began to pray with her eyes on Tanner's face.

"I want him to know You, Lord," Stacy whispered. "I want him to have time to come to Christ, but Your will is holy. Help me to trust." Stacy could not go on.

She was suddenly back at her grandfather's bedside, listening to him tell her that he had believed in Christ. Stacy's eyes slid shut with remembered joy. God had saved her grandfather when he had just days left on this earth, and she knew He could do the same for Tanner. As much as Stacy loved Tanner, she knew God loved him more. This did not give her a guarantee concerning his eternity, but as she'd said to Brandon, God is only good.

"Don't let me forget that, Father."

The young woman standing before Stacy looked shy and a little frightened as she stared up at the Duchess of Cambridge. She had a very tiny baby in her arms, whose color was a healthy pink. Stacy noted that both were clean, and even though their clothing was coarse, it was well pressed and had no stains.

"What is your name?"

"Felicity, my lady."

Stacy could not immediately speak. Felicity had been the name of the girl in Middlesbrough who had been Drew's wet nurse. Stacy had prayed for wisdom concerning this decision and now wondered if this might be God's way of giving her direction.

"Do you feel you have enough milk for both babies, Felicity? I would not want you to starve your own child."

"'e ain't never been able to drink all my milk, Lady Richardson. A've always got plenty to spare."

"Your baby is a boy?"

Felicity's face lit with pride and joy. "'is name's Robert, after 'is pa."

Stacy smiled, even as an ache filled her. She'd planned to feed Alexa for at least six more months.

"Robert is a fine name. Do you understand that I would need you to live here at Winslow, Felicity, and be on constant call?"

"Yes, ma'am."

Stacy nodded, feeling satisfied. "I have just fed Alexa, but I'm certain she is still hungry. Hettie will take you to Alexa's room, and she will be the one to tell you when you are needed. Is everything clear?"

"Yes, my lady."

They discussed a few more specifics before Hettie took mother and son away. Stacy was tempted to watch and see how she did with Alexa, but she didn't think she could deal with the sight of another woman feeding her baby right now.

With a determined move, Stacy returned to the bedroom and Tanner's side. Brandon was sitting with him and seemed to sense that Stacy did not care to talk.

In the next hours trusted servants came and went. The poultice was changed, the bleeding had stopped, and Tanner was made as comfortable as possible. Both Stacy and Brandon prayed that he would wake soon, but it was not to be. By morning Tanner was still unconscious. A fever had begun to rage within his body.

Forty-eight hours later, Stacy's hand shook with exhaustion as she laid a cold cloth on Tanner's brow. His skin was so hot it burned her to touch him, but at least the thrashing had stopped. There had been times when Brandon had all but lain on top of Tanner to keep him on the bed.

Neither Stacy nor Brandon had slept, but at the moment Stacy felt beyond sleep. Brandon had just left to get something to eat, and Stacy now sat alone in the room.

Tanner's hand lay outside the covers, and Stacy reached for it. He was so warm, but she held the hand gently for just a moment and then began to grip it harder.

"I don't want you to die, Tanner," she whispered in some desperation. "Do you hear me?" Again her grip tightened. "I don't want you to die." Stacy's voice was still low but growing almost fierce in intensity. She squeezed his hand. There was still no response.

"Don't you die, Tanner," she now hissed at him. "Don't you dare. You can drum up some of that orneriness that we both know you're so capable of and fight this. Do you hear me, Tanner Richardson?"

Stacy was nearly shouting now and shaking Tanner's arm for all it was worth. A small groan came from his lips. Stacy stopped, horrified over what she was doing.

"I'm sorry, Tanner," she began to sob. "I'm so sorry. I didn't mean that. Please forgive me, Tanner. I'm so sorry." Her sobs were uncontrollable now, so much so that she didn't even hear Brandon come into the room.

"Come on, Stacy," he spoke gently. "Come get some rest."

"Please don't make me leave him, Brandon," she begged, her crying still very harsh.

"All right," he crooned. "Just come over here to the extra bed. Price set this up for you, and you haven't used it. It's time now, come on."

Brandon was afraid that if he called someone to assist him, Stacy would rouse and want to return to Tanner's side. Right now she was nearly asleep on her feet. Wishing Sunny was with him, he urged her onto the bed and covered her with a blanket. He didn't bother with her shoes or anything else, but stood by as she cried into the pillow and finally drifted off to sleep. When he thought she wouldn't stir, he turned his back on her and returned to the bed.

He was tired enough to sleep himself, and would soon, but for right now he needed to make sure that Tanner remained quiet for Stacy. He had tremendous peace that Tanner was going to come out of this and be fine, but Stacy would be of no use to anyone if she continued as she was. An hour later Price came to relieve him, and with Stacy and Tanner still sleeping, Brandon left that room to find his own rest.

Another two days passed before Tanner's fever broke and he awakened. Brandon sat beside him, holding Stacy's Bible open to the book of Luke. It took a moment before he felt Tanner's eyes on him.

"Welcome back," Brandon spoke softly.

Tanner licked his lips. "How many days?"

"About six."

"Stacy." It wasn't stated as a question, but Brandon knew that it was.

"She just went down to get something to eat. I can send Price for her."

Tanner's head moved on the pillow. "I won't be able to stay awake that long."

"All right. Do you remember what happened?"

Tanner's eyes had slid shut, but he still answered. "Yes. It could happen to anyone, Hawk."

Brandon's relief was indescribable. "Be that as it may, I am sorry, Tanner."

Tanner didn't answer then, but Brandon watched his hand lift slightly on the cover and knew that he'd been understood and forgiven.

"Would you like some more?" Stacy asked, holding a cup of strong beef broth for Tanner. He'd sipped half of it, but Stacy could see that he was flagging.

"No." The duke lay back, feeling rather spent. "I'm going to sleep for a while. I hate this weakness," he commented. It was the evening of his first day awake, but Tanner evidently believed he should have been able to jump out of bed from the start.

Stacy smoothed the hair from his forehead and then leaned to kiss his brow. When she sat back, Tanner reached for her hand and searched her eyes with his own.

"Did you read to me while I was unconscious?"

"Yes, every day, from the Bible."

Tanner continued to watch her. "You said something about the wind."

Stacy thought a moment. "That was from Psalm 135. It's a psalm that praises God for His power and provision with the way He brings forth the wind, rain, and lightning."

Stacy waited for a cynical look to cross his face, but it didn't happen.

"Did you pray for me too?"

"Constantly," she told him.

"Thank you, sweetheart."

With that, Tanner's eyes closed, but Stacy didn't move. She sat holding his hand long after it went limp in her grasp.

Forty-Eight

STACY SAW BRANDON, SUNNY, RAND, AND CHELSEA to the door. They had come to see Tanner that morning and stayed for lunch.

Two more days had passed, but he was still feeling very weak. The entire situation made him testy and frustrated. Stacy was thankful that the visit from friends had worked to take his mind off himself for a short time.

Stacy was finding that Tanner wasn't the easiest patient, but she didn't complain. She had been very pleased to see the Hawkesburys and the Gallaghers, as their presence offered something new to her convalescing charge. He'd tried to get out of bed twice but simply couldn't manage it. At those times the staff cleared out because he was nearly impossible to be around.

Nothing was right. The bed was too hard and then too soft. His food was too hot and then too cold. Stacy had never seen him this way, but she weathered it all without so much as a word of protest. She knew it was nothing personal; he was simply frustrated over being kept down.

Some of his ire had cooled during and after his visit with friends, but by the evening he was his old cantankerous self. He had complained to Stacy no less than five times about his dinner, but she still said nothing, only fixed things the way he wanted them and continued to eat her own meal.

"Will you stop treating me like a baby!" Tanner finally snapped at her. Stacy's fork stopped halfway to her mouth.

"I'm not treating you like a baby, Tanner," she said reasonably.

"Yes, you are!" he insisted in a foul humor. "You have this tolerant look on your face as though you were dealing with Drew and just waiting for him to get over his mood."

"Tanner." Stacy's voice was still calm. "I know you don't care to be in that bed, but I'm *not* treating you like a child."

"Yes, you are."

Stacy sighed gently. "If Drew acted as you are, I'd put him across my knee. So you can see that you're not being treated like a child or you'd be feeling the pain of it this instant."

Suddenly they both smiled. That small example of just how self-centered Tanner was acting snapped the tension that had built.

It was just what they both needed. The meal was finished on a lighter note, and Stacy felt for the first time in days that she might be getting her old Tanner back. She was well pleased with this, but the best was yet to come, and it would happen the very next afternoon.

"This letter is from Noel and Elena," Stacy told him. "They obviously haven't received my letter about your wound—they want us to come up for some hunting as soon as we're able. Elena goes on to say that little Noel is getting just huge, and Brittany still asks about Drew every day.

"Now, these two are business," Stacy continued as she sorted the post. "Do you want them here or on your desk?"

"Why don't you give them to Price."

"I'll do that. Oh, I almost forgot—"

"Excuse me, my lady," Reece interrupted them.

"Yes, Reece. What is it?"

"It's Felicity, my lady. She's says her baby has a slight cold and could she please leave and go to the doctor in the village or send for him to come here."

"Send for him, by all means," Stacy told him. "And tell Felicity not to worry. I'll be in to see her later."

"One of our maids has a baby?" Tanner didn't speak until after Reece had left. Stacy nearly laughed at his baffled expression.

"No. Felicity is Alexa's wet nurse. Her baby is just six weeks old. His name is Robert."

Tanner could only stare at her.

"What is it, Tanner?" Stacy asked, not recalling that she and Tanner had never discussed this.

"Alexa needed a wet nurse?"

"Well, yes. I sent for one after the accident because I couldn't be with her all the time."

"But why couldn't you?"

Now it was Stacy's turn to stare. Did he really not understand how many hours she'd spent in this room? Her voice was gentle, however, when she answered him in just a handful of words.

"Because you needed me more than Alexa did."

Tanner's world rocked. Feeding Alexa herself had been very important to Stacy. He knew there was not another woman in all the earth like his wife. She cared for him without complaint. She took his verbal abuse without comment. And now, when he needed her, she had even set her baby aside to be with him. He felt humbled beyond explanation, and for the first time in his life he realized his true feelings for his wife went far beyond respect and admiration.

When Tanner had remained quiet, Stacy assumed he didn't want to hear any more letters. Stacy had stood to bend over him and check his dressing. He spoke while she was poised above him, a study in concentration.

"I love you, Anastasia."

Stacy froze, certain she had heard wrong. Her eyes moved slowly to lock with his.

"Yes, you heard me correctly. I love you, Stacy."

Stacy straightened slowly, and Tanner watched as her hand came to her lips. Huge tears puddled in her eyes and spilled down her cheeks. Tanner had never actually seen her break down before, and all he could do was watch helplessly from the bed.

A door sounded then, and both knew they were going to be interrupted. Stacy turned swiftly from the bed and moved to the window in an effort to control herself. Her whole frame shook as she tried to suppress sobs, but it wasn't working.

Price, who had been the one at the door, sized up the situation immediately and excused himself. Pain ripped through Tanner's chest and shoulder as he shifted to see her. He listened for a long moment to her tears before calling to her.

"Sweetheart. Come back over here."

She did not come immediately. He called to her several more times before she returned and he was able to urge her into the chair near the bed. Tanner gasped his way into a sitting position and handed Stacy the edge of the sheet to dry her tears.

"I just can't...I didn't think you would ever...that is, I hoped, but I didn't know..."

Tanner didn't try to quiet her. Her reaction spoke volumes to him as to how much she'd hoped and waited for him to say the words. It occurred to him suddenly, however, that she had not returned the words. In fact she hadn't said them in many months. Tanner wondered if perhaps she didn't feel as strongly about him as she once had. It saddened him to think that he might have waited too long, but he vowed that as soon as he was able to get out of bed, he would not just tell Stacy, but show her in a thousand different ways that his love was real.

Stacy walked around in a cloud for the remainder of the day. Tanner was feeling remarkably better by dinnertime, and Stacy later found herself pulled in two directions. She wanted to hold her husband and be held in return, but fear for his wound was very real. Tanner, on the other hand, had no such qualms.

After dinner, while Stacy was still checking his dressing, she felt Tanner's free hand in the middle of her back. Before she could even guess what he might be up to, he pulled her down against him and kissed her.

Stacy struggled, thinking that her weight would start the bleeding again.

"Tanner," she gasped. "You can't do that."

Stacy escaped and stepped away from the bed to talk.

"Tanner," she tried to sound stern. "Behave yourself."

"I am behaving myself. I'm behaving like a man in love with his wife. Now come back over here."

"No." Stacy sounded more adamant than she felt.

"Do as I tell you, Anastasia."

There was that tone. The one that always made Stacy feel helpless. She returned, sitting carefully on the edge of the bed.

"I love you," he said again. "And I want the spare bed out of here tonight."

Stacy shook her head. There was no way she was going to jeopardize his recovery by sleeping in the same bed and possibly endangering his wound.

"Yes, Stacy." Tanner's voice was velvety smooth, but even when he ordered, Stacy stood her ground. Tanner was none too happy with her over it, but he saw that he'd pushed far enough.

Stacy was lulled into a false sense of security when Tanner suddenly gave up. She left him for a time to ready herself for bed, feeling distinctly triumphant. She'd have fainted with horror nad she seen Tanner actually standing by the bed after she left.

The effort was almost more than he could take, but once up, he found it not too bad. His injury screamed at him, but he ignored the pain and the trembling in his lower limbs. Just a few minutes was all he could last, but it was enough to give him confidence for the morrow. Thankfully he was back in bed before Stacy or Price could make an appearance.

Forty-Nine

"DO YOU HAVE PLANS TO GROW TEETH any time soon?"

The question was good-naturedly posed to Alexa by her papa. As usual, she grinned and even drooled with delight on the good side of his chest.

Drew had been in for an hour that morning, and now it was Alexa's turn. Stacy was careful to watch Tanner for signs of fatigue, but he seemed a hundred percent better. She smiled to herself when she thought of how swiftly the change had come about. It came with his declaration of love. Stacy's heart was swelling with joy over yesterday's events.

My husband loves me, she told the Lord the night before while spending some quiet moments alone in her sitting room. *It's more than I ever hoped for, Father. You have brought a miracle in this marriage, and I thank You from deep in my heart.*

"Stacy, I think she's doing something." Tanner's voice was distressed, his face chagrined.

Stacy glanced down at Alexa's red, strained features and laughed. She pulled the bellpull, and when Price arrived she asked him to send for Hettie. Hettie was completely undisturbed over the task at hand and crooned softly to her charge as she took her from the room.

"You look like you could use some sleep."

Tanner yawned before answering. “I think you’re right. You wouldn’t like to climb in with me, would you?”

Stacy smiled. “I’ve got some things to do, and then I’ll come up. Do you want anything before I go?”

“No.”

They kissed then, and Stacy made her way around the bed to gather some papers from a small writing desk. She quietly straightened a few things in the room, and then, with a final glance at her sleeping husband, made for the door. She had not reached the threshold of Tanner’s dressing room when Price came in. He stopped in front of her, and Stacy studied his anxious eyes.

“What is it, Price?”

Price glanced at Tanner, and Stacy’s eyes followed his, but he was asleep.

“Lord Stanley is here.”

Stacy stared at him.

“Nigel Stanley?”

“Yes, my lady. He wishes to see you.”

Stacy took a deep breath. What in the world could he want?

“All right. Tell Lord Stanley I’ll be down shortly.”

Price nodded and left. Stacy looked one more time at Tanner. He was on his side, facing away from her; otherwise Stacy would have seen that his eyes were wide open and dark with a myriad of emotions.

Nigel Stanley looked older to Stacy, older than she had expected. It wasn’t that his hair had turned gray or that he’d shrunken in frame, but his eyes and mouth had lost their youth. There was a sadness in the depths of his eyes, and there were deep grooves at the sides of his mouth.

“Hello, Lord Stanley. I understand you wanted to see me.” Stacy congratulated herself over her calm. She wasn’t afraid of this man, but she did not want him in her life or disturbing her marriage as he'd done before.

"Yes, thank you for seeing me. I wouldn't have blamed you if you'd had me thrown from your property."

"Won't you sit down?"

He did, but Stacy could see he was not at ease. Stacy sat also and waited. Nigel cleared his throat at least three times before he began.

"I know that much time has passed, and I'm sorry for that, but I wanted to see you today to express my deepest regrets over my past actions. My actions on that day bring me extreme shame, and I know they caused you great distress.

"I stalked you that weekend, totally thoughtless of your person. It's something for which I have no excuse. I came to tell you how sorry I am for the way I acted."

Nigel stood abruptly, and Stacy did the same. He'd clearly come to say that and no more.

"Thank you, Nigel. I appreciate your stopping. The rumors were evidently false."

A ghost of a smile lifted one side of his mouth. "I suppose you heard that your husband killed me in a duel."

"Murdered you actually," Stacy replied, feeling shame that she'd ever believed such a thing of Tanner. "You did rather disappear."

"Having been raised in Paris, I had not been in London all that long when I attended the party. So when I made such a fool of myself over you, I thought it the better part of valor to make myself scarce."

"But you're back in England now?"

"Only on business. I'm married myself now, just six months, and we make our home in France."

Stacy smiled a very genuine smile. "I'm pleased for you, Nigel, and I wish you all the best."

"Thank you, Lady Richardson. Your understanding and forgiveness confound me, but I am eternally grateful."

He left then, being shown to the door by Reece. Stacy stood in the parlor where he'd left her.

How odd, she mused, but then thought better of it. He needed to make things right, and she admired his doing so instead of pushing that whole incident into some corner of his mind to pretend it never happened.

For the first time, Stacy was able to think of the Cradwell party without pain. The nightmare had come to an end; the problem had been resolved. She understood now that a part of her had still been living in the shadows of that painful time. Stacy felt now a sort of freedom come over her with Nigel's apology. She would have to tell Tanner, in a gentle way, what had transpired.

"Stacy."

Stacy's calm reverie was shattered. Her head snapped to the door. That had been Tanner's voice; she was sure of it. She ran for the closed portal, wrenched it open, and ran for the stairs. He was at the bottom, wearing only a robe. His face was completely drained of color.

"Oh, Tanner. Please go back to bed. Whatever possessed you to get up?"

"Where is he?" Tanner gasped as he sank to the bottom step.

"Who?" Stacy really didn't know.

"Stanley." Tanner could barely talk. "I know he's come to offer for you. I've got to set the record straight—you're mine and we both know it. Unless I tell him, he'll not believe you won't go with him."

Tanner was completely spent then, and Stacy put her arms around him until he caught his breath. She laid her head against his shoulder, and when she looked at him after a moment, found his color improved.

"He came to tell me how much he regretted his actions of the past. Nigel is married now and not even living in England. He's already left."

"He didn't want you?"

"No, and it wouldn't have mattered if he had."

Tanner pulled her head back down to his shoulder. He

held her close for long minutes. Stacy heard him sigh deeply before speaking quietly.

"I'm ready, Stacy. I'm ready to hear what happened."

Stacy lifted her head, and their eyes met. She never looked away as she told her story.

"I was so naive in those days," she began. "I look back now on the way Lord Stanley acted and wonder how I could have been so innocent, but I was.

"He watched me constantly. I realize now that his behavior was obvious to everyone but me. Had I understood, I would have been a little cooler to him, but since I didn't, I was my usual friendly self. Because he was already smitten, he took every smile as an invitation.

"He approached me in the conservatory on Saturday, but I still didn't catch on. Then Sunday, he completely lost his head. When you came in I was trying to push him away, but for all his slim build he was fairly strong.

"I'm sorry I didn't know, Tanner. I'm sorry—"

"Shhh," Tanner cut her off, his eyes still holding hers. "There is nothing for you to apologize over. *I'm* sorry I didn't give you time to explain. The loss has been my own.

"In the last weeks," Tanner told her, "I've figured out much of what you just told me. You're certainly right about Stanley; his actions were peculiar. His eyes looked of blood lust, like a hound on the hunt. I let my emotions run over the top of me, or I would have come to more reasonable conclusions much sooner."

Stacy sighed then and put her head on his shoulder. She'd thought that it was over when Nigel apologized. Now she was certain of it. Content as Stacy was to sit there all day, she remembered just how ill Tanner had been. Stacy was on the verge of suggesting they go upstairs when he spoke.

"I haven't been easy to live with. I know that, and I might be a little late in coming to this, but I'm going to make it up to you, Stacy. When I'm finally on my feet again, I'm going to show you I'm worthy of your love."

"Tanner," Stacy said, lifting her head. "Whatever are you talking about?"

"You've stopped saying it, you know. Not even when I told you I loved you did you say it in return—not that I blame you. But just give me time; I'll win your love back."

"Oh, Tanner. I've never stopped loving you, but when we first came back I knew you didn't want to hear it. I guess I just got out of practice. I'm sorry."

"I love you, Stacy."

"And I love you, Tanner."

He kissed her and then held her close once again. They made quite a sight at the bottom of the stairs, Stacy in a beautiful day-dress and Tanner in his robe, but no one disturbed them and they didn't care.

"I only just thought of something. We never took that trip to France, the one we were going to take for our first anniversary."

"No, I guess we didn't."

"So how about it? I figure we could leave in about a month's time. What do you say?"

The chances of seeing Nigel Stanley were slim to none, but still Stacy could not find any enthusiasm about going.

"Not interested?" Tanner questioned her silence, trying not to read anything there.

"Not in France," she admitted. "But I understand Greece is beautiful in the fall."

"Ah, Stacy," Tanner said with a sigh. "You're so good for my heart."

"Am I?" she smiled.

"Yes. And we'll have no more of this nonsense about your hurting my chest. I'm not up to much, but I want to hold you, and no one is going to stop me."

"All right," Stacy agreed. "I'll ask Reece to have the extra bed removed."

Tanner grinned. "I already did that."

Stacy would have spoken, but Tanner kissed her surprised mouth, and suddenly Stacy didn't have anything to say at all.

TWENTY-THREE YEARS LATER

STACY STOOD IN THE SHADE of a huge willow tree and watched her family's antics. She shook her head at their energy and then turned and made her way toward the house. When she arrived at the back terrace she sat on the swing, from which she was still able to see her children and grandchildren.

Drew, married to a lovely girl for two years now, swung his little daughter, Penny, high in the air and caught her on a burst of giggles. It always took Stacy's breath away to watch, but Penny clearly loved it. Hettie, who was too old now to get around, was sure to be up in her room watching as well.

Next Stacy spotted Alexa as she threw a ball to her son, Joey. Alexa was a Hawkesbury now, having married Sterling, who was the image of Brandon, three years before. Both couples were as happy as they could be. They had found Christian mates and dedicated their lives to Him first and then to one another.

Stacy's mind moved to Chase. He'd come after Alexa by a few years and had been away at school for some time. He had only just finished his studies and was now living in London with Roddy. Lucinda had died five years earlier, and everyone was relieved that Chase would be there to keep company with him.

Lucinda had never been very comfortable with Roddy's talk of Christ and the Bible. On her deathbed, however, she had told Roddy she had made things right.

The girls who had come after Chase were on the lawn now. Kendra was 18 and Pippa 17. They both missed Chase terribly, but it helped to have Drew and Alexa, with their families, near.

The Duchess of Cambridge continued to study her brood, but after a moment she no longer saw them. Her mind's eye had turned to Tanner and his behavior of the past week. Never had she seen him in such a mood. Not that he was usually impossible, but something had definitely changed.

So many years before he had promised Stacy that he would be worthy of her love, and he had been. They had experienced their ups and downs, but Stacy could never fault Tanner's efforts as a husband and father. His children adored him and better yet *knew* him, because he had taken the time in their lives to be there. In fact, before coming home from London that day, he'd planned to check on Chase and see to his well-being.

God's grace amazed Stacy repeatedly when she thought about the way all her children had come to Him, even though their father had had little voice in the matter for all these years.

Tanner still enjoyed his debates with Brandon, and in fact the four of them had only grown closer as the years passed, but Tanner, to Stacy's knowledge, had never made Christ his Lord. Still she prayed, believing.

"Wool gathering?"

Stacy smiled at the sound of that deep voice and rose to embrace her husband.

"How was your trip?" she asked, their arms still tight around each other.

"Good."

"And Chase?"

"Looking well. I think he and Roddy are going to do splendidly."

Stacy gave a heartfelt sigh. "That's a relief." She stood in the circle of his arms just staring at him for a full minute.

Finally she spoke. "Tanner, what's come over you? I can't quite put my finger on it, but you seem quite different."

Tanner gently kissed her brow, his look very tranquil.

"I believe the Scriptures call it being 'a new creature in Christ.'"

Stacy stood in quiet shock for the space of several heartbeats.

"Oh, my darling Tanner," Stacy whispered when she could talk. Her hands came up to frame his face, and she looked at him through tear-filled eyes.

"When did this happen, Tanner?"

"About a week ago," he said, his voice more serene than Stacy had ever heard. "It's been an especially fine year for my investments, and I was sitting in my office congratulating myself as usual for my fine business acumen, when it suddenly occurred to me that without God I would have nothing.

"I felt as if I'd been struck. You, the children—everything is from God. He is the Provider and Savior. I couldn't go on after that. I wrestled for some minutes, but I knew I could never again pretend that I had been responsible."

"But how did you—?"

"I've been listening to you talk to the children for years, sweetheart. I prayed and told Him that I believe in Him and need a Savior for my sins. And you well know He never turns anyone away."

Stacy was overcome then. Tanner could count on one hand the times he'd seen her break down in all the years they'd been married, and now this was one more to add to the list. Tanner led her to a seat then and let her cry. He was thankful that no one disturbed them.

When Stacy could control herself, Tanner began to speak. He told her how empty he'd been feeling inside for the last year and how much he'd begun to think of eternity.

"I'm not a young man anymore, you know. I'm 56 this year and I've lived much of that time for myself. It was more than time for a change, a permanent change."

"Oh, Tanner. Wait until Brandon hears," Stacy sniffed. "You can't know how he's prayed for you."

Tanner smiled. "I'm looking forward to seeing him. There's so much I want to know. So much I *need* to know."

They talked on for some time, and then Tanner stood, eager to go and share with his family. Stacy opted to stay where she was and watch the scene unfold. She smiled, tears coming to her eyes again, as they thronged him, arms hugging amid cries of delight and praise to God.

"I never wanted anyone else, Father." Stacy spoke out loud. "From the moment I laid eyes on Tanner, I knew my heart was lost. Then You chose me, now You have chosen him. In Your love You have given me my deepest desire."

A breeze had come up, and Stacy's words were gently snatched away. Not that it mattered. God had heard them and as soon as her family, who was now coming to see her, arrived, she would gladly say them again.